Clora Lyle

★ ★ ★ ★ THE HOUSE OF WINSLOW / BOOK 1 ★ ★ ★ ★

THE
HONORABLE
IMPOSTER

★

GILBERT MORRIS

BETHANY HOUSE PUBLISHERS
MINNEAPOLIS, MINNESOTA 55438
A Division of Bethany Fellowship, Inc.

Published by Bethany House Publishers
A Division of Bethany Fellowship, Inc.
6820 Auto Club Road, Minneapolis, Minnesota 55438

Printed in the United States of America

Library of Congress Cataloging-in-Publication Data

Morris, Gilbert.
　The honorable imposter.

　(The House of Winslow)
　I. Title.　II. Series: Morris, Gilbert. House of Winslow ; bk. 1.
PS3563.08742H6　　1987　　　813′.54　　　86-31065
ISBN 0-87123-933-7

To Johnnie
We have saved the best
till last

GILBERT MORRIS spent ten years as a pastor before becoming Professor of English at Ouachita Baptist University in Arkansas and earning a Ph.D. at the University of Arkansas. During the summers of 1984 and 1985 he did post graduate work at the University of London and recently took a position as Chairman of General Education at a Christian college in Louisiana. A prolific writer, he has had over 25 scholarly articles and 200 poems published in various periodicals, and over the past three years has had 12 novels published. His family includes three grown children, and he and his wife live in Baton Rouge, Louisiana.

CONTENTS

PART THREE
THE NEW WORLD

PART ONE

ENGLAND

★ ★ ★ ★

CHAPTER ONE

THE MASQUERADE

★ ★ ★ ★

"What! Not ready *yet*?"

Lord Henry North burst into his daughter's lavishly adorned chamber like the brusque February wind that furrowed the Thames and drove the beating waves against the stones of his ancestral home. His outburst made little impression on Cecily North. She gave a quick smiling glance at her father as he stomped in, shaking the snow from his ermine cape, then calmly continued gazing at her reflection in the silver hand mirror. A diminutive maidservant stroked her hair with an ivory comb studded with amethysts and jade.

"We needn't hurry, Father. They won't begin without us."

Only three or four men in England could have taken so little heed of Sir Henry North. At the age of forty-five, he stood high on the pyramid of English culture. Except for the Lord Chancellor, the Lord of Lancaster, and King James the First of England, there was none to question his ways—and *none* who would answer him so casually as this beautiful daughter of his.

His eyes suddenly flashed at Cecily's careless answer, and he strode across the room to her. Taking her smooth bare shoulder with a surprisingly strong grip, he said, "You need a beating, my girl!"

"No doubt I do—and so do you, Father." Then she turned to him, taking his hand in hers and giving him a quick smile.

"We are both too proud for our own good. But then—who's to give us the whipping? There's the rub."

Lord North could not conceal the quick grin that leaped to his lips. The hard grasp on her shoulder softened to a caress, and he grunted, "Know me too well, you do! You should have been a boy."

A touch of regret tinged his voice, and Cecily reached up with her free hand to cover his. No one knew better than she that the one vacuum in her father's life was the lack of a son, and she got up and gave him a quick kiss, saying, "Never mind, Father. If Mother has her way, you'll have a son-in-law soon. Then you can make of him what you will."

North held on to her, staring at her and wondering that she knew him so well. He saw a woman of twenty with hair black and sleek as a raven, highlighted by bold black eyes able to meet any man's glance. Her full red lips needed none of the paint which ladies of the English court had imported from France. They were almost pouting, and smooth as silk. Her complexion, like his own, was olive and flawless. She was not tall, but the full curves of her body made men forget her stature; she had the full-bodied figure of her mother—in the eyes of many, the most beautiful woman in the court.

"A son-in-law?" North released his grip and picked up her white fur mantle from the table, casting it around her shoulders. "I've lost out on the cattle show. Which hunk of prize young nobility has your mother been parading in front of you this time? Young Wentworth?"

"No, Father, that was last month. He fell below the required standards," Cecily laughed. "I think when Mother found out that there was a bar sinister on his mother's side, she threw him to the wolves—along with all the others. Really, Father, I think Mother would marry me off to Lord Findlay—if he could stand up long enough to get through the ceremony!"

"Well—perhaps it's not so bad as *that*." Lord Findlay, nearly ninety, was an enormously wealthy earl of Scotland. "But I must say that Wentworth was the *best* she's dredged up so far."

"He's a cup of cold tea," Cecily shrugged. "Why don't you ever nominate a candidate for the office of son-in-law, Father?"

He was suddenly serious, and there was a faint light of

anger in his eyes. But he said only, "Cecily, your mother and I have disagreed on so many things—but most of all on this. I want you to have a husband who will have three assets—courage, wit, and loyalty."

"What about titles and money?"

"I can give him all he needs along those lines," Lord North shrugged. "But I've seen enough of this marrying a girl off to a scarecrow made of sticks for a fancy title and a few sovereigns. I want your husband to be—the son I wanted. Then—then I can be at ease."

She turned to the door and shot him an arched look, "Well, there's always Lord Roth. *He* has enough gold to satisfy even Mother."

He gave her a quick look and said, "Yes, he has. And enough courage and wit to satisfy me. But what about you, Cecily? Does the Lord Simon Roth have enough to satisfy *you*?"

For one brief moment, Cecily let the habitual smile slip from her face, and she said soberly, "I don't know, Father. I just don't *know*."

He took her arm and led her to the door. "Well," he said gently, "perhaps at the ball tonight you may find out. It's revealing, what a man is in his own castle. Maybe you can look beneath that smooth surface Simon covers everything with."

"Yes, that may be." Then Cecily smiled at him. "He'd do for all of us, wouldn't he, Father? Enough money for Mother, enough courage and strength to suit you—and enough of a *man* for me."

As they went down the stair to meet Lady North, Cecily heard her father say so softly that she almost missed the words, "Strength, money, a title—but what about the *man*?"

Cecily did not answer, but said instead, "Mother, you look beautiful!"

"Thank you, Cecily."

Lady North had heard those words so many times that they slid easily off her smooth face. She was more beautiful than her own daughter, this woman. Even now at the age of thirty-five, the smooth skin, the flawless figure set off by the low-cut gown, the hair without a touch of white, the sleek complexion that put to shame younger women—all was totally admirable.

"We'll be late, Cecily," Lady North said. "But you will be worth the wait for the guests."

"Thank you, Mother," Cecily answered with a rather cold smile. "I suppose it will be the same party, after all."

"Who else would you expect?" Lord North asked. "The nobility doesn't grow a great deal from day to day. Now, the barque is waiting. Let's be on our way before this snow gets worse."

The home of Lord North was on the Thames, and he kept a barque for transport on the river; designed by Henry the Eighth, it was manned by a crew of twelve oarsmen who could send the vessel up or down the Thames as fast as the best carriage. The royal symbol, a lion, was still affixed to the prow, a circumstance that prompted the rather rare wit of the Sovereign, King James. He had once remarked to the court, "North has all the money in the realm—and all that's left is the Crown itself."

"Not so, Your Majesty," North had protested with a wry smile. "As long as I have the money, you may keep the crown!"

Not many dared jest so easily with this dour king. He had grown up with a sour breed of Scottish churchmen who had taken most of the humor out of him, but it was a mark of the royal favor that he had merely laughed at North's jest.

The journey from the palace of Lord North to that of Lord Simon Roth took less than two hours, but it was bitter cold, and the family shivered in spite of the thick furs.

Finally, after what seemed like hours, Lord North pulled the curtain aside and peered out into the swirling drifts. "I think we're about to land. That looks like Simon's palace."

"Good! I'm about to turn into a block of ice!" Cecily said with chattering teeth. "And after all this, I suppose it'll be just another boring affair."

"Not *quite* the same, Cecily," Lady North smiled. She seemed to be impervious to the cold. "Remember, this may be *your* home someday."

Cecily shot her a quick glance and then looked toward her father. Then she said wryly, "Then *Simon* is the next hot-blooded stallion we must consider?"

"You are crude, Cecily," Lady North shrugged without a trace of anger. "Try to be more civil to Lord Roth."

"And to the parson," Lord North added suddenly as he helped Cecily up onto the pier.

"Parson?" Cecily asked suddenly. "What parson?"

"I forgot to mention that a relative of mine—a distant relative—will be one of the guests tonight," Lord North grinned. His face was fixed with the cold, but there was a grim humor in his dark eyes as he handed his wife up to stand on the wharf beside his daughter. "I would appreciate it if you both would be hospitable to him."

As they hurried along the paved walk toward the towering palace of Lord Roth, Lady North asked, "What parson is this, Henry? You haven't mentioned him to me."

"Just a poor relation," Lord North said with chattering teeth. "A son of old Henry Winslow—a younger son, a distant cousin of mine, I might add. I'm thinking of employing him."

Lady North thought about that, then as a footman opened the door to the palace, murmured, "Beware of poor relations, Husband. They can do you no good."

"Must we be concerned only with those who can do us good?" Lord North asked with a humorous look in his eye. He led the two women into a hallway, and they took off their wet cloaks and proceeded down toward a large set of double doors. "Can we not do some good for a worthy relation?"

Lady North did not even acknowledge his question, but Cecily asked pertly, "What possible good can a *parson* do you?"

They had reached the double doors which a footman opened to reveal a large anteroom, and Lord Simon Roth walked toward them.

"He may be of more use than your average parson," Lord North murmured. "I hear he's an able man."

"He's probably a dried up, pinch-lipped piece of dust!" Cecily said, then put a smile on to meet the man who was reaching out to take her hand.

Lord Simon Roth looked a great deal as an English nobleman ought to look, Lord North acknowledged. He took in the tall figure—spare, to be sure, but muscular and youthful despite his thirty-seven years. There was a hawk-like quickness in the brow as well as in the lean face that bent over his daughter's hand. *I should have looked like that*, Lord North thought regretfully.

"Welcome," Lord Roth murmured to Cecily as he touched her hand with his thin lips. "I hope you will feel at home."

"Perhaps I shall," Cecily answered, giving her dark and piercing eyes into his gaze. Both of them knew that he was proffering more than a casual visit, and there was a light in Lady North's face as she nodded slightly at her husband.

"You ladies will want to dress, will you not?" Simon said. "Henry and I have a little business. We will meet you in the ballroom."

"Thank you." Cecily followed the maid who led them down a hall, across a spacious anteroom and up a flight of winding steps. Then, they went down another carpeted hall and finally arrived at a room so large and spacious that it might have served as a ballroom for a lesser lord. It was flanked by a row of tall windows with real glass that let the dim light through quite effectively and illuminated the rich walnut tones of the cupboards, tables and chairs, as well as the massive bed that dominated the room.

Cecily took in the ornate decorations, the tapestries and silver and gold plate that gave a touch of color to the room, then shrugged. "Simon has built quite a place here."

"None in England like it," Lady North agreed, looking at the rich furnishings. "And it may be yours, of course."

"Oh? You're really thinking of Simon now?"

"Of course." Lady North cast a smooth glance at Cecily. "He's the most powerful man in the kingdom—next to your father—or will be, with the proper guidance."

"I see. And what about Wentworth and the others?"

"Not at all possible!"

"No, I can see that," Cecily agreed wryly. "But Simon—he has all the qualifications for a son-in-law?"

"Certainly!" Lady North said. Her smooth composure was broken by a faint surprise. "Surely you must have known that he was the only choice? The others were merely preliminary."

"Of course!"

"Well, now that it's settled—"

"But is it settled?" Cecily asked quickly. "What about Father?"

"Oh, Simon has enough *dash* even for *him*," Lady North said impatiently.

"Oh—and what about *me*?" Cecily asked suddenly. She

picked up the dress the servant was holding up for her approval, then added, "Marriage is a *little* more than money and a title, Mother!"

Lady North seemed to freeze. Her cold face focused on her daughter, and she said almost in a whisper, "No—it is *not*, Cecily! You are engaging in some sort of romantic dream—a poetic fancy—" Her nose wrinkled slightly as if she had smelled a fetid odor. "Your *private* affairs I will not inquire into, but your duty to marry within the realm where fate has placed you, *that* I must see to."

Cecily gazed into her mother's cold eyes and said almost in a whisper, "That is *your* way, Mother. It is not *mine!*"

For a long instant they stared at one another—mother and daughter, so alike, yet separated by a great gulf in mind and passion. Finally Lady North nodded slowly and said, "You will have your own way, Cecily; your father has spoiled you. But in the end, you will do as I have done. You will consider what is best for your own destiny. Have your fling, but do not make the tragic mistake of throwing yourself away for some romantic dream. You are your father's daughter—and he is a romantic fool. I cannot help *that*. But you are *my* daughter as well. I know you do not love me, but it is my way you must follow if you are to survive. So—be cautious!"

"Yes—as you were, Mother," Cecily said, and allowed the maid to dress her for the masquerade.

But as the maid draped her with the ornately bejeweled gown and tried the black mask over her face, she thought bitterly, *I don't need this to hide what I am!*

Then she followed her mother down to the ballroom to join the merrymakers—all adorned, and all masked.

CHAPTER TWO

A PARSON AT THE BALL

★ ★ ★ ★

"Not longing for the days of Good Queen Bess, are you, my dear?"

Cecily turned from the large painting she had been staring at to meet the gaze of Lord Roth. He wore an elaborate doublet buttoned up the side with gleaming pearl buttons. The complicated embroidery on his sleeves alone must have commanded the work of a seamstress for weeks. A black mask hid his face, but there was no mistaking the bold eyes that gleamed at her through the eye slits.

"Yes, I think so, Lord Roth." Cecily held her own mask of Dutch lace away from her face carelessly. "There were men in those days—look at them."

The large painting portrayed a wedding, with Queen Elizabeth carried in a canopied litter borne by courtiers. There was a festive air of celebration gleaming from the painting, and Cecily pointed out the famous men close to the queen.

"See, there's the Lord High Admiral—and there's Edward Somerset, the Earl of Worcester. What a *man* he was! Then I think this must be Lord Hundson, holding his rapier, as usual! I don't know this one, however."

"That's Henry Brook." Roth smiled wolfishly and let his mask fall. "You would have liked him, I think. He had a great deal of that dash and spirit you profess to admire."

"Oh? What happened to him?"

"He was beheaded for treason by Queen Elizabeth, who had first raised him to power." The glittering eyes of Lord Simon held a gleam of humor as he added, "The usual fate of adventurers such as you find so admirable, Cecily."

"You do not find such men necessary, my Lord?"

"No. This is the year of our Lord 1620—not the age of Elizabeth. When she died in 1603, I am pleased to think that the romantic crew she lavished with her praise also went out of style."

"Like Sir Francis Drake—and Hawkins, not to mention Raleigh and the Earl of Essex?"

Lord Roth threw his head back and laughed in genuine amusement. He took her hand boldly and kissed it, then leaned very close to whisper, "I can see I have touched unholy hands to your list of sainted heroes, Cecily! I beg your pardon—though all those men would be out of place in our world."

"The world of King James the First." Cecily gave a sour smile. She waved her fan around the large room and said languidly, "You imitate his horrid taste, Lord Simon. His Majesty thinks that if only one spends enough, the result will be beauty. Father says he will ruin the kingdom if he keeps emptying the coffers on his ridiculous attempts to rival the Roman emperors."

Simon shrugged and glanced around the large ballroom. "Guilty, my Lady, I must confess. It seems to infect us all—the rash and foolish habits of our Most Sovereign Majesty."

They both gazed now at the room, which in itself was larger than many small palaces. Massive walls of stone held up the fan-arching of the ceiling, and on each side huge fireplaces blazed, six of them, and each held logs up to eight feet long. The flickering flames, aided by a great many candles, threw light up among the shadows, and the flash of gilt was everywhere. The rushes on the floor served to deaden the sound of dancers who moved back and forth across the room in the latest Italian steps, and the colors of the costumes almost dazzled the eye—red, green, yellow, all mingled and flashed as the dancers wove intricate patterns in the ever-changing firelight.

Lord Roth drew his gaze from the milling scene of dancers, servants, musicians, jugglers, and a group of Kempe dancers accompanied by three men with taborers and pipes, to draw closer to Cecily.

"It *is* rather *busy*, isn't it? Perhaps we should find a quieter place?"

With an arch smile, she put her mask up and said, "No, Lord Simon, that would be too *romantic*! And you have already informed me that such romance holds no interest for you."

He gave her a sly glance. "I shall hope to convince you otherwise, Cecily. Would you care to try one of those new Italian dances? They are certainly *romantic* enough, even for you!"

She nodded, and they began to move back and forth in the intricate patterns of the newly imported dance that had been accepted by the court of England. There was a seductive quality in the ritual; as Cecily played her role, she felt as if she were the quarry and Lord Simon the aggressive male who must sooner or later corner her and have the way of the flesh.

"Perhaps now that you have finished putting the Wentworth whelp through his paces, you may be more attentive to genuine prospects?"

Despite herself Cecily reacted strongly, throwing her head back to look up at her partner, her eyes growing enormous as she swept his dark saturnine features. Then she attempted to cover up her surprise by murmuring in a bored tone, "I presume you refer to yourself, Lord Roth?"

"You're not surprised at that, surely," he said, holding her even more closely. "Your mother must have pointed out my eligibility to you long ago."

"My mother will not select my husband—nor will my father."

Suddenly Lord Roth drew her through a narrow opening into a small room set in one side of the vast hall, evidently made for storage. In the flickering light of the candles he kissed her, his hard lips pressing against hers, trapping her within the confines of his iron grasp.

Cecily was shaken by his rough passion, but attempted to cover her feelings. She laughed and ducked away from his embrace, saying, "Come, let us dance again!"

As they moved smoothly through the intricate steps past the spectators lining the walls, many eyes were fixed on them—

but none more intently than two men who stood behind one of the long tables filled with food. Lord North watched his daughter with a slight frown on his face, but his companion had happier thoughts.

"They make quite a pair, don't they, Henry?"

Lord North cast a quick glance at the huge form of Bishop Charles Laud. His massive physique swelled out his robe. As the bishop tore at a huge drumstick dripping with fat, North thought, *Laud looks even less like a bishop than I look like a royal duke.* But he only nodded and said quietly, "Yes—quite impressive."

"Money is always impressive, Henry." Bishop Laud paused to wash the meat down with a tremendous draught of wine, wiped his lips, and looked directly at the smaller man. "And power—that's impressive, too. Simon has both, of course, and I suppose you and Lady North will approve of his suit for Cecily's fair hand."

"You would approve, Bishop?"

"Approve? Certainly! He has money and power. You have that, and family as well. What else is there?"

North saw a slightly confused look in Laud's eyes, and he said, "There are those who say that Simon's rise was built on rather unsavory practices. Wouldn't you, as a churchman, object to that?"

"Oh, we'll take care of *that*!" Laud laughed, picking up a hummingbird pie topped with curls of crisp bread shavings. "That's what the church is for, Henry—to wipe out the sins of the successful."

"I stand corrected," Henry North smiled. "I had thought it was a little more complicated than that—from what I've read in the Scripture. And from what the Reverend John Donne puts forth from his pulpit at St. Paul's."

A frown slipped across the heavy face of the bishop, and he shrugged his beefy shoulders restlessly. "Oh, Donne! He's a fanatic! Not much better than those rag-tag Puritans!"

"The Brownists, you mean?" North asked idly. He referred to the followers of Troublechurch Browne, a minister who had filled the land with his idea that all true Christians should separate from the Church of England.

"Yes! And all the rest of them!" Laud's face, usually lit up with good humor, was suddenly ugly, and Sir Henry saw that beneath the sleek, smooth facade of Bishop Laud's cultivated manners lurked a carnivore. "The King has seen the danger of such heresy at last."

"Yes, hanging Penry and Greenwood was a rather strict pronouncement, I thought."

"They won't be the *last*!" Laud snapped. "It was Penry who wrote those scurrilous articles signed 'Martin Mar-prelate,' which attacked the holy Church of England. It must be *stopped*, Henry! It must!" North had heard all this before. His thoughts went to his daughter and Sir Simon Roth—and he was not happy.

As the tapers burned out and were replaced by the servants, Cecily began to grow bored. Simon excused himself, and for over two hours Cecily danced with practically every man of her rank in the room. Finally she sat down with one of her few close friends, Mary Stanhope, daughter of the Earl, and they waved the young men off and talked idly of the ball and other matters.

Cecily yawned and said, "Let's go to our room and talk, Mary. I've never been so bored in my life."

Mary smiled and turned her well-shaped head to one side. She was pretty, but boasted no such beauty as her friend. "Bored with all these men falling at your feet? You're spoiled, Cecily."

"No. They're milksops. Not a red-blooded man in the room."

"Now that Lord Roth is gone?"

"He doesn't have red blood, Mary. Ice water flows through his veins." She said this quickly, but was aware that a flush was touching her cheeks as she remembered his kiss.

Mary caught it, and laughed delightedly. "I can see you don't mean that!" Then she looked up and said, "But—the crop of men isn't much tonight, I'm afraid." Then she paused and added, "Except for *him*, of course."

Cecily followed the direction of Mary's gaze and saw a man dressed in a uniform which bespoke the military, but which she could not recognize. "Who is he? I haven't seen him before," she said.

"He came in about thirty minutes ago," Mary whispered. "He's been watching all the ladies ever since. I think he's trying to decide which one to honor with his presence. My! Look how tall he is! And that hair!"

"Probably cross-eyed and gap-toothed behind that mask," Cecily shrugged.

"Look Cecily! He's coming this way! I think he's chosen *you*! Do you feel honored?"

"I feel he's an insolent puppy who needs to be brought to heel," Cecily smiled slowly behind her fan. "It's a task I delight in."

"I don't know, Cecily," Mary whispered quickly. "He doesn't look like a puppy."

"Watch!" Cecily hissed. "We'll teach him to beg."

"Lady, will you take pity on a poor stranger? I will be lost forever if you refuse to dance with me!"

The voice was low and husky, and the eyes that peered behind the mask were the bluest she'd ever seen—blue as a cornflower. There was a humorous light in them that mocked at the humility of the words, for there was nothing humble in his figure. Tall and lean, like the rapier he wore at his side, there was an athletic smoothness to his bow as there had been to his walk. The mask he wore was thin, not concealing the wedge-shaped face that began with a broad bronze brow and tapered down to a jutting chin bearing a small white scar. The scar drew attention to his wide mouth; a crooked smile exposed perfect even teeth that gleamed in the light of the fires.

Cecily took in the square, well-shaped hands, the strong wrists and shapely arms, the legs set off by the tight-fitting doublet and hose, then said languidly, "A lost soul? Then you must find a priest. There is one over there—Bishop Laud. I'm sure he will help you to find your way."

"Ah, Lady, the bishop can only save a soul; it is not my soul that is lost but my heart."

"Indeed? Then you need a surgeon. I recommend Mr. Deverreaux. He knows all about hearts and their problems."

The wide mouth turned upward in a quick smile, and the blue eyes sparkled gaily as he said, "Not so, fair Lady. He would find nothing wrong with my heart, could he take it out and examine it. For it is not what is in my heart that brings me to death, but what is not there—your lovely self, Lady."

It was the language of courtly love, usually innocent enough. Cecily had seen a performance of *Romeo and Juliet*, and the word play between the two young lovers was light, clever, often stinging. She was quick-witted enough to play the game well, and as for the young man who stood before her, she realized his wit was as keen as his eyes were bright.

Finally she said, "It is my Christian duty to take pity on those who are in pain. Perhaps the dance will restore your health. But your soul will still need the attention of a parson."

Then began a very strange time for Cecily North. For the first time in her life she found a man who could match her wit; indeed, sometimes his words flowed so smoothly she found herself trapped in some of the cunning conceits he laid for her. The ease with which he led her through the dance made the exercise so natural that their conversation—filled with barbed jests and clever innuendoes—was not at all impeded.

Then he said, in that peculiar husky voice that had the unusual effect of sending a shiver along her nerves, "Lady, time is on the wing. Let us not do as yonder tapers and burn ourselves out with nothing to show for all our brilliance."

He had skillfully guided her into the same tiny niche where Lord Roth had led her earlier. *If he had it built for this sort of thing*, she thought with a wary smile, *he ought to keep it locked when he was not in residence*. How the red-haired man had found it she couldn't guess, but she was intrigued by his flow of words and wit as well as by his attractive form.

"What are you suggesting, sir? Surely you are too much of a philosopher to suggest that physical gratification is more important than matters of the soul."

He stepped closer to her and asked, "Do you know Mr. Herrick?"

"No. Is he a minister or a philosopher?"

"A poet, who says better than I what I am feeling this moment—" As he began to quote the poem, Cecily found herself leaning toward him of her own free will. Perhaps she had taken too much wine, or perhaps she was just bored—but as he spoke, that husky voice drew her close to him.

Gather ye rosebuds while ye may,
Old time is still a-flying:

And this same flower that smiles to-day,
To-morrow will be dying.

That age is best which is the first,
When youth and blood are warmer;
But being spent, the worse and worst
Times, still succeed the former.

Then be not coy, but use your time;
And while ye may, go marry:
For having lost but once your prime,
You may for ever tarry.

Then he kissed her—but the encounter was not at all like the one earlier that evening. Simon had held her with his iron arm and battered her lips with force. This time, Cecily was lost in a moment of surrender she could not explain. The room was warm; she had tasted the wine more freely than usual; she was weary—but none of this explained how she suddenly leaned forward and lifted her lips to the stranger who promptly took her in arms that, despite their corded muscle, caressed her rather than bound her. Her own arms seemed to rise of their own accord until she was pressing his head closer and her body closer to his. Cecily had been kissed many times, but never had she given herself like this. The music faded and there was a ringing in her ears, like far-off music heard over water.

"I trust I'm not intruding!"

Cecily pulled back from the man in sudden confusion. The tall form of Lord Roth stood in the opening; his face was pale, and a wild light glowed in his pale eyes.

"I—I—" For once in her life, Cecily North had no quip, no reply; not a single word came to her lips.

"I think this is our dance, is it not, my Lady?" the stranger said suddenly, and she found herself practically pushed through the opening. The red-haired man brushed abruptly past Lord Roth and led her to the floor. He led her through the steps and her head was quickly cleared as she took a glance around the room.

What was I thinking of! she asked herself. Quickly she looked up at her partner to see if he was laughing at her. If there had been one trace of humor, she would have left him at once, but his gaze was sober and he smiled faintly with a lift of one eyebrow. "We must compare poets, my Lady. I'm sure you know a great many."

She felt a quick surge of gratitude as he managed to take the sting out of the moment. Quickly she cast a look toward the wall and saw her father standing with Bishop Laud and another man.

Anxious to speak of something trivial she smiled and said, "There's the parson."

"The parson?"

"Oh, yes. My father said that he had invited one of our poor relations here. I think he's going to make him an object of charity—create some sort of post to keep him from starving. He looks like a parson, doesn't he?"

Her partner took his look at the three men and nodded.

"Most decidedly, a holy man," he nodded, a merry look in his cornflower blue eyes. "He looks sour and unhappy. Quite right. All parsons should look exactly like that."

"Come, I'll introduce you to my father—and to my poor relation."

The three men were watching them carefully, and there was a slight smile on the faces of Laud and her father. The smaller man, who was wearing a common garment, rather the worse for wear, was peering at them also, but narrowly as if he were weak in the eyes.

"Well, now, you've danced the evening away, Lady Cecily," the bishop laughed. "You look quite ravishing."

"Bishops aren't supposed to notice such things, are they?" Cecily smiled, then turned to her father. "May I introduce you to my partner, Father? Except that we have not met. At a masquerade introductions are necessary sooner or later." She glanced at the poorly dressed man beside her father. "I take it this is our cousin, the parson?"

All three men looked a little confused; then her father said, "This is Mr. Tiddle. He serves me in the court from time to time."

"Oh, a lawyer." Cecily looked at him, then shrugged. "I take it you are not insulted to be taken for a parson, Mr. Tiddle?"

"Not at all, Lady Cecily." Tiddle shook his head.

"Your spiritual condition should be considerably better now than at the beginning of the ball," Lord North said with a quick smile at Cecily.

Cecily stared at him and wondered if he *too* had seen the tall man kissing her! "Why, how could that be at a dance, Father? This is no place to practice one's devotion—even if the bishop does attend."

"Perhaps not, but your partner must have given you good counsel, Daughter. That's his business." He took one step forward and put his hand out to the red-haired man. "How are you, Mr. Winslow? I trust you've been quoting holy writ to my daughter as a good parson should."

"I doubt it very much, Henry," Laud laughed loudly; he, too, offered his hand to the man. "Winslow here had a devilish bad reputation at Cambridge. The most *worldly* parson in the whole university, it's said. Well, Lady Cecily, has our parson been effective in saving your soul?"

Slowly Cecily turned to look up at the face of Gilbert Winslow, who removed his mask and was trying not to smile. For a long moment they exchanged glances, somewhat like the clash of rapiers as they searched for weakness; Cecily, especially, tried to cover up her confusion by throwing up a guard.

"I have certainly been highly edified by Parson Winslow's company," she said carefully. "He was just telling me that life is brief—and that all of us must not neglect to use what time we have in the best possible manner. Isn't that so, Mr. Winslow?"

"I doubt that Reverend Donne himself could put it more clearly, Lady Cecily," Gilbert said. His words were smooth, but there was a mocking light in his amazing blue eyes as he continued innocently, "I trust that we will have many opportunities to exchange views on such matters—now that I am the hired drudge of your father."

Cecily's cheeks burned as she remembered his words about the parson, but she made herself smile, and said, "Mr. Winslow, you may depend on it. I will give careful heed to what you have said."

"Then this poor parson is amply rewarded, Lady Cecily. My greatest joy is to pass along a little of what I value most to those I meet from time to time."

This was a new sensation for Cecily North—to be outwitted, especially by a parson! She made herself smile and curtsy, saying before she left, "I shall look forward to your teaching, Mr. Wins-

30

low. The bishop is always encouraging me to attend to my religious duties more strictly. Now that you are here, it will be much more convenient. Good evening."

She left smoothly enough, but she knew that he was laughing at her behind that handsome countenance. That would change, however. He was a man, and no man had ever yet bested her. A smile crept over her face and she murmured, "The next time I'll be ready for our parson!"

CHAPTER THREE

TOURNAMENT OF STEEL

★　★　★　★

Gilbert Winslow slept until the bright February sun pierced the window slit high on the wall, then a servant awakened him. "Sir, you are wanted by Lord Roth."

Quickly he dressed and made his way after the servant along several corridors, up two flights of stone steps, then passed through a set of massive oak doors, probably weighing a hundred stone each, set on hammered iron hinges.

"Well, well, Gilbert, come in!" Bishop Laud was sitting at a low table, perched on a substantial stool eating meat off a silver dish.

"Good morning, Bishop," he said, then nodded his head to Lord North who had turned from staring out a large window to watch him. "Good morning, my Lord." Lord Roth was sitting behind a massive table covered with manuscripts of all sorts, but the cold light in his eyes required only a nod from Gilbert, and a brief, "How do ye?" to which the nobleman did not respond except to turn his head to look at a map lying before him.

Lord North turned to Gilbert. "Sit down, Mr. Winslow. It's time you discover what I have in mind for you. I suppose you've wondered why I sent to Cambridge for you to come to a ball?"

"Yes," Gilbert said. "But for whatever reason, I must admit that the holiday has been a relief."

"You're not content at Cambridge?" Lord North asked.

Gilbert shrugged. "It's not a hard life."

"But you are not happy in your calling—the church, that is?"

"It—was not my choice, my Lord." North saw his firm lips grow suddenly harsh as he added, "My brother, Edward—it was his decision for me to enter the church."

"An able man, Edward Winslow," Laud put in. "He wanted to enter the church himself—but your father had other ideas."

Gilbert bit his lip, turned red, then suddenly smashed a hard fist into his palm, crying impatiently, "That's what Edward has let get out—that my father wanted *me* to go as a churchman— but it's a lie!"

"You think your brother has deceived you?" Lord North asked in surprise. "I have always thought of him as an honorable man. Just as I have thought of your father. You may as well know, Gilbert, I sent for you on your father's account—to offer you a post in return for a service he did for me."

Gilbert stood still, thoughts racing through his mind. He had wondered about this summons from one of the most powerful men in England and what it might mean for him; whatever Lord North's reasons, the words *offer you a post* sent a sudden explosion of release through him.

He shrugged and said more slowly, "Lord North, you know how impatient young men are. In many ways Edward has been a good brother to me. I have been a misfit at Cambridge, but that is not *his* fault. You may know, my Lord, I have had several experiences during the last year which have brought me to the attention of the authorities there."

"Yes," Laud said, trying to look severe. "I have heard of your escapades. According to a report you spend more time gaming, gambling, even chasing local wenches, than reading books of theology. I am shocked!"

"I cannot deny reports, Bishop—since I have been caught in the act," Gilbert grinned ruefully. "But in my own defense I will only say again, Cambridge and the church was the desire of Edward—or of my father, if what you say is true. I have tried to be that man—but it is not my nature, my Lord."

"That may well be," Lord North nodded. "And if that is so, then my offer of a post may be welcome to you. It is not an opportunity without merit, but it will entail your leaving Cambridge and learning to conduct yourself as a man of affairs in business. It will mean travel, and I suppose that will spell *adventure* to a young man such as yourself."

"Sir, I will do it!" Gilbert said, advancing toward Lord North with a light on his face. "I ask not what wages, how hard the work, I ask nothing, for to be set free from my life as it now is, that is a boon from heaven. I will serve you faithfully as well as I can—and I am in your debt eternally!"

"You change careers lightly, Winslow," Lord Roth said. He looked steadily across the table at the younger man and added to Laud and North, "I would think that a young man who can throw over one loyalty so easily would be a rather poor risk. Was there not some sort of vow, some commitment to the church to be made? What of your word there?"

Gilbert flushed and stood stubbornly, meeting the cynical glance of Lord Roth. His voice was even huskier than usual. "A hit, Lord Roth, I must confess. You have me, indeed. I can only say to Lord North, give me the opportunity to prove that when my heart is in the task—as it has *never* been at Cambridge—I will let them take this head from these shoulders before I will betray you!"

"I will have you, then," Lord North said quickly. He advanced and held his hand out, which Gilbert took and gave a hearty squeeze. "Now, we will work out details of your stewardship later in private, but while we are all here, we must make plans. All three of us are involved in an affair which will require your service."

Gilbert looked at the three men, and could not imagine any three more different spirits than North, Laud, and Roth, but he merely nodded and waited for Lord North to explain.

"Lord Roth and I have several trading interests in common, one of them in Holland. We are in need of a man who will give his attention to the venture, and it is for this that I have suggested you to Lord Roth. You will have my clerk, Tiddle, to assist you. He will know the details, but you will handle the affair as well as you can on your own authority. I will rely on Tiddle to keep you out of trouble, but you must learn to stand on your own feet as quickly as possible. Now, you are perhaps wondering about the presence of the bishop in this matter of business," Lord North said. "I will let him explain that to you, and I must tell you that if you take the post, I have promised the bishop he will have your full cooperation. That will be one of the terms of your employment with me."

Bishop Laud began to pace back and forth in front of the window. He had a high-pitched voice, which he ordinarily kept under control, but Gilbert noticed at once that the matter he spoke of angered him so greatly that he spoke shrilly.

"You know of the trouble the Separatists have given us, Winslow. You know it because your brother, Edward, is sympathetic toward that vile movement. I fear he has been drawn into their designs, and one benefit you may reap from this task I am going to require of you is the salvation of his soul—not to mention, possibly his *head*!"

"You're not serious, Bishop!" Gilbert protested. "Edward is no traitor."

"Perhaps not *now*, but others have been destroyed by listening to Troublechurch Brown and others of his ilk. We know that Edward Winslow has had close communication with one William Brewster, and that alone is enough to put him in jeopardy."

"William Brewster? I don't know him."

"If you *did*, you would not be standing here," Laud snapped. "He is a fugitive from justice, from the King's justice."

"What is his crime?"

"He is part of the Scrooby group, a troublesome pack of Separatists and Puritans who fled England ten years ago to escape their obligations to the English Church. They settled in Amsterdam, then moved to Leyden. Brewster was one of their leaders, and in 1617 he set up a press in Leyden." The bishop gave a short laugh and waved his hand toward Holland. "The press was located, poetically enough, on *Stincksteeg*—Stink Alley, in English! He avoided that name by adopting the address of his side door, which was located on Choir Alley—and that is the name of the press."

"What sort of things did he print?" Gilbert asked.

"Violent attacks on the Church of England. Especially one called "Perth Assembly," which our noble Sovereign King James read. He at once demanded that the guilty printer be found and brought to justice!"

"But he was not?"

"No, he escaped. Sir Dudley Carleton, the English Ambassador to Holland, was put in charge of the case. He found the press, and French wine barrels stuffed with seditious pamphlets. Brewster, however, had vanished, and is still at large."

Gilbert stared at the fat bishop. "But—what does this have to do with me?"

Laud stopped pacing the floor and smiled slyly at Gilbert. "Why, my dear young man, *you* are going to find William Brewster for us!"

"I! Why—I am not a sheriff!"

"You will be better to us than a sheriff," Laud said quickly and there was a grim ferocity on his face now. "No officer of the King will ever find the man. Those psalm-singers are too closely knit for that! But there is a way—and it is your employment with Lord North that makes it possible."

"The bishop came up with this idea after I informed him of your employment—and your first assignment," Lord North nodded. "I have a young clerk who is violently in love with a young woman who is a member of the Separatist group at Leyden. His name is John Howland; the young woman's name is Elizabeth Tilley. He has been involved in the Dutch venture in a very minor way from its beginning."

"Exactly! And he is, we think, a member of the church there, although he does not make that public to *me*!"

"He'd be a fool if he did, Laud," Simon grinned suddenly. "You'd have his head in a basket!"

"I would indeed!" Laud nodded vigorously. "But, here is the plan, Winslow. You will go to Leyden with Tiddle and Howland. You will join yourself to that same body and discover the whereabouts of Brewster."

Gilbert stared at the bishop and then at the other two men. North was watching him carefully, interest filling his round face, and Gilbert knew he had no choice but to accept the task.

"I see," he said finally. "I'm to be a spy."

"A spy?" Laud protested. "Perhaps. But this man Brewster is a traitor to English justice. Winslow, you will be doing your country, and your church, a service by turning the man over to the law. And, I might mention, there is a *very* large reward offered by the King himself for his capture. Enough to begin your new career with some dash and style!"

Winslow stood there, caught in a wave of passion. With all his soul he longed to enter the service of Lord North. But—to be a *spy*! It went against the grain, and there was a revulsion that stuck in his throat at the thought of worming his way into a group—then selling the victim for gain!

Lord North was watching him closely, and he murmured, "Gilbert, your father was a good friend to me. If you cannot with good conscience undertake this mission, we'll find another man. And someday I may be able to find other employment for you."

"No!" Gilbert shook his head, swallowed, and said strongly, "I will do it, Lord North. After all, the man is a criminal!"

Lord Roth laughed harshly, and got up, a sardonic sneer on his wolfish face. "And after all," he snapped as he passed through the door into the corridor, "there is money to be made from it!"

"Lord Roth will come around, lad," Lord North said, reaching up with a friendly slap on Gilbert's shoulder. A warm light filled his face. "You'll need to stay tonight. I want to meet with you and Tiddle; we'll give you a good background on the Dutch affair."

Late that evening the Great Hall was abandoned in favor of a small room for the evening meal. It was large enough for the thirty or so who sat around the long tables, with enough space left over for the traveling players to put on their show.

Gilbert could not decide if it were by chance or design that he sat directly across from Lady Cecily North. He had thought at first that Lord North wanted him to be close by so that he could talk more about the Dutch affair, but the nobleman had paid him no attention save a friendly word on the quality of the jugglers.

Cecily had not been as quiet. At first, to be sure, both of them were somewhat reserved, but as the meal progressed and ribald barbs of wit flew around the room, as the wines and ales began to loosen the tongues of most of the guests, she began to show a little more poise. He found it easy to tell her about his slight acquaintanceship with Ben Jonson (whom she admired greatly), and they were soon deep in conversation about that poet and others. Their tastes were a great deal the same, and both were naturally quick-witted. From time to time, Lord North and other guests who were close enough to hear their talk would listen, but a baffled expression soon revealed that such conversation was of no interest.

A faint gleam in Lord North's eyes revealed his pleasure in his daughter's quick wit and wide knowledge; he had educated her as fully as a woman could be taught in his day. He was even more interested in her response to the tall young man he had taken into his service. Looking at Gilbert, he traced the firm line of the determined jaw, the clear blue eyes and highly arched nose, thinking how much more he himself could have accomplished if he had been blessed with a more well-favored body. Not one to waste time mourning over impossible things, however, Lord North had long ago decided that since he would not have a son to pass his name and his fortune to, the next best thing was to find a man who could have the courage, determination, and wit to hold onto it—or even better, to enlarge it. As he watched Gilbert hold his daughter's attention as no other man had, he began to hope that he had found his man. *Too soon to tell*, he told himself. Nevertheless, Winslow was all he longed for in a son. No money, of course—but North had plenty of that, and if the young man proved himself worthy, and could carry Cecily along with him, what could hinder?

After the sumptuous meal Will Stanton cried out, "Well, let's have some excitement! Lord Roth, what say you to some fencing, eh? I volunteer to challenge you—*again*!"

"You are a stubborn fellow, Will," Simon smiled. But his face lightened as he looked at the foils on the wall behind him. "Shall we have a tournament, then?"

A cry went around the room, and the servants appeared to make ready a space for the swordsmen. Quickly they cleared one of the tables, and soon it was filled with rapiers, daggers, broadswords, masks and guards of all sorts.

"Lord Roth keeps an arsenal, Lord North," Gilbert murmured as they heaped the weapons high.

"Yes, it's his one interest—aside from getting richer," North said quietly. "He's one of the best swordsmen in England. He's already killed one man in a duel."

Gilbert watched as the two men chose two foils which were tipped to prevent injury, then set themselves for the contest. There was something deadly about Simon's attitude, even though it was only a fencing match. His eyes narrowed and there was a strange unholy light in his pale eyes as one of the men touched their blades and said, "Engage!"

The hall rang with the sound of steel on steel, and the spectators' cheers began to break the air. "Ah, that's the way, Will!" Waller cried out. "Keep it up! Keep it up!"

But although most of the crowd was cheering for the younger man, it was quite clear to Gilbert that there was no contest. Roth was simply toying contemptuously with his opponent. Several times he almost touched his chest with the tip of his foil, then let it pass so that he could play with young Stanton a little longer.

Then, suddenly, Gilbert saw Roth's face turn cold, and with a wild lunge he forced his younger opponent to the wall and drove the foil against his chest with such force that Stanton gasped with pain and Simon's foil bent nearly double.

"Oh! That's it for me, my Lord!" Will cried out, rubbing his chest. "I see I have a little practice in store before I challenge you again."

A laugh went up, and as Stanton put his weapon on the table, Gilbert found himself staring into the eyes of Lord Roth, and even before the older man spoke, he knew what was coming—and why!

"It's too bad, Mr. Winslow, that you are a man of the church. We might have an interesting match, you and I. Oh!"—Lord Roth pretended to be surprised—"well, you are wearing a sword! How odd for a parson! But surely it's not for use?" Lord Roth's lip curled and he looked up and down Winslow's tall figure, then said with contempt in his tone, "But I never knew a parson yet who could do anything well—anything but hide behind the skirts of the church."

Gilbert stood there in sudden silence, the red of his hair suddenly complemented by the crimson flush that touched his high cheekbones.

He knew it was a foolish thing even to consider. He was to be an employee of Lord Roth, at least for one very important venture. To alienate him would be stupid!

"My Lord, it would not be seemly for me to cross blades with you. I am afraid—"

"Yes, we can all see *that!*" Lord Roth laughed loudly, and slammed his foil down on the table. "Oh, do not be perturbed, Parson. I did not really expect to see a person such as yourself behave like a *gentleman!*"

This time there was no alternative. Gilbert turned pale, but his voice was steady as he said, "I was about to say, Lord Simon, that I was afraid—that you would be deceived if we were to have a match. My studies at Cambridge have been such a source of boredom to me that for the last year I have sought relaxation— in the art of fencing."

Suddenly Lord Roth laughed. "And which of the scholarly Dons gave you lessons, Winslow?"

"Monsieur Paul Dupree."

Lord Roth's face went still and he echoed quickly, "Paul Dupree? You have studied under him?"

"Yes, my Lord."

"Well, in *that* case, we must certainly have a bout!" Lord Roth picked up his foil and said, "Choose your weapon, Parson."

Gilbert peeled off his coat and gave his sleeves a turn up to the elbow. Picking up a thin-bladed rapier already tipped, he slipped his own sword off and turned to face his opponent. "I am ready, Lord Roth."

They touched blades and it could not be said that Simon Roth was a rash man. He knew the formidable reputation of Paul Dupree better than anyone else in the room, and any pupil of his was no novice.

Carefully they circled the room, and the fire threw huge contorted shadows on the masonry walls. Swaying back and forth, they moved catlike across the rushes, their feet making swishing noises, and ever the ring of steel sounded in the ear.

Gilbert knew that he had never faced such a master—except for Dupree, who was not quite *human!* Roth had a fencer's body—lean, muscular; his timing was exquisite.

There were no cheers, in fact, the only sound was the sliding feet of the fencers and the steel pinging out repeatedly. Once Gilbert almost failed to parry, and the button on his opponent's sword almost touched his breast, but he recovered and drove Simon back with a desperate show of physical strength.

It would have ended with a touch had things continued. But the button fell off the tip of Lord Roth's foil—and suddenly Gilbert backed away from a violent rush from the older man, managing to turn aside the needlepoint of Simon's foil by a series of minor miracles.

He had no chance to look into Roth's eyes, but the man *must* realize that he was playing with an uncovered tip! He must! Then, one quick glance during a moment's respite and he saw the catlike cruelty in his opponent's eyes. Roth knew—but he was going to keep on until he buried the blade in the heart of Gilbert Winslow.

It was relatively dark in the room, and by the faint blaze of fires, and in view of the fact that Lord Roth never let his sword stop, no one saw the condition of the foil. And of course, if Lord Roth killed him, he could look sad and astonished. "Poor fellow! I never *dreamed* the guard had fallen off!"

Desperately Gilbert gave ground, his sword arm tiring. Simon drove himself forward, thrusting, twisting, darting like a madman; then Gilbert felt the table strike the back of his legs!

Lord Roth must have seen it, must have maneuvered him into that position, for he lunged forward, ignoring the feeble parrying thrust that Gilbert managed to achieve. The next thrust, Gilbert knew, would go right through his heart! And as he saw the arm of Lord Roth draw back for it, he threw his arms over his head and did a violent and awkward backflip over the table! Dishes and goblets flew everywhere with a tremendous crash, and the top of his head struck the floor with a dull thud—but he was alive!

Several women screamed, and as he started to scramble to his feet, an inspiration struck Gilbert. If he got up, Lord Roth still had that naked point—and there was no doubt about his willingness to use it.

Instead of standing up—which was *exactly* what Lord Roth was expecting—Gilbert rolled under the table. There was Roth, poised and ready to skewer him across the table, and he had time only to catch a quick movement at his feet as Gilbert reached out and slapped Roth's sword wrist with all his strength!

Lord Roth's sword fell, and Gilbert quickly got to his feet. He said with scorn, "You've dropped your weapon, my Lord. Use mine."

He tossed his own blade to Roth, handle first, then in a single motion scooped up the fallen rapier and faced Lord Roth with the naked tip pointed right at his throat.

"Shall we continue, my Lord?" he asked, and Simon saw that he was bested.

Before he could speak, however, Lord North said loudly, "Wait, Gilbert! That sword—the point has been knocked off." He rushed forward and took it from Gilbert's hand. "Why, this could have been most tragic!"

"A good thing you noticed it, Lord North," Gilbert said, not taking his eyes off Lord Roth. "Someone could have gotten killed."

"I can't think how such a thing could happen," Lord Roth said, taking it from North. "They don't make these as well as they should." Then he laughed and said to Gilbert, "Well, Mr. Winslow, you do well—for a parson. Perhaps we can try it again at a later date?"

"At your pleasure, Lord Roth."

Gilbert stared at the man, knowing that he'd made a deadly enemy, and he cursed himself for his foolishness.

He was still angry at himself the next morning when he mounted his horse and rode out of the stable. All night long he'd tossed and turned, trying to think how he could have behaved with more wisdom.

"Gilbert—Gilbert Winslow!"

He pulled his horse up, and there, leaning out a glass window opened to the weather, was Cecily. She was more beautiful than he had thought. The snow on the sill and the white stone of the castle set off her dark beauty like a foil.

"Lady Cecily," he said with a rueful smile. "I must take my leave. Your father is my employer now, and I am his to command."

She laughed and leaned out a little farther. "So? But he is

mine to command! Didn't you know that? I can wind him around my little finger!"

"Him or any man," Gilbert smiled.

"Will you come back soon?"

"If you would have it so."

"You are a daring man, Gilbert Winslow; therefore, I dare you to come again. Come to see me, not my father. We have something more important to talk about than business," she smiled; then loosed a scarf and let the breeze carry it down to where he waited. He nudged his horse with his spurs, caught the snow-white fragment of lace, kissed it, then put it in his inside breast pocket.

"You will see me soon, my Lady Cecily—and the next time we meet, I trust I can think of a better name for you. *Cecily*—that's for parents, for friends. I must think of something much better."

"You'll steal it from some poet, Gilbert," she laughed, then turned quickly to look inside. "Someone is coming. Don't forget—I'll be waiting!"

As Gilbert rode toward London to meet with the lawyer, he thought himself a very fortunate fellow. His future now was secure! No more pettifogging little parson's life for him—no, indeed! With a man like Sir Henry North to favor him—and a woman like Cecily North to inspire him—to what could he *not* aspire?

If he could have seen, at that moment, the face of Lord Simon Roth, he might not have been so cocksure. Simon had not missed Winslow's leavetaking with Cecily, and for a long time his pale eyes remained fixed on the road where the young man had disappeared. Finally, he nodded as if to himself, and a strange smile of satisfaction appeared on his thin lips. "I think the parson must be seen to," he said softly.

CHAPTER FOUR

A MATTER OF HONOR

★ ★ ★ ★

"You know London, do you, Mr. Winslow?"

Gilbert felt a sudden pull at his arm, and looked up just in time to avoid being flattened by a coach-and-four driven by a haughty driver in livery. "Well, I've not been in this part of the city." The lawyer nodded and plunged into the thick of the heavy traffic, skillfully threading his way between vehicles and pedestrians.

"This is Cheapside," Tiddle said out of the side of his mouth. "Our man lives not far from here. Step lively, Mr. Winslow! Our ship weighs anchor in three hours!"

"I think you'd best call me Gilbert—since we're to be together so much, Mr. Tiddle."

"Fair enough. I'm Lucas." He lowered his head and led Gilbert down the street almost at a lope. Carts and coaches made such a thundering it seemed as if all the world went on wheels. At every corner they encountered men, women, and children— some in the sooty rags of the chimney sweeps, others arrayed in the gold and gaudy satin of the aristocracy, gazing languidly out of their sedans borne by lackies with thick legs. Porters sweated under their burdens, chapmen darted from shop to shop, and tradesmen scurried around like ants, pulling at the coats of the two men who fought their way through the human tide that flowed and ebbed on the street.

"Watch yourself!" Tiddle said sharply, pulling Gilbert back just in time to avoid a deluge of slops that someone threw out of an upper window. "Nearly got you, lad! But now that the city's put the drain in the street, why every rain will wash away all this garbage." He waved his hand at the ditch about a foot wide and six inches deep in the center of the cobblestoned street. "That carries all the slops and garbage away quite nicely, you know? Wonder what a change modern improvements make, isn't it? Why, most cities just let the garbage and slops pile up— but not London! No, sir!" Tiddle paused in his admiration of the open sewer to wave his hand and say, "There. I think that's it."

Gilbert followed him up two flights of rickety wooden steps, then down a dark corridor. The lawyer knocked firmly on the oak door and at once it opened, as if the young man who stood before them had been waiting for their appearance.

"Mr. Tiddle, I saw you coming up the street." He was a husky fellow, perhaps twenty-five, with warm brown eyes set far apart under a pair of bushy brows. Turning his head to one side like a bird to stare at Gilbert, he asked, "Be this Mr. Winslow?"

"Yes," Tiddle said. "This is John Howland, Winslow. We must hurry. John, I suppose you're ready?"

"All packed," Howland said. He picked up a wooden chest bound in brass and followed the two men into the corridor, pausing only to fasten the massive padlock on the door.

"We'll take a coach," Tiddle said. "Wouldn't do for us to miss our ship." He gave Howland a sharp grin and said, "You've been away from that wench of yours so long I daresay you'd *swim* the Channel to get your hands on her, eh, John?"

The young man's tanned face grew rosy, and he answered, "You mustn't talk like that 'bout her, Mr. Tiddle; she' not one of your tavern wenches!"

Lucas laughed and slapped the husky young man on the shoulder. "I know she's not, John. I know." Then he glanced at Gilbert. "John's got himself a real preacher woman, Gilbert. Got him so holy he won't even *spit* on the Sabbath! But she's a good cook—and a fine figure, too! You *did* notice that, I trust?" He dug his elbow into Howland's ribs and gave a piercing whistle at a coach which stopped as if the horses had run into a wall.

Tiddle and Howland kept the conversation rolling as they threaded their way through the narrow, crooked streets of London. Gilbert had seen only a little of the city, but he felt a warm glow as he realized that before long he would know it as well as Tiddle.

Winslow had left the university with a sense of adventure rising in him. Tiddle met him at his office, and the next three days were spent learning the rudiments of the business affairs that would occupy him in Holland. They had packed and left to pick up Howland for the journey.

Tiddle was a talker and Gilbert was a listener. The lawyer was not impressive in appearance, but he had a mind like a razor. He was, after all, the most trusted advisor of the second most powerful man in all of England, and Gilbert wanted to gain his confidence.

Once Tiddle stopped abruptly in the middle of a complicated explanation and gave Winslow a straight look. "This is tedious, Gilbert—but you must learn it if you are to become the man Lord North desires." Then he grinned and peered up at Gilbert in his shortsighted fashion, adding, "And I do not mean a man of business!" He laughed aloud at Gilbert's blank look, then continued, "You may be aware that North is shopping for a son-in-law?"

"Well—I hardly think he need look my way," Gilbert said with a rueful laugh. "He's got the pack of English nobility to pick from!"

"He's already sorted through that crowd," Tiddle sniffed. "Nothing there for him. No, he's a man who'll pick his own raw material, pour money into the man he likes, and that'll be *it*!"

"Modesty forbids me to say how much I think I deserve such an honor, Lucas."

The shrewd eyes of the lawyer held a sly twinkle, and Lucas smiled as he said, "You may just do it, Gilbert. It wouldn't be the first time a young fellow such as yourself made his way to the top by way of a rich father-in-law." He paused and added, "I see that doesn't trouble you; but have you made up your mind as to this business with William Brewster?"

Gilbert shifted uncomfortably. "Well, I must admit it seems pretty raw. I'll be a spy no matter how you try to refine it."

"That's the way of it, I'm afraid. I'm thinking you may have too much religion for the world of business, Gilbert. You were preparing for the church at Cambridge, and the world is no church!"

"It's not that," Gilbert answered slowly. It was difficult for him to explain his distaste for the mission, but he felt he had to try. "I'm not really a churchman. That was my brother Edward's idea. And I would never have fit into that world in a million years! But—well, church or no church, Lucas—there *is* such a thing as honor! What I'm being asked to do is beneath a gentleman!"

"Oh." Tiddle stared at the young man as if he were scrutinizing a rare animal. He took a pinch of snuff, then said gently, but with a barb in his tone, "A gentleman, is it? If you'd seen as many 'gentlemen' as I have—selling their souls for a shilling, all ready to step on anyone who gets in their way—well, you might have to adjust your ideas somewhat."

"But there is such a thing as honor!"

"There's such a thing as doing the job Lord North has assigned to you! You will either do it or you may as well go back to Cambridge. It's not at all complicated, Gilbert." Tiddle lifted his hands in an abrupt gesture and spoke to the young man before him as he would have to a slow-witted apprentice. "You either pack your rather antique sense of honor away and do what you have to do—or you leave the world of business alone."

Gilbert bit his full lower lip and stared out the window. Finally he said, "All right, I'll do it."

"I thought you might," Tiddle nodded dryly. Gilbert felt as if he had parted with something that had been quite valuable, and the emptiness which he carried about in its place sobered him considerably. Tiddle patted the young man's broad shoulder. "Don't feel too bad, Gilbert. The loss of innocence is rather painful—but I assure you the time will come when you will cease even to think of it." He stared at Gilbert soberly, then shrugged and ended, "And the good news is that no man ever died from losing it."

Gilbert stared at Tiddle and finally gave a tight grin, saying in his husky voice, "Well, now that I've sold my soul, when may I expect to gain the whole world, Lucas?"

The lawyer laughed suddenly, but there was a note of sadness in his face as he looked at Gilbert. "Now that you have put the next world out of your plans, Gilbert, I think you will soon see your barns begin to fill up. I'm a little sad to see a young man like you sell his soul for a mess of pottage, though!" he jested to take away the sting.

"A mess of pottage!" Gilbert exclaimed, then grinned at Lucas. "Why, I'm getting a much higher price for my soul than that! I'm new in business, but even such a novice as I can drive a better bargain with the devil than a mess of pottage!"

Tiddle stared at Gilbert for a long time, then spoke so quietly that the young man almost missed it: "Well, I trust you will enjoy your bargain—but it may be more expensive than you think now, Gilbert Winslow!"

"There's Leyden just ahead, Gilbert," Lucas nodded out the carriage window. He turned to look at the young man slumped in the seat beside him and gave a wink in the direction of Howland sitting across from him. "Don't tell me you're still seasick, lad? Come now, you can't have anything left in your stomach— not after the way you heaved all the way across the Channel!"

Gilbert raised a hollow-eyed face the color of old ivory. The voyage had been a nightmare for him, for he had discovered with the first roll of the twenty-ton merchantman that he was no sailor.

By the time the ship touched at Amsterdam, Gilbert had long ceased to be afraid that he would die—he only wished he could! Howland had practically carried him off the ship and put him in a carriage, and he had been unconscious for most of the trip to Leyden. They had stopped for a meal at a small inn, and while his companions had wolfed down a huge meal of veal and cheese, Gilbert had managed to keep down a half pint of cold ale and a few swallows of fresh bread. Deciding he was going to live, he finally managed to sit up and take in the scenery that unrolled as they made their way toward Leyden—mostly flat fields silvered with winter's touch. Windmills everywhere turned their huge sails, and neat stone and clapboard houses dotted the fields. "We'll put you off at your brother's house," Tiddle said. "He's expecting you. I wrote to him myself."

"When will we . . ." Gilbert began, then glanced at Howland and bit off what he was about to ask. The husky young man with the innocent face was to be his key to opening the mystery of William Brewster, but the plan to infiltrate the church fellowship was to be between him and the lawyer.

Tiddle said quickly, "You have your visit out, Gilbert, and John here will be courting his young woman. Just make yourself at home." Lucas's face did not change, but at the words *make yourself at home*, a light touched his small bright eyes, and Gilbert nodded slightly, knowing that it was his role to become a familiar figure in the little community of Separatists.

When the coach finally pulled up in front of a snug little cottage set in the midst of a small grove of trees, Gilbert felt ill at ease. "We'd better hurry," Lucas said. As Howland got the baggage from the boot, he whispered to Gilbert, "Remember, we must be quick. Don't go too fast; your brother is no fool— and neither is Bradford. But the thing must be done quickly before the man gets away for good. I'll probably leave you here for two or three days." He got in the coach with Howland and they rolled away, leaving Gilbert feeling very much alone.

There was nothing to do but go on, so Winslow moved to the door. He had raised his hand to knock when the door opened, and he found himself face-to-face with his brother, who reached out and pulled him into the house.

"Gilbert! Why, you've grown into a fine man!"

Edward Winslow was in the prime of life, thirty-two years old. He had long red hair, a smooth, good-natured face, a neatly trimmed moustache and a powerful frame overlaid with a layer of fat. His eyes were the same cornflower blue as Gilbert's and seemed to look right into the soul of the person before him. He was wearing a fine lawn collar turned out from his throat, tied beneath a silk, red-tassled cord. A fine corduroy coat with a double row of silver buttons and silk breeches in the Dutch style completed his costume.

Gilbert took only a quick glance at his brother's dress; he was staring at his beaming face. For six years Gilbert had made this man the villain in his little drama. Now looking at his brother's face, he could not find the evil foe he had slain in his thoughts a thousand times.

"Elizabeth!" Edward called, and kept his arm around Gilbert's shoulders as he turned to a woman who came through the low doorway at the end of the hall. "Elizabeth, he's here! Gilbert's here!"

"I'm glad to see you, Gilbert," Elizabeth said, holding out a bony hand for him to clasp. "But you don't look well."

"I was seasick, Elizabeth," Gilbert stammered. His brother's wife was a frail woman, specter-thin and possessed of numerous ailments, real and imaginary. She was a startling contrast to her husband, who was blooming with vitality.

They took him into a large comfortable room with a huge fireplace, and for a time Elizabeth plied him with remedies for his ailments while Edward questioned him about his activities. When Elizabeth left it seemed to make the air a little freer, and both men breathed more easily. Edward once again clapped his younger brother on the shoulder and smiled warmly. "I hear you're changing careers."

It was a critical moment, for Gilbert realized that if he were to gain entrance into the Separatist fellowship it would have to be through Edward. Now he stammered as he tried to explain. "Well, Edward, I know you always thought that I should be in the church, but—"

"Just a moment, Gilbert," Edward said quickly. "Father wanted that, and I have tried to carry out his wishes—but it was never *my* design."

This put Gilbert at ease and he went on more smoothly with the speech he had planned. "I have tried to find my place in the Church of England, really I have. But, it's not for me, Edward. Let me explain. For the past two years I have grown to be more unhappy with the practices of the English Church. Now, there are many good men who serve as priests, and I have no quarrel with them if they are content. But I *cannot* in all honesty continue to follow what I believe to be unsound Christian practice!"

"I see."

Gilbert noted the quick look of interest Edward took in this, and worked himself up into a pitch of excitement, loathing himself for his pretense. "To be quite frank with you, I find the Church of England to be a huge mass of old and stinking works—a patch of popery and a puddle of corruption! The Lord has said, 'Come ye out from among them and be ye separate, and touch not the unclean thing!' " Gilbert had learned this speech by rote from the men at Cambridge who were known as "precise men" who advocated separation from the state church, and he hoped fervently that his face pictured the outrage that his words stated. He finished with the defiant words: "The true church must be restored to purity!"

Edward was staring at him with burning blue eyes. "You really mean that, Gilbert?"

"Yes!"

"Then I welcome you into the fellowship of those who are on just such a quest!"

There were tears in the eyes of Edward Winslow, and he threw his arms about Gilbert, saying huskily, "I have prayed for this, Gilbert! It was not our father's way—but it is the way of God!"

"You're not angry with me?"

"Angry? No! It is the way of courage, Gilbert. I welcome you into the ranks of God's warriors!"

"I—I will try to be faithful, Edward," Gilbert said, but there was a heavy weight on his spirit. This man, this brother—whom he had trained himself to hate—this was no hypocrite! If he was a true sample of the Brownists in Holland, the task he had vowed to accomplish would violate the very foundation of a truth held sacred! Gilbert remembered suddenly the words of Lucas Tiddle: *It may be more expensive than you think!*

Then he thought of Cecily and Lord North, their glittering world of excitement—and he smiled and took his brother by the hand. "I will join you, Edward!"

Edward Winslow's face was bright with a sudden happiness, and he gripped his younger brother's hand, saying, "I have prayed for you, Gilbert. Now that the Lord has opened your eyes, like the great Apostle Paul you must begin your race. We will go to the meeting tomorrow, and you will meet your companions on the quest. They will welcome you into the fellowship of saints and receive you as a brother beloved—as I do now!"

Gilbert Winslow had violated most of the Ten Commandments with enthusiasm. His life had been a careless affair insofar as doing *right* was concerned. He had defiled himself almost cheerfully, tasting of forbidden pleasure at will. But never had he felt the condemnation of spirit as he did now—holding his brother by the hand, committing himself to the society of those who had renounced the world to follow Christ. And as Edward embraced him again, he could almost hear the words *thirty pieces of silver*! They seemed to echo from heaven—or from hell. He resisted the impulse to put his hands over his ears to shut out the sound.

Instead, he stepped back and made himself smile. He said, "I trust I may prove myself worthy to be a part of God's band of saints, Edward."

He was thinking, *Thus I begin my new career! Gilbert Winslow—spy and hypocrite!*

CHAPTER FIVE

AT THE GREEN GATE

★　★　★　★

Gilbert took a long drink from the pewter mug and slammed it down on the oak table, exclaiming, "I never thought it would be so easy to be a Judas!"

Tiddle leaned back in his chair and gave Gilbert a tight smile. He shook his head. "So, that *honor* of yours is bruised already, is it? Well, you'll have to be more of a Judas than that before you're of any use to us here in Leyden, Gilbert. You've been here three days and nothing you've found out is worth a farthing."

Gilbert shook his head stubbornly, took another drink of the dark red wine, then said, "Why, I don't see any problem—Edward has already accepted me as one of the *saints*. Doesn't appear to be too difficult to join this congregation."

Lucas shrugged his thin shoulders, pulled a large watch out of his vest pocket and stared at its face. Replacing it, he pulled his cloak around him and said, "I must hurry to catch the ship—but let me tell you this, young man—these aren't fools you're dealing with! I notice you haven't heard the name of William Brewster mentioned, have you?"

Gilbert shook his head. "Well, no, but that's only—"

"That's only because these people are not going to give the man up!" Tiddle got to his feet. "I'll be in London reporting to Lord North in two days. I'll tell him what we've accomplished, which is precious little!"

Lucas threw a coin down on the table, turned and left the inn without another word. When Gilbert followed him outside, he saw a frown on the face of the lawyer and was taken aback when Lucas said in a voice absolutely harsh, "This is the world of business, Gilbert Winslow! You'll do what you have to do to find this man Brewster. Lie, cheat, steal, deceive—whatever is necessary. That's what it will cost you to make your place with Lord North. You have my address—don't bother to write until you have something to say!"

Winslow stood there, struck dumb by the harshness of Tiddle's manner. Caught short by the savagery of the attack, for a moment he considered getting on the ship and going back to England, forgetting the whole thing. But it was too late for that! For better or for worse, he was committed to the world of business—and as he turned and made his way slowly down the cobblestone street toward the house of his brother, he pondered—not for the first time—the end of this strange business.

He forced himself to smile as Edward and Elizabeth came to meet him. "Am I very late?" he asked.

Edward took his arm and smiled, "Why, as it happens, we just have time to stop by Elder Bradford's house before the service if we hurry."

As they walked down the linden-shaded avenue he asked, "Did you get your lawyer friend off properly, Gilbert?"

Gilbert nodded and said with a sigh, "Yes. He left me here for a few days to finish some business. I trust I'll not be an inconvenience to you and Elizabeth."

"An inconvenience!" Edward flashed him a brilliant smile, struck him lightly on the arm and said with enthusiasm, "We'll have time to get acquainted, brother! And I'd have you know and be acquainted with your fellow saints. Come now and we'll have time to talk a little with Bradford and his wife."

They made their way to a poor section of town, passing through crowded quarters, the street cut by many winding lanes and alleys. At the end of the street they came to a small brick house covered with moss up to the eves and topped with dull red tiles. As they paused in front of the cobblestone walkway, a man and a woman came out and made their way down the sidewalk. Edward said, "Ah, William, we're not late I trust—

and Dorothy—you look well today! Let me make known to you a new seeker—this is my younger brother Gilbert, about whom I have often spoken. Gilbert, Elder William Bradford and his dear wife Dorothy."

William Bradford was a middle-aged man with a full beard and a large wart on his right cheek. He had the air of one impatient with those who were not quick and he pulled at his nose nervously, nodded shortly and said, "It is good to have you in Leyden, Brother Winslow. I trust your stay here will be profitable."

"We'd best hurry or the services will begin," Dorothy said. She was much younger than her husband, not at all the type of woman Gilbert expected in a Separatist. She was blonde, with large blue eyes; the frilly lace at her bodice reflected a taste for finery that clashed with the stern grays and blacks of the rest of her costume and with that of her husband. The fine planes of her face spoke of an aristocratic background, this also in contrast to her husband. His features were craggy, rough and deeply creased.

"Dorothy is right—we must hurry," Bradford said, leading them down the street and across a series of small intersections.

Whether deliberately or not, Gilbert could not tell, but Bradford fell into step beside him, leaving Dorothy to follow with Edward and Elizabeth. He commented briefly on Gilbert's arrival, asking several rather pointed questions about his business in Leyden, and there was a faintly suspicious light in his eyes as he glanced at the young man and asked, "You are, I understand, a member of the Established Church?"

At once Gilbert realized the snare that was laid. Edward had, of course, accepted him at face value as being an earnest seeker, but this man had no reason to trust him. Carefully Gilbert said, "That has been my history, Elder Bradford, but along with many others, I've had serious doubts of late concerning the integrity of the way I have been taught to follow."

Bradford's head swiveled and his eyes bored into Gilbert, his question sharp, "You intend, then, to leave the Established Church and become a Separatist?"

Fighting the impulse to blurt out a quick agreement, Gilbert allowed a note of regret to creep into his voice. "No, I cannot say that at this time. It's too soon. I have hopes that the Lord will give me a word of wisdom on this subject soon—but as for now I am, as my brother says, merely a seeker for the truth of the kingdom of God."

The sharp light in Bradford's eyes, Gilbert saw with relief, softened and he nodded, saying in a more genial tone, "As the Scripture says, 'Ye shall find me when ye shall search for me with all your heart'!"

"Amen!" said Gilbert and as they walked along, Bradford gave him a few details on the meeting place.

"For many years, we met in the homes of individuals. It was not until May of 1611 that we acquired a permanent place of worship—this is it up ahead. It's called the Kloksteeg—or Bell Alley, as we would say it. For a long time it was known as the *Groenepoort*, or Green Gate, and so it is still called by most of the natives here. It is a fine house, and it serves both as a meeting place and a parsonage for our pastor and his wife and three children."

"We're late," Bradford said. "Come and let us join in and afterward, my brother, you will have an opportunity to meet the congregation."

Nothing about the meeting that day suggested the Church of England to Gilbert. The first shock came when he discovered that the saints were not allowed to sit as they pleased in cozy little family groups. As they filed in, the men took their seats on the hard wooden benches to one side, the women sat apart across the aisle, while the children were placed off by themselves under the stern and restless eye of the deacons. Gilbert learned that this was known as "dignifying the meeting."

The saints prayed, and during the prayer the members of the congregation stood up, for kneeling was, as Gilbert learned later, an idolatrous Roman practice. After the opening prayer, which continued a little longer than an hour, a small, pale-faced man identified as Pastor Robinson took up a huge Bible and read aloud. He paused often for comment and exposition, and after this a psalm was sung without any instrumental music of any kind, nor did the congregation have musical notation of any kind to aid its singing. All tunes were sung from memory. Someone set the pitch, usually one of the deacons, then all lifted their voices together, with the men taking the lead in the simple melody. The saints evidently shared Calvin's aversion to any frills in a religious service.

After several hours of the singing came the sermon, preached not from a pulpit but a low dais supporting a simple wooden table. Here, in black clothes and black gloves, Robinson expounded his text with a quiet and moving eloquence, a deep human understanding, and a wealth of apt illustration.

When the sermon was concluded, the congregation sang another song, and the sacraments were then administered. Two men came forward to pass the collection plates, and the morning exercise ended about noon with a benediction.

Gilbert felt rather awkward, but he was led by Edward through a small garden behind the house where the congregation met to talk briefly before their noon meal. He was, of course, an object of curiosity to the congregation, and most of them gathered around to be introduced. Isaac Allerton, a thin man of about thirty-five, his wife Mary—a little younger—both bowed deeply and introduced their children—a young boy named Barth and a girl with the strange name of Remember. Standing beside them a couple named White, William and Susanna, whose son was dressed in black exactly like his father, although he was only five. He bore the unusual name of Resolved. Noticing that Gilbert was taken slightly aback by the unconventional names of the children, Bradford brought forth a slender woman with a dark olive complexion, accompanied by two small boys. A twinkle appeared in the elder's eye as he said, "This is Sister Mary Brewster, Gilbert—" and Gilbert looked up swiftly, recognizing this woman as the wife of the man he had been sent to ferret out. "And these are her two boys, Love and Wrastle."

A large, thick-bodied man with a black beard and a pock-marked face shouldered his way through the crowd surrounding Gilbert and said in a voice that thundered, "Well! So this is the young scholar we've heard so much about, is it, Edward?" His massive hand swallowed Gilbert's, and a solid thump on the shoulder shook the newcomer to his heels.

"Careful there, Deacon!" Edward laughed, and turned to say to Gilbert, "This is Samuel Fuller, one of our deacons."

"And a physician, sir!" Fuller's large eyes gleamed with

humor, and he stepped back to survey the visitor shrewdly. "Cambridge, is it now? Well, I'd spend some time with you, young master Winslow—to see if your stay there has left any brains in your head!"

Bradford smiled gently and with a shake of his head said, "Now don't wear the young man down, Samuel—he's not one of your patients, you know."

"Well he will be, soon or late!" Fuller smiled and said to Gilbert confidentially, "I'm not the best physician in the world—but my fees are reasonable, so come to me when you have an ailment for body or soul! Sam Fuller's your man!"

The burly physician seemed to have taken a liking to Gilbert, for he pulled him toward a table set with a light meal of round loaves of fresh bread, butter, cold cuts of several types and large containers of fresh milk. It was a time, evidently, of fellowship and of simple relaxation, and Gilbert allowed himself to be ushered to a stone bench in the garden while Fuller ran on with his mouth full, usually concerning the church—of which he was obviously very proud.

"Now, you'll not understand some of our ways, Winslow, but if you'll pay attention to the Holy Discipline, why you'll soon find your way!"

After listening for an hour to Fuller expounding the views and beliefs of the Brownists, they got up and went again into the house where Gilbert was introduced to "prophesying." Pastor Robinson chose a text, spoke on it briefly, and then opened the meeting for general discussion. Despite himself, Gilbert was impressed at the broad and deep knowledge of the Scripture possessed by most of the men and was likewise struck by the gentlemanly nature of their bearing.

By three o'clock Gilbert had dozed off several times, losing track of the sophisticated arguments that went around the room. But his attention had been attracted by two young women who sat well toward the front of the room on the women's side. The one closest to him was a small girl with brown hair and a pretty face. From the looks she exchanged with John Howland, who sat on the men's side across from her, Gilbert assumed this was the Elizabeth Tilley whose praises he had heard from the husky young man. The other young woman was hidden behind Elizabeth, but when the final "amen" was said and the congregation rose and filed out into the afternoon air, Gilbert made it a point to tell Edward that he would walk for a while around the town before returning to the cottage. Most of the congregation took time to stop by and say a friendly word of greeting, and out of the corner of his eye, he saw Howland and his young woman leaving through a gate to the north of the house, accompanied by the other young woman. Quickly he made his way through the gate and caught up with them as if by accident.

"Oh, there you are, Gilbert," Howland said with a broad smile. "I don't believe you've met these two members of our congregation. This is Elizabeth Tilley, and this is Humility Cooper. May I present my friend Gilbert Winslow."

Gilbert was taken slightly aback as the young woman turned her eyes upon him and said in a low voice, "How do you do, Mr. Winslow?" She was far more attractive than any of the other women of the congregation. And even the strict dark colors of her long black dress did not disguise her womanly figure. She had green eyes with a broad face and her coloring was glorious— red lips, bright cheeks, eyes very wide spaced and the whitest teeth he had ever seen. Her hair was tied up under her bonnet— as was the custom with all the women—but the blonde tresses that escaped had glints of red that caught the fading afternoon sunshine. A slight dimple appeared on her right cheek when she smiled at him, and she had honest frank eyes more like a man than a woman. She looked directly at him, and there was something bolder in her appearance and her appraisal of him than he had expected.

"I'm walking Elizabeth and Humility home, Gilbert," John Howland said. "Won't you walk with us for a way?"

"You're very kind, John," Gilbert said with a smile. He allowed Howland and Elizabeth to go on and the girl named Humility fell in beside him as they strolled down the street.

Gilbert Winslow had enjoyed some success with women, and he was prepared to begin his tactics by charming this girl with the strange name of Humility in his usual manner. But she looked at him and asked in a most serious manner, "The Spirit of God moved quite wonderfully among us this morning, did He not, Mr. Winslow?"

Gilbert's jaw dropped open, and for one moment his mind was totally blank. The girls he had known had had nothing to say about the Spirit of God, and he coughed slightly before he managed to answer, "Why—ah, yes, I think that is very true, Miss Cooper."

"And what was your opinion of Reverend Robinson's concept of sanctification?"

It was fortunate for Gilbert that at exactly this moment Howland turned and said, "This is the street where the Tilleys live, Gilbert." For Gilbert had nothing to say in response, and he was furious at himself at being taken off guard. *This is one of those holier-than-thou wenches who has forgotten how to be a woman!* He managed to stammer out a few words as they watched the young women go into the house; when they turned to head back toward the center of town, Howland did not notice Gilbert's discomfort. He was too busy singing the praises of Elizabeth and encouraging his friend to see all of her virtues.

After Gilbert put the matter of Humility Cooper aside, he began to listen more closely to John, and to lead him into a description of the members of the congregation. Howland was so simple that Winslow had some difficulty ascertaining the basic facts about the various individuals and their families. All the same, Gilbert noticed that not even Howland mentioned William Brewster. Gently he brought the young man's mind on the track by saying, "I don't remember meeting the dark lady's husband— what's her name? Oh, yes, Mrs. Brewster. Is she a widow?"

Howland looked disconcerted, bit his lip and said, "Oh, no, her husband is one of the elders of our congregation—Elder William Brewster."

"Oh? I don't believe I met him, did I, John?"

"No," Howland stuttered, and the words came slowly from his lips as he attempted to explain. "You see, Elder Brewster has been away. Humility and her brother Henry are servants of Mr. Tilley, but the Brewsters are really like parents to them—especially to Humility."

With a little urging, Howland told the complete story without being aware in the least of his friend's interest. Gilbert knew from his earlier reports that the leadership at the Green Gate Assembly had been under close surveillance by spies of the crown from time to time. None of them had had any direct contact with William Brewster—that much was certain. But Brewster *had* to maintain some kind of communication with these people. *If this girl is that close to Brewster*, Gilbert thought suddenly, *how possible, even likely, it is that Brewster's contact with the leadership might be through her!* By the time Gilbert said goodbye to Howland and turned to go to Edward's cottage, a scheme was fully formed in his mind.

He hastened to the small upstairs room that had been allocated to him, threw himself down before a table, and with bold strokes wrote a letter to Lucas Tiddle. There was a cruelty of sorts on the broad lips of Gilbert Winslow as he set down the following words:

> My dear Tiddle,
>
> You left me under a cloud, suggesting that I would be rather useless so far as Lord North's mission is concerned. I must confess, my dear fellow, that I was both hurt at your rather pointed and barbed statements and somewhat fearful that they might prove to be true!
>
> I write hastily to inform you that you may soon expect to hear from me very good news! I am no detective, and must confess that my talents for spying have not been developed by my earlier career—however, one discipline I have studied and pursued with alacrity, and that studying now stands me in good stead.
>
> In a word, there is a member of this congregation, Humility Cooper, who is in the confidence of our friend Brewster. She appears to be quite an attractive girl, and perhaps intelligent, but I have taken dead aim upon Miss Cooper, and if she can withstand the wiles of this novice spy, she will be unique! Expect to hear from me by the next post more concerning the elusive Mr. Brewster and the decline and fall of Miss Humility Cooper!
>
> Your most obedient servant,
> Gilbert Winslow

CHAPTER SIX

HUMILITY

★ ★ ★ ★

Edward Tilley pushed his chair back from the table and looked around at his family—his wife Anne, his daughter Elizabeth, called "Bess," Humility Cooper, age eighteen, and Henry Sampson, age sixteen. Humility and Henry were his adopted children and served as servants in his household.

"Anne, be sure you have enough bread baked to last over the Sabbath," he said quietly, pushing back from the table. "I'd not like to run short as we did last week."

"I will see to it," Anne replied quickly.

"Papa, will it be all right if I go with the group to Bargsteen?" Bess asked. "All my friends are going, and I must let them know right away."

"I don't believe you should, Bess," Edward Tilley said thoughtfully. "We have heard some evil reports of the activities of young people who go on these trips."

A frown swept across Bess's pretty face and she said petulantly, "Oh, Papa, don't be so narrow-minded! Nothing wrong happens on these trips; I've told you that a hundred times!"

Anne Tilley looked nervously at her husband, nodded shortly and said, "I think it would all right, Husband. They are very nice boys and girls, and there's not much for Bess to do in the town."

Humility rose from the table and began collecting the dishes as the argument went on. When she got back from the kitchen, Mr. and Mrs. Tilley were gone, and Bess looked up with a mischievous smile on her rosy lips. "I think you ought to go with us this time to Bargsteen, Humility. You never go anywhere, and we'll have such fun!"

Humility gave her smile and said, "I'm too busy this time, Bess. Maybe later."

"Oh, all you ever do is read the Bible and talk with Pastor Robinson about it," Bess said in disgust.

She got up and began to help pick up the dishes and when they got into the kitchen with them Humility said, "I've got to go down to the harbor for a few minutes, Bess. Would you please mop the floors in the bedrooms for me?"

Bess gave her a sharp look and tapped her chin with her forefinger, then asked in a teasing voice, "Going to the harbor *again*? It seems everytime a ship comes in you have to run down to meet it." She laughed gaily and said, "You must have a sailor for a sweetheart, Humility! Or maybe more than one, from the way you meet all the ships."

Humility flushed slightly and shook her head. "Don't be silly, Bess. Will you do the bedrooms for me?"

"Oh, of course I'll do them," Bess said, "but you be careful about meeting those sailors—you know their reputation!" She gave Humility a playful pinch on the arm and said as she went from the room, "I've got to go down to the Millers and get that flour we're short of, but as soon as I get back you can go to the harbor—for *whatever* reasons you have!"

Bess made her way to the Millers which was only a few blocks away, got the flour, and was within a block of her house again when someone spoke to her from behind.

"Good morning, Miss Tilley."

Bess turned to see Gilbert Winslow smiling broadly. He seemed to tower over her, and as she leaned back to look up into his wedge-shaped face, her heart fluttered as it always did in the presence of a handsome man. "Why—good morning, Mr. Winslow! My, you're out early this morning."

Gilbert walked down the street with her and after exchanging pleasantries, he mentioned Humility's name, and immediately Bess turned her head and looked at him. "Well, you needn't waste your efforts pursuing Miss Cooper," she smiled. "She's a very virtuous girl and absolutely man proof!"

Gilbert laughed and said, "Come now, Miss Tilley, no beautiful woman is absolutely man proof—no one should know that better than *you*!" He began to flatter her, and before they had gone ten steps she was giggling at his remarks.

"Surely Miss Cooper must have many suitors?" he asked.

"Oh, no, not Humility! Though of course, I *have* been a little suspicious of her for the past few months."

Gilbert quickly asked, "Oh, she has been seeing someone, then?"

"No, not really," Bess shook her head. "But I have noticed that every time a ship comes into port, Humility doesn't waste any time getting down there."

"Oh, you think she has a sailor as a sweetheart?"

"No—no, not that—but I believe she is getting letters from someone abroad—probably England. As a matter-of-fact, I'm hurrying home now so she can go to the harbor."

Gilbert said hurriedly, "Well, here you are, but I must run, Miss Tilley. I'll see you again soon."

Gilbert walked rapidly down the street, took the first turn to the right, and paused, thinking hard. He had to gain a closer standing with Humility Cooper, but that task seemed almost impossible. Grown girls were watched so closely in this community of saints that is was rare for a strange young man to have access to any of them. But what he had heard from Bess, however, made him hopeful. If his guess was correct, and Brewster was getting information to the elders, this might be the lucky coincidence that would lead him to find the source.

He loitered around the neighborhood, always keeping out of sight of the Tilleys' front door, and within fifteen minutes Humility Cooper came out and headed directly toward the harbor, a twenty-minute walk. He kept well behind, although it was not likely that she would be suspicious. When she reached the wharf, he saw her stop a man, ask a question, and walk along the stone wharf until she came to a small two-masted schooner. Several sailors were on deck, and she called to one of them and then stood waiting. A portly man, obviously the captain, came down the gangplank, and Gilbert saw them nod to one another then carry on a short conversation. He handed her an envelope, which she placed in a small bag she was carrying, then nodded, and went back up the gangplank.

She did not come back toward him but took another route, and Gilbert said to himself as he followed her, *I'll bet my last farthing she heads right for the Reverend John Robinson!*

He would not have lost the bet, for in a few moments she went up to the door of the Green Gate and, without knocking, passed inside. Gilbert thought quickly, and without hesitation walked down the street, turned into the door, and knocked briskly.

He recognized the small woman who opened the door as the wife of Pastor Robinson, and said, "Good morning, Mrs. Robinson; may I see your husband, I wonder?"

She hesitated then said, "Come in, please. Someone is with him now, but I think he will be glad to see you."

She led him across a large open hallway. On the left he recognized the meeting room where services were held. They walked to the end of a long hall, and Mrs. Robinson tapped at a massive heavy door on the right.

"Yes, what is it?" Pastor Robinson himself opened the door, and from where he stood, Gilbert could see Humility standing near a large desk in front of some high bookcases. She gave him a startled look, but he kept his eyes fixed on the man in front of him.

"I'm sorry to intrude, Pastor Robinson. Perhaps I should come back later?"

"No, no, come right in, Mr. Winslow."

Robinson stepped back and nodded to his wife, who turned and left. Gilbert went in to stand in front of the desk, saying, "Why, it's Miss Cooper!"

Pastor Robinson said, "I think Miss Cooper was just leaving—"

Gilbert waved a hand hurriedly and said, "Oh, no! I only wanted to stop by and see if you could spare me a little time, Pastor."

"Time for what, Mr. Winslow?"

"Well, I have been much aware of late of my need for a deeper knowledge of the Word of God, and if you could be my mentor, I believe it would be a great blessing to me."

A willing smile crossed Pastor Robinson's face, and he said, "Why, certainly! Why don't we begin to meet on a regular basis—say, at three this afternoon? Perhaps that would be suitable?"

"Excellent!" Gilbert cried, and he shrugged slightly, saying, "I'm afraid you'll find me dreadfully stupid! My time at Cambridge seems to have been totally wasted!"

"Oh, I doubt that," Robinson said, "but I can recommend a list of books that we might begin with." He leaned over his desk, wrote rapidly across a sheet of paper with a goose quill pen, then handed it to Gilbert. "These will do to begin with—if you need to purchase them, I believe you'll find them at the bookshop down by the market."

Gilbert gave a negative shake of his head, "I'm afraid I don't know the place." He did, but he was hopeful that he could lure Humility Cooper away. He was totally successful.

Robinson nodded toward Humility. "Humility, would you be so kind as to show Mr. Winslow the bookshop? It isn't out of your way, I believe."

She gave Winslow a quick look, then said, "Of course, Pastor. If you're ready then, Mr. Winslow—?"

As Pastor Robinson led them out the door, he asked by way of parting, "Humility, are you going on the trip that Bess has been pestering me to death about—over to Bargsteen with that group of young people? I doubt her father will permit it."

Humility smiled and shook her head, "Oh, she's going, all right. Did you ever know Bess to fail at doing exactly what she wanted to do?"

The pastor shook his head. "I wish you'd go with them, Humility. I'd feel much better, and I'm sure your parents would also if you would accompany Bess."

"If you say so, I'll be glad to."

Immediately Gilbert said, as if in surprise, "Bargsteen—Bargsteen? Why I have to make a trip to Bargsteen! That's one of the cities I'll have to make a business trip to for Lord North."

"Why, perhaps you can serve two purposes, Mr. Winslow," Robinson said quickly. "If possible, perhaps you might go along with these young people as sort a companion and see to your

business at the same time. They leave day after tomorrow—
would that suit your purpose?"

Gilbert nodded and appeared to think about it. "Day after
tomorrow—let me see—why, the very thing! It will work out
admirably! And I'll have the opportunity to do some small service for the congregation—perhaps the first of many, Pastor Robinson."

"Fine, fine!" Pastor Robinson said. "Well then, Humility, if
you'll show Mr. Winslow his way, he can get his books, and
we'll begin to make a theologian out of him—and thank you very
much, Humility."

"Come, Mr. Winslow, I'll show you the bookshop."

As he walked along the cobblestone streets toward the center of the village where the bookshop was located, Gilbert said,
"You're looking lovely today, Humility."

His use of her first name made her cast a quick glance at
him, but the pleased expression immediately changed to a
frown. "Thank you, Mr. Winslow." She slightly emphasized the
word *mister*, but Gilbert had seen the startled expression of pleasure.

"Mr. Winslow, I'm happy to hear that you're starting to
study the Word of God with Pastor Robinson. I feel he is the
most able minister in the whole world."

She had shown, Gilbert realized, a defense against men, and
there was no quick way to penetrate it. He thought then of the
trip proposed by the young people which he had agreed to participate in, and determined that he would break her resistance
down one way or another on that trip. For the present he had
another scheme, so he said when they got to the bookshop and
she turned to leave, "Thank you very much, Humility, for your
assistance. I'll see you again soon, the Lord willing."

He felt no guilt at the religious expressions he used, for he
was convinced that Humility Cooper was playing one game—
the game of being a Christian saint. He was simply playing another game in order to achieve his own ends. If he could find
out from this girl the whereabouts of William Brewster, it would
be simply a matter of winning a game—and he was better at his
game than she was at hers.

"I'm glad you're going on this trip with the young people,

Mr. Winslow. Pastor Robinson tells me you're studying theology with him, and I'm quite pleased that you are choosing to do so."

William Bradford had drawn Gilbert aside on the morning of the departure for Bargsteen. Gilbert had been aware that there was a reservation in Bradford's manner, and he had gone out of his way larding the elder with scriptural quotations and pious talk on every occasion. Now he felt sure that he had gotten the confidence of the man, and he said modestly. "I do feel that God is speaking to me in an unusual way, Elder Bradford. I trust that I will be found worthy to join your congregation before too long."

Bradford shook his head and said, with more openness than he had shown in the past to Gilbert, "I fear, Mr. Winslow, that our congregation stands on precarious ground here in Leyden. We are here by the permission of the Dutch government, and as you know, Holland and Spain have erupted into open warfare several times already. There are two powerful forces struggling for control of this country, and if it comes to an open conflict—well, we still remember the horror of the Spanish Inquisition when it was introduced to this country in the 1570s."

Gilbert stared at him and asked, "You may have to flee for that reason, Elder Bradford?"

"Not only for that reason, for even if that situation never developed, we are troubled over the future of our children. You see, a new generation has grown up here without memories of England. The discipline of our congregation bears down hard on the spirits of the young. They watch their Dutch friends having entertainment on Sundays, while they are expected to spend the day listening to sermons. It is inevitable, I suppose, that young people will be attracted by the high-spirited traditions of Holland. You have seen, I'm sure, Mr. Winslow, the women of these parts give great liberty to their daughters. Sometimes they stay out until the gates of the city are locked, and the young men entertain them at inns all night or until they please to take rest. The young men and women go by horseback and in carriages to cities ten or twenty miles distance and there feast until late at night—and this they do without all suspicion of unchastity. That is why I am glad you are going on this excursion," Bradford said with a smile. "And I exhort you to take care of the virtue of our young women."

"You may trust me for that," Gilbert Winslow said with a straight face. "If there is anything in this world that interests me, it is the virtue of young women!" Then, lest Bradford should see any humor in his eyes, he asked quickly, "And this situation is so serious that you may move out of Leyden?"

"It is indeed; necessity forces most of our young people to labor in shops and mills. It is hard work, and they have no economic gain to look forward to in this country."

"But—where would you find a place for your people?"

Bradford stared at him for a moment, pursed his lips, and then said quietly, "The New World." He seemed to be lighted inside by the thought, and his eyes gleamed as he went on. "We are engaged now in such an investigation that may prove profitable." Then suddenly he stopped and looked straight at Gilbert, and the open manner disappeared from the elder as he said quickly, "This is all confidential, Mr. Winslow, and I urge you to say nothing of it."

"Why, of course not," Gilbert said at once. He filed the matter in his mind, knowing that it was the sort of information the authorities of England would be glad to have.

Later that morning, Gilbert and John Howland were packed into a carriage with several other young people as they made their way across the brilliant countryside. Bargsteen was a large village some ten miles from Leyden, and when they arrived, the village square was packed with people. Gilbert reached up and handed Humility down, an action which caught her unawares and brought a faint flush to her cheeks. She nodded to him and said in almost a whisper, "Thank you." And he held on to her hand a few seconds longer than absolutely necessary.

They all went to a large inn and were shown to their rooms, Gilbert sharing a common room with Howland and two other Dutchmen, and Humility and Bess doing the same with some of the young women. They met together for a supper at the long table in the inn; after supper, just as darkness was beginning to fall, Gilbert noticed that Humility got up and walked out of the room through the large front door. Glancing around, he saw that no one was paying any attention, so he rose up and went after her. When he got outside, he saw that she was walking slowly, head down, toward the long canal that intersected the center of the marketplace. It was a narrow canal, no more than six feet across, spanned at frequent intersections by arching stone bridges. He let her get a few hundred yards from the inn and managed to come up quite close before he called out, "Humility."

She turned in surprise and said, "Oh, it's you, Gilbert." The use of his first name did not pass unheeded, and he stepped up beside her, noticing for the first time that she was taller than most women.

He said, "It's beautiful tonight, isn't it?" Then he added, "May I walk with you for a while?"

She hesitated then said, "Well, only for a little way—I must go in soon." He walked beside her, and the red flashing sun threw rippling streaks along the surface of the water in the canal below. The cool breezes of evening brushed against their faces. As they went farther from the center of town, a quietness spread out, and their voices seemed loud in the silence. Once he allowed his arm to brush against hers—apparently by accident and noted that she did not draw back. They spoke idly of the things that had occurred on the journey until finally they came to one of the arched bridges, and Gilbert said, "Let's cross this bridge and pretend it's London Bridge."

She smiled at him quickly and he recognized with a shock, *Why, she's beautiful*! Taken aback, he did not speak until they reached the crest of the bridge. They stood staring down at the rippling water beneath.

"I've never seen London Bridge." Humility took a tiny stone, threw it over the side, and watched as it hit the water and the circles spread to the sides of the tiny canal. "I suppose you've been there many times, Gilbert?"

"Oh, yes, I've been to London. I've been to many other places, too—but, I suppose places are about the same." He hesitated, then looked down at her and added softly, "People are born, they grow up, they fall in love—" Gilbert paused at this last word and watched her face carefully for any response. Finally, he smiled and went on, "—they marry, they die—and that's what life is, Humility." He looked at her face and asked gently, "Isn't that what you want with your own life, Humility?"

She looked up at him and said breathlessly, "Oh, I don't

know! I really don't know, Gilbert—" She bit her lip, shook her head, and there was a note of desperation in her voice as she went on quickly, "I've thought about—about love—and, and—" She seemed to have trouble with the word, but forced herself to go on. "I've never been able to get it straight in my mind how I can love God best and love a man at the same time." It seemed to shock her that she had said something like this so bluntly, and she gave a little gasp and started to draw back.

Gilbert Winslow was never a man to miss a golden opportunity like this. He drew her close with a smooth, practiced motion—not so recklessly that he would frighten her nor so gently that she could pull away. Her eyes opened wide as he pulled her into his embrace, and she seemed unable to move as his body pressed against hers. Her lips opened slightly in shock, and he strongly suspected that never before had Miss Humility Cooper ever felt as she was feeling at this moment. He lowered his head, and let his lips fall upon hers. They were lips soft by nature, and soft as a result of the surprise and shock that came to her as his arms met, closed around her.

At once a resistance stiffened her backbone, but as the warmth of Gilbert's lips touched hers, it seemed to spread like a fire through her veins; he felt her resistance melt, and she allowed him to pull her even closer. Humility's heart was beating fast; unconsciously, her arms raised and went behind the back of Gilbert's neck, and for one moment they stood there embracing, caught in the powerful magnetism between a woman and a man.

Then she drew back with a gasp, her eyes staring; her face, at first pale, took on a crimson flush starting at her throat and sweeping up over her face. She said in a stammering voice, "I— I can't—" Then she put both hands to her face and turned blindly away.

Gilbert instantly took her arm and said what he knew must be said. "Humility! Forgive me—I don't know what came over me!" He led her down the bridge and continued as she walked blindly down the lane. "I can't tell you how I regret such behavior! I've *never* treated a young woman in such a fashion in all my life!" This was true enough, for the young women Gilbert Winslow had kissed in such a fashion had never been let off so lightly, and he had to conceal a quick grin that swept across his features.

He continued apologizing all the way back to the inn; finally she stopped and turned to face him, her composure restored to some degree. Her eyes were still wide and her lips trembling, but she did not appear angry. She was, Gilbert perceived, shaken from her complacency, and he rejoiced to see it. Finally she said, "We were both wrong, Gilbert."

Gilbert shook his head, "There can be no wrong on your part! I have never known a young woman who has such depth of spirit; I must say the thought that came to me when I first saw you: a woman of virtue and of such beauty is a pearl of great price."

Humility touched her cheek with one hand, then, confused, turned away from him and went through the doorway, leaving Gilbert standing outside. He stood there for a few moments; then a broad smile flashed across his lips and he said under his breath, *"Well, Humility, my dear! Underneath that drab exterior and strict Puritan behavior lurks a tiger! I'm glad to discover it; and it will be my duty as well as my pleasure to tame the beast!"* As he followed her into the inn, he knew he had won the game.

CHAPTER SEVEN

THE INNER RING

★ ★ ★ ★

"Oh, Gilbert, I'm so glad you returned in time for my birthday!"

Dorothy Bradford leaned forward, put her hand on Gilbert's arm, and swept the crowded room with excitement in her eyes. She was wearing a bright green dress full in the sleeves and trimmed with yellow silk. The other women, for the most part, wore bright colors also, and even some of the men were decked out in gay array. Gilbert had been surprised at first, thinking that the Separatists wore only black or dark gray; he soon discovered, however, that the more somber dress was only donned on the Sabbath—and on festive occasions they loved to wear brighter colors.

"My dear Sister Bradford," Gilbert said with a smile and a nod, "you did not think I would miss it, did you? After all, when a beautiful lady issues an invitation, it becomes, in effect, a royal command!"

Dorothy lowered her eyes, then looked up with a brilliant smile. "Oh, you're such a flirt, Gilbert! I don't see how Humility can put up with you!" She slapped his hand playfully, then looked up, saying, "Oh, here come the Tilleys—I must go speak to them." She turned to leave but paused for one moment to give him an arch look. "And now that Humility's here, I suppose none of the rest of us will be able to get your attention for one moment!"

Gilbert watched her go to greet the Tilleys, then made his way through the crowd toward where Humility stood. The hot June sun had warmed the Bradford house, and the heat from the packed bodies made a sweltering furnace of the large living room. As he approached Humility, he wiped the sweat from his brow, thinking how quickly he had entered into the life of the little fellowship. Only two weeks had elapsed since the trip to Bargsteen, but he had spent almost every day since in her company. The lifestyle of the Separatists was simple, composed primarily of work and services that lasted all day on Sunday, and from time to time a celebration such as this birthday supper for Dorothy Bradford. He had achieved the distinction of being accepted as Humility's suitor, so that they were spoken of together often. It was common to hear the phrase, "Gilbert and Humility," when plans were being made for such events. Pushing his way through the crowd, Gilbert smiled and thought: *Almost any time now Mr. Tilley is going to corner me and demand to know what my intentions are!* He reached out, took the hand that Humility extended to him, and raised it to his lips, delighted as always with the blush that rose to the girl's cheek when he made any gesture of affection. Her eyes dropped, and she hesitated as he held her hand a moment longer, then she murmured, "You—you shouldn't do that, Gilbert. It's—"

He laughed easily, his white teeth flashing against his ruddy skin, and said, "I can't think why not! Doesn't the Scripture say to greet one another with a holy kiss?"

"I'm not sure how *holy* your greeting is," Humility responded quickly, but there was a light of pleasure in her wide green eyes.

"Well, I suppose it's my fate to be forever misunderstood. As the Scriptures say, 'Man is born to trouble as the sparks fly upward.' " He took her by the arm and piloted her through the crowd toward the long table laden with food, saying cheerfully, "You aren't fasting, I trust? I'm practically starved to death! Let's try to get something into our stomachs before these gluttons devour it!"

They filled their pewter plates with coldcuts of beef, fish, mutton, and fresh vegetables of a bewildering variety, then found a tiny vacancy in one corner of the room. Sitting down, they ate and enjoyed the noisy hum that ran around the room. Gilbert looked around, thinking again of how mistaken he had been about the habits of the Separatists—not only in the matter of dress but in their character and social habits. Somehow he had formed the idea that all they did was sit around in dark clothes, looking mournful and trying to think of new ways to keep people from enjoying life. He had, however, soon discovered that though they worked terribly hard, when they got together on festive occasions, they put equal energy into that part of their lives. They loved to eat and to fellowship and not only the children, but the adults as well loved games of all kinds—a trait which gave some misgivings to the more sober leaders of the congregation.

He had discovered quickly, too, that the same energy with which they worked and played carried over into their services when they worshiped God. Accustomed as he was to the staid and formalized rituals of the Established Church, Gilbert had been taken aback at the emotional fervor with which the Brownists approached God on the Sabbath. There was a sense of excitement as they sang; he was shocked to find that they actually *believed* the words of the Psalms they sang with such gusto! He himself had long since failed to relate the words he sang in the services of the Established Church with anything having to do with real life! When he had heard the Green Gate congregation sing Psalm 150 for the first time, enthusiastically singing the words: *Praise ye the Lord! Let everything that hath breath praise the Lord!* the volume and pitch almost lifted Gilbert out of his seat. And all through the long sermons (which sometimes numbed his brain), an alertness illuminated the eyes of the hearers, and a little refrain of sound echoed the minister's words: "Amen! Yes, that is true! Bless the Lord!"

Gilbert Winslow's experience with formal religion had not been of this nature. These people looked forward with anticipation to celebration when they went into the house of God. Most Christians Gilbert had known left church with the feeling, *Well, now that's done—I can get on with the things that really matter!* But to the worshipers at the Green Gate, worshiping and serving

God seemed to be the things which *did* matter, and they went through the rest of their duties in order to get to this experience. It somehow made him feel uncomfortable, but try as he might to attribute their fervency to some sort of emotional disorder, when he sat in the service, looked about, and saw the pleasure written on the countenances of the worshipers, he felt himself out of step with some deep reality.

When Gilbert finally took his leave, he said goodbye to Dorothy, leaning forward to whisper in her ear, "Many happy returns, dear lady!" He gave her hand a squeeze, kissed it, then added, "Elder Bradford is a fortunate man indeed to have such a beautiful rose planted in his garden."

At first a wave of pleasure swept across Dorothy's face, then a cloud touched her eyes and she shook her head. "Thank you, Gilbert. It is nice to hear such things—though I suppose it's vanity that makes me like it. I fear that my beauty—such as it is—will not remain long in view of what's to come."

"What's to come?" Gilbert paused, looked down at her, and asked, "What could possibly take the bloom from those cheeks?"

"Why, if we make this terrible journey, if we live through it, there's little likelihood that neither I nor anyone else will have anything resembling beauty!" A mixture of anger and sorrow drew her lips down and she shook her head, adding, "Don't mind me, Gilbert. I know it must be done."

Gilbert wanted to press her, for this attitude was unusual. He suspected it had something to do with the proposed journey to the New World, and it was imperative that he find out anything he could about such a project. But he could not talk with the crowd around, so he took his leave from Dorothy, bade goodbye to Elder Bradford, arranged to meet Humility the next day for a walk, and left the house. Making his way along the cobblestone streets that twisted and wound through the city, he was greeted by a smallish boy on a path beside one of the canals. "Mr. Winslow, I've been waiting for you!"

"Oh, it's you, is it, Tink?" He looked down at the boy, fourteen years old and undersized. The boy had tow-colored hair that shot off in all directions almost covering a pair of jutting ears, and bright blue eyes. He had a large purplish birthmark on his right cheek that marred his face and ran down onto his neck.

Despite the smile in his face, there was something vulnerable about the lad.

During the long afternoons with nothing else to do, Gilbert had taken Tink strolling along the canals, catching the small, silver-scaled fish. The boy, who had been painfully shy at first, had opened up in the warmth of Gilbert's attention, and Gilbert had the impression that Tink communicated more with him than with anyone else, for he seldom saw him with the other young people his own age.

Now as Gilbert put his hand on Tink's shoulder and they walked toward the canal to find a favorite spot, Gilbert said, "Well, how was it today, Tink?"

"It was all right." Tink helped his father, a wool carter, and if he ever complained about the long hours or the arduous work, Gilbert had never heard him. The idea of using the boy as an informer somehow still lingered in Winslow's mind but it would be difficult now, for he had developed a genuine affection for the lad.

"Mr. Bradford says that in the New World it won't be hard to make a living like it is here," Tink said enthusiastically. "My father will have his farm like everyone else and they do say that the ground is so rich that the fruit falls off the trees all year round! Won't that be wonderful, Mr. Winslow—just to have apples— or even bananas—anytime you want one?"

Gilbert shrugged his shoulders and said, "That will be good, Tink, but is it all settled? I mean grown-ups talk a lot about things like this—about moving, about finding a new place and bettering themselves, but often it never happens."

Tink shook his head violently. "Oh, we're really going! I heard Mr. Carver tell my father that the ship to take us there has already been bought!"

Winslow saw that the boy was in deadly earnest about the journey to the New World. If the departure was to be soon, that meant to please Lord North he had to find Brewster at once. It made no sense to think that Brewster, one of the founders of the Green Gate congregation, would be left in England while the rest of the flock went to seek new homes. He would somehow make an attempt to get aboard one of the ships.

He was so deep in thought that when a man standing beneath a dimly flickering light at the intersection of the main street called his name, he did not hear. Tink caught his arm and said, "Mr. Winslow—I think he wants you."

Winslow came to himself with a start and turned to see a large burly man dressed in dark clothing approach. "Mr. Winslow, is it?"

"I'm Winslow—and who are you?"

The husky man stepped even closer and by the flickering light Gilbert saw that he had a broad face with one eye turned outward in such a fashion that it was difficult to keep from staring at it. He had huge hands, thick, broad, and short stubby fingers—butcher's hands, they seemed.

"May I have a word with you, Mr. Winslow?" The straight eye glanced quickly at the boy, and he added in a high tenor voice, "Alone, if it's all the same."

Curiosity touched Gilbert, and he said, "Run along, Tink. Here, take these fish and leave some of them with Mrs. Winslow for tomorrow—off with you, now!"

Tink took the string of fish, gave the stranger a quick glance, then nodded at Gilbert and turned to move off quickly down the darkening streets.

"What's your business?" Gilbert asked sharply. The man did not seem to be dangerous—but at the same time he was a stranger and there was a furtive air about him. Gilbert thought perhaps he was a beggar of some sort, but his clothes were not worn enough. A gold ring on one thick finger of his right hand and a gold watch chain gleamed dully in the light of the lantern.

"I'm Johnson." He nodded his heavy head quickly three times, searched the dark shadows with one eye suspiciously, turned back and said suddenly, "My business is the same as yours, Winslow—Brewster!"

Gilbert stared at him and said cautiously, "Brewster—which Brewster is that? I know no Brewster."

"You'd best know one and quick or your master will be displeased, Winslow!" Johnson winked his good eye, bared his large teeth in what passed for a grin, and again nodded sharply with a firm movement of his chin. "You've wasted too much time, and they're getting restless."

"Who is *they*?"

Johnson reached into the recesses of his coat, pulled out an envelope, and handed it to Gilbert. "It's all in here, Winslow. But I'll tell you what it says—it says that you're to be on that ship that came in this morning and report in person to Tiddle in London."

Opening the letter, Gilbert scanned it and saw that it was indeed a short note from the lawyer instructing him to return as soon as possible and give a report. Characteristically, the lawyer made no eloquent pleas, but phrased the request in blunt language, and signed his name simply—Tiddle.

Johnson said, "Ship weighs anchor tomorrow at three. Be sure you're on it, Winslow!"

"But I've got to stay here, Johnson! I've got to keep an eye on a girl that may lead us to Brewster."

Johnson nodded his head savagely, and winked his glaring eye. "Aye—I know the wench! You get to Tiddle and I'll watch her! If I have to, I'll break her neck to find out what we need to know!"

Gilbert reached out, and although Johnson was a massive man, he was jerked up on his toes by the powerful grip that gathered the front of his coat. "Keep your hands off her—you hear me!" Thrusting Johnson back, Gilbert turned and walked away, throwing over his shoulder the words, "I'll be at the ship when it leaves!"

As he walked swiftly toward Edward Winslow's house, Gilbert's mind swam and he tried to make some sense out of Tiddle's request. He did have some business affairs to report on, but there was an urgency in the lawyer's reply that seemed uncalled for. He somehow felt it had more to do with Brewster than with business.

It was not late when he got to the house, and as he entered, Edward greeted him, saying, "Come in here, Gilbert—we need a word with you."

Gilbert followed Edward into the dining room and saw that Bradford and Carver were seated at the carved oak table. "Why, good evening Mr. Bradford—Mr. Carver."

Edward moved to his chair, sat down, and motioned for Gilbert to do the same. There was an air of tension in the room, and Bradford's craggy features were set in lines of discouragement. Looking across the table, he said, "Mr. Winslow, we have decided to accept you into the fellowship of our congregation."

Gilbert's heart leaped—his mission was accomplished! He covered this exaltation by nodding his head and saying humbly, "I am honored, Elder Bradford. I trust that my devotion to the church will be proved by my faithfulness in service."

John Carver spoke up at once. He was in his sixties and his hair was a beautiful silver. There was a placid air in Carver that Gilbert had noted and envied, and now the older man said evenly, "You have heard, Gilbert, of the voyage to the New World, I suppose."

"Have you obtained a charter, Elder Bradford?" Gilbert inquired.

"Of sorts," Bradford admitted, nodding his head slowly. "At this very moment we have two men making the final arrangements for the voyage—Elder Robert Cushman has arranged for a ship called the *Mayflower* that is being fitted out even now in Southampton. Another ship has been purchased called the *Speedwell*, which will take our people from Leyden to Southampton."

Gilbert said, "It is a tremendous undertaking, gentlemen! I know that you have sought the will of God in the decision."

"Indeed we have, Gilbert!" Carver said, and his face lit up with a holy light. "And we have wondered if perhaps you could be of some service at this time to the congregation?"

Gilbert said at once, "Anything—anything at all."

"There is an urgent necessity for getting the mission underway," Edward said, striking the table with his fist. "This is the fourteenth of June and we must leave in July or we will come to the New World in the dead of winter."

"Do you plan to make a visit to England soon, Gilbert?" Carver asked.

"Why, yes, as a matter-of-fact—my business calls for me to return home tomorrow."

"Wonderful! Surely it is the hand of the Lord!" Carver cried out. "Could you perhaps go to Southampton and carry this message to Elder Cushman?"

Gilbert reached out and took the bulky envelope that Bradford held, looked at it, then said firmly, "It will be my pleasure to be of some small service. We weigh anchor tomorrow afternoon, and I should be able to convey the message instantly upon arrival." This agreement made all three men beam and when he left the room, a warmth and a friendliness shone in the face of Bradford that exceeded anything Gilbert had seen before.

Gilbert slept fitfully that night and was up early getting his few belongings packed. He spent the morning working on the reports of business that Tiddle would expect, then went shortly after noon to find Humility, only to discover that she was gone. He was disappointed, but there was nothing he could do but to take ship without saying goodbye.

As he walked up the gangplank that afternoon, Winslow heard his name being called. He turned to see Humility approaching the foot of the gangplank carrying a small box. When he turned and went quickly to meet her, she shoved the box at him, saying, "It's a lunch for you for your crossing, Gilbert. I'm sorry I missed you earlier today, but I thought you might like something to eat."

Gilbert laughed and tucked the box under his arm, then shrugged his shoulders. "Many thanks, Humility, but if I'm as sick as I was on the way over, all your efforts are for naught."

Humility looked up at him and smiled. "It will be different this time—I'll pray for you to have a good crossing."

Gilbert looked down and saw that her hands were trembling. "I'll miss you, Humility," he said gently. "Every foot that ship takes me away from Holland will be like a million miles."

He was speaking the language that he had learned to practice on young women, and as she had done often before, she caught him off guard. Looking up straight into his eyes, her lips trembling slightly, she said, "I'm learning to love you, Gilbert."

Gilbert Winslow's jaw dropped and he felt as if someone had struck him a solid blow in the pit of the stomach. Twice he tried to say *something*, but the words that came to his lips seemed silly and futile and unworthy. He looked down into Humility's sea-green eyes, noting the steadiness of her gaze, and the firmness of her lips now that she was under control, and he knew what it had cost this girl to say those words. She was not, he knew, a woman given to light language—what she said represented the very depths of her heart. Now as never before, he felt the heat of perfidy and despised himself thoroughly. But he said only, "And I'm beginning to love you, too, Humility."

"I'll pray for you that you won't be sick, and I'll pray for you to come back soon, and I'll—I'll pray for our life together." Humility did that which would have been impossible for her only a short time before. With a swift gesture, she reached up and pulled his head down, kissed him lightly on the lips. Then with a bright smile and tears in her eyes, she whirled, ran down the gangplank, down the street, and around the corner. Even as he stood there, Gilbert saw the burly form of Johnson suddenly appear and follow her, and the appearance suddenly brought all the sordid details of his life into focus.

As the ship crossed the channel, the waters grew rough, and the winds drove the ship hard—but so deep was he in thought that he took no notice. It was only when they came within sight of England that he suddenly stopped dead still, looked wildly back toward the land across the channel, and said out loud: "Why, I wasn't sick a bit this time!" And quite unreasonably, he was angry and ashamed.

CHAPTER EIGHT

BACK TO BABYLON

★ ★ ★ ★

Great skeins of tattered clouds were drifting raggedly across the horizon as Gilbert disembarked and made his way along the Southampton quay. He took little note of the fishermen unloading their catch of cod, stopping only long enough to ask of the ship he sought.

"*Mayflower?*" a barrel-shaped sailor pulling a small dinghy up on the beach scowled. He jabbed a stubby thumb at a ship sitting low in the green water, then asked, "Take 'ye aboard for a shilling?"

"Good enough." The price was high, but Gilbert had determined to have an interview as quickly as possible with Cushman, the elder from Green Gate.

The *Mayflower*, he judged, was not more than eighty feet long. Being a typical apple-cheeked boat, perhaps twenty-five feet across in the beam—only a little over three times as long as she was broad—she had a stubby, awkward appearance. She would have a crew of about twenty, he guessed, and being low in the waist, would certainly be a wet ship. Carrying the usual three masts, the fore and main were square-rigged in the simplest manner, while the short mizzenmast behind on the poop was rigged to fly a lateen sail. Built across the foredeck was a roomy forecastle, like a small house that had been forcibly jammed forward. A set of steps were rigged on the flat down the sloping side, which the outswelling curve of the ship caused to stand out from her several feet at the bottom.

The two crafts touched, and Gilbert said, "Wait for me! I'll not be long," then scrambled aboard. Swinging over the low bulwark, he stepped onto the deck. Three of the crew standing at the rail had been watching him, and the tallest of them—a thin blade of a man with sharp features and a huge beak of a nose, snapped querously, "What's yer business?"

"I'm looking for Mr. Cushman."

"Another one of them holy psalm-singers, Coffin," a thick-bodied tar grinned. He spat over the side through a large gap in his teeth, and added, "Looks like a proper parson, don 'e now?"

"Belay that, Daggot!" the man called Coffin snapped. He stared at Gilbert then said in a surly tone, "In the Great Cabin—up there."

"Better hold 'is hand, Coffin," Daggot jibed. "He might fall overboard!"

"No great loss if the whole pious bunch drownded," Coffin said with a glare at Gilbert. "Too many parsons in the world, I say."

Gilbert gave a curious look at the man, then shrugging, he made his way up a short stair to the poop deck and knocked firmly on the heavy oak door that led to the captain's cabin.

In response to Gilbert's knock, a voice called, "Come in!" The Captain's Cabin, or Great Cabin, was shaped to fit the rounded swell of the ship's side, and a row of windows along the stern allowed the last rays of the sun to light up the low-ceilinged room. A brass lantern hung from one of the ribs over-head, and there was a Spartan simplicity in the furniture—a single bed in one corner, two chairs and several stools ranked along one bulkhead. Pegs driven into the sides of the inward sweep of the ribs served as a wardrobe for shirts, oilskins, and various items such as a highly polished sextant and a broad-sword of the old style.

"Well? Have you got a tongue, man?" Gilbert took in the man, whom he took to be Captain Christopher Jones, sitting behind a mahogany desk—a solid, tightly built man in his early thirties. Bronzed to a ruddy color, he had a full head of brown hair, slightly curly. "Speak up, man!"

"My name's Winslow. I have business with Mr. Cushman."

"I'm Robert Cushman." A slight man dressed in brown broadcloth was standing beside the desk. He had a thin face, and a tic in his right eye drew up that side of his face from time to time. "You come from Leyden?"

"Yes."

"I don't believe we've met," Cushman said tentatively with a trace of suspicion in his thin face.

There was a tension in the room that Gilbert didn't understand, but he needed to assuage any doubts if he were to get any information. "I'm new to the Green Gate, Elder Cushman. But you know my brother, Edward, I think."

The name had the power to remove all doubt, and Cushman smiled at once, stepping forward to offer his hand. "Of course, of course. You'd be Mr. Gilbert Winslow. I've heard much from Edward about you! Come with me, Mr. Winslow," he said quickly, then walked to the door and stepped outside, closely followed by Gilbert. He walked with quick nervous steps to the far rail of the poop deck, then asked, "How are things progressing at home?"

"I have this letter from Mr. Bradford and Mr. Carver." Gilbert took the large envelope from his pocket, then watched while Cushman eagerly slit the seal, opened it, and read the contents with darting eyes.

"You know the contents of this?"

"No. I was coming to London on business and the elders asked me to bring it. It has to do with the voyage, I assume."

"Yes. In order to hire the ship to take us to the New World, we must have a full company. Mr. Thomas Weston has organized a group of Merchant Adventurers who will provide the funds for our venture, but he also insisted that the new colony be sufficient in number."

"Aren't there enough volunteers from the Leyden church?"

"Not half enough—and Mr. Weston has recruited a group to fill out our number."

"Are they of the Brownist persuasion?"

"Mr. Winslow, they're *nothing*! Many of them are poor—weavers, tanners, shopkeepers, and the like. But that's not the trouble. They have no faith! Most of them are members of the

Established Church—just what we are sailing across the ocean to escape from!" A wry smile creased Cushman's thin lips and he added, "Why, already there's a name for the two groups—saints and strangers!"

A smile touched Gilbert's lips, and he repeated the phrase. "Saints and strangers—I'd lay a gold angel to a lead shilling there'll be trouble between those two groups!"

"I do fear it, Mr. Winslow! But, let me ask, do you return to Leyden soon? I must send an answer as soon as possible."

Gilbert hesitated, then said, "I'll see it gets there, Mr. Cushman. But I'm pressed for time at the moment."

"It will take only a moment." Cushman scurried off to find writing material, and Gilbert spent twenty minutes struggling with his conscience, for he had decided to open the letter on the off chance that it might have valuable information concerning the whereabouts of Brewster.

He took the envelope which Cushman handed him, but when the thin man said, "God bless you, Mr. Winslow! I am grateful to God for your help in this matter!" a wave of shame swept through him. He mumbled goodbye hurriedly, and as the sailor oared him back to shore, he almost decided not to read the letter.

"Fie on it!" he said to himself angrily as he sat down in the small room he hired for the night. But after tossing and turning for two hours, he got up, lit the candle and read the letter. It said nothing of Brewster, being a plea from Cushman to make all haste possible in winding up the affairs at Leyden. The postscript added, *Mr. Gilbert Winslow is a welcome addition to our small fellowship. He will be one of the saints—not a stranger!*

Cecily pulled the dappled mare to a halt with a sharp tug on the bridle that brought the lathered animal to an instant halt. Slipping to the ground with a careless grace, she tossed the reins to a short stable boy who led the exhausted mare toward the stable. If anyone had ventured to suggest that she had been cruel to the animal, Cecily North would have been incredulous. "But it's *my* horse," she would probably have said.

A tall man was stepping out of a coach in front of the wide steps that led into the boxy mansion designed by Inigo Jones,

England's most sought-after architect. As she advanced, the man turned, and she called out, "Gilbert!" and a quick smile touched her lips as she ran forward to greet him.

"Cecily!" Gilbert took her hands, and her beauty caught him off guard, so much that he stood there staring at her, speechless. Finally he said, "You're lovely in the morning!"

"Morning! It's almost noon!"

"Well, you're even more beautiful at high noon!" he grinned.

"Come inside. I demand to know why you've stayed away so long. I warn you that I have an unerring ear for a romantic lie, so you may as well confess to all your indiscretions!"

As she pulled him into the stately foyer, he said, "I've thought about you since we parted."

"And you came only to see me, didn't you? Nothing to do with my father or business?"

Gilbert faltered slightly. "W-well, to be truthful . . ."

Cecily threw her head back and laughed. "Oh, you perfidious creature! Caught in the act! And I thought you were such a *romantic* suitor!"

"I trust to prove myself just so—but I do have to see Lord North at once."

"Tomorrow," Cecily said firmly. "Tonight you'll escort me to the Duke's ball!" She called loudly, "Thomas, show Mr. Winslow to the guest house and make certain he's taken care of."

"Cecily . . ."

"We'll leave at seven, Gilbert." She swept out of the room, and Gilbert followed the servant out of the house.

For the ball Gilbert wore clothes provided by his host: red velvet coat and breeches, yellow waistcoat with ruby buttons, and yellow hose above his shoes with gold buckles. The red hat with the large yellow plume was almost too much, but he shrugged and tucked it under his arm as he walked across the garden to meet Cecily.

Cecily achieved a triumph by choosing a simple gown ornamented with very small pink roses against vertical stripes of silver set off by sky blue. He took the scarlet cape lined with dark blue from her maid and as he slipped it over her smooth shoulders, said, "I didn't think it possible for anyone to outshine your beauty, Cecily, but I fear it has come to pass."

She shot him a smoky glance and asked in an icy tone, "And who has eclipsed my beauty, may I ask?"

Gilbert made an elaborate gesture with his plumed hat, sweeping it downward to indicate his elaborate dress, and said with a grimace, "Me! I feel like a tailor's ape, Cecily—fool of a coxcomb in ribbons and hose!"

Her lips curved into a smile, and she said, "You look well enough." She took in his lean athletic form, the slightly crooked smile and the coppertoned hair that framed the intensely masculine wedge-shaped face, and then added, "You are a beautiful man, Gilbert—you're most likely to charm the ladies of the court, I fear."

Gilbert was embarrassed at her comment on his appearance, but turned it off by saying with a rueful laugh, "Faugh! If your father finds me unsatisfactory for his service, I can always become a gigolo, can't I?"

The ball was a blaze of splendor that Gilbert could afterward remember as some sort of fantastic dream. He brushed shoulders with the demigods of British royalty, and was amazed—and somewhat shocked—to find out how strictly human they were. The Countess of Wentmore, fabled like Helen for her fabulous beauty, looked well enough at a distance of twenty feet under artificial light, but Gilbert was repelled to discover that she had apparently never discovered bathing. "Scratch me!" he exclaimed under his breath to Cecily. "But she smells like a hog in a ditch!"

Simon Roth turned from a group to stare at Gilbert, and Cecily quickly led him away.

"Why did you do that? Pull me away?" Gilbert asked.

"My dear, I didn't want another duel like the last time you met." She took the glass of wine he got for her and looked over it at him, her eyes catching the gold of the plate and the glare of the chandeliers. She took a sip, then murmured, "You know he hates you, don't you?"

"It's quite obvious. And there can only be one reason."

"Yes. He wants me." It sounded crass, but she shrugged and added, "He's always gotten what he wanted—and I suppose he'll get me, too."

"Do you love him?"

"No. But he's rich and attractive in a strange sort of way. Mother wants him for a son-in-law. Father wouldn't object."

Gilbert stared at her and said angrily, "You sound like love doesn't enter into it!"

"I don't think it does." Cecily reached up and touched his cheek, then said with a sad smile, "You are such an innocent man! You would be terribly shocked if you knew how rarely love is a factor in marriage."

"You're different, Cecily!"

She gave him a warm smile then, and pulled his arm close. Looking up at him she said quietly, "You think I am, don't you, Gilbert? Perhaps that's why I'm drawn to you—a penniless man with no title. But it's so *good* to find one man who's not blinded by money or my father's position!"

"You're woman enough for any man," Gilbert said, and would have pulled her into his arms in the center of the crowded room.

She laughed, bit her lip and drew back. There was the glimmer of tears in her eyes—the first Gilbert had seen, and in the softest voice he'd heard her use, she whispered, "Thank you, Gilbert. I—I'll treasure that!" Then she swept her hand across her eyes and with a laugh pulled him to the floor and made him dance with her.

The following day, Thomas handed him a letter. Cecily watched as he opened it, and the summons from Tiddle to be at Whitehall the next day was a cold shock.

"You have to go, don't you?" Cecily asked.

"I fear so."

She walked to the window and stared out, saying, "It will be lonely here without you."

"And even more lonely for me." He turned her around to face him, and said, "I'll come back."

"Will you?"

"I would always come back for you, Sweet."

He kissed her then, tenderly, yet she clung to him fiercely, like a lost child. Finally she drew back and said, "I'll have Smith drive you to London. What time must you be there?"

"As soon as possible, I fear. Tiddle urges all haste."

Cecily bit her lip and nodded, then they parted. Gilbert threw his things together, ignoring Thomas's attempts to help, and in half an hour was in the coach on his way to London. He did not see Cecily, and there was such confusion in his mind that he had to be spoken to twice by the coachman when they arrived.

He got out of the coach, gave the man a coin, and went inside the large inn Tiddle had mentioned. The clerk informed him that instructions had been given for him to occupy a room next to that of Lord North. "And I think—yes, there's a letter for you."

Gilbert took the letter, opened it, and read Tiddle's blunt script. "Come to Whitehall as soon as possible. The clerk will give you directions."

"Have these things put in my room, please; and can you tell me the way to Whitehall?"

"Well, sir, will you walk? It's not far."

"All right."

"You'll have to pass through a pretty bad section, sir," the clerk warned. "Perhaps a coach . . ."

"I'll walk; just tell me the way."

A high wind was whistling down the Strand from Charing Cross, driving the sooty drizzle from chimney pots. It endangered hats and flapped the curls of periwigs, then set the street signs dancing. Gilbert paid no heed, but passed through the half-deserted streets in the falling twilight.

Passing east along Pall Mall, he passed into a section the clerk had called Dead Man's Lane—one of the many old sections of London grown gray with age and mossy with time.

Darkness was filling the sky, and he was caught off guard when a voice said, "Would you pass by here, Mister Jackanapes?"

Instantly a sense of danger scraped across Gilbert's nerves, as he saw a tall man blocking his way. He responded harshly, "The only pass I make will be through your rotten heart!" He drew his sword and whirled to face the man who had accosted him. He was lean, his tattered coat fastened tightly to his body with pewter buttons to the neck. He wore an old scabbard, but the sword in his hand was new, and there was a leer on his face as he crowed in a harsh voice, "I heard you fancied yourself as a good blade. But cock of the hectors am I, that can spit a running fowl through the neck, and am here to do quite as much for you!"

"Your health will remain good if you step aside," Gilbert smiled grimly.

Instead the man shouted, "God rot ye!" and lunged in quarte for his opponent's chest. Gilbert's hand swept to the left across his own chest knocking the thrust wide, yet so close to the body that the blades hissed together.

Twice more the blades darted and rattled, and then Gilbert did something that Paul Dupree had taught him. It was a secret *botte*, a sword trick. If a man fights closed-up, and ventures little more than a half-lunge, his antagonist comes to underestimate his reach. But if he draws his right-angled foot up close to the left foot, as Gilbert did, he has an incredibly long leg-lunge when he goes forward. His arm and sword, rigid as a rod together, seems far longer.

As his long-legged opponent launched his own thrust, Gilbert's blade tapped that of the other, then swiveled upward, and the extra distance he gained from the *botte* allowed Gilbert to stretch just far enough. The tip of his blade caught the man through the upper throat not far under the chin. It ripped up behind the teeth, crashed through the roof of his mouth and lodged in his brain. In the next instant Gilbert ripped the blade free; it came away in a gush of blood that spattered heavily on his hands and cuffs.

For half a second the long-legged form stood upright, hardly swaying. The gaunt corpse tried to take a step, but he was already dead. He fell full length, face down, and Gilbert asked bitterly, "Still cock of the hectors, are you?" Then Gilbert remembered his words: *I heard that you fancied yourself a good blade!* and he knew at once that the fine hand of Lord Roth lay behind the attempted murder!

Quickly he wiped his blade on the dead man's clothing, sheathed it, then hurried away before the watch came. Twenty minutes later he walked up the high steps of Whitehall palace, the London residence of King James, the royal majesty of England. Glancing down at the drying blood on his cuffs, he thought, *first a betrayer, now a manslayer!*

Winslow was aware that there was no way under heaven to prove that Roth had any connection with the attempt on his life, but he was in too deep to back out, so he marched up to the guards bearing silvery armor and said, "Mr. Gilbert Winslow of Leyden to see Lord North!"

CHAPTER NINE

AT WHITEHALL

★ ★ ★ ★

Gilbert spent the night in a small room after being unable to contact either Tiddle or Lord North. Rising at dawn, he found both men eating a sumptuous breakfast after which North led the way through the maze of rooms that made up the palace.

"We have an audience with the King in one hour," Lord North said. He led them through a tremendous ballroom with fully a thousand lights in chandeliers and iron-gilt holders.

Gilbert trailed along behind as North led them down several corridors to the southeastern corner of the hall into a shut-off space with a fireplace built in the very angle of the wall. Four high folding screens, of heavy leather with brass nailheads and thickened with three inches of padding, had been drawn around to form an intimate space in the large room. There were several Oriental chairs, draped and padded for comfort, and seated in two of them, Gilbert saw, were Lord Roth and Bishop Charles Laud.

"Ah, North, there you are . . ." the portly clergyman beamed. He waved a fat hand toward the chairs, saying in his rich baritone, "His Majesty will arrive shortly—but before he comes, perhaps we can have a brief report from Mr. Winslow, eh?"

"Have you discovered the whereabouts of Brewster, Gilbert?" Lord North asked quietly.

"I regret, sir, that I have not."

"No progress at all?" Tiddle rapped sharply. "You had enough time, it seems, to find out *something*."

Gilbert plunged ahead to explain how he had attained membership in the Green Gate assembly, and made the most of the fact that he had been entrusted with a message to Cushman. While he was trying to explain that Brewster would try to join the expedition to the New World, the door swung open, and James the First, dread sovereign of England, walked into the room.

As Gilbert joined the others in making a low bow, the King said, "No ceremony! No ceremony, if you please!" As he seated himself on one of the chairs, Gilbert took occasion to examine the ruler of England.

He was of middle stature, more corpulent in appearance than in reality, for he wore his clothes large and easy, the doublets quilted for stiletto protection, his breeches in great pleats and fully stuffed. There was something of a timorous disposition in his face, which no doubt explained his dagger-proof doublets, and his large eyes rolled over the men in front of him with a trace of suspicion. His beard was very thin, and as he began to speak, Gilbert noted that his tongue seemed too large for his mouth, which made his speech muffled. He took a cup of wine from one of his attendants, and seemingly had to wallow the liquid to the sides of his mouth in order to drink.

As Lord North replied briefly to a question, the king got up and walked in a circular manner, and Gilbert remembered having heard about the weak legs which some attributed to some sort of foul play on his youth, or even before he was born, for James had not been able even to stand before the age of seven.

"Enough of that, North!" James interrupted, and his eye fell on Gilbert. "Is this the spy?"

Hearing the matter stated so bluntly, Gilbert turned pale and North said quickly, "This is Mr. Gilbert Winslow, Your Majesty, a very accomplished gentleman who has generously agreed to interrupt his own career to help root out Your Majesty's enemies."

Roth said in a strident tone as if Lord North had not spoken, "Yes, this is the fellow I told you about, Sire. I believe I mentioned he left Cambridge after developing a distaste for the ministry."

A wave of anger shot through Gilbert, and he opened his mouth to make a defense, but Tiddle hurriedly said, "I must add to that, my Lord, that Mr. Winslow left the university in order to enter the service of Lord North under my care. He has made an excellent beginning, and will prove a useful subject to the crown."

"I believe you are acquainted with Mr. Winslow's brother, Edward?" North asked.

"Oh—Edward Winslow? Yes—yes—an able man!" James nodded rapidly, and the suspicion in his weak eyes faded. He sat back and asked, "Well, what has been done about this Brewster fellow? I'll have him drawn and quartered, d'ye heed me?"

Catching the slight nod from Lord North, Gilbert plunged again into his report which the King listened to carefully. A murmur of approval went around the circle as he ended by saying, "The Separatists will leave England soon, Sire; in fact, they *must* leave by August if they are to make landing in the New World before the dead of winter."

"What then, Winslow?" James snapped. "How does that bring Brewster into my hands?"

"Why, it is certain, my Lord, that he will make this journey," Gilbert answered. "He is the leader of the congregation—and besides, he must know that he will be apprehended sooner or later if he stays in England! I have made a close acquaintance with one of the Separatists. Brewster has written to this young woman often, and is sure to do so again. Sire, I must return at once to Leyden, for time is running out! Brewster will be contacted—he must be! They may wait until the last possible moment to attempt to get him aboard the ship, but that will work to our advantage."

"How is that?" the King asked.

"I am in the confidence of the leadership of the group at Leyden. They are aware that I know the country and that I travel freely. I will put it in their way to ask for my assistance. Be assured, Your Majesty, the moment I find the man, he is as good as in your hands!"

"That soundeth well, Winslow!" the king cried out and got

to his feet. Moving toward the door, he exclaimed, "I said at the beginning I'd *make* them conform or harry them out of the land! See to it, man, and ye'll not go unrewarded!" He left accompanied by the bishop, and a silence ran around the room after the door closed. Then Tiddle said, "You've not mentioned your adventure last night, Gilbert."

North nodded and there was a serious look on his face. "We got a report early this morning on your encounter in Dead Man's Lane. When they found you were connected with me," he added, "the authorities brought me the report—and left it in my hands."

"Otherwise you might be cooling your heels at Tyburn prison," Tiddle nodded grimly.

"It was a matter of self-defense—the witness made that clear," North mused. "A robbery, I take it—but the woman said she never saw anything like the way you dispatched the varlet."

"What then?"

"Murder—or an attempt at it." Gilbert carefully kept his eyes away from Lord Roth as he added, "The varlet knew me, my Lord. He made it clear that I was marked as a victim."

North had a puzzled look on his face. He glanced at Tiddle and said, "That makes things more difficult, I suppose?"

"Could be the Puritans saw through your masquerade, Winslow," Lord Roth remarked carelessly. He picked a piece of lint off his tunic and gave a thin smile. "Such things frequently happen to informers, I'm told."

Gilbert nodded slowly, locking eyes with Lord Roth, and finally he said, "Anything is possible, my Lord."

"Once again, Winslow, I must pay tribute to your blade," Roth said smoothly. "We must have another match soon."

"At your leisure, Lord Roth."

"Gilbert, you'd best get back to Leyden," North interrupted. If he caught the tension between Roth and his young friend, nothing of it showed in his smooth face. "The King's eye will be on you—and a success in this matter will open many doors for you."

"Yes, my Lord, I'll return at once."

Lord North said a hearty "Godspeed," and clapped Gilbert across the shoulders with a rare show of affection. Roth did not even glance at him as the two left the room.

"I'll go with ye to the ship, my boy," Tiddle said at once. "Get your things and I'll engage a carriage."

They left shortly, Tiddle going over detailed aspects of business that Gilbert would need to attend to in Holland.

"Your mind isn't on business, is it, Gilbert?" Tiddle asked suddenly. "I see you're still not easy in your mind—on this business of turning Brewster in."

"It's different from the duel in Dead Man's Lane," Gilbert said vehemently. "I'll lose no sleep over that one! But if William Brewster is like the others I've met, he's no criminal!"

"He is in the eyes of the King."

"Then the King is wrong!"

"Hush, man!" Tiddle said with a glance upward toward the driver. "D'ye not know men have gone to the Tower for saying less!"

Gilbert shrugged, then forced a smile. "I know you're a lawyer, Lucas, and accustomed to putting moral questions in neat little boxes. Well, I can't do that! To me Brewster is a human being—from what I hear, a fine one! I can't hand him over to torture and death because he printed a sermon that offended the King!"

Sadly Tiddle shook his head. "I fear it's like that. The world's a bad place for romantics and idealists, Gilbert. As I once told you, you must pack your sense of honor away, retaining only the name and join the rest of us who are busily selling our souls to the devil."

"This world or the next, eh, Lucas!" Gilbert sighed. Then he turned to face the lawyer. "Let me ask you, are you a Christian?"

"I am a member of the Established Church, Gilbert," Tiddle said evenly. "I pay my tithes, take communion when I am obliged to by the bishop, and do not give aid to dissenters. That is my religion. Having done those things, it is up to the Church of England to keep me out of hell!"

The coach rattled along, and Gilbert watched a high-flying falcon stoop to take a field sparrow in an explosion of feathers.

Finally he said heavily, "The world would be a much simpler place—if it weren't for God and all that."

"No doubt—but it's the only world we have, lad!" Tiddle echoed sadly.

CHAPTER TEN

HUMILITY FINDS A MAN

★ ★ ★ ★

Humility made her way along the canal, and if the water below was calm and glassy, her thoughts were not. Since the moment she had confessed her love for Gilbert Winslow, fierce restlessness had distracted her during the days and kept her tossing for hours after she went to bed.

"Daydreaming, are you, lass?"

She glanced up to see the burly form of Sam Fuller, and greeted him with a wan smile. "I suppose so."

His sharp black eyes took in her pale face and the fatigue that marred the wide-set green eyes. He picked up a pebble, tossed it in the water, and smiled at her, "I do a bit of daydreaming myself. Brain gets all messed about with cobwebs, eh?" He gestured at the widening gyre of the wave below, and said, "Now you take that bit of a circle there—perfect! Nothing out of line in it." He smiled sadly, saying, "But us human beings, why, we ain't so simple as that, I reckon."

"I—suppose not, Sam," Humility said slowly. She stared at the circle below, then tossed in another stone. It made a *plop* and a second circle radiated outward, crossing the line of the first. "Look—Sam!" she exclaimed. "If you throw one pebble in the water, you only have one circle—but if you throw two, the circles interrupt each other."

"I take it you're making some sort of comment on life,"

Fuller stated. "You seem to be saying, 'Just let me alone, and things will be smooth; don't let my life get all complicated with other people.' But you can't live like that, Humility."

"I thought I could, Sam," she murmured uncertainly. Biting her lower lip, she said, "I had my life all planned out. Since I was a little girl, Sam, I've thought never to marry, just serve God."

"But along comes young Gilbert Winslow, eh, lass?"

"Why—"

"Tut, Humility, no shame in it!" Fuller answered warmly, seeing the guilt in Humility's face. "The Apostle said that not everyone is fitted for a single life. And if I ever saw a young woman made for love, I'm looking at her now!"

"Oh, Sam—I'm so unhappy!"

Fuller had held her in his arms when she was barely able to walk, and now he put a fatherly arm around her and she grabbed at him blindly. He held her close for a long time, and when her tremors finally ceased he reached down and picked up a handful of pebbles. He threw one in, then another. "See how the two circles cross? I guess if those circles could talk, they'd complain about how they'd been confused. And look here—" He tossed a small handful of loose gravel into the water, and the concentric circles began to intersect and fragment. "Now that is confusing, eh, lass? But that's the way life is. We have our own little circles, all nice and neat. But there are other lives, too, and if we live with people we'll sooner or later have our little circles all inter-rupted—over and over by all kinds of relations—friends, lovers, husbands, wives, enemies—but there's this one thing, Humility. We serve a God who knows every little circle, and when our little lives get rocked and the pattern goes by the board, why, He's not at all confused!"

Humility watched the water until it cleared, then looked up and smiled at Fuller. "Thank you, Sam."

They turned and began to walk along the canal. "How does your young man feel about this, Humility?" Sam asked.

"Oh, I think he cares for me—but we've not talked about such things as marriage."

"Well, he seems like a fine young fellow," Fuller nodded, then added stridently, "I'll break the pup's neck if he tampers with your affection, I will!"

She laughed and squeezed his thick arm, saying, "I'll threaten him with that, Sam! Maybe a little push wouldn't be unscriptural!"

They said little as they wound their way through the crooked streets, but when they came to the intersection where Fuller left her, he patted her arm and said, "D'ye know the verse that says, 'He that findeth a wife, findeth a good thing, and obtains favor from the Lord'?"

"Yes."

"Well, lass, that could as well read, 'She that findeth a man—a husband, that is—findeth a good thing!' You take my meaning?"

"How could I help it?" Humility smiled at the burly man. "You're about as subtle as a broadaxe, Samuel Fuller!"

He gave her a wide smile, then said with a sudden sadness that darkened his cheerful face, "Marry a man that will make you smile, lass!"

Then he left her with a lurching walk down the cobblestones.

Slowly she turned, and as she walked home she knew that until she had made up her mind about Gilbert Winslow, nothing in the world about her would have any significance.

When Gilbert returned two days later, Humility found his presence did nothing to settle the restless spirit she could not shake.

He caught her off guard, coming up behind her as she was hanging clothes to dry on the line. She was totally unaware of his presence when suddenly two strong arms reached around her waist and she was plucked up and whirled around like a child.

When he set her down, breathless and flaming with indignation, he laughed at her, embraced her and gave her a resounding kiss, daring her to be angry.

"You—you mustn't do that!" she protested, her smile threatening to break through the sternness she tried to assume.

"I promise not to," he said with his lopsided grin that made her feel strangely happy. "Not until the next time!"

She broke into laughter, put her hand on his cheek in a rare gesture of affection, and said, "You *are* a fool, Gilbert Winslow! The elders will have you up for discipline for this sort of thing!"

"If they try to clap every fellow in love with a beautiful girl in the stocks, they'll have to cut down the forest for new stocks!"

She looked up at him, her face almost translucent, and with a husky quality in her voice, she whispered, "*Are* you, Gilbert? In love with me?"

A dusky flush swept across Gilbert's high cheekbones; there was a slight hesitation, then he smiled warmly, put his hand on her cheek and said, "Can you doubt it? A man would have to be dead not to love a woman like you!"

She took a sudden deep breath, then nodded. It was hard for this girl who had kept her emotions under strict control to let them slip, to let the warmth and pure love she felt so deeply rise to her lips. Twice she tried to speak and failed; then she swallowed and said in a whisper, "Do you know what I'm thinking?"

"What, Sweet?"

"Of the scripture—The Song of Solomon." She looked full in his face and quoted the ancient script with a passion that leaped out at him like a living thing:

> Let him kiss me with the kisses of his mouth: for thy love is
> better than wine.
> My beloved is white and ruddy, the chiefest among ten thou-
> sand.
> His mouth is most sweet, yea, he is altogether lovely.
> He brought me to the banquet house, and his banner over me
> was love.
> My beloved is mine, and I am his.

Winslow stood there like a man in a trance. There was something so sensual in the words—yet something so *pure* in Humility's uplifted face and in her whole attitude that he could not speak.

"That's—that's very beautiful, Humility," he said finally. He dropped his hands, and she saw that the playful spirit had left his face.

"Gilbert—I embarrassed you!"

"No! It's just that—well, I'll have to get accustomed to a woman who makes love out of the Bible!"

"God made love," she said simply. "Male and female, created He them."

"And does He have one particular woman in mind for every man?"

"Of course!" she exclaimed, surprised that he asked. "Have you not ever read in the Scripture how God chose Rebekah as a wife for Isaac?"

"I see." Gilbert gazed into Humility's green eyes, flecked now with fragments of gold around the iris, and mused, "What if a man takes a notion for the wrong woman—one that God *didn't* intend for him?"

"Then—then it's terrible and very sad!" She glanced at him, and could not but think of how much he looked like his brother—who had, she felt, married the wrong woman.

"Gilbert, did you ever hear the old Persian myth about how marriage began?"

"I'm not really up on my Persian myths, to be truthful."

"Well, according to the story, God made a creature in the very beginning. But the creature did a very wicked thing, so God cut His creation right in two pieces and scattered the fragments out into the wide world."

"Pretty lonesome, I'd say," Gilbert mused. He was fascinated with the piquant animation that stirred her face as she spoke.

"Oh, yes! There were lots of the creatures in the world, all torn in two. One part of the creature—according to the story—was man, and the other part was woman, so you see what happened!"

"Well, not quite."

"Why, one of the man pieces had to search all over the world to find the piece that fit him—the woman who had been his other half. And none of the others would do—it had to be the very one!"

Gilbert stared at her, then said soberly, "That's pretty hard doctrine! One man—one woman. No substitutes."

"You don't think love is that way?"

He hesitated, then smiled, saying, "I hope so, Humility. It's a nice thought."

For the next few days they spent most of their waking moments together. Except for short visits on business to neighboring towns, Gilbert could be found either at Pastor Robinson's studying the Scripture or walking the countryside with Humility.

The closeness of community made for talk, some feeling that the affair was progressing much too rapidly. The silver-haired elder, John Carver, however, expressed what most felt about the couple when he said, "If we're going to make a new world, we'll need new blood—and Winslow blood is better than most."

Humility was happy, but from time to time grew restive— almost worried. Gilbert had spoken of love—and for her that meant marriage. But on that subject, Gilbert had said nothing.

Once when he had fallen into one of his moods—not angry but withdrawn—she said half joking, "You're so *quiet*, Gilbert! I believe you must be thinking about some girl you have in England."

"No!" Gilbert stated, then his face reddened and he forced a smile. "No, I'm just concerned about the future. Humility, are you going to the New World?"

"Why, of course!"

She waited, expecting him to state his declaration, but he said nothing. Finally she asked in a small voice, "Are—are you going?"

He hesitated, then stated, "It's such a big decision, Humility!"

"I'll be there," she said, then waited for his response. When it came she was disappointed.

"I haven't much time, have I?" was all he said.

On the next Sunday morning, Elder William Bradford's face was slightly pale as he preached the sermon. He was distinctly more subdued than usual, and after the last *amen* was spoken, he held his hand up and said, "I have something to say to you." The congregation, sensing the tension in his face, grew absolutely still. "The time is now here for us to leave this place. We will leave on the 22nd of July in the *Speedwell*."

There was a tumult in the room, and for the next hour Bradford and the other elders answered questions on the venture.

There was nothing but the voyage on the lips of everyone the next day, but for Humility there was something else.

Getting word that a certain ship had docked during the

night, she quietly slipped away and picked up a letter from a sailor, taking it directly to Pastor Robinson.

He broke the seal, scanned it quickly, then said, "Humility, can you find Mr. Bradford and ask him to come here? Then come back with him?"

She left, and was fortunate in finding Elder Bradford at home. When she told him her errand, he asked at once, "A letter from Brewster?"

"Yes."

"I'll come with you."

Bradford and Pastor Robinson secluded themselves at once, and Humility waited until after nearly an hour, the pastor called her.

She went into the study, and Robinson said without preamble, "We have a problem, Humility, and it may be that you can help us."

"I'll do anything. Is it about Mr. Brewster?"

"Yes, we must see to it that he makes his way to the dock at Southampton and gets aboard one of our vessels before we sail."

Bradford said heavily, his brow creased, "That would be difficult under any conditions—but we have word that the search for Elder Brewster has been stepped up. It will be very difficult to get through the lines to the coast."

"We think you might be the one to make the attempt, Humility."

"Me!" She was amazed and began to make excuse, but the pastor interrupted her.

"Not alone. That would be too dangerous. You don't know England well enough for such a mission. But if you had someone to help you, someone who *does* know England, and who has legitimate business—that would be different, would it not, Humility?"

"Why, yes, but whom would you mean?"

"Gilbert Winslow," Pastor Robinson said.

"Gilbert!"

"I've already sent for him," Robinson said. "Most of us are known to the searchers in England, but Gilbert is a businessman—in the service of Lord North—perhaps the most powerful man in England next to the King himself. No one would question him!"

"Just one word." Bradford faced Humility with a stern look on his gaunt face and stated, "I am against this move, but Pastor Robinson has convinced me that it is our best—nay, perhaps our *only* hope of getting our brother on the ship and to the New World."

There was a knock at the door, and he said, "That will be Gilbert now, I should think."

He opened the door and Gilbert entered with a wary look on his face.

"I must be direct, Mr. Winslow," William Bradford stated flatly, not taking his eyes from those of Winslow. "You are an alert young man; you must know pretty well what is happening in our community."

"The move to the New World? Certainly, sir, I am aware—"

"I ask if you are familiar with the name of William Brewster?"

Gilbert could not conceal the shock that ran along his nerves. Hesitating for an instant, he said with a slow nod, "I will not deceive you, Elder Bradford. I have been aware for some time— even before I came to Holland—of Mr. Brewster. It's common talk in England, I believe."

"Mr. Winslow, we have observed your conduct well, and Pastor Robinson indicates that you have a respect for the Word of God which does you credit. We feel that you have some intention—honorable, of course—for this young lady."

"Thank you, sir," Gilbert nodded. "If I may boast, I would say that any task you might care to set, I will undertake."

"Very well. We ask you to do a dangerous thing, Gilbert Winslow. We must get Elder Brewster out of his hiding place and to Southampton as quickly as possible. We think that you and Humility might be able to accomplish that." He frowned and added, "Ordinarily we would not permit an unmarried couple to make such a journey unchaperoned—but we face a crisis."

"I agree," Gilbert said, "but let me urge you to let me undertake this mission alone. It's too dangerous for a woman." He argued valiantly for ten minutes, but to no avail.

"Both of you must go," Bradford insisted stubbornly.

"Very well." Gilbert shook his head. "Where is Elder Brewster hidden?"

"We think it best that no one know that—or as few as possible," Bradford said smoothly.

Gilbert saw in a flash that he was on trial—and that it would require more doing than he had thought to do the job. But he said only, "A wise decision, Mr. Bradford. When do we leave?"

"As soon as possible. A ship is due in two days. Will that be satisfactory?"

"Perfectly."

Gilbert spent much time during the next two days sequestered with Bradford and Pastor Robinson, going over details. Not once did they allude to the location of the elder. Humility spent the time tying up that part of her life that had been spent in Leyden—saying goodbye to those who would remain, making plans to be reunited with those she would see again on the *Mayflower*.

Finally, after a tearful parting at the dock, they stood on board a three-masted schooner, headed for England.

They said little for the first few hours, but after the moon came up, they stood in the bow, watching the white waves break, flashing with a rich golden light. The tang of salt was in the breeze that whipped through their hair, and there was a hissing sound as the schooner slid through the water.

"Are you afraid?" Gilbert asked suddenly.

Humility turned to him and thought about his question. Her blonde hair billowed in strands like golden threads, and she smiled as she said, "Not of being caught and sent to gaol."

"Of what, then?"

"Of something happening to us."

He bit his lip, and asked quietly, "To us?"

"You remember about the Persian myth?"

"Yes."

"That's what I'm afraid of most, dear. That we'll be torn apart—and never find each other again." Then she leaned against him, saying, "I'm like that myth, Gilbert. If I got lost from you, I'd never have anybody—not anybody! I never wanted to marry, and I never expected to love anybody as I love you."

He stood there, staring into her eyes, and finally said, "Humility, I have to tell you something—"

She waited, then when he said nothing, she asked, "Yes, what is it, Gilbert?"

"Nothing. Things will be all right."

He pulled her into his arms to prevent her seeing the twitching of his face as he said the words.

"It will be all right," she murmured, pressing her face against his heart. "It will be fine—now that I've got you, Dear Heart!"

The ship faltered, changed course, and as the sails slipped and the masts creaked, a silence wrapped around the pair in the bow of the ship.

CHAPTER ELEVEN

A TRAITOR UNMASKED

★ ★ ★ ★

After getting ashore at Dartmouth, Humility and Gilbert caught the mail coach, then rolled along the Great North Road, huge plumes of dust rising like waves behind them. The fine grains of whitish dust coated them from head to foot, and even the water tasted dusty in the hot July weather.

They passed Cambridge on the left, and hours later the Boston Road flanked west, but they rolled steadily toward the north.

They changed teams three times, and shadows were growing long as the coach pulled into a quiet hamlet on the bank of the River Ryton, within sight of its junction with the Idle, both sluggish small streams in the watershed of the Humber which drains the moors and lands of the middle eastern counties.

"We leave the coach here," Humility said, catching Gilbert off guard.

"What place is this?"

"Scrooby."

Gilbert stared at the cluster of cottages and small houses. "He's not *here*! It's the first place they'd put a watch on!" He knew that because Tiddle had mentioned that the only wise thing Dudley Carleton had done was to set a man to keep close watch on Brewster's former home where he still had distant relatives.

"No, but we can get word of him," Humility said. She led

the way past a small parish church, well built of cut stone, and a great manor house of timber.

They went past the last lights of the small town, and for nearly half an hour groped their way along the stony road. Finally Humility said, "We go in here," moving toward a dim light set well off the road.

"Who's there? Stand and declare!"

Out of the small cottage, a huge man with a tremendous beard appeared, holding a flickering lantern high. He had a large cudgel in his fist, and he called again as the pair approached the house, "Who be ye?"

"It's me, Gabriel—Humility."

"Is it now!" the giant exclaimed, then leaned the club against the side of the house and took her shoulder with his free hand. He towered over her, but there was a warm smile on his craggy face as he said, "Well, now? Is it a ghost you are? Appearing like a spirit in the middle of the night?"

"This is Mr. Winslow, Gabriel."

Gilbert put his hand out and it was crushed in a fleshly vise. "Gabriel was Mr. Brewster's servant in the old days."

"Still am, Lady! And always will be!" He stepped back and urged them inside, saying at once when he put the lantern on the handmade table, "Ye'll want to see him, I take it?"

"As soon as possible," Humility nodded. "Tonight if we can."

"You stay close here tonight," Gabriel said at once. "Tomorrow old Simon will get word to Mr. Brewster—then he'll bring word back of what to do."

After a meal of bread and cold meats, Gabriel put Humility in the single small bedroom, and Gilbert slept on fragrant hay in the loft above the half-timbered cottage.

The sun was warm on his face when Gilbert woke up, and he hastily descended the small ladder into the house below.

"Good morning, Gilbert," Humility smiled. She came to him and lifted her face for a kiss, then went back to the small hearth where she was warming fresh bread and stirring a black pot hanging over the fire. "Try some of this porridge—straight from Scotland."

After cleaning the dishes, they wandered through the fields

and woods, taking pleasure in a staggering, newborn fawn crossing the path. As they went deeper into the woods, Humility took him to a small stream, and sitting on the green, mossy banks, they talked until the sun reached its zenith, then realized with a start that the whole morning had passed.

"I wish every day could be like this," Gilbert said suddenly. "Life gets so *complicated*!"

Humility, thinking of the time she'd stood on the bridge at Leyden watching the circles in the water ripple and clash, smiled and put her arm around him. "One day it will—when we get to the New World."

Gilbert started, then gave a rueful laugh. "I expect it will be a little more difficult than this."

"Even so, we'll be together!" she said. Since Gilbert had agreed to undertake the mission they were on, there had been no doubt in her mind that he was committed to the voyage, and the hardships did not frighten her. She was so complete in her happiness, she failed to notice the awkward silence that inevitably followed any reference she made to the exodus to America.

Gilbert had his mind made up to one thing, at least: he would turn Brewster over to the authorities, but he would keep Humility free of the business. Somehow he would pull her away before the actual arrest.

It was a little after one the next day when Gabriel returned, accompanied by a gnome of a man named Simon Lee.

"Simon will take you to the place," Gabriel said. "It's a goodly walk."

The "goodly walk" turned out to be a twelve-mile trek through brambles, bushes, and jagged paths that stabbed at the feet like dragon's teeth! Simon led them upward from the table land to the foothills south of Scrooby, the beginnings of Sherwood, until finally they crested a rise, and there in a valley below was a small stone house, and beyond, a large meadow spotted with sheep and goats.

"It's an abandoned sheep farm," Humility explained as they made their way down the winding path. "It was too far away from market, so it was abandoned years ago."

Fifteen minutes later they approached a man sitting on a large buff stone outcropping, and Gilbert got his first look at

William Brewster, fugitive from the King's justice.

He was of medium height, and had that healthy thinness that old men sometimes achieve. Over a broad forehead, mild eyes were set rather narrowly, and he had a full brown beard streaked with white. The hand he raised in greeting had the long fingers of an artist, and a stubborn set in his chin was the only evidence of the iron determination that lay like bedrock in his character.

"Daughter, it's good to see you," he said in a high-pitched, pleasant voice, then turned a pair of inquiring eyes on her companion and put out a thin hand, saying, "And this is Mr. Winslow. God bless you for your aid, sir."

Gilbert nodded, unable to reply, but Humility threw her arms around Brewster's neck, and cried out, "Oh, just think, soon we'll be in the New World."

Brewster gave Winslow a quick smile over her shoulder, saying, "Well, this old world isn't all that bad, actually."

Brewster took Gilbert by one arm and Humility by the other, turned them toward the cottage, saying, "I'm thankful you've come—both of you. I've been alone so much I talk to the hares—and even they go to sleep! Come, let's go to the cottage."

The next three days were a strange time for Gilbert. The mornings and afternoons were spent doing little but wandering the beautiful hills with Humility, while the nights provided good talk with Brewster. The old man had lived a great deal and had known many famous people. Gilbert had nearly fallen out of his chair when Brewster casually mentioned being rather close to the poets Spenser and Sir Philip Sidney. But that was nothing to what he felt when Brewster said, talking about the old days, ". . . They were not so good as they remember," he had mused. "Why, I remember once when Bess had a half dozen of her ministers cooling their heels in the tower at the same time. I recall it was at that time that Essex came to see my master, Mr. Davenport, and we were talking in the parlor—"

"You spoke with *Essex*?" Gilbert stared at him as if he had said he talked with Moses.

Brewster's eyes twinkled and he nodded, "Oh, yes, but he wasn't much—Robert wasn't. A tailor's dummy—beautiful to look at, but not enough sense for a nit!"

"But Elizabeth—Queen Elizabeth—you actually saw her?"

"Many times, lad—but she wasn't much to *see*," Brewster smiled. "She was getting pretty long in the tooth, but she'd bed down with anything that caught her fancy! And curse? Why, she would put the roughest sailor in the fleet to shame!"

Gilbert stared at the old man, then shaking his head in sad wonder, said, "You don't think about people like that having flaws—temper, or bad teeth."

"Ah, that's because you're a romantic at heart, lad!" Brewster chuckled. "You'll choose to think of something long ago rather than today, because time dulls the rough edges of things. And a true romantic will always think the land across the sea will be much more wonderful than Scrooby or London. It's only when he gets there and discovers that garbage and leaky roofs occur about as often in a far-off paradise as they do in England!"

Humility said, "Why, you seem to be saying that all of us who are going to the New World are romantics, Mr. Brewster!"

"Why, bless you, child," Brewster hooted with laughter. "Of *course* we are! Every pilgrim is!"

"I never thought of it that way," Gilbert mused.

"Rich, successful men don't become pioneers, Gilbert. They are settled down in this world with both feet. It's only those who have a dream who tear up and risk everything in a new world."

"I suppose that's why the Scripture says, 'Abraham looked for a city which hath foundations, whose builder and maker is God.' "

Brewster nodded approval. "Ye know your Bible, son. And you'll mind the verse in that same chapter that says all the pilgrims 'died in faith, not having received the promises, but having seen them far off, and were persuaded of them, and embraced them, and confessed that they were strangers and pilgrims on the earth.' "

"Not a happy prospect, is it?" Gilbert mused.

"Because they didn't get what they wanted?" Brewster demanded, and there was a fire in his fine old eyes. "Son, the most miserable man in creation is the man who has everything he wants! Ye've heard of Alexander who wept because he had no more world to conquer? Well, he deceived himself, because there was one world—more wonderful and rich than Greece or Persia—that he never conquered!"

"Which world, Elder Brewster?"

"Himself." The answer came quietly, but there was such fervor in Brewster's manner that he seemed young, and Gilbert had a sudden hope that he would have the spirit of William Brewster when he came to the end of his life.

Humility had not taken her eyes off Gilbert's face. Now she put her hand on his, and said gently, "Strangers and pilgrims on the earth." She smiled at him with a faith so steady it shook him, and added, "It's better, though, to be on the pilgrim way *with* someone, isn't it?"

Gilbert put on an evasive cheerfulness, and the moment passed.

As the days passed, Gilbert was drawn to the spirit of Brewster, and the idea of betraying the good old man grew increasingly repulsive.

On the third night the thing got the best of him. He was sitting beside Humility listening to Brewster read from the Scriptures, as he did each night. He was reading the account of the last hours in the life of Jesus, and when he came to the story of Judas, an icy fist seemed to seize Gilbert's heart: "The Son of man goeth as it is written of him; but woe unto that man by whom the Son of man is betrayed! It had been better for that man if he had not been born."

It would have been better for that man if he had not been born!

The words echoed in Gilbert's brain with an eerie cadence— an anthem straight out of the Pit!

He stared across the room, and the holiness etched on the face of William Brewster was an indictment of his own wretched soul—and one glance at Humility as she smiled at him with love and confidence was enough to fill him with a self-loathing such as he had never known!

"Gilbert, don't you feel well?" he heard Humility ask.

"You look pale as death, boy—are you ill?" Brewster asked.

Gilbert got up, averting his face and lurching toward the door. "I—I am a little sick—don't come—I'll get some air!"

He wandered blindly along the path, paying no heed to anything save the agony of guilt that had suddenly exploded within his soul. Finally he threw himself face down on a grassy knoll and bit his lip to hold back the cries that rose from within him, and there was such a power in the storm of emotion tearing at him that he was drenched in sweat and his hands were scratched from beating on the earth unconsciously.

How long he fought that battle he never knew, but finally he rolled over on his back, drained and empty, staring up at the sky. Then a decision came—like the return of an old friend who had been long on a journey; he felt his honor come back. He lay there, wondering why he had ever thought he could sell another human being for his own gain and hope to be a man.

Getting up, he looked to the sky and said, "I may never be lord of any land—but by my honor, there's *one* thing I'll rule over, and that's myself!"

The stars seemed friendly, and he made his way back to Brewster's cottage. He felt clean, refreshed, as if plunged into a pool of water that washed away all the stains the past had marked him with.

But he also felt a twinge of fear, thinking that he would lose his place, lose the main chance that had come to him in life if he did not deliver up Brewster. He laughed aloud, saying to the night, "Why, let it be, then! If Lord North turns me out for being an honorable man, why, he's none himself! If Cecily boots me out for refusing to be a man-seller, I'm best off without her! Let Tiddle prate on about how a man can do without honor—but I notice that he's none too happy for having sold his for a place!"

He found light still burning in the window as he burst through the door and said to Humility, who was sitting at the table with Brewster, "Well, I feel much better! Must have been that third chop you forced on me for supper, Elder Brewster."

He stopped abruptly and the smile left his lips as he saw that Humility's face was pale as a sheet of paper, and Brewster looked very disturbed.

"What's the matter? You have some evil tidings?"

"Why, I think not!" Gilbert whirled in time to see Lord Roth step from behind the door that had swung back to conceal him. There was a savage joy in his piercing eyes as he stepped forward, sword in hand, and said, "The tidings are good for the loyal subjects of King James—evil for traitors such as William Brewster—and those that are involved in his escape."

Gilbert stood like a man turned to stone. It was like a nightmare! Coming as it did on the heels of his decision to aid Brewster, he could not find any avenue of escape.

"Ah, you are speechless?" Roth stated with mock sadness. He whipped the foil in his hand through the air idly, then nodded to the pair at the table. "I salute you, Mr. Brewster. You have outwitted the law for quite a long time. As a matter-of-fact, if it had not been for the help of Mr. Gilbert Winslow, it is likely that you would have made your way to the New World after all."

"No!" Humility cried. She rose, hands at her breast, and the pain in her eyes was unbearable to Gilbert. She stepped to his side, and said in a voice strained to the breaking point, "He's lying! Tell me he's lying, Gilbert!"

The inside of his mouth was dry as toast, and the words stumbled to his lips, but he had to try!

"I—I did agree to help the law find Elder Brewster—that's true—but—"

"Oh, that's true enough, Lady," Roth said with an oily smile. "I see he's used you for his evil purposes—as he has used another lady!"

"Another lady?" Humility stared at Roth, then at Gilbert. "What lady?"

"Lady Cecily North, the daughter of Winslow's employer. He has led her to believe that his affections were due only to her." Roth shrugged and added with a show of sadness, "But that has been Mr. Winslow's downfall—by his own testimony. I hear he has been a womanizer of terrible proportion."

"Gilbert, is it true? Have you made love to this woman—all the time that we—"

"Humility!" Gilbert said hoarsely, "I know how you must feel—and I've been wrong! But just tonight, I decided that I couldn't go through with it! That's why I looked ill, and when I got alone, I took a close look and decided that I could not betray you!"

"Dear me!" Lord Roth sniffed. He gave Gilbert a sad shake of his head, saying, "I regret that you must resort to the final excuse of all evildoers! I never knew one who did not cry, 'I was just going to repent'!"

One look at Humility's face, and Gilbert knew that she hated him. His mind raced, and suddenly he saw his sword hanging from a peg on the wall. With a sudden leap, he pulled it from the scabbard and set himself on guard against the form of Lord Roth.

"You devil!" he whispered. "No matter what I've done, one thing is certain—you'll not take this man!"

Simon Roth did not seem alarmed at the threat of Gilbert's sword. He said easily, "Well, now we see, don't we? First you betray this woman, then you betray Brewster. Now you intend to betray your employer, the bishop, the law and the King of England. There's nothing in you of truth, is there, Winslow?"

The raw truth of Roth's speech raked across Gilbert's nerves, and he could have wept at the foolish decisions that had brought him to this time!

But he shook his head and said drily, "You mistake me in one thing at least, my Lord—and I will now prove to you by my sword that my honor may be tattered by my foolish choices— but there is enough remaining to stop *you*!"

Gilbert advanced to engage swords with the lean man in front of him, but to his surprise, Roth did not lift his blade. Instead, he called out, "Johnson!"

Aware suddenly that his back was to the bedroom door, Gilbert whirled to find the man he had encountered on the dock at Leyden framed in the doorway, in his hands a heavy blunderbuss, trained right on Gilbert's chest!

"We meet again, eh?" he said with a wide grin. "Thought we might."

"Well, well, we must get on with it," Roth said. "As you must have guessed, Johnson followed you and the woman here all the way from Leyden. Followed you here, also, then came to get me. So we'll have your head on a pike on London Bridge, I shouldn't wonder, Mr. Winslow. It'll look well enough—until the crows pick out those bright blue eyes!"

"We better chain this one 'till morning, Lord Roth," Johnson suggested.

"Quite so, Johnson. I believe you brought the irons?"

"Right enough! Here, you put yer arms behind yer back!" Johnson commanded, bringing a set of heavy manacles out of a roomy coat pocket.

He kept the blunderbuss trained carefully on Gilbert's middle, and there was no chance of avoiding being torn in two at that range. "Just drop the sword!"

Gilbert gave up hope then, and his sword clattered to the stones of the floor. Turning to face Lord Roth's triumphant gaze, he heard Johnson approach and felt the touch of the iron on his wrists.

"Don't grieve over Cecily too much, Winslow," Roth said. "I'll see that she gets the proper consolation. As a matter-of-fact, it—"

Roth's words were drowned out by a tremendous *bonging* sound almost in Gilbert's ear, and the weight of Johnson's body came crashing into his back. The blunderbuss hit the floor, exploding with a tremendous boom! The shot tore huge chunks of plaster from the wall next to Lord Roth, and the nobleman's face turned pale.

Gilbert whirled to find Elder William Brewster holding a large chamber pot made of solid brass in both hands and staring down at the still form of Johnson whose head was beginning to bleed from a large gash over his left ear.

Brewster looked a little stunned at his own action, but a gleam came into his mild eyes, and he said distinctly, "The Lord is a man of war!"

In a heartbeat Gilbert snatched up his sword, but barely in time, for Lord Roth recovered his senses in time to make a lunge that would have pierced the heart of Winslow had he been one fraction of a second slower!

They met in a fierce instant, hilts locked, their faces not six inches apart. They strained fiercely, then Gilbert thrust his opponent backward, sending him against the wall with a tremendous crash that rattled the dishes.

There was a silence, the two men frozen for one brief moment. Then Lord Roth said, "I had thought to see you hang, Winslow, but this way is better!"

"Lord Roth, look to yourself. One of us will be in the presence of God in a few seconds!"

Gilbert lifted his sword, the creation of master swordsmith Clemens Hornn, a gift from Paul Dupree. He stood sideways, right foot straight forward with knee bent, left foot sideways and a little behind him, creeping to the right leg. The rapier, so balanced to his hand that it seemed to carry its own weight, was as steady as if it were carved in stone.

The adversaries moved forward, the blades rang; then they disengaged and fell back. This was no tournament with buttoned foils; both men knew that one error would be fatal.

Time and time again, Roth's blade circled slowly, then like the strike of a snake it drove straight toward Gilbert's heart; each time Gilbert used just enough pressure on Roth's blade to deflect it.

Once Gilbert saw his opportunity, and made a lunge, but the long arm of Roth made it ineffective.

Roth was fencing according to all the rules, and Gilbert was caught off guard when suddenly, instead of lunging in a classic thrust, Roth bent to one side and slashed viciously at Gilbert's leg. A sudden pain ripped through Gilbert's thigh, and blood spattered the floor, making it slippery.

"A foretaste, Winslow!" Roth smiled. He wiped his sweating brow, and glanced at Brewster and Humility who were backed up against the outside wall, saying, "Just a moment more, and we can have our tea!"

Pain was running through Gilbert's leg, sending its message through live nerves. He knew at once that he was cut to the bone, and was aware that if he put his full weight on that wounded right leg, he would go down. Backing up slowly, parrying Roth's now frantic thrusts, he saw that his opponent knew as much and was bearing down with all his might to end the fight with one thrust. He need not fear Gilbert's blade, for the wounded leg meant that he could not thrust at all.

Then Gilbert felt the wall against his back, and saw instantly that Roth was uncoiling that long body of his ready for the final thrust that would pin his helpless opponent to the wall!

Throw the rule book away, Mon Ami! The words rang in Gilbert's mind—words he had heard a hundred times from his master Dupree: *When you are losing, what good are rules?*

As Roth gathered himself into a coil of muscle, Gilbert knew that the last thrust was coming. Then Gilbert did what he had never done—what he had never seen done, and what he had never heard of; and he did it smoothly as though he had practiced it every day of his life.

As Roth's blade drove toward him, Gilbert's left hand flashed out, grasped the tip of the flat sword. It was pure chance that his finger's closed on it, for no man is fast enough to achieve that sort of reaction on purpose.

As Roth came in for the kill, Gilbert twisted his blade to one side. It sliced through his palm, cutting to the bone with each edge, but that was a small thing. At the same time, Gilbert simply lifted his sword and Roth, sensing at the last moment what had happened, opened his mouth to cry out, "No!"

But he was too late. The force of his lunge brought him in range, and Gilbert felt his blade penetrate the tough membrane of the chest, grate on bone, then slide easily up to the hilt.

Roth stood there staring at Gilbert with a terrible brightness in his eyes. Then he looked down at the hilt of the sword nestled against his chest. For a long moment he seemed to be meditating what to do about it. He put his hand up, touched the hilt of Gilbert's sword tenderly—then his legs buckled and he sprawled limply on the floor, a bright crimson flood spreading out from beneath his body.

Gilbert stared at Roth's body, took one step forward on his wounded leg, and fell headlong, his legs tangled with the body of his adversary.

He looked at his left palm, noting impersonally the white gristle and bone in the red slashes, then at his thigh which was pumping a throbbing stream of his blood on the floor with each steady beat of his heart.

He heard Humility say, "We must leave! There'll be others!"

Looking up, he saw her face, but it was as if she were behind a thin red curtain. Her voice was thin and reedy, as though she were in a distant far-off room.

He knew he was dying, bleeding to death, and he desperately wanted to tell them both how he had changed out under the stars—but when he opened his lips, no sound came out.

He heard Humility say, "Leave him!" Then came a roaring in his ears, and then—nothing.

CHAPTER TWELVE

"THEY KNEW THEY WERE
PILGRIMS . . ."

★　★　★　★

Consciousness came to Gilbert suddenly. One moment he was unaware of anything; then he was looking up at a crude picture of a horse with very stiff legs. Fascinated, he stared at it, thinking, *I could draw a better horse than that!* Then he felt a thrill of fear, for he realized that he didn't know where he was—nor even, for a fraction of a second, *who* he was.

"You're awake," a voice said, and he rolled his head to one side to see a face that looked familiar—an elderly man with a full beard and eyes that were kind. "About time, my boy!"

Then it all came back—the cottage in the valley and the duel with Lord Roth. "Elder Brewster . . ." he croaked, and could not say more, so parched were the tissues of his throat and lips, until Brewster held his head up and gave him a few swallows of tepid water from a pewter tankard. "Let me sit up."

"Careful with your leg!" Brewster warned as he helped pull Gilbert into a sitting position. "We've got too much invested in you to lose you now."

Gilbert's head swam as he sat up, but that passed and he stared around the room, a small, low-ceilinged affair with one small window allowing a thin shaft of sunlight through a dingy glass. "This isn't your house! Where are we—and how. . . ?"

"Now, there's time for that," Brewster said. He got up and brought a bowl from the small chest by the door. Taking a large wooden spoon he said, "You try to eat some of this broth, and I'll tell you what's happened."

The broth was cold, filmed with grease—and the most delicious thing Gilbert had ever tasted! He gobbled down the contents, and Brewster refilled it twice from a black pot as he talked.

"Well, when you went down bleeding like a slaughtered steer, we got the bleeding stopped; then we did the needlework. We had no way of knowing how soon somebody would appear looking for Lord Roth and Johnson, so we managed to get you into my little two-wheeled cart, hitch up my donkey, and somehow—by God's grace!—we got you back to Gabriel's house."

"Is this it?"

"Oh, no, Gilbert! That would have been fatal! We stayed until dark the next night; then we put you in a wagon, covered you with fresh cut hay, and Humility and I lay beside you to keep you still. Gabriel has a brother with a tiny farm about ten miles from Scrooby, and that's where we are now."

"How long have I been here, Mr. Brewster?"

"This is August 6—that makes it five days."

"Five days! Why, you can't stay here—you've got to get to Southampton at once! The *Mayflower* is due to sail—"

Brewster pushed Gilbert back into bed, and said in a gentle voice, "The ship sailed yesterday, Gilbert."

"Oh, no!" He struggled to break the grip of Brewster, but he was too weak, and finally fell back, despair etched on his face. "What will. . . ?"

He stopped abruptly when the door opened and Humility came in.

He almost failed to recognize her, so changed was she from what he remembered. She was very pale—he could not see how anyone could lose so much color in such a short time! The rosy cheeks and the pert cherry lips were washed to a pale gray, faded and lifeless, and there was none of the sparkle in her green eyes that had been so beautiful. She gazed at him as she approached, and there was no anger that he could read, but more of a stolid indifference. Her eyes seemed cloudy, obscured by a thin film that blocked out all the warmth and charm of her spirit. "I found some food," she said quietly, and there was the same deadness in her voice that was in her eyes—none of the vivacious element that had been there before.

Gilbert swallowed and said with an effort, "Humility—and Mr. Brewster—it may not mean anything to you now—I suppose it doesn't—but what I said to Roth, about deciding not to deliver you up? It was the truth!"

"I believe you," Humility said, but it seemed to have no meaning to her; there was nothing in her voice or in her face to remind him of the woman he had known.

"And so do I, Gilbert!" Brewster patted his shoulder. He gave Humility a quick glance and then said hurriedly, "You must put it all behind you, and start all over again, my boy!"

Gilbert put his hand out to Humility and said huskily, "I'm sorry for all of it!"

She took his hand, but it might have been the hand of a marble statue he held—so cold and motionless it was. And her eyes were somehow brittle and empty as she said tonelessly, "I forgive you, Gilbert." Then she turned and left, saying, "I'll be downstairs if you need me."

Brewster waited until she was gone, then said, "Don't despair, Gilbert. She'll change."

"Why should she?" Gilbert asked angrily. "I've pulled her world apart—yours as well. If I hadn't been involved, you'd both be on the *Mayflower* right now!"

"You can't *know* that, can you? A thousand things might have happened to keep us from being there. Do you remember the word from the Bible: 'All things work together for good to them that love the Lord'? So this tragedy is part of God's plan."

"Doesn't seem possible!"

"And did it seem *good* to Joseph when his brothers threw him in a pit to die? But years later when he saved his whole family, he told them not to worry about what they'd done. Remember that? He said, 'You thought evil against me, but God meant it unto good, to save much people alive.' "

"I can't see how murdering a man and wrecking your life can be *good*!"

"Well, to be honest with you, my boy, neither can I—right now. But I'm an old man, and one thing I've learned is that God has a sovereign will in every situation. So we must wait and see what He plans to do with *this* one!"

He was out of the bed in a week, dizzy and clinging to the wall for support. But it took three more weeks for him to move with anything like a normal walk. He used the days to exercise in the small room, and after dark he limped painfully around the confines of the small farm. There were other farms so close that there was always a chance of someone seeing them, so Gabriel came to bring them food and give them news.

Gilbert had given up on any response from Humility. She was locked in, barricaded behind a wall that baffled his many attempts to get through. Brewster had said, "Give her time, Gilbert. She'll come out one day and be herself again."

He marked a little calendar that he had made, checking off each day, and on the 4th of September Gabriel came bursting into the house, calling, "Mr. Brewster! Mr. Brewster!" in stentorian tones loud enough to rattle the dishes.

Gilbert fell downstairs and saw the huge Gabriel practically shaking the slender form of Brewster, his face wild with excitement.

"I tell ye, she's not gone yet!"

"Who's not gone, Gabriel?" Gilbert asked.

"The ship—the *Mayflower*—she's at Plymouth!"

Brewster was trying to read a note, apparently a letter that Gabriel had passed to him. "It's true, Gilbert! This is from Bradford . . ." He paused to scan the contents, and then looked up with excitement in his face. "The two ships left Southampton together, but the *Speedwell* proved to be unseaworthy, so they turned back to have her repaired."

"And they're at Plymouth?" Gilbert demanded.

"Yes—but Bradford says that the new plan is to leave the *Speedwell* here—to put as many as possible on the *Mayflower* and make the trip in one ship."

"When do they sail?"

Brewster looked at the letter and shook his head. "By the 6th—that's day after tomorrow!"

"You'll be on that ship!" Gilbert exclaimed.

"Impossible!" the older man exclaimed.

"With God, all things are possible," Gilbert grinned. It delighted him to have a hope; the waiting had been terribly hard on his nerves, but the worst was the total lack of any possible action. Now he took Gabriel by the arm, and said rapidly, his face glowing with excitement, "Gabriel, get your wagon piled high with hay."

"Why, it's here—I was bringing a wagon load to my brother for his stock!"

"Good! Where's Humility?"

"Gone to the stream for fresh water," Brewster said.

"I'll go get her—you throw everything we've got in the way of food and clothing together!"

He lurched out the door, breaking into a half-run. Pain ran along his leg, but ignoring it, he drove himself through the gate and halfway to the creek when he met Humility coming back in the darkness.

"Humility!" he shouted, grabbing her by both arms. "Come on! We're leaving!"

She dropped the clay pot and it smashed on the ground. "What are you talking about?" Her voice held more animation than he'd heard in a month.

"The *Mayflower* is at Plymouth, and you and Brewster will be on her when she sails in two days!"

"Oh!" That was all she said, but in the dim starlight, Gilbert could see an animation change the dead set that had fixed her features. She held a trembling hand against her cheek, and suddenly tears gathered in her eyes and trickled down her cheeks— silver tracks in the dim light.

He paused, then said, "You'll get to your New World, Humility—I promise you!"

After collecting their meager belongings, they all piled onto the farm wagon drawn by two draft horses, and Gilbert took charge of the expedition, speaking crisply, "We'll have to go through without stopping to rest the team. Gabriel, do you know any places where we can change teams on the way—maybe twice?"

"No trouble there," Gabriel nodded. "I got relatives most counties from here to Plymouth. But they'll be watching the roads pretty close."

"Do you know where the most likely checkpoints will be?"

" 'Course!"

"All right, here's the way of it, then—we'll ride in the wagon until we get close to a checkpoint. Then we get out and follow Gabriel. If he gets stopped, we go around and meet him on the far side."

"A fine plan!" Brewster said. "I have faith in it."

He had, perhaps, more faith in the plan than Gilbert, but it was the only hope. They left at once, and all night long they lurched along the narrow country road, striking the Great North Road at dawn.

Three times during the journey they had to abandon the wagon and they changed horses twice, with great difficulty the second time. It was close to dawn when they pulled up with footsore animals at the dock in Plymouth.

"She may have sailed!" Gabriel whispered.

"Let me have a look," Gilbert said. "I got a look at her at Southampton."

He began walking along the wharf, peering desperately into the dusky darkness. By the starlight and part of a moon, he could make out several ships anchored, but none of them seemed to be the *Mayflower*. He went to the end of the wharf and began the search in the other direction. He was about to give up hope when a cloud that had obscured the moon shredded and there she was—rising lightly at anchor not two hundred feet off-shore—the *Mayflower*!

He hurried back to the wagon and said, "She's still here—just off shore!"

"Praise God!" Brewster breathed, then asked, "But we must get aboard without being seen—and quickly!"

"There's a dory that will serve," Gilbert said. "Let's get our things in it."

Soon they were ready, and after bidding farewell with many thanks to Gabriel, they were underway, the dory sliding easily over the small swells as Gilbert rowed.

They were almost to the ship when Brewster exclaimed, "This boat, Gilbert—it will be missed!"

"No, I'll bring it back as soon as you're aboard."

"But—how will *you* get aboard?"

Then Gilbert finally expressed what he had long since decided. "I won't be coming with you, Mr. Brewster." He saw Humility look at him with a strange expression, but he paid no heed. "The New World's not for me. All I wanted was to make up a little for what I'd planned to do to you. Maybe getting you here will do that!"

Brewster was struck dumb for an instant. He had never considered but that Gilbert would go with them. He said then, "Why, my boy, there's no need to speak of *that*! You must go! There's no place for you in England!"

"I'll be leaving," Gilbert said, "perhaps I'll go to France."

The prow of the dory bumped into the hull of the ship, and there was no more time for talk. Gilbert stood up, grabbing the small steps on the side of the *Mayflower* and held the dory still while the other two climbed awkwardly out. "I'll go aboard with you," he whispered. "Maybe there's no watch tonight. It would be good if you could get aboard without their knowledge. You won't be safe until you're underway."

That would have been well, and indeed there was no watch. Humility made the long step that brought her to the top rail, and cleared it despite her skirt, but when Elder Brewster attempted it, he lost his footing and fell backward, driving into Gilbert, who was caught off balance.

They fell into the dory, and Gilbert's bad leg took the full force of both their weights. The gunnel of the small boat struck his thigh a sharp blow, and Brewster's body crashed down, striking exactly on the wound.

Gilbert felt the wound gape open, and the warm rush of blood confirmed his worst fears. He lay there struck dumb by pain and sick to the heart with despair.

"Gilbert—I'm so sorry! Are you hurt?"

"Yes—you'll have to get some help to row me ashore!"

"Yes!"

Brewster scrambled up the ladder, and was gone so long that Gilbert feared the morning watch would come. Finally, however, he heard sounds, and then Edward's voice said, "Gilbert! What's the matter!"

He looked up in the growing light and gasped, "Edward, you've got to get me ashore!"

Edward looked down at the bloody trousers, shook his

head, and said, "You'd be helpless with that wound, Gilbert. You must go with us."

"No! I *can't!*"

Edward paid no heed, but called out softly, "John? Lend me a hand—help me get him aboard!"

John Howland's face appeared, and his strong arms plucked Gilbert up as if he were weightless.

The two men carried him aboard, and there was Bradford, who looked at Gilbert with a strange expression.

"The leg's torn open," Brewster said. "Can you hide us someplace where we can work on it, John?"

"Are you certain you want this man to go with us?" Bradford stood there, his face stern, and Gilbert would have given his hope of heaven to have been able to get off the boat.

"Let me go!" he cried out, thrashing wildly, but was held in the vise of Howland's mighty arms.

"Gilbert, you have no choice," Edward said. "We have to get that leg fixed *now.*"

Gilbert was half carried down to the main cargo deck. Bradford led the way with a candle. He led them past rows of wooden barrels carrying the water supply to the forward end of the cargo hole. "This is the sail locker, William," he said, opening the door and holding the candle up to illuminate the interior.

Howland helped Gilbert inside, and put him down gently on a thick slab of folded canvas. "I'll get Fuller to take care of the wound," Bradford said, and Gilbert lay there gritting his teeth against the pain.

Brewster spoke a word of comfort once, and Edward pressed his shoulder, saying, "This will be a good place for you and William, Gilbert. The crew never comes here—except after a sail's been damaged. We'll not mention your presence to Captain Jones—not until we're several days out of Plymouth."

Fuller came quickly, his dark eyes burning. "Let me see . . ." he said brusquely. "Ah—need some restitching." He set to work, but Gilbert saw that there was a difference in his manner. He had been a warm friendly man at Leyden; now there was a hardness in his attitude.

"Get it done, Fuller!" Gilbert gasped. "I won't stay on this ship!"

Then Fuller put the needle through his flesh, and the pain was unbelievable. Halfway through the operation, Gilbert went limp.

When he woke up, Brewster was sitting beside him, reading from his Bible.

"We've left England!" Gilbert gasped.

"We'll be out of port soon, Gilbert." Brewster put the book down. "Lie still now. Fuller said the damage wasn't as bad as it might have been—but you don't want to pull the thread out again!"

"Oh, God!" Gilbert cried out, and the tears ran down his cheeks as he rolled his head helplessly. "I can't bear it! I must get off this ship!"

"Easy, son—rest easy!" Brewster said. His thin face was filled with compassion for the young man who writhed in agony of spirit before him, but he knew that for the present, there was little that anyone could do to comfort him. "There's no turning back now. You'll just have to cast in your lot with us psalm-singers."

"But everyone on this ship knows me for a traitor!"

"Not so. There's *one* who doesn't—" Brewster struck his breast lightly, then pointed upward, adding, "And there's another!"

"God? God doesn't care about me!" Gilbert moaned. He had been braced for the danger that lay before him in England—but not for the prison of the New World!

"God cares, Gilbert," Brewster said evenly. "We're not wrong, you know. All of us leaving homes and friends to risk death in a strange land, why, God knows our names! And He cares, Gilbert, oh, how He cares!"

"I can't believe that!"

"You must believe it." A prophetic light appeared in the old man's face, and he said in a soft cadence, "What's happening in the world, Gilbert? Right now? How interested is anyone in a little group of 'psalm-singers' on a tiny ship headed for an obscure corner of the globe? In London, they're talking about King James's deplorable weakness in dealing with Spain; war has broken out in Bohemia, and Spain will send a terrible army rampaging across the Continent. The English court is in an uproar, with the king hysterically denouncing Spain and vowing that the long-talked-of marriage between the Spanish infanta and Charles, the Prince of Wales, is forever cancelled. Along the borders of Holland, Spain is ready to launch an attack on the Dutch."

Brewster paused, and his beard moved lightly as he shook his head; then he looked at Gilbert and asked, "With Europe about to go up in flames, who will stop to notice a handful of tattered exiles sailing west in a weather-beaten freighter under the absurd delusion that God is interested in their endeavor and will protect them in their amateur assault on a wilderness that has swallowed thousands of tougher, better-equipped pioneers?"

Gilbert had risen on his elbow to stare at Brewster as he spoke these words. Now he thought of them, and in a voice filled with doubt, yet with a fragment of hope in his eyes, asked, "And you still say that God is in all this, William?"

Brewster's lips moved silently; then he touched Gilbert's hand and said, "God is in everything, son. He's in your life and He will bring you to harbor. You're tied to us now, and I'd like you to remember a phrase that was in Bradford's letter, when he spoke of the saints that left Leyden—risking life and all for God in this voyage."

"What did he say, Elder Brewster?"

Brewster quoted the lines softly: "They left Leyden, that goodly and pleasant city which had been their resting place for near twelve years—" and here the old man's voice broke as he completed the sentence . . ."*but they knew they were pilgrims!*"

Gilbert Winslow, fugitive from the King's justice, his life in ruins, every dream dead—gazed at the old man's face. The flickering yellow flame of the candle that guttered in a flat dish highlighted Brewster's features, forming a corona of golden light around his face. The wash of golden shadow threw his face into deep relief so that only the gleam of his black eyes was seen; and against the dusky gloom of the sailroom, his face seemed to be coated with thin gold foil, incised with tiny wrinkles etched by time.

Gilbert sat there listening to the creaking of the ship's timbers as she strained from side to side in a slow roll. He felt the plunge as she nosed down, then the rise as she rose like a phoenix and crested the waves. He thought of England, of the wreckage of his career—and he thought with a keen, almost physical pain of Cecily.

He was a Winslow, and the men of his family had been molded by the hard life of the Middle Ages. They had died amidst the ring of sword on shield; they had enriched the soil of England with their blood, their sweat. Part of that blood, at least, went back to the golden-haired Vikings who came to plunder the land; part of it to the lowly Saxons, men of the soil, and some to the proud-eyed Normans who breached the land in 1066 under William.

None of them had been cowards as far as Gilbert had heard.

Slowly he set his jaw, pulled himself up to a sitting position, then looked at William Brewster with a fierce light in his light blue eyes—perhaps like that in the eyes of his forefather when with Drake he had boarded a mighty Spanish galleon with his dirk between his teeth and his cutlass cutting down his enemies like ripe grain.

"So be it then!" he said with a mixture of exaltation and sadness in his tone. Brewster looked up in surprise at the steely note in Gilbert's voice.

"I'll be a pilgrim, too!"

Brewster smiled, his eyes filling with tears, and he said in a voice not quite steady, "That's wonderful, Gilbert! And God will be your guide!"

"No, Mr. Brewster, not God. I've tried God—and although I honor your faith, it's not for me."

Brewster raised a hand in shock, let it fall, then in a weary voice asked sadly, "No God for you, Gilbert? What will you trust, then?"

"This!"

With a cry, Gilbert reached down and unsheathed the sword made by the hand of a man long dead. The blade gleamed with reflected light, and there was a strange beauty in it, deadly as it was.

"This, Mr. Brewster," Gilbert said intently, as he lifted the blade toward heaven. "This is where I put my faith!"

"Gilbert! I thought you'd chosen the pilgrim way!"

Gilbert Winslow gave a slight salute with the blade, then said in a voice as cold as the steel itself: "So I am—*a pilgrim with a sword!*"

PART TWO

THE
MAYFLOWER

★ ★ ★ ★

CHAPTER THIRTEEN

THE SWEET SHIP

★ ★ ★ ★

The *Mayflower* was a "sweet ship," her hold full of pleasant odors, in contrast to the foul fumes that rose from some ships. She had carried cargo rather than passengers for most of her fourteen years—taffeta and satins from Hamburg, hats and hemp to Norway, wine and cognac from France.

In the gray light of morning a crowd of Plymouth people gathered on the quay to bid farewell. The tide rose full and began to drop as the male passengers gathered on the waist deck. The heads of the families, along with Bradford, Carver, and Sam Fuller, watched the thin rays of morning cut through the haze that lay over the harbor, talking quietly in low voices.

After nearly an hour Captain Christopher Jones appeared on the high aft deck. His black figure climbed out of the poop hatch and turned abruptly before the mizzenmast; with his hands on his hips, he looked down on the ship. His face was pale in the morning light, and his stiff hair was plastered down with water. He put his hands to his mouth and sent his voice bellowing down the length of the ship: "Mr. Clarke, Mr. Coffin, Mr. Duff! Break out the anchor. We get underway."

Six sailors in breeches, shirts open to the waist, and bare feet, trooped back through the hole; after working the 'tween-deck capstan to lift the forward anchor, the stairway was cleared for them to pass above.

Women and children awoke and began stumbling about as the heavy square doors of the ports, held up by chains on the outside, were dropped; they had been open day and night since anchoring; now they thudded down until darkness filled the first hold.

"Let fall your main!" Mr. Clark, the bosun, yelled.

Coffin gave William White a hard shove when the small man got in his way. White was driven forcefully against the broad chest of young John Alden who prevented him from falling, then said in a slow Yorkshire brogue, "Ye needn't be so rough, mon!"

Coffin whirled and appeared to consider giving the same rough treatment to Alden—but the immense shoulders and heavily corded arms of the young man gave him pause, as did the steady look he received from Alden's deep-set blue eyes.

"Stay clear or get stomped!" Coffin sneered, then moved to the forward mast.

Susanna White had come to stand beside her husband, and as his thin body was racked with an explosive series of coughs, she put her hand on his arm and said, "Don't mind him, William. Go lie down for a while."

"No," White said when he got his breath. "This is my last look on England, Susanna. I'll not miss that."

Susanna shot a quick look at Edward Winslow who had moved toward the scene, and something in her husband's word carried a foreboding of gloom. Winslow caught Susanna's eyes, shrugged imperceptibly, then said, "We'll be back, William, never fear."

William White looked at Winslow, gave a small shake of his head, and said quietly, "No fear, Mr. Winslow. God is with us. But it's the New World for me—I'll not look on this old one again."

The fore and main topsails were flown, as were the two big square sails and the lateen sails on the poop; the ship moved slowly down the water and the town diminished into the distance, a sharp black outline of rooftops against a cold sky.

As they came around, trimmed, into the wind so that a sudden gust filled the mainsail out with a resounding slam, William Bradford said to Dorothy, "We are free at last! Now the New World!"

"I'm afraid, William!" There was something pitiful in the small figure of Dorothy Bradford as she stood hunched over the rail, filling her eyes with the dim outlines of her homeland. "I'm so afraid!"

But an expression of exhilaration filled William Bradford's craggy face as the *Mayflower's* blunt cutwater rose and fell heavily, smashing through the dark frills of water. He was rejoicing that the thing was done at last. They were out on the open sea to live or die.

If he had taken his eyes from the horizon to look down at Dorothy's face, he would have seen exactly the reverse—for she stared wild-eyed at the rolling ocean as if it were a demon out of hell. As it was, he did not notice at all when she wheeled and ran below, her hands over her face in a helpless gesture of futility.

The day proved bright and fresh, and the sun shed warmth upon the ship as it drove into the deep swells. After the crew had set the tackle and cleared the deck, the women and children began to come up, peering fearfully at the vast expanse that met their eyes. They had their first meal at sea at noon—biscuit-bread, smoked bacon, and mugs of beer served in the first hold by candlelight.

On a ship for the first time in her life, Dorothy Bradford lay on her plank bunk in the tiny cabin shifting from hot to cold and hot again, not caring if she lived or died, while her husband wiped up the mess. Then he himself took sick and had to lie down, and Humility came into the cabin to take care of them.

Humility waited until Dorothy fell into a fitful sleep, then left the cabin. Below deck the enclosed air was soured by seasickness, although those women who were well kept the spruce planking swabbed clean with salt water. Walking was not easy, for the great width of the *Mayflower* in proportion to her length made her subject to the push-and-pull of the waves. With every change of wind, she waltzed with a thunderous flapping of canvas. The ship was built for roominess and carrying capacity. Below the deep hold and the upper deck was a gun deck about twenty-six feet wide and seventy-eight feet long. It was here that most of the passengers were settled. Humility had to step carefully, for most of the deck was covered with quilts and bedding. Beyond the gun deck the ship's sides bowed together until she was only nineteen feet wide on her upper deck.

Humility wandered aimlessly over the ship, hoping to take her mind off her queasy stomach. She peered into the forecastle, where the crew lived. A good portion of it was taken up by the galley, and the foremast came through the forward end of it. *Not much space for thirty men,* she thought. But sailors traveled light, and half the men were always on duty.

She did not go below the poop deck, the sailors being active in that area, but later she discovered it contained the poop house, a cabin about thirteen by seventeen where the master's mates dined and relaxed. There also was the Great Cabin where the captain slept and ate in lonely splendor.

Humility had heard a fragment of discussion between Captain Jones and Elder Bradford, learning that the poop house had been divided in half and that about eighteen passengers were accommodated there—a situation that did not endear the pilgrims to the crew! But some arrangement was necessary, for there were eighteen married couples, and eleven unmarried girls, many in their early teens, as well as eight or ten very young children aboard. Most of these were in the after-house cabins, where there was some degree of privacy. That left, Humility figured, as she made her way downward to the lower parts of the ship, about fifty-four people to be taken care of on the gun deck—married men without wives, bachelors, and grown boys. Some slept in the shallow, a large fishing boat taken apart and stored in sections; others had crude bunks built into the ship's sides, and a few imitated the sailors in their hammocks.

In one of the dark passageways she suddenly encountered one of the crew, a swarthy thick-bodied sailor, who deliberately pressed his rank body against her in the narrow space. He grinned broadly, exposing a wide gap in his upper teeth, and said in a thick, slurred voice, "Well, naow, looky 'ere wot we finds!" He put out a stubby finger to touch her face, and when she whirled and made her way quickly back toward the gun deck, he roared with laughter, calling after her, "You can't run far, can yer now, missy? And the gals don't get away from Jeff Daggot—no, they don't!"

In her haste to get away from the man, Humility ran headlong into the arms of a surprised Sam Fuller. He held her up as she fell backward, gave a deep laugh, and said, "Well, where could you be going in such haste, Humility?"

"Oh, it's you, Sam!" she gasped, taking a deep breath. She glanced over her shoulder and decided it would do no good to complain, so shrugged and gave him a smile. "Just exploring a little. What are you doing?"

"A mite of doctorin', lass." His large eyes crinkled in a grin, and he shrugged, adding, "Nothing to do for seasickness."

"Dorothy is very bad!"

"Yes—and I'm thinking it's a bit more than just the usual trouble at sea." He leaned back against the bulkhead, and there was a frown on his broad face. "I've said all along that some people ain't fitted for the hard life. Mrs. Bradford, why, she's a fine lady, but she is pretty delicate. I told William all along he ought to leave her home until we get a little comfort built into the new land."

Fuller looked at the tall girl with sudden interest. "You had some pretty rough handling, Humility—the business with young Winslow?"

"I'm all right, Sam."

He shifted uncomfortably, for there was something in her brief statement that did not seem good to him. He pulled at his beard, finding it hard to put into words what he wanted to say, and finally murmured, "Don't be a sour woman, Humility."

She managed to give him a smile, and patted his arm, "I— I won't get sour, Sam. I promise!"

"There's my girl!" He nodded vigorously and then said, "I don't think anyone has given any thought to our two *friends* in the sail locker. Wouldn't do, either, for the captain to be introduced to them this close to England. They must be getting a mite hungry, eh, lass?"

She saw his design, testing her to see if she could face Gilbert, and she laughed suddenly, saying, "You're not very subtle, are you, Sam? All right, I'll see to it."

"God love you, lass! That's the sweet spirit I like to see in a gal!"

Humility made her way to the galley and wheedled some biscuits and two portions of cold meat from the gnome of a cook. Thomas Hinge was very slight and crippled, but was friendly, especially with the children who crowded around his small fire hoping for tidbits as he cooked. He smiled crookedly at Humility, saying in a surprising bass voice, "You 'as quite an appetite for a young lady!"

"Oh, that's because you're such a fine cook, Mr. Hinge!" she laughed, and was rewarded by a dish of plum duff from the little man.

Finding her way below was easier now, though she had to grope her way along until she got to the cargo hold. There she found a small door at the forward end of the cargo hold.

When the door opened, William Brewster peered out, holding a candle high, and when he saw who it was, he smiled and said, "Ah, Humility! Come in, come in!"

She entered the small room, and found herself looking down at Gilbert who was sitting on a bundle of sailcloth with his back against the bulkhead.

He was, she saw, very pale, and the leg stretched out in front of him was wrapped in a thick roll of bandages. He looked startled as she stood over him, his eyes widening as she entered and set the lantern down on a small table—the only furniture in the compartment.

"Hello, Gilbert," she said steadily, willing herself to meet his eyes. She nodded and asked, "How's your leg?"

"I'm all right," he said finally. "Leg hurts some."

"You must be hungry," she said quietly and set the food down.

"You thought of us," Brewster nodded with a smile. "That's like you, Humility." He took a bite of biscuit, then nodded to Gilbert. "Try to eat, Gilbert. You lost a lot of blood."

She was not comfortable, and got up to leave.

"Can I get you anything, Mr. Brewster?" Humility asked.

"I have what I need, thank you." He held up his worn Bible.

"Can I bring you anything—" she faltered for the first time over his name, and covered up the omission by saying, "Maybe you'd like your Bible, too?"

Gilbert did not lift his head as he answered, "No Bible—but my green notebook I would like."

She did not miss the bitter note in his voice as he mentioned the Bible, but said only, "I'll bring it."

She left quickly, and the two men ate the food. Brewster noted that Gilbert was only picking at his meal, but said nothing. Finally he ate his share of the duff and handed the bowl to the younger man, saying, "Eat all the rest of this, Gilbert. It's fine duff; it'll help you get your strength back more rapidly."

"For what?" Gilbert asked, his voice full of bitterness. Impatiently he spooned the food out of the dish, then flung it onto the sailcloth. "What difference does it make? I'm not going anywhere—have nothing to do!"

William Brewster was too wise to rush the young man. He knew that Gilbert Winslow was, for all his swordplay and toughness, finely wired and as sensitive as a woman. The old man made no attempt to speak to the despair that shrouded Gilbert, but spoke of other things until Humility came back with a leather-bound book which the young man took with a curt nod.

"Mr. Bradford said to tell you he'll come and talk with you tonight. He said it would be better if you didn't leave this room for a day or perhaps two."

"Yes. I expect that would be wise."

"I'll bring your food in the morning," she said, and left without a glance at Gilbert.

Brewster sat down and opened the large black Bible with a sigh of contentment. There was a swallow of light beer left in his cup, and he drank it down, saying wryly, "I'm a very carnal man! Look, here's the Word of God—and here's my beer, and you see which of the two I mind first?"

"Man shall not live by the Bible alone—doesn't it say that somewhere?"

Brewster glanced swiftly at his companion, well aware that the caustic remark was the fruit of a bitter spirit, but he only smiled and answered gently, "Well, something like that, I think."

He read steadily, immersing himself in the Scripture, noting after a while that Gilbert had found a worn pen and a small quantity of ink. He had hitched himself up painfully with the book on his good knee and was slowly writing.

Brewster had slept little since they had scrambled on board the *Mayflower*, and now as the regular rocking of the ship rolled him in a soothing cadence, his eyes grew heavy, and the last thing he knew was the sound of Gilbert's pen making a thin scratching in the small cabin.

September 7, 1620

The keeping of a journal is the business of lovesick maidens.

Yet here am I, Gilbert Winslow, sitting in the dark sail locker of the *Mayflower*, scribbling away by the light of a stubby candle, my only companion a religious fanatic.

The cabin is no darker than my own heart. How quickly life can reverse itself! Was it only a few brief hours ago that I was secure in the certainty of place and fortune in the service of the most powerful Lord in all of England, happy in the hope of the love of a beautiful woman? And now, here I sit in this dank hole with my life wounded far worse than my leg—which, by the way, throbs as if a demon were pounding a white-hot spike into it!

Brewster has gone to sleep, and I do not need to write any longer. I began writing to keep him from talking to me, nothing more. He is so confounded *cheerful* in the face of everything! Of course, *he* is safe now, bound for his New World where he can preach to the naked savages to his heart's content. To give him his due, he is an honest man, quite convinced that this world is but a bit of practice for the world to come. They all think that, actually seeming to *enjoy* suffering! They claim hardship endured for God is like money in the bank, that it will build up compound interest until they get there to enjoy it!

But trying to talk to these fanatics about hard *fact* is like talking to a tree! They just give you a smile dripping with sweetness and ask, "Why, where's your faith, brother?"

In a few weeks, after scurvy hits and teeth start dropping out, I'd ask a few of them, "Where's *your* faith, brother!"

No, I will not. That's the bitterness of my own heart.

I pity them, for it will not be as they think—no paradise on earth!

I have only one hope. I am strong and I will endure this voyage. I will endure the beginnings—and I will be aboard the first ship that comes to the accursed place!

One thing I will *not* do—I will not join these people in any way. My lad Tink is a likely chap. But I will be leaving him as soon as I can, so no need to get emotionally involved in him. Brewster is a fine man—one of the few in this earth who would forgive another for such as I planned to do to him. But he'll starve or be killed by savages like the rest. Humility—I cannot write about her . . .

I will give these people the strength of my arm—but not one inch of ground in my heart—so help me God!

CHAPTER FOURTEEN

STOWAWAYS

★　★　★　★

Gilbert's wound began to knit almost at once, and three days after leaving Plymouth, he began to get sick of the sailroom. There was nothing to read but Brewster's Bible, and when the older man was absent, Gilbert was driven from sheer boredom to read the mystic visions of Ezekiel and the lists of clean and unclean food in Leviticus.

He spent long hours thinking of Cecily and of the lost opportunities of their life together. Now that she was lost to him, she seemed more desirable than ever, and the wealth and power which had been a mere possibility as Lord North's man, in his imagination became more solid and real than ever. A dark streak of fatalism imposed itself on his spirit, and the optimism that had been a part of his character faded as the lonely days dragged on.

William Brewster noted this, of course, and he said to Edward on the first Sunday at sea, "Edward, I'm worried about Gilbert. He does nothing but lie in that little place and mope."

They were standing at the starboard rail, watching the passengers come up for the first service since leaving England. The small deck was crowded; everyone who was not seasick came topside, most of them rather pale from the close confinement below.

"There's no help for it, I suppose," Edward answered

shortly. There was a reserve in his face that was unusual as he said, "I'm still finding it hard to believe that my own brother betrayed us!"

Brewster pulled at his grizzled beard and in his gentle voice said, "There's one thing we can take comfort in, Edward."

"What's that, William?"

"He couldn't go through with it. When the time came, there was something in him that *refused*! He has great good in him, Edward."

Edward studied the face of the older man; then a smile touched his lips. "There is that, isn't there? It gives me hope that he may come out of this business a man."

"I'm sure of it, Edward—but it's going to take all our prayers. He's bitter now, you know. I think if you'd have a word with him, it might help."

"All right, I'll do it." Edward saw that Bradford was mounting the poop deck, and said, "I think the service is beginning."

As Bradford was preparing to speak, Brewster looked down from the upper deck, seeing for the first time all the passengers together, and it gave him a sense of uneasiness to see how small the Leyden group was. Only twenty-seven in all, less than a sixth of the church—a minority that showed up clearly as he saw the bulk of the *strangers* on the crowded deck.

There were about eighty of these, volunteers whom Thomas Weston and his business friends had recruited in London and its vicinity to fill out the plantation's quota.

Some, like Christopher Martin, were dissatisfied with the Church of England and quite ready to join the kind of church the Leyden exiles had created. Others had obviously succumbed to the Weston vision of profits in the wilderness and, like millions who would follow, were headed for the New World to make their fortunes. Stephen Hopkins, Brewster thought, was certainly one of these. He had already made one voyage to Virginia, and had survived a harrowing shipwreck in Bermuda. Now he was sailing on the *Mayflower* with his pregnant wife Elizabeth and their three children. He was a man of considerable means and had brought along two servants; Edward Dotey and Edward Leister, both of London.

Another "stranger" was John Billington, a surly, contentious character, Brewster knew, with a viper-tongued wife and two unruly teenaged sons.

Scanning the crowd, Brewster nodded with more approval on William Mullins, boot and shoe dealer of Dorking. He was a devout man bringing his wife and two children, Joseph and Priscilla. Mullins had bought nine shares in Weston's company—equal to an investment of about one hundred pounds—and he had a large supply of shoes in the ship's hold—the last of his stock.

Some of the men were servants hired by more affluent members of the group, such as husky John Howland hired to do the heavy labor in the wilderness for Carver. Twenty-two-year-old William Butten was to do likewise for Samuel Fuller.

Important to the venture were two master mariners—Thomas English and John Allerton—two ordinary seamen who were to man the ten-ton shallop stored between decks on the *Mayflower*. They were under contract for one year, and were essential for helping explore the shallow waters along the coast.

One other hired man of considerable importance was Captain Miles Standish, a short, stocky, tough ex-soldier who had been assigned to handle the plantation's defenses. Now thirty-four, Standish had served with the English army sent by Queen Elizabeth to aid Holland against Spain. The last English troops had been withdrawn from Holland in 1609, about the time the first of the Scrooby exiles were making their way to Amsterdam and finally Leyden. Standish had met some of the leaders of the Green Gate congregation in Leyden, and Bradford had remembered the pugnacious warrior as the right man to superintend their military affairs. For Standish, whose only trade was soldiering, it was a welcome offer; between wars, the English government had an unpleasant habit of discharging its best men, leaving them either to steal or starve. Childless, the captain brought along only his wife Rose.

Bradford raised his voice and began a hymn, and as the others joined in, the crashing of the green waves on the plunging bow, the whistling of the wind through the rigging, and the creaking of masts and spars muffled the reedy voices.

After several hymns and a long reading from the Bible, Bradford preached a short message. He took his text from Deuteronomy 8:7: "For the Lord thy God bringeth thee into a good land, a land of brooks of water, of fountains and depths that spring out of valleys and hills."

Bradford raised his seamed face and said, "This is the promise of our God—we will rejoice and be glad in it!" Then he exhorted the people to remember that it was God and not man who had delivered them and would provide for their needs. He spoke briefly, ending by saying, "I call your attention to verse 11 of this chapter, where we are warned: 'Beware when thou hast eaten and art full that thou forget not the Lord thy God, in not keeping his commandments!'"

He closed the Bible, and the service closed with a long prayer from Bradford. Edward said, "William, there's a meeting called by Martin. You had better come."

"More complaints, I take it?"

"What else?" Edward growled as he led the way toward the stair.

The meeting was to be in the section of the poop house used by several of the passengers, and by the time Brewster and Winslow got there, Bradford was ringed by Billington, Martin, Hopkins, and several others, none of them from the Green Gate congregation.

Billington, a tall, heavy man with thick features and only one tone of voice—a half shout—was waving his thick forefinger under Bradford's nose, saying, ". . . Let no mistake be made, Mr. Bradford; we won't be put upon! Your man Cushman found out I'm a man wot's gets 'is rights! I got me rights, see?"

"No one denies that, Mr. Billington—" Bradford tried to interrupt, but was overpowered by the weight of Billington's foghorn voice.

"We ain't in Leyden, I says, so don't think we a'goin to be like them sheep wot you brought with yer!"

"Not likely," Steven Hopkins piped up. He was as small as Billington was large, and his small, pointed face was in contrast to that of the larger man. He waved his hands about as he talked, his features working nervously as he insisted, "I been a traveler, Mr. Bradford, all the way to Virginia. Was shipwrecked and made my way home safe despite it all." He nodded and looked around proudly, and then he said shrewdly, "What it comes to,

Mr. Bradford, is this: on a trip like this there's got to be some 'justments made!"

"Adjustments?" Bradford asked quietly. "What sort of adjustments?"

"Why, ain't it plain? All this talk about who's the governor and such! When that time comes, it'll be up to *all* of us to have a say, won't it?"

"Certainly you are entitled to have a voice in the government," Bradford nodded, but then he added with a trace of iron in his voice as well as in his dark eyes, "but we began this voyage under the hand of God—and God, Mr. Hopkins, is not a democratic leader. He is a Sovereign King."

"Oh, *that's* the way it's going to be!" Christopher Martin, tall, cadaverous, and usually angry over some imaginary slight to his dignity, grew red and swelled up. "Why, I didn't leave England for a New World to be lorded over by nobody! No more lords and nobles for me!"

"That's *treason!*"

Every man in the group started at the loud voice that cut through the argument, and the crowd parted to allow the captain of the *Mayflower* to stand in the center.

Captain Jones was a solid, tightly built man, though neat and short, in his early thirties. He had a pair of direct gray eyes that ran around the crowd with no attempt to conceal the anger in them.

"I warned you, Mr. Bradford, there'll be no treason on my ship!"

"There is none, Captain Jones," Bradford said quickly. "Mr. Martin was speaking in general terms."

"I heard what he said!" Jones snapped. "And I heard what you said as well. Did I not warn you there'd be no fanatical treason preaching on my ship? Why did you ignore my order?"

"Sir, it was Sunday. We merely had our usual worship."

"You spoke against the King!"

"Not against the King, Captain Jones."

"Did I not hear you talk of freedom for every man? What would that be if not treason? Is not every Englishman under the King?"

"I spoke of the soul of man, Captain, not politically."

Jones stared at him, then shook his head stubbornly. "The King is the King—no matter about *souls*!"

"I must disagree. Only God can rule over our souls."

"I am the master on this ship. Every soul 'board ship stands under the master, and likewise every Englishman stands under the King!"

"Their souls?"

"Yes!" Jones nodded emphatically, sending his curly black hair wildly bobbing. "Know, sir, that I am aware of your views. I am not unaware that some of your group offended the King and are fleeing his wrath! Deny it not to be so. You would lead people away from their duty to the King under your pretense of holiness. Beware, Mr. Bradford, for you will not do so on my ship!"

"Captain Jones!" Edward Winslow moved to stand directly in front of the captain. "There is no treason here. You are not unaware that I have been for many years in the King's service. Would such a man as I be a part of any group bent on treason?"

Jones faltered, for there was an air of distinction in Winslow's bearing, in addition to which Jones was aware of the service of this man to the King.

"I make no accusation against *you*, Mr. Winslow," Jones said in a calmer voice, "but you are not in good company. I urge you to take heed to yourself!"

The captain felt that he had made his point, so saying bluntly, "I have my eye on you—do not provoke me!" he left the hold.

"I see no point in this meeting," Winslow said, looking with distaste at the group of dissidents. "We are bound to one another, and we must have a ruler. Otherwise we are no better than beasts!"

"But who's to say who's to be the ruler?" Billington asked loudly.

"God will always raise up a man," Bradford said at once. He nodded and said, "I have nothing to say to you on this matter."

He turned and left, followed by Brewster and Winslow.

When they got up on deck again, Winslow said moodily, "That'll not satisfy them, William."

"It will have to be prayed about, I fear." Bradford looked across the rolling ocean, then down toward the hold, saying sadly, "If we cannot agree on matters before we reach our land, how will we manage there?"

"God will make our way plain!" Brewster said at once. "One step at a time, William!"

William Bradford nodded, but there was a break in his intense air of faith. He finally looked up and said, "God is all!" and then he walked away to stand beside the mizzenmast staring moodily into the west.

Humility had not felt easy over her failure to visit Elder Brewster. He was as much of a father as she had known, but to avoid contact with Gilbert, she had kept away from the sail locker for nearly a week.

Now it came to her that she was being unfair, so she made her way toward the galley to wheedle a goody or two from Hinge for the pair.

She was by now familiar with the manner of cooking aboard ship. Every third day a charcoal fire was lighted over the sand on an iron hearth, a cauldron of porridge made from soaked oats and another cauldron of stew; the porridge was eaten hot every third morning, cold every other two. Fumes from the bad charcoal made them cough, but this was thought a small inconvenience in return for a steaming bowl of food. The porridge was eaten for breakfast with a lump of biscuit-bread and a cup of beer or water, everyone sitting down around the hold with their bowls on their knees. The midday meal was usually cold stew or mush, or biscuit-bread with a slice of smoked bacon or smoked beef.

In the evening their frugal meal was again mainly biscuit-bread, with which they could have a small portion of cheese, heavily smoked, and salted sausage meat, soaked peas, raw onion, finnan haddie, kippered herring, or dried tongue, and a mug of beer.

The few delicacies—apples, prunes, raisins and pickled eggs, of which the store was small—were given only to the children, the sick, and the pregnant. All food was carefully rationed out by the orderlies. Meals took a long time; the food was small in bulk but tough in substance. Most of the meat had to be chewed at great length, and even then was hardly digestible. They were always hungry, but it lay in their own hands; they could eat well now, if they chose, while idle, and starve later on when perhaps they would have heavy labor to perform.

Humility had made a fast friend of the little gnome of a cook, Thomas Hinge. He was a lonely fellow, twisted in his legs, and most of the crew looked upon him as a menial servant.

She found him stirring a pot of stew over a small fire, and with a smile she said, "Hello, Thomas."

"Why, here you are, miss!"

"We have a sick man who would get well on a bowl of this wonderful stew."

He squinted at her, grinned and gave her a helping in a large vessel. "See you bring that bowl back, now!" Then as she rose to go, he teased her, "Sure that ain't for some young gentleman you're sweet on, miss?"

She looked at him directly, her green eyes suddenly losing their light. "No," she said evenly. "No, there's nothing like that, Thomas."

After she left, the little cook stared after her for a long time, then said, "Scratch me now—I reckon I said the wrong thing, but bless me if I know what it was!"

Making her way down the dark stairs, Humility bit her lip to keep back the tears. She had never cried a great deal, but lately she had found her eyes flooded for no reason, and now she forced herself to blink the stinging tears away.

The odors of the ship were rank, thick with the air of unwashed bodies, stale bedding, night soil, and the old grease. On land it would have been unbearable, but it had become part of the world for her and she paid no heed.

She had reached the cargo hold, and as she made her way along the dark passageway, a man moved out of the darkness ahead of her.

"Well, if it ain't my gal!" Jeff Daggot grinned broadly, moving to block her way. His massive body completely blocked the passage, and she drew back at once. He had taken every opportunity to force himself on her, brushing against her whenever they happened to meet, and more than once reaching out to touch her face with a blunt finger or give a tug to her clothing. She had heard him make a coarse remark about her to Mr. Coffin, and had tried to avoid him.

There was an unholy gleam in his small eyes, and she took a step backward, only to have him reach out and take her by the arms.

"Let me go!"

"Not likely!" he grinned through his broken teeth. "It took me a while to figure it out, but finally it come to me. I been watching you come down here, and so here I am."

He pulled her forward; in his massive arms she was powerless. His arms went around her, and she cried out, "Let me go!"

"Why, sure—in a while!" Daggot said. He put his hand behind her head and forced his huge lips on hers—fear shot through Humility in a way she'd never known. She dropped the bowl of stew, and with both hands beat against Daggot's broad chest, trying to break free from his embrace.

"That's right!" he grinned, holding her even tighter against his body. "I likes it when a gal fights a bit—makes it all the sweeter!"

He pulled her to one side of the corridor and attempted to force her to the deck. With both hands she reached in blind fear for his face, raking as hard as she could with her nails.

"Ow!" he cried out, and instinctively released her, his hands flying to his eyes. "I'll show you . . . !"

She realized the door leading up to the next deck was too far, so she ducked under his arms and plunged straight down the dark hall. She heard his heavy footsteps right at her heels, and he was cursing in a vile way as she reached the door of the sailroom, opened it, and fell inside with a gasp.

Brewster and Gilbert had heard the noise of the struggle, but had not dared open the door. Now the older man stood there and as Humility fell against him, he held her protectively as Daggot plunged into the room.

The huge sailor stopped abruptly, for he had not supposed anyone was on the cargo deck. "What's this!" he shouted. "Who are you?"

"I think you'd best be going," William Brewster said. The

frightened girl was weeping in his arms, and his face was stern as he said, "I think the captain would be most severe on you if he were to discover your treatment of this young woman!"

Daggot stared, his piggish eyes suddenly filled with apprehension. He knew what the old man had said was true. All the crew made fun of the pilgrims, but it went no further, for Captain Jones had made it clear that any of the crew actually molesting the passengers would be flogged.

But then Daggot had a thought. "Wait a minute," he growled. "I ain't never seen you—nor him either." He stared at Gilbert who had risen to a sitting position and was standing up, his face pale with the strain of standing on the wounded leg. "What you doin' here?"

"That's none of your business," Brewster said. "Just be on your way and we'll forget this."

Daggot shook his head, a frown on his face. "Stowaway, ain't you?" He caught the look that the older man and the younger man gave one another, and then he laughed hoarsely, "Well, I caught you fair, didn't I? Come on, up with you!"

Daggot grabbed Brewster by the arm, and the power of his grasp shot the frail body of the older man toward the door. Humility quickly took his arm, saying, "I'll report you to the captain, Daggot!"

"Haw! We'll see who gets reported," Daggot sneered. "Come on, now. You're all goin' to the Great Cabin!"

"Why, you can't take this man up those steep stairs!" Brewster protested. "He's got a severe wound."

"Ain't that a *shame!*" Daggot grinned. He shoved Brewster and Humility out of the compartment and grabbed Gilbert by the arm. "Now, you can walk topside, or I can drag you!"

Pain ran down Gilbert's leg, but he said steadily, "I'll walk."

It was one of the most difficult things he could remember, climbing the three flights, even with Brewster and Humility helping him. By the time they got to the Great Cabin, and Daggot rapped sharply on the door, his leg was aflame and a red mist had dropped before his eyes.

"What's this, Daggot?"

"Stowaways, Cap'n!" Daggot said. "I been seeing this gal

take food down to the cargo hold, so I sets me a trap, and these two is what I caught!''

"What's your name?" Jones demanded.

"William Brewster.''

The name meant something to Jones. He nodded and said, "Wait outside, Daggot.''

When the burly sailor was outside, Jones said at once, "You are a fugitive from the King's justice, Mr. Brewster.''

"Yes."

The simplicity of the reply caught Jones off guard, and he said angrily, "You think I will shelter you on my ship?"

"Will you put about, Captain Jones?"

Christopher Jones reddened and snapped, "You know I can't do that—but I can take you back with me—in irons! And you, sir, what is your name?"

"Gilbert Winslow.''

Captain Jones stared at the young man, shook his head and said in wonder, "It seems I have a pair of fugitives. You, too, are sought by the King.''

"I have no doubt.''

Jones stared at Gilbert, and there was a guarded admiration in the captain's eyes at the courage of the two men.

"Well, you are more likely to bleed to death than to hang, if I'm any judge.'' He looked at Humility and said, "Get that Fuller who passes for a doctor.''

As they waited for Fuller, Captain Jones seated himself in the chair behind his desk and stared at the two men. There was a vague air of wonder in his face, and with a hint of humor he said, "I've hauled many a cargo in this ship, but none that gave me so much trouble as you good Christian folk. Why do you suppose that is, Mr. Brewster?"

Brewster smiled at him, and said with a touch of wry humor in his thin voice, "Why, I suppose that people are always more trouble than *things*, Captain Jones. Souls are, after all, trouble-some things!''

"True, sir,'' Jones nodded and added under his breath, "and in the future I will haul a cargo that does not have such pesky souls!''

Brewster heard him, however, and said, "The real trouble,

Captain Jones, is that you have a soul of your own."

Jones stared at him, and said nothing to that, but there was a nervous air in the way he ran his fingers up and down the cord that looped his neck, and he did not speak again to the old man.

CHAPTER FIFTEEN

ON DECK

★ ★ ★ ★

Christopher Jones sat in the Great Cabin munching on an apple. He swallowed a tot of gin and ran his eyes over his log.

Log: September 12.
Yesterday two stowaways were discovered. One of them, Mr. William Brewster, has been a fugitive from the King's justice for some years as a result of certain writings. The other is a young man named Gilbert Winslow. Since there is no possibility of escape, I have not placed them under arrest, but on the return to England, I will do so and turn them over to the proper authorities.

A knock on his door interrupted his reading, and he closed the log, saying, "Come in."

Edward Winslow entered, nodded and said, "Good morning, Captain Jones."

"Yes, what is it?"

Ignoring Jones's gruff reception, Winslow said evenly, "I want to speak to you concerning my brother, Gilbert, and Mr. William Brewster."

"There's naught to be said!" Captain Jones snapped. He slapped his palm hard on the desk and there was an angry light in his gray eyes. "They are criminals and will be so treated!"

Winslow shook his head, saying mildly, "I realize you have been put in a difficult position, but as you get to know these two men, I'm sure you'll realize that they are not criminals in the strictest sense of that word. Mr. Brewster is a godly man of impeccable character with years of faithful service to his King and his country. His *crime* is a matter of a fine theological point." Winslow was a trained diplomat and used his full powers of persuasion as he spoke. "There was a great theological argument, I believe, among the Pharisees in the Lord's day, over how many angels could dance on the point of a needle."

"The charge against Brewster is not so frivolous as that—he is charged with sedition and plotting against the King of England!"

"Technically, that is true, but as you get to know Mr. Brewster—and my brother—you will see that they are both honorable men. Since you are an honorable man yourself, Captain Jones, I feel sure that you will find their true qualities."

"They will go back to England under arrest, Mr. Winslow." Captain Jones had been brought up in a hard school, and he was not about to gamble his ship or his reputation for the sake of two fanatics.

Winslow saw the folly of forcing the argument, so he merely smiled and said, "I hope you will see things differently before the voyage is over, Captain Jones."

He bowed, left the Great Cabin and proceeded along the deck to where Gilbert stood at the rail, staring glumly at the waves.

"Well, here you are!" Gilbert turned to face his brother, and grudgingly admitted that Edward's face was open, without a trace of the accusation he half expected to see there.

"Hello, Edward."

"Leg is doing *very* well, isn't it?"

"Yes. Much better."

"Good! Good! Expect this fresh air and exercise will work miracles for you, Gilbert. But we Winslows are a tough breed, eh?"

Gilbert smiled briefly, appreciating that Edward was doing his best to restore brotherly feelings. "By the time Captain Jones gets me back to England, I'll be in excellent health—just right for the hanging."

Edward stared at him, then laughed shortly. "Nonsense! You're not going to hang."

"No? I hadn't heard that King James had stopped executing those convicted of treason." Gilbert despised himself for unleashing on the one person who *did* have an affection for him, but the confinement had soured him, and he seemed to have no control over his tongue. He slapped the rail with his hands, then, saying sheepishly, "Your pardon, Edward. I'm not fit company for anyone."

Edward's face relaxed and he clamped his large hand on Gilbert's shoulder. As the two stood there, the family resemblance was very evident. Both were tall, and though Edward was heavier, there was a natural grace and athletic air about them both. The cornflower blue eyes were common to all the Winslow men, and the auburn hair of both glowed like burnished gold in the sun. Both had strong features, defiant cheekbones rising to broad foreheads, and both had the wedge-shaped face, and a slightly jutting jaw which suggested a deep and stubborn will.

Edward, the more intellectual of the two, was quick to reply, "No reason why you shouldn't be pretty tightly strung, I'd say. You must be out of your mind, being tied to that bunk so long."

"Well, it is getting pretty boring, Edward."

"Been catching up on your reading, I expect?"

"No. Nothing to read."

"What? Why, that's a *crime*, Gilbert! I have plenty of books. What'll you have?" He allowed a glint of humor to crease his broad lips, and suggested gently, "A good book of sermons?"

Gilbert laughed despite himself, "I'd read *tombstones*, Edward!"

"Well, some of the sermons I've heard aren't as interesting as a good stone," Edward laughed. "What would you say to a folio of Master Shakespeare's work, eh?"

"Now, that's business!" Gilbert smiled. "Thank you."

Edward turned to go and said, "I'll get it for you . . ." He paused, then said in a hesitating manner, unlike his usual forceful speech, "I say, Gilbert, don't—well, don't expect too much of us." He pulled at the lace on the front of his shirt, embarrassed, and added, "I mean to say, it may take a little *time* before people forget . . ."

Seeing Edward bog down, Gilbert gave a tight smile and finished the statement, ". . . forget that I sold Mr. Brewster for thirty pieces of silver?"

"Well . . ." Edward still could not find what to say, so he shrugged and murmured, "I know. It's hard, Gilbert. But you have to remember that all of us are flesh and blood. If you cut us, do we not bleed? But it's in your favor that when the time came, you put your life in jeopardy to save William and Humility. That will sink into people's minds after a time. Give them a chance, man!"

"Of course," Gilbert said; Edward gave him a good smile and left to get the book.

Gilbert found a place to sit down and spent the next hour reading a play about two "star-crossed lovers." The confusion that brought the youthful Romeo and Juliet to such a disastrous end caught at his mind, and from time to time he would lift his gaze to follow the drifting clouds. Once he murmured softly, "Mr. Shakespeare, you know the heart—at least the confusion of it!"

The *Mayflower* was a little world, sailing through the rolling, trackless water much as a single star cleaves through the ebony blackness of space. There was a difference, however: the star had fellows (invisible though they were to the eyes), while the ship was solitary.

Bobbing like a cork on the tossing waves, she was smaller than the leviathan that sometimes surfaced close enough for the passengers to see the waterspouts. But though dwarfed by the miles that lay beneath her keel, by the sky that unscrolled blankly over her mainmast, and by the mighty ocean stretching in every direction, she kept a life and order running through the ship— an image of the macrocosm of the planet.

Captain Christopher Jones was the archtype ruler: master, potentate, king, prince, emperor, congress, parliament, court. He ruled the little world with the power of an absolute despot, the Great Cabin no less the seat of authority than the Vatican or Buckingham Palace.

The ship was its own cathedral, chapel, monastery, nunnery; there were as many divergent views among the inhabitants of the bobbing little world as the babble of tongues in the larger one. From the dim, superstitious thought of Richard Salterne— common sailor, little better than a half-wit, who thought of God only as a sort of murky stew engulfing the earth—to the profound meditations of William Brewster, philosophies of God were as diverse on the little ship as were the staggering varieties of life that teemed beneath her keel.

Sam Fuller, sitting on the edge of the poop deck with his feet dangling, felt godlike as he watched the teeming quality of the deck. He was a man not given to idealism, and was constantly amazed to find himself on such a preposterous voyage. In truth, Fuller was an incurable romantic—and terribly ashamed of it! He covered the soft streak with a hard shell that fooled all but a few who knew him best.

Now as his eyes swept the deck, he saw half a dozen dramas unfolding, and his wise old eyes took them in—weighing, balancing, judging.

He saw Edward Winslow approach his brother Gilbert, and it was clear from his face that he was trying to cheer up the younger man. Then, after Edward left, young Tinker, who had been watching the pair from behind the mizzenmast, edged out, and Fuller saw the fear and grief in his pale face turn to joy as Winslow apparently made something right with the lad.

A smooth talker! Fuller thought grimly. *He put it over all of us— even me! But he won't do it again! Not likely!* There was a hard streak in the burly man's makeup, and he was especially sensitive since he took pride in his knowledge of men. He had taken to the young fellow as he had to few, and it had hit him hard when his faith had proved to be misplaced.

He saw William Mullins, his wife Alice, and his daughter Priscilla in a tight group over on the starboard side. And he saw husky John Alden leave his seat on the forecastle and amble along toward them, whistling, apparently quite aimless.

Fuller smiled, thinking: *Young Alden ain't so simple as he seems! Looky there how he was all surprised to see that pretty Miss Mullins sitting there—as if he didn't have the foggiest idea she was on the ship at all! Why, I've seen the young buck mooning over her since the day she come on board, and now, look at that! She's just as surprised to see him! And poor old William Mullins and Alice—why, they're so fuddled by this journey they ain't got the sight to see that pair being drawn to each other like magnets! Well, they'd better keep their eyes on that young woman! She ain't bad, but she ain't above usin' her eyes on a man, either!*

He grinned at the thought, a ribald streak running through his spirit.

Then he saw a group knotted beside the mainmast, and he frowned. The physician knew men, and the men who were engaging in a meeting were objects of scorn. Hopkins' pale blue eyes were darting constantly toward where Bradford and Carver sat in the bow, and it was obvious that Hopkins' companions—Martin and Billington—were speaking of them.

As eminent a set of ditch dogs as I've seen! Fuller thought. *They'll bring this ship to grief if they're not stomped on—and soon. I've warned Bradford, but he's so full of theology he can't see a mutiny when it's taking place under his nose. Winslow can, though!*

Sam Fuller shook his head wearily and pulled himself up to leave the poop deck.

He encountered Captain Jones who was scanning the horizon with a glass, and would have passed by, but the captain glanced at him and said, "Would you like to take a look, Mr. Fuller?"

Fuller shook his head. "Nothing to see, I know that."

"There's a school of dolphin—see?"

Fuller took the glass and watched the creatures come racing by the ship, plunging and diving in something of a marine minuet, and said grudgingly, "That's pretty, ain't it now?"

"Never get tired of watching the beasts of the sea," Jones said. He looked down at the thick knots of passengers on the waist deck and sighed. "It would be nice if people were as regular as dolphins. You always know what a dolphin's going to do, every time. Can't say as much for people, can you, Mr. Fuller?"

"No."

"On the other hand, maybe one way you can count on them."

Fuller saw that he was watching Humility Cooper washing some clothes in seawater, and the captain added, "You can count on there being trouble when a pretty woman is on ship—never fails!"

"She's a good girl!"

"Don't doubt it, but look at that," Jones pointed to where Daggot and some of his mates were lolling on the forecastle deck.

"Daggot is a fool. He's after that girl, and he'll keep it up until there's trouble."

"Keelhaul the swine!" Fuller snapped.

The captain shrugged, his gray eyes taking in the scene. "Can't keelhaul a man for what he's *going* to do—or for what wrong things he *wants* to do." He smiled suddenly at Fuller. "Guess we'd all be keelhauled if that happened, wouldn't we, Mr. Fuller?"

Sam Fuller felt weary. He looked out over the crowd below and said, "I thought we were going to the New World to work for God. Now it looks like we may never get there with a principle left intact."

"You've lost your faith?" Jones asked instantly. He was highly skeptical of the Separatists—indeed, of religion in general—and he would not have been displeased to find one of the pillars of the church beginning to crumble; it would confirm his belief that it was all humbug.

Fuller pulled himself up, looked at the people, then said, "No, Captain Jones, I've not lost faith—not in God."

He turned to leave, but said with a shrug of his heavy shoulders, "But I wish sometimes God would speak to me a little louder so I could get a better idea what He's up to!"

Jones watched the big man lumber below deck, and there was a strange smile on his lips as he looked down at his passengers, then up toward heaven. He said in a quiet voice, "Amen." Then he laughed at himself and went back to studying the dolphins.

CHAPTER SIXTEEN

CAPTAIN SHRIMP

★ ★ ★ ★

A driving wind scoured the deck as Captain Miles Standish looked with disgust at the ragged line made by the settlers along the waist deck, waiting impatiently for Mr. John Carver to finish his speech.

The snow-white hair of the man chosen as governor two days earlier blew over his face, and several times he had to pause to brush it away from his mouth. He was small and thin, but there was an erectness in his figure and a clear light in his brown eyes.

"We must be prepared to defend ourselves as soon as we land," he said in a clear, thin voice, "and we are very fortunate to have Captain Standish as our military advisor. He has served in the wars against the papists."

"Don't need no man to teach me how to fight!" John Billington rapped out sullenly. "Besides, I thought we was a Christian settlement!"

"David was a man of war, Mr. Billington," Carver said. "We will hope that we shall make a quick peace with the savages— but we must know the use of our weapons. And you must remember that we will have need of skill with weapons to bring down game for food."

Gilbert had joined the group at the urging of Edward, though he had no hope that would gain the good graces of the settlers by such an action. But his leg was improved, and he was bored with reading and staring at the empty horizon, so he agreed.

Now looking at the old, rusty matchlocks leaning against the rail, he thought with a quick grin: *I think I'd rather be in front of one of those relics than doing the firing!*

He did like the looks of Standish, though. The captain was a small, sinewy man with bright red hair and a florid complexion, wearing seasoned leather breeches and a leather-lined jacket belted and buckled. A burnished steel helmet sat on his head, decorated with a crimson band. *He looks like what he is*, Gilbert thought, *a seasoned veteran*.

Standish waited until Carver had finished, then picked up one of the matchlocks. Holding it up, he said, "You will learn to use this weapon. This is a matchlock, the most simple made. It is touched off with a wick or a match cord. There are no wheels, flints, or steel to misfire. Treat it well, and it will not fail you—unlike human beings."

"Ho, now, hear how the soldier boy talks!"

Gilbert looked up to see half a dozen of the crew gathered on the forecastle deck, grinning down at the little group. Daggot was in the center, flanked by his mates Salterne and Bart O'Neal—a stubby Dubliner with a fierce black beard and one eye milky. The pilot, Coffin, was there, standing to one side with a sardonic look in his muddy eyes.

Standish ignored the crew, and proceeded to give a stiff lecture in a crisp voice. "The first rule is to carry your length of wick in your left hand, your gun under your right arm, or on your right shoulder. You will never touch your weapon off by accident if you do this." He gave detailed instructions on how to take care of the weapon, washing out the barrel with boiling water, keeping the powder dry in rainy weather, how to form lead into shot with a ball mold, how to measure a charge. He illustrated the use of a ram, with dire warnings on the danger of putting home second and third measures of powder on previous, unexploded charges and the risk to life and limb occasioned by carrying gunpowder carelessly near the fire.

Finally, he sent John Howland below to light the slow match, and when he returned with end aglow, Standish poured a charge of powder down the muzzle of a gun, slid in the ramrod and patted it gently home and dropped in a ball. He shook a few grains of black powder over the touchhole, put some more in the flashpan by its side, and slid the flashpan cover while he screwed the glowing end of the slow match into the movable arm, which would jerk it down and dab the spark in the primed pan.

"Get below deck, mates!" Salterne shouted. "The soldier boy is likely to blow us all to kingdom come!" He was a slow-witted young man of twenty with the vilest vocabulary on board, and he loosed a few choice specimens of lower-deck language as Standish stared up at him.

Standish turned his back to the wind, holding the gun above his right hip and pointing upward, to port. Deftly he cupped his powder-blackened hand around the flashpan, protecting the powder from the wind as he slid back the cover; and all in one movement changed his position, gripped the gun with both hands and squeezed the trigger. The serpentine and wick jabbed down, a little puffing explosion of muffled fire and black smoke hissed up out of the flashpan, followed by a red belch of flame and sooty smoke from the muzzle. The heavy weapon buckled back under his arm alarmingly. A cloud of soot and sulphur fumes drifted across the deck and some of the group applauded the feat.

"Gor! 'E done me in!" Salterne shouted and fell back, clasping his heart as one with a deadly wound. His mates rocked with laughter, and Standish looked up to see Captain Jones standing on the poop deck, arms folded and wearing an amused smile on his lips.

"Captain Jones," Standish called. "Can you not find work for these men?"

"They are on their own time, Captain Standish."

"They are disturbing the drill!"

"The ship is small. Where would you have them go? Besides, you would not begrudge them a little amusement, surely."

Standish stared at Jones, his face dusky with anger. But he understood military law, and the captain of the *Mayflower* was the iron law of discipline.

Ducking his head, he bit his lip and said, "Very well. Now, who will be first to practice?"

Billington stepped forward, his eyes ugly. He towered over the small, neat form of Captain Standish, and there was a bullying light in his closely spaced eyes. "You got no right to rule over us, Captain Shrimp!" He used the term some of Standish's enemies used to deride the small man, but it brought instant retribution to Billington.

Quick as flash, Standish reached out, and grabbing the larger man by the arm, he whirled him about as if he weighed nothing. Avoiding with ease a ponderous blow that Billington made toward his head, the little captain with a smile on his face gave a hard shove with his hands and at the same time drove his boot upward in a hard kick that caught Billington in the haunches. The force of those twin blows shot the bulky form of the settler toward the longboat, and he crashed into it with his arms cartwheeling helplessly. His big belly took the force of the collision, and there was an audible *whoosh* as the air was driven from his lungs. He flopped over, sliding to the deck, and he looked like a huge sick frog as he sat there with his wide mouth open trying to draw air into his lungs.

There was a dead silence on the deck as Captain Standish ambled across the deck, with one motion grabbing Billington by the collar and jerking him to his feet. "Now, sir, *you* load that gun!"

Gagging and gasping, Billington stood there, and then Governor Carver said gently, "I believe you received a command from our captain, John."

That settled the question of the captain's authority, and one by one they took their turns, loading and firing the weapons.

Most of them had no experience at such things, but when Gilbert loaded the gun with practiced ease and got his shot off in a remarkably quick time, Standish glowed with pleasure. "Well now, Mr. Winslow, you've done that before!"

"I've had some experience," Gilbert said diffidently.

"Good! We can use some of that! And is it possible that you've handled a sword as well?"

"A bit of that, also."

"Splendid! Perhaps you might be willing to help the others with that part of the training?"

Gilbert shrugged, but said, "Well, *I* would be willing, Captain. As to whether the others would accept . . .?"

"I'll plant my foot in their backsides if I hear one word!"
The words were rough, but there was a kindly twinkle in the
little man's eye, and he clapped a friendly hand on Gilbert's
shoulder. He lowered his voice, saying, "I've heard all the gossip
about you, Winslow—but it's my way to judge a man on what I
see—not on scandalmongers!"

Gilbert warmed to the man, admiring his bluff honesty, and
for the next three days he spent much time in his company.
Standish's wife Rose was a tiny, silent woman who seemed
oddly mismatched with her firecracker of a husband. They had
no children, and Rose Standish spent much of her time caring
for the children of the settlers.

"She loves the little ones," Standish said to Gilbert while
they were sitting on deck late one afternoon. "Lost three of them,
and none has come since." He shook his head sadly. "Nothing
a man can do to help a woman in that way."

Humility Cooper, Priscilla Mullins, and Bess Tilley were sitting by the mizzenmast, laughing and talking, a pretty sight to
the captain, who had been quite a dandy in his younger days.
He caught a glimpse of Gilbert looking at the women, and asked
softly, "Now any one of those three would be a fine wife for a
young fellow, would you agree?"

"I suppose so, Miles," Gilbert said. He moved his shoulders
nervously and added, "I don't think about such things."

"And why not?" the fiery little man demanded. "I'd like to
hear your story, Gilbert—if you'd care to tell a stranger."

"You really would?"

"I would, lad. I've taken to you."

Gilbert had kept his own counsel, but Miles Standish, for
all his toughness, had a good heart, and for the next hour Gilbert
spoke steadily, reliving the history of the past few months.

He faltered at first, but Standish simply waited, and then it
began to flow. They were alone on their corner of the deck, and
as the wind luffed the square sails, slapping them with powerful
gusts that drove the little ship along swiftly, he lost himself in
the story. He made no attempt to defend his actions; indeed,
there was such bitter self-accusation in his words that more than
once Standish stared at Gilbert and gave a silent shake of his
head.

Finally he ended, almost out of breath with the effort. "And here I am, a fugitive with a guilty past—and no future to speak of."

Standish did not speak at once. He dug into his pocket, found an old pipe, then a black tobacco pouch, slick with age. Filling the bowl, he rose and walked over to where some of the matches were still glowing from the day's practice, lit the pipe, then returned to sit beside Winslow.

Finally, he said, "Boy, you can't scare me with your tales of a misspent youth. When I was your age I was studying for the gallows." He smiled at some fleeting memory, and there was a furry soft quality to his voice as he said, "I'm not a man for preaching, but one bit of scripture I think is straight . . . how does it go? Oh, yes: 'Though a just man should fall seven times, the Lord will lift him up again.' Now *that's* good sound walking around theology!"

Gilbert stared at him, seeking to understand what the soldier was saying. "Are you telling me that it doesn't count—what I did?"

"Not that!" Standish protested. "I guess what we do stays with us—in some ways. But I'm one of the roughs, lad. Maybe I've had to be. And I don't rightly know as I understand much about the God these preachers keep talking about. I read the Bible, right enough, but only about the Man."

"The Man? You mean Jesus Christ."

"That's it. Oh, I know what they say, that He's God. And so He is, but what strikes me is that when the good Lord on earth gave himself a title, it was 'The Son of Man'! Now, that's what I'm putting my hope in—the Son of Man!"

"I—I guess I'm too dense to understand, Miles."

"Not you, Gilbert," Standish smiled. "You're maybe *too* smart! Get yourself all tangled up with all kinds of high thinking about God! What I say is, Jesus Christ came here to be a *man*! And that meant He found out what it was like to be in the middle of this life! Don't you know He got dirty, got tired? People let Him down, didn't they? He bled and died, just like I've seen many a fellow do!"

Gilbert nodded slowly. "That's all true, Miles, but . . ."

"Well, that's my religion, lad! Jesus Christ was a man who

knows what this world's really like. So when I fall, which is pretty often, I just say something like, *Lord, you were a man, so you know all about this!*''

Seeing that Standish was finished, Gilbert shook his head, saying stubbornly, "That's too *easy*, Miles. There's got to be more to it than that!"

"See? I said you were too smart! But I've been there where the last drop of blood was dripping out, lad, and men who are dying get *simple*—they just come down to one thing. Have they served God or not?"

The words of Standish caught at Gilbert. He had heard of repentance many times, but as he stood there, he experienced a stab of remorse at his past sins in a way that was almost a physical pain. He yearned suddenly for a new heart—a cleanliness of spirit. And he felt with all his being that this was to be found only in Jesus Christ! But *how*? He shook the thought off regretfully.

Then Standish laughed and slapped Gilbert on the shoulder. "Bless me, lad! We got a ship packed with preachers, and here's a reprobate of a soldier preaching to you! A plague on't it now!" He saw that Winslow was biting his lip with a worried scowl on his smooth brow, and added, "You'll be all right, Gilbert. I know men, and you and that brother of yours are two I'd stand for!"

They sat there talking, unconscious of the glances that touched on them from the three young women on the deck.

"I wonder how Captain Standish ever came to marry such a pale little creature?" Bess Tilley mused. "He's so full of fire and she's so drained and pale."

"Maybe she was pretty when she was young," Priscilla shrugged. "I think being the wife of a soldier would be very hard. Always traveling to strange places."

"No," Bess shook her head vigorously. "She's never been pretty, you can tell." She was a girl of strong opinions and often got into trouble for voicing them. "Lots of good-looking men marry women that are homely. Look at Edward Winslow. Why, he's so handsome it's a sin—and there he is married to poor Elizabeth!"

Priscilla pulled at a strand of her honey-colored hair and argued in a dulcet voice, "I don't think looks are very important,

Bess. It's what's in a person's heart that counts."

"Oh, you little tease!" Bess laughed. She looked at the shining hair, the startling violet eyes, and the flawless complexion of Priscilla, saying, "That's what the preachers say, but I notice you won't have anything to do with that ugly little man Richard Warren. He follows you around like a lap dog, and you don't even know he's alive! You're too busy keeping your eyes on that *beautiful* figure of Mr. John Alden!"

"Why—" Priscilla's mouth opened and her cheeks flushed scarlet. "You mustn't *say* things like that, Bess!"

"Why not? Everybody on board knows you're moonstruck with him!"

"Bess, don't tease her," Humility said quickly. She patted Priscilla's hand and smiled at her, adding, "Don't mind Bess."

"Why, you're just as bad, Humility," Bess began and then thoughtlessly prated on. "Didn't you fall head over heels in love with that Gilbert Winslow?" Instantly Bess clapped her hand over her mouth and her eyes flew open wide.

Humility did not say a word, but her face went pale, and then she got to her feet quickly and said, "I promised to take care of Resolved for Susanna."

The two girls watched her go, and as soon as she was out of hearing, Priscilla said in exasperation, "There, you see what you did, Bess! I declare you ought to have your tongue cut out!"

"How can I be so stupid?" Bess mourned. "She never liked any man before."

"No, she didn't, did she?"

"And she's the kind who sticks to things! If she were flighty like some, it wouldn't be so bad, but I'm afraid she's the kind you see sometimes who never get over a first love."

"It's too bad! He's such a handsome man, and his brother Edward is so nice." Priscilla rose and said, "You're right about the way I feel about John, Bess." She laughed and added, "I just get goose bumps looking at him!"

Bess rose with a laugh. "Isn't it *awful*? I do the same thing with my John! But I'd never let him know it!"

They left the deck, giggling and talking. After they disappeared, the sound of coarse laughter rose from the poop deck. Salterne, Daggot, and O'Neal had been lying down flat, invisible to the young women, and they had kept silent, eavesdropping.

"Now we know why you ain't never been able to get a hand on that Humility Cooper, Jeff," O'Neal crowed. "She's pinin' away for her true love—that Winslow fellow!"

Daggot's gap-toothed smile was savage, but he laughed and said, "This voyage ain't over yet, mates. I'll have her eatin' out of me hand before we drop anchor!"

"You'll get yourself a flogging, Jeff. You know how the captain is."

"Oh, I knows that, right enough," Daggot said with a wave of his meaty hand. "But all I got to do is show that little gal how much more of a man I am than that stick of a Winslow!"

"Aw, you're just sounding off, Jeff!" Salterne said. "You ain't got the guts to do nothin'!" Salterne looked thin and pale, and he loosed his customary string of blasphemy adding, "I feel like a dying buzzard. You reckon I ought to see that sawbones?"

"Drink a quart of gin, Salterne!" Coffin's voice grated behind them. Then he warned Daggot, "Do what you want to that Winslow—but be slick, Jeff!"

"Oh, I got me a plan, Coffin. You know how Winslow's teachin' them to use swords every day?"

"Yes. What then?"

"Why, I'm gonna wait until he's doing that—and until Miss Humility Cooper is watchin'—and then I'm gonna give him a lesson of my own!"

Coffin said, "You'll hang if you kill him, Jeff."

"Who said anything about killing him?" Daggot spread his hands expressively. "But if I'm letting him *teach* me, why, you know how it goes, Coffin—a man can get pinked through the shoulder—or maybe even in a bad leg, eh?"

"Now that's an evil thing!" Coffin said, but there was a cruel smile on his lips. "And besides, you don't know but what he's a better blade than you."

"No fear, Coffin! I been watchin 'im, and I can touch him anytime."

Coffin liked the idea. Winslow was not unlike the man he'd killed in a duel, and there was a perverse hatred in the pilot for all aristocrats.

"Do it then, Jeff!"

CHAPTER SEVENTEEN

THE STORM

★ ★ ★ ★

The storm that struck on the morning of September 17 was like nothing Captain Jones had ever seen. Coming out on deck, he stopped dead still, so suddenly that Sam Fuller rammed into him. "Look at that!" he breathed in a small whisper.

"What is it?" Brewster asked.

"Storm coming—faster than I've ever seen!"

A black cloud dropped down, making a shelf across the horizon and moving so fast across the choppy waters they could trace its progress.

"All hands!" Jones shouted. "Man the sails! Batten down! Batten down!" As the crew came tumbling out of the ship, Jones said, "Get to the passengers, Brewster! This is going to be pretty bad!"

In a matter of minutes the main top sail ripped up one side and blew out in ribbons, cracking like gigantic whips.

The ship began beating back and forth before the terrible force of the headwind, like an animal running up and down. The light of day failed as the blackness of the cloud wrapped a sable blanket around the plunging ship, and the last flag of daylight, a thin streak of silver-white, was blotted out by the rolling cloud. The dull roaring rose at times to a high-pitched scream, drowning out the creaking of the timbers and the fluttering of the tattered sails.

The seamen fought their way along the tilting decks, grabbing desperately to rails, masts, lines as they tried to control the ship.

"Take in sail! In with your top sails. Lower your main sails, lower the foresail . . ." Jones shouted.

Stripped of all canvas, the *Mayflower* was thrown about like a ball. "Get a few feet of canvas up on the poop or she'll founder!" the captain shouted, and Coffin was nearly washed overboard as the crew rigged a small sail.

The masts swayed crazily against the dark sky, and the bow lifted over mountainous swells, a terrific shudder shaking her as she plowed into the head of the mountain of water. She was flooded below as wave after wave broke over her.

Below deck there was bedlam. Water ran everywhere—through the hatch covers, under the two doors opening out onto the waist deck, and through many loosened seams in the main decking, trickling and seeping down from deck to deck till it reached the bilge in the bottom of the ship.

William Brewster peered through the darkness cut only by the occasional glow of a single candle through panes of an opaque lantern, thinking with the others that each roll of the ship might be the last.

Many of the women were crying as well as the children, but suddenly William Bradford's voice rang out over the screaming wind, "Lord, do not grind our people and let them be lost! Deliver us, as you delivered Jonah and Daniel!"

Then he raised his voice in a psalm, and there, in the depths, the voices of others joined in:

> Jehovah feedeth me, I shall not lack
> In grassy folds he down doth make me lie
> He gently leads me quiet waters by
> He doth return my soul, for his name sake
> In paths of justice leads me quietly.

But still the wind thundered and the ocean smashed at the ship; then as their quaking voices began the next verse, with a crash like a cannon shot, a main beam amidship cracked and buckled!

Dorothy Bradford raised a face pale as death, and cried out, "Oh, God! The ship is breaking up!"

Pandemonium broke, both from men and weather. The captain and mates rushed below to gaze up from the gun deck at the sagging beam, the splintered deck around it. Water gushed from the new openings, and the terrified passengers huddled against the ship's sides to escape it. Half a dozen of them put their shoulders to the job while the freezing water poured down on them. It was like trying to raise the roof beam of a house. The massive piece of timber only sagged a little more. A spare beam was dragged up from the hold, and the men tried using that as a ram. No success.

For two hours they fought the waves, and the carpenter exhausted his resources trying to pull the ruptured beam into place.

"We'll have to go back to England, Captain!" Mr. Clark insisted. "There's no hope of a repair where we're headed!"

"We've come too far," Jones said grimly. "She'll never make it—to the New World or the old."

A great cry went up from many of the passengers to turn back, while forward in the hold, out of the way, Bradford, Carver, Brewster, and Edward Winslow held a conference.

"We must not turn back," William Bradford said quietly. He was the type of man who performed better under pressure, and now there was a rocklike set to his craggy features.

"I agree," answered Brewster. "It will be the end of our dream. Ruin for all of us!"

Gilbert had not been invited to the meeting, of course; it was mere chance that he happened to be in the hold close to where the men met. He sat on a box, and his eyes met those of his brother. Edward said, "It's beyond the power of man, brethren. We must seek God!"

Gilbert's lips turned up sardonically, and he did not bow his head as the three men began to pray for deliverance. He got up and left, hearing William Brewster pray fervently, "Oh, God, give wisdom to deliver this ship!"

Shaking his head, Gilbert thought, *Too late for that. We'll never make it back to land.* He made his way to the spot where the carpenter, together with John Howland and John Alden, was trying to lift the beam with a long board for a lever. Putting his hands on the lever, he threw his weight on it, and the sudden strain snapped the piece.

Howland and Alden sprawled out as the deck collapsed, then got to their feet. The carpenter said, "I didn't think it would work—that beam must weigh two tons!"

"Where are the others?" Alden panted, his huge chest rising and falling with the effort.

"Up there . . ." Gilbert nodded, then added, "praying for a miracle."

"You don't believe in miracles, Winslow?"

Gilbert whirled to see the captain, his face a mask, standing behind him.

"No."

"Well—neither do I," Jones said, biting his full lower lip. "But that's about what it's going to take to get that beam in place!"

They stood there racking their brains, trying to find a way to lift the beam. In a few minutes William Bradford and Brewster came in followed by Carver and Winslow.

"We have had an answer from the Lord, Captain."

Jones started, and almost looked overhead for the Deity, but quickly covered this with a sardonic smile. "Well, it's good to have men on the ship with a direct line to God. What is the answer?"

"It came to Brother Brewster and Brother Carver almost simultaneously," Bradford smiled. "A word of prophecy based on Acts, chapter 27 and verse 24: "Fear not, God hath given thee all them that sail with thee.'"

"Yes, and then the 25th verse says, 'I believe God that it shall be even as it was told me,' " Brewster nodded.

Captain Christopher Jones stared at the wreck of the beam, settling slowly, knowing that it would sooner or later snap, and that when it did the *Mayflower* would break in two. He heard the cries of the women and children, and the shouts of the seamen on deck trying to keep the ship aright. The look he gave to Brewster was filled with unbelief, and he grated out in a harsh voice, "You are like all prophets that I've met—filled with pompous words that have nothing to do with living in this world!"

At that moment the ship spun her head out of the wind and lay broadside to the crested swells, instantly battered by a gargantuan wave that tore its huge weight over the deck, snapping cleats and ropes and heeling the ship so far onto her beam-ends that her spars almost entered the water and the men in her hung on a vertical wall.

Tons of water muffled the screams and cries of the women and children, and Gilbert was flung so hard against the bulkhead his head rang and pain shot through his bad leg.

Pulling himself upright, he waited for the ship to right itself. There was a long moment when he was sure that the slow roll would continue, but the *Mayflower* came upright. He shook his head and left the first hold to go to the sail locker.

He passed through the cargo hold, went to the sail cabin, pulled on a heavy coat that was drenched already, then left. As he passed through the cargo hold, there was a tremendous groaning as the timbers creaked, and only a feeble light from the swinging lantern gave any illumination.

His eyes running over the barrels and equipment, he wondered how long it would be before they slipped loose and went crashing through the planking.

Back in the first hold, he found the captain urging the carpenter to come up with a solution, and it was clear to Gilbert that Jones was a desperate man.

He joined the others as they tried to wedge a piece of heavy timber under the ruptured spar, but it was evident there was no hope.

Then something happened in Gilbert's mind. He could never explain it afterward, but it was as close to a vision as he ever came in all his days. Suddenly he saw an object—as clearly as he had ever seen anything in his life with physical eyes.

Then—the sound of the breaking sea rolled back into his head, and he looked up, startled to find himself still pushing at the futile timber.

"Wait!" he shouted, and the strident tone of his voice brought the crew to a halt.

"What is it?" Edward asked at once. "Are you all right, Gilbert?"

"I know how we can brace that timber, we can . . . !"

"Mind your business!" Coffin rasped acidly. "This is ship's matter."

"What's your idea, Winslow?" Captain Jones asked quickly.

He stared at Gilbert with a faint glow of hope in his eyes. Not much, perhaps, but he realized more than anyone there, unless that timber was braced immediately, they were doomed.

Gilbert said quickly, "Alden, you remember you were showing me the equipment in the cargo hold?"

"Yes, but . . . ?"

"I wasn't very interested, but now I remember one thing—that big iron jack!"

"That's it!" Alden shouted. He struck himself in the forehead with his palm and started for the ladder at a run.

"What are you talking about?" Jones demanded.

"It's some kind of device used for jacking up boats for repairing the hulls—that's what Alden told me. It's big enough to do this job, Captain."

An optimistic hubbub of talk ran through the hold, and when John Alden came back bearing the heavy black jack in his powerful arms, Jones shouted, "That's the thing! Get it under this beam!—Where's that timber, Mr. Clark? All hands bear on here!"

"Put this timber crossways, to rest it on," Alden said. "Otherwise it'll shove right through the decking."

They laid a heavy timber down, put the jack on it, then balanced another timber on its flat lip. "Get a short piece to put under this thing!" Jones urged, and when that was done, he commanded, "Raise the jack, Coffin!"

A cheer went up as the upright jack pressed against the beam and slowly pushed it up until it was even.

"That'll hold until calm weather," the carpenter said. "Then we'll spike a splint across that break and repeg it to the upper deck."

Suddenly William Brewster's voice cut through the hold like a trumpet—feeble, perhaps, but reaching every ear: "The Word of the Lord has come to pass! He has sent deliverance!"

Christopher Jones was flooded with relief. The *Mayflower* was his livelihood, his love, his security. Five minutes ago, he would not have given a farthing for the chances of saving her; now it was a matter of riding out the storm.

He raised a hand that was not entirely steady to wipe the water from his face, then he turned to face Brewster who was standing knee-deep in water with his hands raised to heaven and a light of joy on his thin face.

"I think Mr. Winslow really deserves some credit," he said softly. "It was quick thinking, man, and I'm in your debt!"

Gilbert stood there, staring at the jack, saying nothing, and then he felt a hand on his shoulder and looked up to see William Bradford standing beside him.

"Mr. Winslow, we are all in your debt."

Gilbert was caught off guard. Bradford had said not one good word to him since he had come aboard, and yet the honesty of the man was not to be doubted. He looked at the angular planes of Bradford's face, and asked impulsively, "Surely you can't think the Lord would use a sinner to do his work—with so many saints around?"

William Bradford was a strong man, but he bowed his head at that question, and there was a look of pain in his dark eyes as he looked around at the people in the hold—saints and sinners.

"I am not as certain as I once was in some things. When I was younger, I felt that it was a simple matter to identify God's children. Lately, I have wondered if I was not often hasty in my youthful judgments."

Gilbert stared at him, then said in a hard tone, "Well, there's no doubt in *my* mind about this business. I saw the jack, and when we needed it, I remembered it. Nothing of God in it!"

He sounded like a man trying to convince himself, but Edward put a hand up and said quietly, "There's some of God in everything, Gilbert—as you'll know before He's finished with you!"

Gilbert made a brief entry in his journal:

September 17

I am not sure of anything. I suppose a man has two sides and there never will be a world which will please both sides. One side of him is going to be hot and the other side cold. Maybe this earth is for right-handed folks—maybe for left. In the world of right-handed people, the left-handed ones will cry in it!

Which is my world? England seems as alien as Venus. Would I go there, get rich, marry Cecily? Why do I still look in Humility's eyes and think of New Testament verses?

I guess there is God and the devil in me—maybe in everyone.

What happened today in the hold? They prayed and I thought of a jack. Did the God who flung those millions of stars in space give a hang for this fragment of a ship on an insignificant journey to savage land? Brewster says God stepped in. He claims that I was given the answer, and that may be true—but I can't believe it! Whatever God is up there has forgotten about us long ago. But how comforting it would be to believe in Brewster's God!

CHAPTER EIGHTEEN

ANOTHER KIND OF STORM

★ ★ ★ ★

The sun breaking through the next day brought calm weather, but there was a taste of snow in the air. For the next three days Miles Standish drove the men hard at musket practice. His sharp voice harrying the settlers rang out for long hours, and more than once, one of the elders found it necessary to reprove him for his language.

"Aye, Reverend Bradford, it's not best for a man to use foul language, but do ye realize we'll be moving through enemy territory in a few days? Our lives will depend on these butter-fingered yokels! Why, sir, the whole colony could go down if these men don't do better!"

"I'll pray about it, Captain," Bradford said; his giving way marked how determined he was to plant a colony for God. He spent night and day going about the ship, encouraging the weak, nursing the sick, and for long hours he retreated to the lower deck to pray.

Standish gave Gilbert, who was standing by, a sly wink, saying, "Right! You do the praying and I'll do the drilling!"

The first day of sword drill, Gilbert had been challenged by Standish, who said, "Let me see what stuff you have, Winslow!" There had been astonishment in his eyes, however, when Gilbert toyed with him, balancing on his good leg. Time and again Standish had tried to drive through for a touch, but Gilbert had smiled and with the tip of his blade sent that of Standish wide. It was obvious that the younger man could have won at any time, and finally Standish stood there puffing with effort. It was a tense moment, for the little man fancied himself a fighter and did not like to lose.

Then he had smiled and said, "I'm not much on religion, Winslow, but if I get around to prayers any time soon, I'll give a thanksgiving for you! I've never seen a better blade—where'd you pick up the skill?"

Gilbert had not gone into details, and no one had seen the encounter, so Standish had not been shamed before the crew.

Most of the men were on deck for the drill, as were many of the women and children. There was no danger from flying lead, and quite a bit of rivalry had sprung up. The saints, Gilbert had learned at Leyden, loved simple games; and the fencing and drill, pitting man against man, took their fancy, breaking the dull monotony of the long days.

As Gilbert gave a few instructions and stood back to watch the participants, he glanced around the deck, noting that the voyage had not dissolved the factions and sects on the *Mayflower*.

The saints were crowded together in a group over on the starboard rail—the Allertons, Carvers, Tilleys, Tinkers, Whites.

The strangers, perhaps not by chance, took station on the port deck—the Billingtons (the largest family on board), Chilton, Eaton, Hopkins, and Mullins families.

Ranging around the poop deck many of the ship's crew lounged, taking in the sight with half-whispered jokes from Daggot and O'Neal. Captain Jones and First Officer Clark leaned against the mizzenmast.

Jones had requested that those members of the crew who wished might be instructed, and Smith had agreed. It was obvious that of the crew only Daggot had any skill, though there was a light in Coffin's eyes that warned Gilbert that he was no beginner.

Daggot had clowned through the basic instructions, entertaining his mates and some of the passengers with his remarks. He had attempted several times to engage Gilbert in a debate, but had been disappointed.

"He's not bad, Winslow," Standish had said, watching care-

fully as Daggot ran through the preliminaries with careless skill.
"And he's not in love with you, I see."

"No."

"He'll try to show you up. Don't let him have a chance."

Although there was no doubt in Gilbert's mind about his
ability to meet any challenge from the seaman, he knew only
mischief could come of a direct conflict with the man.

As he called the men off from practice, he saw a glint in
Daggot's eyes, and followed his glance. He saw Humility watching from the rail, and the sudden swagger in Daggot's walk
warned Gilbert that he was going to have trouble from the man.

"All right, heed this now," he said clearly. "You've not got
to face skilled fencers or trained swordsmen . . ."

"Which is a good thing, ain't it now?" Daggot said loudly,
with a wink at O'Neal. " 'Cause if any of these babies ever did
face a *real* man, they'd run 'ome to their nannies!"

Gilbert ignored the laugh from the crew, and continued with
his lesson.

"But the principles are much the same. If you have a sword
in your hand in a fight, your man will come at you with *something*—a rock, a spear, a stick. And you need to be so familiar
with your blade that you don't even have to think about it . . ."

"Ain't no need to warn these babies not to think!" Daggot
called out, casting a contemptuous look at the passengers.

". . . your blade must become like a member of your
body . . ."

Daggot laughed and made a rude remark, and a ribald laugh
went up from the crew, even from some of the strangers.

"Must we put up with this?"

Gilbert looked around to see that Peter Brown, his best
pupil, was glaring at him. Brown had had some training in the
use of the sword, and in the man-on-man exercises had easily
won. He gave one quick glance over his shoulder to where Humility was standing, and then looked back to Gilbert. "Mr. Winslow, I think we might do without the crew for the exercise."

"Why, you ain't very polite!" Daggot spoke up, again winking at O'Neal. He took an aggressive step forward, adding, "But
I guess you preachers ain't used to bein' around *real* men."

Gilbert saw the thing getting out of hand. He shot a quick

glance toward Captain Jones, who merely shrugged his shoulders. The affair amused him, and he whispered something to Clark that made the First Officer nod and smile.

Miles Standish, his face red with anger, stomped up to Daggot and stared up into the large seaman's face. "You want a little action, Daggot? Come on, then!"

Daggot shook his head as the fiery little soldier whipped out his blade. He raised his hands in a gesture of innocence, protesting, "Why, Captain, you're a professional soldier! You wouldn't take advantage of a poor ignorant sailor boy, would you now?" There was an arrogance in his tone, but the words were nothing that Standish could challenge.

"Well, *I'm* not a paid soldier!" Peter Brown cried. He whipped out his sword, and lifted it in the air. "Let me have a bout with the fellow, Winslow—if you won't do it yourself!"

He's calling me a coward, Gilbert thought. *But I'm no boy to rise to a foolish dare. I know more about my courage than he does.*

He was about to dismiss the men when Daggot suddenly whipped out his blade and said, "Why, then, sonny, let's just find out who's the real man!"

A circle was formed when the others drew back, and as the two men touched blades, Gilbert had an evil thought. *Daggot hates me and will sooner or later try to kill me. Brown is in love with Humility and will do what he can to show me up for a coward as well as a traitor. No matter which one of them wins, or even gets pinked with a blade, why, it's no problem of mine!*

He shook his head at the wicked thought and stepped forward to prevent the match, but was stopped by Standish's iron grip. "Let 'em have at it, Gilbert!" he said. "They can't hurt each other much with those blunted tips—and it wouldn't matter much if they *did*! These lads need to see a little blood to get 'em ready for what's to come!"

Gilbert shrugged and watched as the two men circled each other. The space was small and there was a vivid contrast in the antagonists. Daggot was broad as a door, bulging with muscle, while Brown was tall and lean as a sapling.

The blades rang again and again as the two met, engaged, then stepped back. Ordinarily Gilbert would have picked Brown to win easily. He had the reach and some formal training, but they did not serve him well.

Daggot's bulk did not allow him to cover ground as fast as his smaller opponent, but his reflexes were amazing, Gilbert saw at once. His blade ran in and out like the tongue of a serpent, and he had been well taught in the art of defense, probably by Coffin, Gilbert decided.

The contest soon became uneven, as Brown weakened, no doubt, from the bad food and inactivity of the voyage. He began to breathe with a rasp, and his arm began to droop with fatigue.

Gilbert moved quickly forward, seeing the young man about to be humiliated, but Daggot saw him coming and with a lightning parry drove home a stroke straight at Brown's face—a violation of the rules.

The blunted tip of the blade caught the young man in the mouth, splitting his lower lip and breaking off a tooth.

"Enough!" Gilbert cried, springing forward furiously. "You swine! I ought to run you through!"

Daggot stared at him, malice in his hot eyes. He said softly, "Why don't you, Winslow?" He waited, then when Gilbert hesitated, he raised his voice loud enough to carry to the poop deck, "Come on! Are you a man or not?"

There was a silence then, broken only by the rasping wheeze of Brown's breath, filled with pain as he held a handkerchief to his broken mouth.

Gilbert had come upon a stag once, worn down by the chase and surrounded by a pack of red-eyed wolves, their eyes cruel as death. Something of that was in the faces of the onlookers—some of them, at least. The quick look showed him that most of the crew of the *Mayflower* wore that cruel lupine expression, wanting only to see a good fight. Billington, among the strangers, looked much the same, even crying out, "Go on, Winslow, give the scoundrel a foot of steel in his belly!"

Brewster and Bradford, standing together, seemed struck dumb by the violence that had exploded in their faces, but Edward's face was red with fury, and he nodded at Gilbert, saying, "Have at him, boy!" in a voice shaking with anger.

The one face that seemed to leap out at him was Humility's. Her green eyes were enormous in her wide face, and her lips were stretched tightly against her teeth. She was not a girl to let her emotions show, Gilbert knew, but now she was holding back her feelings so strongly that the knuckles pressed against her wide mouth were white with strain.

Gilbert felt the pressure on his back, and suddenly he was tempted to cut the man down. It would not be difficult, he knew, for while Daggot was a good journeyman with the sword, he was not in Gilbert's class.

But he waited, and as he did, a mutter went across the crowd, and he heard the word *coward* several times.

It raked across his nerves, and he looked around the deck, hating the look in the eyes of most of the spectators.

I won't put on a show for you! he thought grimly, then put up his sword, saying, "Put your weapon away, Daggot. You know better than to make for a man's face. Even with a blunted tip, it's possible to blind or cripple. Stay clear of the drill in the future."

Daggot waved the sword in his hand in front of Gilbert's face, his voice filled with contempt, "And if I don't?"

Gilbert said, "Captain Jones will have something to say about it, I would think."

He looked up and saw something like disappointment in the captain's face, but Jones said, "Daggot, stay away from the passengers. I'll not warn you again!"

Angrily, Daggot threw his sword to the deck, glared at Gilbert and said, "You're a coward, Winslow! Hiding behind the captain!"

"Daggot! Did you hear me!" Jones bellowed. "One more word and we have a keelhauling!"

Fuller stepped forward, a bleak light in his face, but he said nothing to Gilbert. "Let me have a look at that mouth, Peter," he said, and he led the wounded man off to one side for a closer examination.

Standish waited until the deck had cleared, then said, "Bad business. I thought for a minute there you were going to skewer the rogue!"

"That's what everyone seemed to want!" Gilbert said wearily. "And didn't you warn me, Miles, not to let the man trap me?"

The answer came slowly. "Aye, you did the wise thing—but it must be hard to be labeled a coward."

Gilbert smiled grimly down at Standish. "I'm getting used to it, Miles. First a traitor, now a coward. Not much left, is there?"

"You're none of that!" the doughy little soldier snapped. "Why didn't you cut the man to ribbons?"

Gilbert stared out at the sea, watching the gray expanse unbroken and creased by myriad whitecaps. There was no more expression on his face than on the blank sky that stared down on the little ship bobbing on the waves.

"It didn't seem to matter much, Miles." He lifted his cornflower blue eyes, startling in his tanned face, and there was a sadness that ran deep in his husky voice that caught the attention of Standish.

"Why, you're too young to be so tired of life, Gilbert Winslow. You've got a whole lifetime ahead of you!"

Gilbert gave him a short, bitter smile before turning to leave the deck. "I know, Miles—and do I dread it!"

CHAPTER NINETEEN

LAND!

★   ★   ★   ★

As the temperature outside fell, so did the strength of Young William Butten, Samuel Fuller's servant. He had remained in the sail cabin with Brewster and Gilbert instead of returning to his bed behind the shallop, Fuller hoping that the relatively warm, dry conditions would help him.

"He don't seem to get on," he said to Humility as they ate the meager portion of beef passed along by the cook. "I wish I'd not brought him on this trip."

Humility said quickly, "You meant well. It's the late start that's brought us into this cold weather."

"Maybe—but it's a rough life we're heading into, lass." He chewed on the tough piece of stringy beef thoughtfully, and there was a rare discouragement in his voice as he added, "We're in bad condition, Humility. Half the passengers are down with some ailment now—and what it will be like when we're put ashore in the dead of winter, I hate to think. I'm going to see to Dorothy."

"I thought she was better since she got over her seasickness."

"There are worse things than upset stomachs, lass," Fuller grunted. He pulled his hand through his tangled beard, and added, "Dorothy has problems in her mind."

"I know, Sam." Humility got up, took the man's dish and

added, "She sometimes talks—well, in a peculiar way."

"She'll lose her mind if something doesn't happen."

"Sam! No!"

"I know you work hard, lass, but I wish you'd spend all the time you can with her. Try to encourage her if you can. She needs a friend." He paused and said tightly, "Far as I can see, she opens up more to that Winslow fellow than to anybody else—which is not right!"

They parted and Humility, passing across the deck, saw that Dorothy was talking to Gilbert Winslow in the bow section. She hesitated, then made her way forward.

"Oh, there you are, Humility," Dorothy said brightly. The cold air nipped at her cheeks, grown thin during the voyage, and she smiled faintly. "Sit with us, won't you? Gilbert was just telling me about a ball he attended at St. James Place."

"I can't stop now, Dorothy, but later on maybe we can read some more out of the book you liked so well."

"All right," Dorothy said, and added as the girl disappeared down into the lower parts of the ship, "Humility's such a sweet girl! I hope she gets settled with a good man who'll take care of her."

"What book is that she spoke of?"

"Oh, a book of poetry. I don't understand much about it, but Humility reads so well, I just love to listen."

"How's your husband?"

Her face, which had been lively, tensed as if in fear. "He's very ill."

"He and I are not well acquainted, but I admire him greatly."

"Oh, he's very admirable. I—I sometimes wonder that he married me. I mean, he was older and a great scholar and I was just a silly girl—only sixteen."

Gilbert hesitated, fearing to go too far, but he had a brotherly feeling for Dorothy, and he finally asked, "Have you been happy?"

"When I was a little girl, I was very happy!" she said, and her small face lit up with pleasure at the memory.

"I mean since you married."

"I don't know," she said slowly. And then a strange thing happened, something that Gilbert didn't understand. Dorothy was staring across the rolling sea, apparently thinking of her past as a child, and suddenly she turned and said in a voice very different from her normal voice, "I want some melon, Papa!"

A chill ran over Gilbert. She had a blank look in her eyes, and her features sagged, making her look older, but the voice was that of a child.

"Can I please have some of the melon, Papa? Robert has had *two* pieces already!"

Gilbert had never encountered a disturbed mind, at least not in such a form, and he sat there petrified. There was no *danger*, of course, from this frail woman, but a streak of fear cold as ice ripped through him. He wanted nothing so much as to get up and flee from her, but could not move.

He said carefully, "Dorothy—are you all right?"

Instantly her eyes cleared, and she said in a normal voice, "Why, yes, Gilbert, I'm fine. A little cold, perhaps."

At once he said, "I'll get you a coat."

"No, I must go inside and see about William." She rose, and there was a terrible fragility in her face that Gilbert understood. She patted his arm, saying, "If I didn't have you to talk to, Gilbert, I think I'd lose my mind!"

He sat there, his mind in a whirl, and finally he rose and sought out Elder Brewster. But he found him deep in conversation with Governor Carver, and feeling that he must say something to somebody, he made his way to the small cabin that Edward and Elizabeth shared.

"Gilbert? Come in—if you can get in, that is." Edward's face was lined, for he had lost his cheerful expression. His tremendous vitality had been sapped by the illness of his wife, and he had a haunted look as he turned to say, "Gilbert's here, Elizabeth."

There was no answer from the woman who lay on her back covered to the nose with a mound of blankets. She was staring at the ceiling dully, and did not respond when her husband said, "I'll just go along with Gilbert for a time. You try to sleep."

"How is she?" Gilbert asked as they stepped out on deck.

Edward filled his large chest with fresh air, lifting his head to meet the stiff breeze. "Ah, that's good after that foul cabin!" he exclaimed. He began walking vigorously up and down the deck, swinging his arms and stamping his feet. His face grew flushed and the tension left, smoothing his features. "Elizabeth is as well as she's going to be, I suppose."

It was as close to a critical word as Gilbert had heard from his brother concerning his wife, then Edward paused and said in a softer voice, "She's not fitted for this life, Gilbert. I shouldn't have brought her."

"I think there are several who shouldn't have come. Fuller is much afraid for William Butten—and I wanted to talk to you about Mrs. Bradford."

"Dorothy?" Edward shook his heavy head, muttering sadly, "She's not doing well, is she?"

Gilbert hesitated, then told his brother of the incident that had so shaken him. He saw that it disturbed Edward greatly.

"It's not the first time, Gilbert. All of us who are close to her have had forebodings."

"Something must be done!"

"What?" Edward shook his head sadly. "Fuller can give her a purge or a blood-letting, but who can minister to a broken heart—save the Lord himself?"

"Does her husband know?"

"Why, William knows she's unhappy and not well, but he's been so busy ministering to the needs of others, he's had scarcely a word with her. I've tried to tell him, as has Elder Brewster— but he's such a single-minded man it's almost impossible to catch his attention."

Gilbert's anger flared out suddenly. "Doesn't he know the Scripture says that he who doesn't care for his own is worse than a heathen?"

Edward frowned and there was a puzzled look in his eyes. "I tell you the truth, Gilbert, I think that William Bradford is a great man—greater than we know. If this venture succeeds at all, it will be his doing. Others have been more visible, but he's been the hub on which the whole thing has turned."

"But his own wife . . . !"

"He's a great man, but great men can destroy others with their dreams!"

Edward struck the rail with his hand, and there was a fire in his blue eyes as he said angrily, "Bradford can see a New

World and all its destiny—but that vision so fills his eyes he can't see that his own wife is going insane!"

"Tell him!"

"He's a *great man*, Gilbert; you don't simply tell that breed something. It's like trying to reason with a glacier that's slowly moving along, taking everything with it—trees, rocks, hills. William must love his wife—but his vision fills his heart and his soul. He won't allow anything or anyone to come before what he sees as God's will for his life!"

"Well, I'm happy that I'm not one of the great men," Gilbert said moodily, then grinned at his brother. "Like you."

Edward spat over the rail and stared moodily at the horizon. "I'm in worse shape than Bradford in a way, Gilbert."

"I don't believe that!"

"No? You aren't blind, so you must have seen that my marriage is a farce."

"Well . . ."

"Oh, don't bother to be polite!" Edward said, almost angrily. "It would be a relief to have somebody say just once, 'Edward Winslow, you are a fool!' "

Edward's passionate speech broke off abruptly. "I'm—sorry, Gilbert," he said finally, and managed to dredge up a smile of sorts. "Don't usually let myself go like this." Then he said, "It's too late for me—but not for you. When you marry, Gilbert, be sure you get a woman who won't *bore* you to death—better to have one who'll smash your head with a chamber pot!"

Gilbert had to laugh at the idea. "Not much for me to worry about, I suppose. Can't see myself married at all."

"You're thinking about being hauled back to England? God won't let that happen. You'll marry, and I'd give anything if you'd find a woman that could keep you entertained for a lifetime in two ways."

"Two ways?"

"In body and in mind!" Edward nodded. "Now, you're not a blabbermouth, so you just keep what I've said about myself under your bonnet."

Dorothy Bradford sat below deck with the Whites, playing Fox and Hounds with Resolved, listening to Susanna and William with part of her mind. They were talking about the problems that would beset them when they arrived, and Susanna was trying to encourage her husband.

"I can't see how we can get anything planted before May," White was saying. He coughed almost constantly now, his weak lungs unable to stand the harsh air of the Atlantic. "Then we'll have to wait for the harvest—if there is one."

"God will provide for us." Susanna was close to her time, and most women would have been in need of support, but there was no fear in her eyes. She leaned forward, still graceful in spite of her girth, and held William's thin hand. "Remember the Scripture cautions us to trust in God, not in the arm of flesh."

White lifted his arm and stared at it, saying with a wry smile, "This arm hasn't got much flesh on it, has it, Susanna? Not much to trust in!"

"You'll get better, William."

"I wish I had your faith." He stared at the emaciated arm, coughed sharply, then said in a low voice that Dorothy could barely hear, "It's not myself I fear for—you know that. It's you and Resolved, and the little one. Who will care for you if I die?"

"God." Susanna smiled and put down her sewing to move to his side. "If it did come to that—God would be my help. He is the father of the fatherless."

Dorothy looked at them, and thought, *Why can't I ever talk to my husband like that?* Then she looked down at Resolved and the sight of his face brought memories of her boy John, and she began to cry. She was always crying it seemed, and she was ashamed, but there was no help. She rose and left before the Whites could see, thinking, *If only this journey were over!* But then the thought struck her, *What then?* And terror filled her, for she realized that when she got off the *Mayflower*, she would not leave the dark fears behind, but would take them with her, ghastly things that pulled at her mind and dragged her spirit downward. *Why can't it all end?* she cried out in her heart over and over, but there was no relief.

"How's the boy, Fuller?" Captain Jones asked. He was attempting to shoot the sun with his cross-staff, a graduated bar of wood about thirty-six inches long, with a sliding bar about twenty-six inches long attached at right angles.

"Bad, I'm afraid. The miserable diet of salt meat, biscuit,

and dried peas we've had for weeks hasn't been any help."

Jones did not take his eye from his staff. Absently he remarked, "Try a little extra of dried fruit and lemon juice."

"He can't keep it down." Fuller stepped closer and watched as the captain jotted down a figure in a small notebook, and asked, "Does that thing tell where we are?"

"Not exactly. Gives the latitude pretty well, but there's no way to get the longitude."

"Well, doesn't that thing the seamen fool with every day tell how far we've come? If you know how far the New World is, seems as though you could subtract and tell when we'd get there."

"All that does is judge the speed." The log line was a quadrant of wood weighted on one side with a line about 150 fathoms long attached to it. The line was knotted at regular intervals, and by counting how many knots ran out while the line ran through the log glass, the number of knots or miles per hour could be roughly figured. But in heavy weather such as they had experienced it was useless.

"We *must* be getting close!" Fuller insisted.

Jones suddenly grinned, and jibed at Fuller, "I thought you people all believed that God was in control—fall of the sparrow and all that?"

"So He is—but He gave us intelligence to look to our ways. 'A wise man looketh well to his going,' the Scripture says."

"Well, I'm keeping the Scripture then," Jones argued good-naturedly. "I'm looking well to our going—that's what a captain does." He leaned against the mast and studied Fuller, wondering for the hundredth time what went on inside the Separatists. At the beginning of the voyage he had been adamantly certain that they were only another crew of wild-eyed fanatics, but his views had changed. He had discovered that the leaders were better educated than he, and men like Edward Winslow always excited his admiration. William Bradford he did not like, but William Brewster and Governor Carver were men of such evident piety he had to believe in their sincerity.

"We'll get there, Fuller," he said gently. "I know it seems long to you—the sea seems evil at times, even to me. He waved his hand at the rolling swells, and went on in a soft voice, "What can we know about the sea? We seem to be caught in the same old circle, always the same in every direction. Sometimes it seems that no matter how we feel the ship move through the water, we haven't made any progress—just glued in place while the sky and sea moves under and over us!"

Fuller stared at him, then smiled. "Well, now you know how we feel about God, Captain Jones."

"What's that?" Jones asked in surprise.

"Why, you sail your ship toward some spot you may have never seen and you have plenty of doubts, I see. Wonder if you'll make it? Get to looking at that huge, trackless ocean and it all seems very unlikely you'll ever arrive?" Fuller's broad face broke into a smile and he said, "That's what we call 'faith,' Captain Jones!"

Jones shook his head and mused, "Sounds dangerous to me, Fuller—I mean the way you people are leaving hearth and home. I have my charts and the stars to steer by, but what do you have?"

"We chart our course by the Word of God, Captain Jones— which is more stable than all your stars. 'The Word of the Lord changeth not, it endureth forever!'"

Jones considered this, then said seriously, "You will need all your faith, Fuller. It's very late for an endeavor such as yours. You should have timed your voyage to arrive on site in May or June. Winters in this latitude are fierce as tigers, I understand. How will you live—what will you eat?"

Fuller dropped his head and for one instant he looked tired and defeated, but then he looked up at the rolling banks of clouds that raced overhead, and then back to Jones.

"God is not dead, brother."

The simplicity of the reply was exactly the sort of thing that both disturbed the captain and paradoxically drew him to the settlers. Being a practical man, he was irritated at what appeared to be improvident planning—yet he longed to possess that serenity of soul that kept them secure.

"We cannot be many days out," he said firmly. "You'll be in your new Eden in a week, I'd venture."

Fuller nodded, then a figure caught his eye. Gilbert Winslow had appeared on deck and was making for the poop deck. "What will you do about that fellow?"

"Take him back to England."

"And Mr. Brewster?"

The captain hesitated, then was spared making an answer as Gilbert approached. "Mr. Fuller, I think you'd better come."

"Is it Butten?" Fuller asked quickly.

"Yes. He's having some sort of spell."

Fuller left without a word, and Gilbert turned to follow, but paused when Captain Jones caught his arm. "Is the boy dying, Winslow?"

Gilbert gave a slight shake of his head, his eyes cloudy, and he said briefly, "He looks very bad, Captain."

"Too bad! Too bad! I wish I could do something."

Gilbert stared at the captain curiously. His impression had been that the seaman was a rather hard specimen, but now there was a concerned furrow on the face of Jones. He said, "It does you credit to be concerned, Captain."

Jones gave him a direct look. "You think I am a heartless man, I take it."

"I don't know you, Captain Jones," Gilbert shrugged.

"No, nor I you. And with a certain matter between us, we may never get to know one another."

"You mean the matter of a gallows in England to which you will take me?"

Jones bit his lip, then nodded. "I could wish it were otherwise, Winslow. But as captain I am accountable to the Crown. If it became known that I allowed a fugitive to go free, it is not inconceivable that I might take your place on the gallows."

"I believe our Royal Sovereign is quite capable of such an action," Gilbert remarked with a grim smile; then he said, "I hold no malice toward you, Captain. But surely you must have some feelings about returning Mr. Brewster to the executioner?"

The question stung Jones and he said defensively, "He is an enemy to the Crown!"

"You know how false that is, Captain, I think." Gilbert shrugged and added, "You have spent much time with him on this voyage. I know that, for he has told me. Now can you, on your honor as a gentleman, say that there is anything in William Brewster that could possibly harm King James?"

Jones struggled for an answer, then rapped the deck with

his staff, saying fiercely, "No! On my honor, he is no threat to anyone on earth!" Then he paused and there was pain in his gray eyes as he turned to leave. "I wish the two of you would sprout wings and fly off my ship!"

Gilbert watched him leave, then descended from the poop deck. He was turning to go below when a small body shot up the stairs and collided so abruptly with his legs that he nearly fell.

Gaining his balance, he saw Tink, his face white with fear, trying to scramble around him. Catching his arms he said, "Tink—what's wrong?"

At that moment the huge form of Jeff Daggot appeared on the landing below. He was evidently chasing Tink, but stopped abruptly when he saw Winslow.

"What's this about?" Gilbert said.

"That boy stole me tot!" Daggot said. He advanced up the stairs in a threatening position, pointing a dirty finger at Tink. "See? That's me own ale—and I'll have a piece of 'is skin! Teach 'im to steal from Jeff Daggot, I will!"

"Hold it right there, Daggot," Gilbert said at once. "What about this, Tink?"

Tink kept his small body behind Gilbert. He held up a pewter tankard and said in a frightened voice, "Dr. Fuller sent me to get some ale—for William. And I found this—but I didn't know it was *his*!"

"Liar!" Daggot spat out. He reached out a thick hand for the boy which Gilbert knocked away. "Keep your hands off this boy, Daggot! Tink, give me the ale!" Taking the tankard from the boy, he handed it to Daggot, saying, "There's your property."

Daggot stared at it, then suddenly threw it straight into Gilbert's face, shouting, "*You* can 'ave it yourself, Mr. High-and-Mighty!"

Gilbert gasped as the ale caught him open-eyed, and as he threw his hands reflexively to his face he felt Daggot's mighty hands close on his throat, then a smashing blow caught him full in the mouth driving him backward to sprawl helplessly against the steps. He cried out, "Run, Tink!" at the same time kicking out with his good leg.

He had guessed that Daggot would follow up and, blinded though he was, he caught the sailor a solid kick in the groin. Daggot yelled and staggered backward, and Gilbert wiped his eyes free and leaped to his feet.

Daggot's face was a red mask of pain and rage as he started up the stairs with his hands held out like claws. "I'll pop yer eyeballs out like a pair 'o grapes!" he yelled, and with a curse threw himself up the stairs.

Gilbert was struck in the stomach by Daggot's huge head, and the back of his legs struck the top stair. He fell backward, rolling his head to one side just in time to avoid the jabbing thumb which Daggot drove toward his eye. It caught him on the cheek, the dirty nail slicing a gash as neatly as a blade along his cheekbone. He felt the blood well up, but ignoring the pain he drove a knee into the man's belly. It was tough as a board, but it gave. Daggot's wind belched out and he went lax just long enough for Gilbert to roll free and get to his feet.

Daggot was up instantly, and drove a hard blow that crushed Gilbert's mouth against his teeth. He was hit in the belly and lost his wind, then fell backward as he took a low blow. Great sheets of pain flowed upwards and he pulled his knees up to protect himself from the kick he felt sure was coming. It caught him on the bad leg, and when he scrambled to his feet, he was in bad shape.

Daggot was a barroom brawler, and he was out to kill or maim. Gilbert backed away, knowing that he had no chance in such a fight. Someone cried out, but he could not make out the words. Daggot did not hear; he had lain awake nights thinking of this time, and now he would smash the man before him even if he were flogged for it. "I'll smash yer pretty face so she won't love you no more!" he grated between clenched teeth, and he drove toward Gilbert in a rush of flailing fists.

He battered Gilbert's tipped-down head and his fist scraped along the smaller man's chin and nose. He hooked into Gilbert's temple, and then the blows came like deadly rain, starting up a blaze of lights in Gilbert's brain. He felt them and he heard them, but could not stop them and was driven back against a hard object.

His hand closed on an object, and when he pulled at it, it

came loose in his hand—a belaying pin. He had only strength enough to lift it, and as Daggot came roaring in, he brought the heavy weapon down, catching Daggot on the side of the head.

It was a blow that would have knocked a lesser man unconscious, but Daggot's matted hair and thick skull protected him. He went to one knee, his head down, and blood sprinkled the deck from the gash over his left ear.

Gilbert backed away, and Clark came running up. He grabbed Daggot's arm, yelling, "You fool! You'll be . . ." He was not able to finish, for Daggot came to his feet and striking out blindly, caught the First Mate in the stomach with such a powerful blow he fell to the deck gasping for breath.

Daggot stared at the belaying pin in Gilbert's hand, then his eyes drifted to the oak cabinet to his left, just under the rim of the poop deck. It was a small closet used for gear, but Standish had persuaded the captain to let him use it as a storage place for the weapons of the settlers. It was locked, but Daggot ripped the door open with a mighty heave, and when he turned, he had a sword in his hand.

Other voices were crying out, and Gilbert thought he heard the captain, but his vision narrowed until he saw only the glittering blade in Daggot's hand. A silence fell on his ears, and he heard the ragged breathing of the man who was moving toward him with murder in his eyes.

Daggot lunged, blade lowered, and it was a good thrust. Only barely did Gilbert manage to turn the blade aside with a quick movement of the belaying pin, and Daggot recovered quickly, saying under his breath, "That's all right—that's all right—Daggot will get you—that's all right!"

To stand was to die, so Gilbert took his only chance. As Daggot fell into position for another thrust, Gilbert waited until the last possible moment, then threw the pin straight into the man's face. It caught Daggot in the chest, and Gilbert whirled and ran around the longboat making for the bow.

Daggot laughed then, and Gilbert heard the sound of bare feet close on his heels! He reached the forecastle and in one mad leap scrambled on top, hearing the hiss of Daggot's blade as he made a cut.

He rolled over, and looked wildly around, but there was

only the sea in front, and now Daggot was on the deck, his sword poised.

They stood there outlined against the sky, Daggot crouched in the classic pose of the fencer ready to drive home the final thrust; Gilbert standing on the edge of the deckhouse, his hands widespread and waiting.

Daggot laughed, ignoring the voice of Captain Jones. "I'm a'goin' to kill you now," he said, and moved forward.

Gilbert awaited the thrust, knowing that Daggot was too good a swordsman to miss, and there was no fear in him—only regret that it had to end like this. Then a voice cut across the air like a trumpet.

"Gilbert!"

Looking up, Gilbert saw John Howland's head just over the lip of the forecastle deck—and in his hand was a sword!

"Here!" Howland yelled and threw the blade toward Gilbert.

It cartwheeled in the sun, sparkling like glass as it rose. Twice it turned and Gilbert thought, *It's too high!* but he gave a leap and the hilt slapped into his palm with a solid sound.

His feet touched the deck just as Daggot made his lunge, and it must have seemed like magic to the man's eyes.

One second he was driving his blade toward the body of an unarmed man—the next moment he was facing a sliver of steel that drove his own blade to one side and rammed through his chest like an icy dart.

Daggot's lunge carried him face-to-face with Gilbert, and for one moment he stared into the blue eyes, and then the incredible pain wrenched at him. He opened his mouth and said, "You— you ain't . . ." and then his body arched over backward, ripping the sword out of Gilbert's hand.

His body twisted as he fell, and he seemed to be trying to reach the hilt of the blade that nestled against his chest. His own sword hit the deck with a clatter, then he fell.

His lower body hit the top of the forecastle deck, but the heavy torso cleared the side, and he turned a complete somersault, striking the deck a lifeless hulk.

Captain Jones was on the far side of the deck, and he rushed around to find John Alden standing there, but no Daggot.

Alden's eyes were blazing, and there was blood on the front of his jerkin. As the captain stopped short, Alden nodded toward the sea, and there was a challenge in his face as he said calmly, "Man overboard, Captain."

Log: September 20
Sighted land at dusk. It appears to be Cape Cod, somewhere off the high bluffs at Truro. It being late, we will search the coast for a harbor on the morrow.

Seaman Jeffery Daggot was lost at sea after falling overboard. Attempts to recover his body were in vain. May God have mercy on his soul.

CHAPTER TWENTY

MUTINY ON THE *MAYFLOWER*

★ ★ ★ ★

They were sixty-five days out from Plymouth, ninety-seven from Southampton. Shouts of joy and tears of relief rang on the morning air as the entire company met to view their new home.

They were close enough to see high brown bluffs and the tops of tall trees, but all was in outline. Captain Jones dared not venture too close to shore, and the leadsman was hard at work feeling for the bottom. "Forty fathoms, thirty fathoms, twenty fathoms."

For half a day they continued this cautious progress down the coast, and it was late when the lookout from the maintop shouted, "Breakers ahead!"

"We'll find a harbor tomorrow," Jones said to the anxious group, and then there was an anticlimactic lull. Passengers wandered over the small deck interfering with the work of the crew, and had to be driven below by orders from the Cabin.

Far into the night the leaders talked, planned for the coming days, and they were caught off guard when a group led by Billington demanded an audience.

"We ain't satisfied with the way things is going, Mr. Bradford," Billington said bluntly. "And we have come to a decision."

William Bradford lifted his head slowly, taking in the group, and he asked quietly, "What is your decision?"

"Why, when we come ashore, we intend to use our own liberty."

"That's right!" Stephen Hopkins piped up, his rabbit-like face twitching eagerly. He nudged Billington, adding, "There's none with the power to command us—not if we land at this spot."

"And why not?" Bradford asked.

"Because this ain't Virginia like we signed for."

"In that you are correct," Bradford nodded. "The charter calls for us to settle south of latitude 41. But we are hundreds of miles north of the Hudson River, and the captain informs us that to beat our way there would be very dangerous. In addition, the captain insists on taking the ship back to England as quickly as possible."

"What this amounts to," Carver said gently, "is that we really have only two choices—settle here, or go back to England."

"We signed for Virginia!" Hopkins said stubbornly. "And if we stay here, we don't see as how we're under your authority."

"It's all Virginia," Bradford said steadily; "this part is called New England."

"I don't know anything about New England," Billington said loudly. "We won't be bound by any power if we don't settle in Virginia."

"We'll elect our own governor!" Hopkins said.

"And you are a candidate, I take it?" Bradford asked acidly.

"Why . . ."

"You were on a voyage to Virginia once before, I believe." Bradford pinned the little man with his eyes.

"Why, yes, I was, and . . ."

"And there was a rebellion against the authority of Sir William Gates, was there not?"

Hopkins' mouth dropped open, and he wiped his chin with a nervous hand. "I don't remember . . ."

Bradford's voice chopped at the little man relentlessly. "And there was a trial in which the members of the conspiracy were convicted of mutiny and rebellion."

"Yes." Hopkins' face was sallow now, and his voice could hardly be heard.

"And all were executed—with one exception, I believe. The man who organized the entire affair was let off because, as the record says, 'He made so much moan alleging the ruin of his wife and children in his trespass.' And the name of that man is—Stephen Hopkins!"

"It wasn't my fault!" Hopkins began to cry, his face contorted with shame. "They made me do it, I didn't want to!"

"And are *they* making you lead this mutiny?" Bradford asked sternly. He pointed his finger at the group, saying, "You will drop this matter at once, do you hear me!"

He did not wait, but pushed by them, saying, "Mr. Carver, Mr. Brewster, come with me."

The rest of the day they spent in the captain's Great Cabin, and the ship was abuzz with rumors. When Bradford stood on the poop deck late in the afternoon and called for a meeting, there was a rush to get a place.

The cabin was crowded, for although no women were there, most of the able-bodied men were. Discontent was in the air, and the faces of the leaders were gray with strain. The thing was settled when Brewster said to Bradford, "William, some sort of terms must be offered to all, strangers as well as saints. We must have a written document embodying the idea that everyone would have fair treatment under the new government."

That paper was in the hands of William Bradford, and he waited until the room grew quiet, then in a steady voice read the Compact:

IN THE NAME OF GOD, AMEN

We whose names are underwritten, the loyal subjects of our dread Sovereign Lord King James by the Grace of God of Great Britain, France, Ireland, King, Defender of the Faith:

Having undertaken, for the Glory of God and advancement of the Christian Faith and honour of our King and country, a voyage to plant the First Colony in the northern parts of Virginia, do by these presents solemnly and mutually in the presence of God and of one another, covenant and combine ourself together into a Civil Body Politic, for the better ordering and preservation and furtherance of the ends aforesaid, and by virtue hereof do enact, constitute and frame such just and equal law, ordinances, acts, constitutions and offices from time to time, as shall be thought most meet and conve-

> nient for the general good of the Colony, unto which we prom-
> ise all due submission and obedience. In witness whereof we
> have hereunder subscribed our names at Cape Cod, the 11th
> of November, in the year of the reign of our Sovereign Lord
> King James of England, France and Ireland, the eighteenth,
> and of Scotland the fifty-fourth. Anno Domini 1620

"This will be the foundation of our government," Bradford
said. He put the paper on the captain's desk, picked up a quill
and signed it. Those that were entitled to the term "Master"
stepped up, led by John Carver, followed by William Brewster,
Edward Winslow, Isaac Allerton, Miles Standish, Samuel Fuller,
William White. Then the leaders of the London group signed—
Christopher Martin, William Mullins, Richard Waren, Stephen
Hopkins.

Then the goodmen were invited to sign—the next social rank
below master. Twenty-seven of these signed; then four servants
signed on orders from their master. A total of forty-one of the
sixty-five males aboard signed. The women were excluded, of
course, for they were not free agents, being legal chattel and
servants of their husbands.

"We will now proceed to elect a governor who will serve for
one year," Bradford said. He stared straight at Stephen Hopkins
and John Billington, daring them with his dark eyes to speak,
then added, "I offer the name of John Carver."

"I second that name," William Brewster said, and almost
before Carver knew what was happening, he was the first pop-
ularly elected official in the New World.

Brusquely Bradford dismissed the meeting, and they all
trooped up to take a look at their New World.

Captain Jones had invited himself to the meeting, and since
it was *his* cabin, there had been no way to exclude him. Now he
sat with his back against the bulkhead watching as William Bradford remained to gather up the documents and writing materials.
Rising to his feet, he walked to the table and stared down at the
long sheet of paper the men had just signed.

Finally he looked up with sober eyes, saying, "This is an
unusual thing, Mr. Bradford."

"Yes, Captain, it is—but then, we are leaving the *usual* behind in our venture."

"A Civil Body Politic," Jones read aloud. "That would not

be pleasing to His Majesty, I think. Nor would your manner of choosing a governor. The Crown has always appointed governors of the colonies."

Bradford gave the captain a curious smile, saying, "It is the way we choose our pastor for our congregation—by popular vote."

Jones laughed suddenly. "Well, *that* doesn't sit too well with the King either, you know." Then he added, "Carver is a good man—but it is obvious, Mr. Bradford, that you are the natural leader of the group. Why were you not elected?"

"I would be unacceptable at this time," Bradford said. "Carver is not as—" he sought for a word, then found it. "Not as *direct* as I."

"He is a meek fellow," Jones agreed. "But you will be the power behind the throne, so to speak?"

"I will serve as best I can," Bradford said slowly. "But the heart of our government will lie in this: the people will elect their own rulers."

"That is a dangerous practice!" Jones said. "What if they elect a man who is not able, or who is dishonest?"

"Then others may get together and elect a better man in his place!" Bradford smiled at the perplexity on the captain's face, and added gently, "The Greeks called it 'democracy.'"

"Sooner or later the King will realize that the end of this 'democracy' is the abolition of his own power. What then, Mr. Bradford? Will you deny the power of the Crown?"

"We will follow God's leading, Captain."

Jones stared at him, then shrugged, "Well, I wish you well, Mr. Bradford. I had little use for your ideas when we first met—but I have been most favorably impressed by the behavior of your people."

"Thank you, Captain Jones," Bradford nodded, and then with a look of rare humor in his sober eyes, he asked suddenly, "Does this charitable spirit extend to allowing Mr. Brewster to remain with us when you depart?"

"You *are* a polititian, Bradford!" Jones laughed and slapped the table with his hand. "Well, officially he does not exist on the *Mayflower*—at least under that name. I feel safe enough on that score, so he may stay."

"And Mr. Gilbert Winslow?"

Captain Jones bit his lip and shook his head. "Ah, that's different. He is a violent man—as Mr. Brewster is not."

"He is not really one of us, Captain," Bradford said slowly. "I suspect that you have found out most of his story . . ."

"I have some of it—and it does him no credit." Jones looked inquiringly at Bradford, asking, "He betrayed you—and yet you intercede for him, Mr. Bradford?"

" 'If the Lord should mark iniquities, who should stand?' " Bradford quoted. "I behaved in a very uncharitable manner to the man when he betrayed us—but there is something good in him. His brother Edward is one of the best men I have ever known, and I see some of him in Gilbert Winslow."

"The business yesterday with Daggot—!"

"Surely you of all men will not hold that against him? Your man gave Winslow no choice, did he?"

"No—the fellow was always a troublemaker! And I would have done the same," Jones admitted. "I have noted in my log that he was lost overboard—which is the truth, in a way."

"You must follow your own way in this matter, Captain," Bradford said. "But it is a serious matter to hold a man's destiny in your hands. I suggest that you pray much before you commit yourself to any action."

"Pray?" The suggestion came as a shock to Jones. "I've not been accustomed to praying about such things."

"It is not a bad way," Bradford nodded. He rolled the Mayflower Compact into a tight roll, and there was a stoop to his shoulders as he turned to go topside.

Preparations for the first exploratory voyage were underway. Miles Standish scurried around the deck, seeing to the arms of the men selected to participate, and the crew labored to swing the longboat over the side.

From the crowded decks, the passengers gazed out at the long white sandhills that reminded them of the dunes of Holland; on the other side, bristling forests marched to the water's edge. They roamed from port to starboard, from stern to stem, studying the land before them, their faces a mixture of joy at the arrival and apprehension of what was to come now.

Humility did not join those that watched. She was in the galley begging Hinge for some broth for William Butten.

"Ah, well, we can have a *real* fire now!" the little cook grinned. "Plenty of firewood instead of this cursed charcoal!"

"This is good, Thomas!" Humility said, taking a sip of the steaming broth. "It may help the boy."

"How is he now, miss? The doctor was none too hopeful yesterday."

Humility bit her lip, and there were diamonds in her wide green eyes as she said, "He is very bad, Thomas. Very sick."

"Ah, too bad! Too bad!"

She hurried down the ladder past the crew's mess, then down one more flight to the cargo hold. Balancing the bowl carefully, she pushed the door open and entered.

"Hullo, miss." Tink was sitting in the gloom of the tiny cabin, and he had a frightened look on his face. "William—William is real sick, miss!"

Humility took one look at the pale face of the boy under the blanket, and put the soup down. She knelt by the sick boy and laid her hand on his chest. It did not move, and she was suddenly paralyzed with the thought that he was dead! Then the frail chest heaved, and there was a rasping rattle in William's chest and his eyes opened. He moved his lips and she had to lean forward to catch his words.

"Are—we there? Are we—at—the New World?"

"Don't try to talk, William," she said. Then she rose and whispered, "Has Dr. Fuller been here?"

"No, miss." Tink wiped a tear from his eyes, saying, "William, he keeps askin' for Mr. Winslow. Do you know where he is?"

"I'll get help, Tink," she said quickly. She ran along the lower deck, then up to the waist deck where Fuller was busily engaged in getting ready to go ashore with the party.

"Sam! You've got to come with me! William is dying, I think!"

Fuller stopped probing at the musket in his hands, then he looked directly into Humility's eyes and said, "The boy, he don't need me, lass." Then he dropped his eyes and fumbled with a button on his frayed black coat. "I can't do anything for him now."

"Sam!"

"You ain't blind, lass," Fuller said. "He's been sinking for two days now—I expected to see him go last night."

"But you can't go with him dying!"

Fuller looked haunted, then he sighed and shook his heavy head. "I'm a coward, lass. I just don't have the heart to see the boy go. Get one of the elders to go—Carver would be good. He can pray for the boy—" He broke off abruptly and stepped away from her, joining the small group at the weapons cabinet.

Humility stared at him, angry and frightened. She turned blindly and tried to think, but her mind was spinning.

I can't go back and see him die! she thought wildly, but there was no other way. With the faint hope that Fuller might be wrong, she turned and went down the ladder.

When she got to the cargo deck, a thought came to her, and she turned to enter the water cask room. Directly behind it was a tiny room where a few things were stored, including spirits— mostly beer and ale. *Maybe some wine will help him*, she thought, and with a faint hope she opened the door and began feeling around blindly for a bottle.

She had been there before, watching Alden as he checked the water barrels and the stores, but there had been light then. Now the only light was a faint glow from a lantern that swung halfway down the cargo deck.

The wine—it was in a case by the wall, she thought, and she groped her way along the wall.

She was almost there when her extended hand touched warm flesh!

She gasped as a pair of strong hands grasped her and pulled her into a hard embrace. Blank terror filled her as the smell of alcohol on the man's breath came to her, and the pressure of his body on hers was like fire.

"Let me go!" she cried out, and with both hands she beat at her captor, but she was helpless against his strength. "Help me!" she screamed, and then he spoke.

"Go on—scream all you want, Humility!"

She stopped struggling and whispered, "Gilbert? Is it you?"

"Who else would be getting drunk and attacking innocent girls in the wine cellar?"

The reply was bitter, and his voice was slightly slurred with the wine. He pulled her even closer and suddenly kissed her before she knew what he was doing.

The touch of his lips was a shock that ran along her nerves, and suddenly she felt herself yield to his embrace! There was no reason in it, and her mind was screaming, *No! Don't let him touch you!* but her body rebelled and she felt herself relax as he pulled her closer; to her horror she felt herself raising her arms to put around his neck.

With a cry of disgust—not at him, but at herself—she pulled herself back and slapped his face with a quick blow.

"You—you *beast!*"

He laughed, and pulled her closer. "The scum of the earth!— and he's holding you in his arms, Humility." Then he added, "And you don't hate it as much as you pretend, do you?"

She felt her face burn, for he had sensed her response to his embrace. She ceased to struggle, and said quietly, "All right, Gilbert, shame me if you will—you can't say anything to me I haven't said to myself."

At once he dropped his arms, and they stood there in the darkness, memories of the past brushing against them.

Finally he said, "Don't blame yourself, Humility—you've done nothing wrong."

"The way I let myself love you—*that* was wrong!" she cried out.

"No, you just didn't have any defenses against a scoundrel," he said wearily.

She could not beat the scene, so she said, "William is dying—I came to get him some wine."

"All right." His voice was dead, and he said only, "Let's go to him."

They left the room, and she saw by the pale amber light of the lantern his face was swollen, the raw wound made by Daggot's thumbnail crusted with blood that he had not bothered to wash away.

"You'll get an infection if that cut isn't taken care of."

He had a brown gall bottle in his hand, and he looked at it, saying, "This may help him."

She stared at him. "You could die from that kind of infection. Don't you care?"

"No."

She stared at him, then wheeled and led him swiftly to the sail room. William lay still, his breath coming in a short, choppy rasp. He opened his eyes, and whispered, "Are we—home—Mr. Winslow?"

Gilbert knelt beside the boy, lifted the thin body hot with fever and poured a few drops of brandy into the trembling lips.

"You're almost home, William."

"Mr. Winslow—I—I—" He broke off, and his eyes rolled backward for a moment, then they came back to fasten on Winslow's face. "Me—and Tink—we're going to—to have—" He faltered again, and his body was suddenly rent by a racking cough.

"We'll have us a place, William!" Tink cried. He wiped the streaming tears from his thin face and patted the dying boy's hand. "We're home."

"Will you—take me—to see it—Mr. Winslow?" William gasped.

Gilbert looked over the boy's head and met Humility's tearstained face. The anger toward him was gone, and she nodded numbly, her lips forming a *yes*!

Gilbert scooped the thin form up, and Humility tucked the worn blanket around him; they made their way along the dark corridor and up the three flights of steps.

The sky was dark, but William closed his eyes tightly. "It's so bright!"

Everyone stopped to stare at them, and a quiet fell on the busy deck. Gilbert's bloodstained, beaten face, Humility's expression of grief, and the thin form of the dying Butten threw a blanket of silence over the deck.

Gilbert carried the boy to the bow, and he felt Humility close beside him. When they got in the very apex of the deck, he turned and held the boy high, facing the shore.

"There's your New World, William," he said gently.

The boy's eyes opened slowly, and as he stared at the shore, a smile came across his parched lips.

"Ain't it—ain't it—*good*—Mr. Winslow?"

"Yes, William," Gilbert said hoarsely, his voice breaking so that he could say no more.

As the sea lifted the *Mayflower* gently, Gilbert felt Humility press closer, and Tink grabbed him by the waist sobbing uncontrollably.

The sky was gray as ashes, featureless and stark. Gusts of cold wind swept across the deck, and the shore seemed alien and hostile where it touched the sullen breakers. The harsh cry of a gull seemed an evocation of doom, and there was a brittle, fragile quality about the ship thrown into relief against the eternal whisperings of the sea.

Bradford saw that the scene was evoking sharp fears in the spectators. He raised his voice, piercing the gloom with his words, "Put away your fears, dear brothers. It is true we have no friends to welcome us. We have no shelter at hand, and winter is nigh. We hoped for a paradise, but we will be content with a desert if God so wills."

The sharp wind caught at his words, making them weak and ragged, so he cried out in a powerful manner, like an Old Testament prophet, "One day our children will say, 'Our fathers were Englishmen who came over this great ocean and were ready to perish in this wilderness. But they cried unto the Lord and He heard their voice and looked upon their adversity.' Let us therefore praise the Lord because He is good and His mercies endure forever!"

As Bradford began to pray, Gilbert felt a slight movement in the frail body he held, and then heard a single brief sigh.

"William?" Humility whispered. She gripped Gilbert's arm tightly and then looked up into his face.

He looked down into William's still, pale face, now relaxed with no trace of strain—then he looked back into the face of Humility and spoke in a gentle voice, the tears running freely down his scarred face:

"William has gone home, my dear."

PART THREE

THE
NEW WORLD

★ ★ ★ ★

CHAPTER TWENTY-ONE

FIRST LOOK AT EDEN

★ ★ ★ ★

They buried William Butten at sea, sewn into a canvas tarp with a bag of sand for ballast.

Gilbert's face was set like flint as the tiny body slid off the board, making a small splash in the sea, and as he turned to go, he met Humility's eyes, but she at once whirled and turned to avoid him.

The next day was washday, the women being put ashore early under an armed guard to do the family wash. While they were beating, scrubbing, and rinsing heaps of dirty clothes and bedding, the children ran wildly up and down the beach under the watchful eyes of sentries. The men brought in the shallop stored between decks on the *Mayflower* and beached her for repairs, for she had been badly battered and bruised by the storms at sea and her seams had been opened up.

As a gang went to work under the direction of Francis Eaton, the ship's carpenter, the rest prowled the beach and tidal flats in search of shellfish. Ravenous for fresh food, they made a great feast that night on tender soft-shell clams and succulent young quahogs, and also put away many large mussels—which proved to be a grave error, for the mussels made them deathly sick.

That night, against Governor Carver's will, they decided to send an exploring party inland. "There is a river, the captain says, and it would be safer to take the shallop in by that means."

"The craft won't be ready for days," Edward Winslow objected at once.

"And the weather is getting foul," Bradford added. "We *must* find our ground as quickly as possible."

"But what about the savages?" Carver asked.

"And the wild beasts?" William Mullins shook his head fearfully. "There may be elephants!"

"Elephants?" Standish snorted in derision. "Nonsense, Mr. Mullins—there are no fabulous beasts here."

Mullins triumphantly lifted a book, crying, "But here is proof!" He opened the book and showed them a crude picture of very fat animals being hunted by savages. "This is the book by John White, his pictures, the first ever made in Virginia!"

The men crowded around to stare, and he flipped the pages proudly. "See, there's the prince of the savages, Saturiba, walking with his queen!" He pointed to an engraving of mostly naked figures of noble-looking Indians. By the chief's side walked young men carrying great fans, while behind him walked another wearing gold and silver balls hanging from a little belt around his hips.

"I've seen those books!" Miles Standish growled. "They're made to sell—not to tell the truth."

They argued back and forth, and finally Bradford said waspishly, "Well, we can't sit here in this ship waiting for a royal welcoming committee. Tomorrow, Captain Standish, you will take fifteen men on an expedition. We must locate as soon as possible!"

The next day Edward put a hand on Gilbert's arm. "I want you with us on this exploration."

"Why? I'll not be staying here." There was a bitter light in Gilbert's eyes, but Edward ignored it.

"You need to get away from this ship. And who can say about what's to come?"

Gilbert stared at him, then smiled. "All right. I'll come."

Fifteen able men joined on deck at dawn, including Miles Standish, William Bradford, Edward and Gilbert, John Alden, Stephen Hopkins, William White, John Billington, Christopher Martin, Isaac Allerton, Sam Fuller, and the three hired sailors, English, Trevore, and Ellis.

The distance from the *Mayflower* was something under a mile, a matter of thirty minutes' pulling. The men piled out on the sandy beach, sending the boat back with the sailors.

The party turned down a gully where the growth was sparse and proceeded up through the trees. There were evergreens here and there, but otherwise the dead hand of winter had stripped the trees. Nevertheless they managed to identify a goodly number of species: boxberry, shrub oaks, oaks, aspen, beech, wild plum and cherry, holly and juniper.

As they filed across a stretch of marshy ground, a huge crane rose into the air, followed by the quicker flight of a cloud of waterfowl. Early winter dusk was already darkening the air, and they had seen no sign of human life. Confused in the wasteland, they unwittingly turned north and came upon the beach again, and decided to advance, hoping to find a better path inland. Again the men began to straggle so that Gilbert and Standish forged ahead about four hundred yards.

Suddenly Gilbert lifted his head, and squinted into the falling darkness. "Look, Miles!" he said, pointing down the beach.

Three quarters of a mile away Standish saw the black dots of human figures. Five or six men were coming along the shore toward them, and they had a dog with them. "Come up! Come up!" Standish called to the party, and as they halted, he passed his smoldering slow wick and each set a glowing tip to the end of his own cord and clipped it into his gun in readiness.

"Tightly, now," Standish commanded, and led the little troop forward. As they progressed, the figures in the distance suddenly turned and disappeared.

Standish led the group to the spot, pointing down at imprints of bare feet in the sand.

"We'll follow," he said, and stalked up the incline toward the sand hills. The men plunged over the dunes, and Standish called out, "Be ready for attack!"

"This is a little dangerous, Miles," Gilbert panted as they slid and stumbled through the undergrowth. "A perfect spot for an ambush."

"So it is, but I want to make contact—find what we're up against."

They found nothing, though, and by noon when they were

permitted to rest, they were hungry as bears. Washing down
their cheese and biscuit-bread with water from a spring, they
rested for almost two hours, then Standish roused them up, and
they thrashed around all afternoon, coming back to the beach to
make night camp. William Mullins was so afraid that he slept
little, muttering deliriously and crying out in fear at every owl
hoot, but most of them lay like stones. The stars came out, and
Gilbert rose once to feed the fire with juniper sticks. He relieved
Standish who was standing guard, and the two talked quietly
for a short time sitting under the distant stars. So the night
passed.

They were up at dawn, and traveled a long distance, but
mostly in wavering lines; they never got more than five miles
from the beach, and it was about two in the afternoon when they
found the cornfield.

Standish spotted it first, and called to the others, "Here's
something!" He was standing on the edge of an irregular field
of stubble. It was a large-stalked, thinly spaced stubble, but obviously not wild. "A planted field!" Bradford exclaimed. They
spread out and found another field adjoining, and there, half
buried in the sand, were four weather-beaten timbers—ship's
planks, obviously the remains of some sort of man-made hut.

"See here!" John Alden cried, stooping to scoop something
up. "A kettle!" He held up a rusty iron pot, and insisted on
taking it along as they continued their exploration.

At the edge of the field Billington found a small mound, and
called them over, saying, "Maybe it's buried gold!"

"Looks more like a grave to me," Mullins muttered.

They fell into an argument, Billington leading those who felt
they might find something valuable, and Bradford reluctant to
disturb a grave. Finally, he agreed, and they began feverishly
throwing the earth high in the air.

"Who knows?" Billington cried out. "Maybe an Indian king
with jewels in 'is ears! Maybe gold nuggets!"

Finally they came against a hard surface, and scooping out
the last of the dirt, Billington pulled out a woven basket. He
instantly turned it over and a shower of yellow fell to the ground.

"Gold!" Billington shouted, and they all took it up.

"Corn, you fool!" Standish said in disgust.

Bradford picked up a handful of the grain and there was a prophetic gleam in his dark eyes as he said quietly, "To think that God led us to this very spot—out of all the vast empty spaces in this land!"

"We ought to put it back, cover it up as we found it," Edward said.

"No!" Billington shouted. "It's ours now."

"Take it," Standish said at once, and there was a sharp debate; Gilbert exchanged amused glances with Edward as the men wavered between greed and their holy duty. They finally dug farther into the mound and found a larger basket also filled with corn.

Finally Bradford said, "Very well, we'll take what we can carry—for seed corn. But we'll make every attempt to find the natives and explain our intentions—to pay for what we have taken."

Since such a thing seemed highly unlikely, Billington's faction agreed, and they left with bulging pockets filled with corn.

They got sick of the kettle, for it was heavy and awkward, and by nightfall they were glad to make their second camp. The next morning they wandered back toward the shore, discovering the river mouth that had been seen from the *Mayflower*, and later on a sandy bank, a dugout canoe, consisting simply of a tree trunk shaped by fire into a long narrow boat. Mullins suggested they might put the heavy iron pot in it and paddle back to their starting point, but Bradford insisted on leaving it in place, and Standish led them back toward the harbor. Night overtook them, and they were forced to make camp again. The next afternoon, Friday, the seventeenth of November, they reached the harbor and fired the signal shot that brought the longboat to return them to the *Mayflower*.

As they were on their way back to the ship, Edward leaned forward and said quietly, "Not the paradise most people are expecting, is it Gilbert?"

The sober look on Gilbert's face was broken as a wry grin drew his broad lips upward, and he murmured, "As Edens go, I expect it's about average."

"You're right, but dreams don't follow logic," Edward mused. He cast his eyes back toward the barren shore, then shook his head sadly. "This place is likely to break the spirit of the fainthearted."

"Are you having second thoughts, Edward?"

"*Second* thoughts!" Edward frowned. "Man, I've had a *hundred* thoughts, wondering what in God's name brought us to this place!"

"A dream, Bradford says."

"Aye, a dream, but is it a good dream—or will it turn out to be a nightmare?"

"I wonder if Bradford or Carver ever have doubts?" Gilbert asked. "They seem so certain that God is in all this."

"I doubt they ever think of it," Edward snorted. "They're visionaries, Gilbert. Prophets who've heard from God. The rest of us are risking everything on their vision."

A cold wind stung Gilbert's face, and he stared at the rolling water that tossed the longboat like a chip. All morning the sun had been muffled with fat, dark clouds, and even now there was an ominous keening as the winds gathered up and cut across the sea. He stared at his hands, red with cold, and then looked up, saying, "I've never been much for dreams, Edward. Right now the whole thing looks pretty grim to me. I won't be here if Jones has his way, but if I were staying, there'd be some fear in my heart, I think."

"Don't give up, Gilbert," Edward said instantly. He put his hand on his brother's shoulder and added, "I'm not much on theology myself, but I can't think God brought you this far for no purpose."

"You think God is in such dire need of men He has to use a traitor and a murderer to build a New World?"

"Ah, Gilbert!" Edward shook his head and said energetically, "Forbear that, I beg you! You're no murderer, nor traitor either, not in your soul. You've taken a fall—well, what young man doesn't, I ask ye?"

As the men piled onto the deck, there was an excited hum of voices, and Priscilla Mullins caught at John Alden with her eyes wide, saying, "John, what was it like?"

The big cooper smiled down at her, and pulled her off to sit beside the rail. He did not note the hard look that her father gave him, but began spinning the tale to the delighted girl.

Bradford smiled at the crowd, but shook his head. "We have good news. The land is fertile." He reached into the kettle held by Allerton and Billington, allowing the golden grain to trickle through his fingers. "See, the grain of the new land!"

As everyone crowded close to see, Brewster came close and said in a low tone, "William, you'd best go see Dorothy."

"Dorothy? Why? Is she ill?"

"I think so."

Bradford nodded, and leaving Edward to tell of their findings, he followed Brewster into the first hold. "What's wrong with her, William? She was fine when we left."

Brewster stopped so abruptly that Bradford bumped into him. "No, she was not. She hasn't been well for some time."

Bradford stared into the eyes of William Brewster, perplexity scoring his craggy face. He tried to think, then said, "I hadn't noticed she was ill."

"You must pay more heed to her, William. She's not strong."

"Why, I hadn't thought . . . !"

"No, you've been so caught up with the people, it's escaped your notice. But she needs your love and assurance more than anyone else on this ship."

They found her in the tiny cabin, sitting on the bunk with her hands folded in her lap. The light of the flickering candle threw a shattered light over her face, and the sight of her drew a sudden gasp from William Bradford.

She was staring emptily at the wall, her face etched by the rigors of the journey. She had been plump and pretty, but there was a cadaverous look about her as she sat there. Her cheeks were drawn in, and the outline of her teeth could be seen through her thin lips.

But it was not that which shocked Bradford so much as the emptiness of her eyes. She had always had bright eyes, her best feature, but now they were dull, almost as if filmed with some opaque material.

She was singing under her breath, so faintly that Bradford had to lean forward to hear. It was a nursery rhyme, one he had heard her sing often to John when he was an infant.

Bradford leaned forward and caught the faint words: *I'm a*

little lost lamb—a little lost lamb—Far, far away from home!

"Dorothy," he said gently. "Dorothy, are you all right?"

She did not respond, but kept her eyes fastened on the wall, and sang again, *I'm a little lost lamb . . ."* Then she smiled and murmured softly, "I found the doll you made me, Papa. It was under my bed."

Shock raked across Bradford's face, and he could not seem to move. He stood there, leaning over his wife, his eyes wide, his heavy lower lip drooping. Finally he straightened up and stared blindly at William Brewster. He formed the words with his lips: "She's mad!"

William Brewster's face was filled with pain as he nodded.

"She is indeed a little lost lamb, William. A little lost lamb!"

CHAPTER TWENTY-TWO

DOROTHY

★ ★ ★ ★

Log: Friday December 4
    Cape Cod. Weather continues to worsen. Temperature falling, and rain threatening to turn to snow. Settlers have been in conference daily trying to make a decision on place of final settlement. Many want to settle at Corn Hill, while others cite its want of adequate water supply. They would have to depend on fresh-water ponds which would dry up in summer. Coffin has volunteered to guide an expedition to a good harbor not far across the bay. Much weakness among people. Thompson, servant of William White, dies.

The news of Edward Thompson's death came as no shock, for he had been failing for days. The men were in one of the endless debates on where to settle when Sam Fuller entered the hold, sat down heavily, his head bowed.

"What's wrong, Mr. Fuller?" Hopkins asked.

"Edward just died."

A silence settled on the group; then Billington shrugged, saying, "He'd not have lasted the winter."

The death of Thompson sobered both sides, and they finally agreed to make one more exploration. Coffin, the man who knew the coast best, vowed there was a navigable river and a good harbor less than twenty-four miles around the coast.

O'Neal asked the pilot why he was giving aid to the settlers when he'd never had anything but contempt for them.

"Because I'm interested in my own hide, that's why!" Coffin cursed and went on, "The captain, he's bewitched by these whey-faced psalm-singers! You ain't heard him say nothin' about going home, have you? No! Gone soft, 'e has! He'll stay around this cursed place all winter, and what'll we have to eat on the way home, I ask you? We'll starve, that's what! And that's why I'm gonna' show 'em a good spot; then they'll be off the ship and we can get away from this place!"

As soon as the expedition left, the weather began playing diabolical games with the *Mayflower*. Rolling swells and gusty blasts of freezing rain combined to roll the ship till she heaved and strained at her anchor. There was no possibility of going ashore, and what was happening to the small force caught in such weather, they dared not think.

Gilbert had not gone on the expedition, his place being taken by Peter Brown. The only warmth on the ship was in the small galley, and he had joined Tink there on the second afternoon after the departure.

They were hugging the small fire when Samuel Fuller came in and poured himself a cup of the hot tea that Hinge kept for a favored few. The burly physician was thinner than when they had left England, and Gilbert noticed that his hands were not steady.

He drank the tea silently, not seeming to taste it, then looked at Tink and said, "You know the forecastle, lad?"

"Yes, sir!"

"Well, there's a small leather bag in a wooden box under my bunk. Go fetch it, and I shouldn't be surprised but what there was a treat in it for you. Run now!"

Waiting until Tink dashed away in search of his prize, Fuller stared moodily at the fire, then lifted his broad face to Gilbert. "I've no liking for you, Winslow."

"That's clear enough, Mr. Fuller." Gilbert stared at him, shrugged, and said, "I can't blame you."

Fuller slapped his thigh angrily, and said loudly, "I'm too hard—too hard! That's what I am!"

Gilbert asked, "Something's wrong, isn't it?"

"Yes!" Fuller turned the cup over in his hands nervously, then looked up and said, "It's Mrs. Bradford."

"She's worse?"

"Every day she slips a little deeper into that black pit that's swallowing her up. I told Bradford not to go on that expedition!"

"Doesn't he know how sick she is?"

"He don't know anything but his New World! Blind—blind as a mole!"

"Can't you do anything?"

"You're a smart man, Gilbert Winslow. You know doctors can't do much, even for physical ailments. What can we do about a mind that's dying?"

Gilbert stared at Fuller. "It frightens me, Fuller. I suppose I have as much courage as the average man, but this is—well, it sends cold chills all over me when I look into her eyes."

"Ay, that's the way it strikes all of us."

"Is there nothing that can be done?"

Fuller squinted at Gilbert, nodded slowly, and said, "Stay with her, man. I know it's hard, but she likes you. You and Humility—she seems less likely to go into one of those spells when someone she likes is there."

"All right." Gilbert stood up and gave a long look at the physician. "I'll go see her now."

Fuller mustered a small smile. "Good man!" and there was a warmer light in his brown eyes than Gilbert had seen for some time.

Leaving the galley, Gilbert made his way along the deck slippery with rain, then down the ladder to the first hold. With an effort of will he knocked on the door, and when Dorothy said, "Come in," he entered the small cabin.

She got up and put her hand out, a smile on her face. A wave of relief swept through him as he saw that she was herself—pale and wan, but without the blank expression he had dreaded to find.

"I thought you went with the others," she said. Her hand in his was fragile, like a tiny bird's bones, and her face was hollow and sunken. Only her eyes were alert, and she pulled him toward a chair. "Sit down and put that cover over you. You must be frozen!"

They sat and talked for thirty minutes, mostly of things they had left behind in England. She seemed to have blocked the new life out of her mind, for she spoke only of her garden in Holland, of her friends she had left, of the activities of the Green Gate Church—never of anything in the future.

When the conversation lagged, Gilbert spotted a folio on a shelf and picked it up.

"Ah—Mr. Shakespeare's play, *The Tempest*, have you been reading it?"

"Oh, I don't understand such things," she answered. "Mr. Bradford says that such things are dangerous."

Gilbert scanned the pages, and she watched him. Then she said, "Read some of it, Gilbert."

He paused at the page he was on, looked up, then began to read:

> Our revels now are ended. These our actors,
> As foretold you, were all spirits, and
> Are melted into air, into thin air:
> And, like the baseless fabric of this vision,
> The cloud-capp'd towers, the gorgeous palaces,
> The solemn temples, the great globe itself—
> Yea, all which it inherit—shall dissolve
> And, like this insubstantial pageant faded,
> Leave not a rack behind. We are such stuff
> As dreams are made on, and our little life
> Is rounded with a sleep.

He lifted his eyes, about to comment on the lines, but she said in a weary tone: "That's what I've been feeling, Gilbert."

"What, Dorothy?"

"Why, like the poem says, everything is so frail! The earth is going to dissolve. That's what I've been feeling lately." She gave him a trembling smile, then brushed her hand across her eyes. "It's true, isn't it? Nothing lasts."

Gilbert was trapped, wishing desperately that Carver or Brewster were on hand to handle the question. His own mind was not clear on such things, but he knew he had to give her some encouragement.

"Why, things change, of course," he said. "But when the old things pass, new ones come along. Like your garden in Leyden," he said quickly. "It was beautiful, but you'll have one here, too."

She did not respond, but kept her eyes fixed on the candle that threw a flickering light over the dark room. It seemed to fascinate her, and as she spoke, her speech was slower, slurred as if she were very sleepy.

"But—it's not real. Like the poem says, we are made of stuff like dreams. That's what life is, Gilbert—a dream—like a dream. . . ."

Her voice trailed off, and he saw with a shock that her eyes were fixed and glassy. Taking her arm he gave her a shake, saying loudly, "Dorothy! Life's not like that at all!"

She did not hear, and her hand was limp and lifeless as he took it, cold as ice.

"It's all a dream . . ." she murmured, and then she started singing the song he had heard her sing before. "I'm a lost lamb . . ." and over and over in the darkness she sang the song and said, "It's a dream."

He sat there holding her hand, from time to time saying her name, and the horror of it rived him like a sword. This was not Dorothy sitting beside him, he knew, but something else. Where was the attractive, witty woman who had charmed him in Leyden? What held her in such a fell embrace and left him sitting with an empty shell of a woman? As time dragged on, he fought valiantly, forcing himself to remain when every nerve cried out to flee the dark cabin and the thing that sat beside him.

Finally, the door opened and Humility stood there. She was outlined against the door, her face still and yet moving as she looked into the countenance of her friend. Then she entered and asked, "She's bad, isn't she?"

"Very bad!" Gilbert breathed. He got up, and his hands were trembling.

She looked up at him, and there was some of the old affection in her eyes as she said, "You've been good to stay."

"I wish—!"

She shrugged and sat down, taking Dorothy's thin hand. "I know. It's in God's hands. I'll stay with her now."

He nodded, and the last thing he saw was Humility pulling Dorothy's head against her breast as she would a sick child.

Humility remained with Dorothy in the small cabin for twenty-four hours, and finally dropped, exhausted, into sleep.

Dorothy had slept off and on, but when she awakened and found her hand released and Humility lying on the floor asleep, she lay there for a long time staring at the candle.

The winds were whistling through the sails, and the motion of the boat was hypnotic.

"I'm a poor lost lamb—I'm a poor lost lamb . . ." she breathed softly, then put the cover aside and stood up. The cabin was cold, and she shivered as the air struck her. She leaned forward peering at Humility intently; then a small smile touched her lips and she put a finger on her lips and whispered, "You sleep, Mama—I'll go outside and play with my dolls."

Softly she tiptoed through the cargo hold, carefully avoiding the sleeping forms, and when she got to the ladder leading upward, she giggled with her hand over her mouth. She climbed the stairs and went out on the deck.

The ocean was a beast, rolling from side to side and growling deep, but she did not heed the crashing of the waves against the sides, but made her way quickly to the bow. There she leaned out and stared down at the water that seemed to be alive.

"I'm a little lost lamb . . ." she murmured, and leaned farther to see into the green depths of the great water that licked the sides of the dark hull.

The prow went down sharply, and then rose high in the air, and the sudden movement frightened her. She began to cry, calling out, "Papa! Papa! Where are you, Papa?"

Her thin cries were swallowed up by the roar of the wind, and waves licked higher up on the hull. She turned to go back along the deck, then came to a large box beside the rail.

Carefully she climbed up on top of it, then turned to look over the rail, now up to her knees. The ship seemed to drop, then lurched sideways as she started to step down, and the sudden movement threw her off balance.

Her feet slipped, and she shot over the rail crying once before she reached the freezing water, *Oh, William!* Then she struck the hard green water; darkness enveloped her as she went down, head over heels. The icy coldness seared her lungs, and she opened her mouth to scream, but it filled with salty water. Then she slid into utter darkness, dragged down by the claws of a powerful undercurrent.

The tide rolled her gently toward the deep sea, her skirts wafting slowly, a sea flower, her hands white fingers of coral, her hair fine streaming sea grass.

When the shallop approached the *Mayflower* on Wednesday, the sun shone brightly and the air was milder than it had been for days—almost like a fine fall day.

Gilbert was standing in the bow, his head down, exhausted from the search he had made in the small boat for Dorothy's body. He had driven himself long after Fuller and Humility had said, "It's no use, Gilbert—she's gone."

A shout rang out, "There's the craft!" and a moment later the rail was lined with women looking for their husbands. They waved as the shallop came in, bending on the wind, crying out to the small figures in it.

Nearer and nearer came the craft, until they could be identified: old John Carver, Alden, Edward Winslow, Hopkins, Billington, White, and the rest.

As the boat was made fast and the men started up, Brewster made his way forward, his face a mask. He must be the one to tell Bradford.

Hopkins jumped to the deck, yelling "Arrows!" and began to tell of the Indian attack; then the others piled on deck.

William Bradford was one of the last to mount the ladder, and as the others were shouting and hugging their wives, Brewster took him and drew him beneath the projecting weather-beaten deck of the poop.

Bradford looked quickly at the older man, noting the sorrow in his eye and the silence in the midst of the uproar.

Quickly he said, "Dorothy—she's worse?"

Brewster took a deep breath, then said quietly, "She's gone, Will—our Dorothy's gone to be with the Lord!"

The rawboned, harsh-featured man stood there staring at Brewster, and then without a word he turned and made his way below, going down into the dark recesses of the deck, into the cabin where her things still were, and shut the door. He stumbled about with little half-formed cries, seeking a corner in which to hide, finally falling on his face, grinding his forehead into the rough planking and calling her name again and again.

CHAPTER TWENTY-THREE

"IT WILL BE ALL RIGHT!"

★ ★ ★ ★

"I think we must go to Plymouth Harbor, Captain."

Christopher Jones, looking up in surprise to see William Bradford standing before his desk, did not answer for a moment, so shocked he was at Bradford's appearance. It had been three days since the party came back, and Bradford had kept to his cabin all that time.

There was something pitiful to Jones about the way the minister held his back straighter than usual, but he said only, "I agree, Mr. Bradford. Are your people agreed on settlement at Plymouth Harbor?"

Bradford stared at him, then said quietly, "I will do the agreeing, Captain Jones. Please get underway as soon as is convenient."

Bradford wheeled and marched directly to the lower deck. As he came to the small area used for meetings, a silence fell on the group of men who had been loudly debating the issue of choosing a harbor.

"Well, Mr. Bradford," William Mullins said haltingly, "you've come to help us decide on which harbor we will choose for our permanent settlement." Mullins cast a look around, seeking encouragement from the others, and added, "Some would have us settle at Corn Hill, while others would like—"

"We set sail at once for Plymouth Harbor." The tone of Bradford's voice was no softer than the rocks on the harbor half a mile away; he settled back on his heels, rifled the group with a steady gaze, and said, "We have no choice. Corn Hill has no permanent water supply, and that alone is sufficient reason to eliminate it."

"But we must discuss . . ." Billington raised his voice, but was cut off at once by Bradford.

"Governor Carver has made the decision, and we sail at once."

Every eye turned to the elderly Carver, who suddenly seemed uncomfortable. He twisted this way and that, and finally nodded reluctantly, saying, "Yes, that is what we must do."

Everyone knew instantly that Mr. Carver was incapable of such a radical decision, that William Bradford was the power behind the throne; but none dared challenge the direct stare of the small man standing there like a rock.

Suddenly there was a loud rattle as the anchor chain began to draw, and Bradford said with a nod, "We will begin work on our first building as soon as Captain Jones can drop anchor."

As the group broke up, Edward said to Sam Fuller, "He's changed, Sam."

"Right enough! And for the better, I say!"

"I thought he'd die in that cabin for three days. I don't think he ate a bite."

"He's always been a driving man, but he's got a look in his eye, ain't he, Edward?"

Edward nodded slowly. He stared at the departing Bradford, and said, "He's the one man who can make a plantation in this place, Sam. Too bad it took the loss of his wife to get a fire built in him."

"There's going to be more than Bradford losing their people—and not as far away as all that, either." The heavy face of the doctor reflected the strain that he'd worked under, and he gave a helpless gesture with his hands as he turned and left Winslow alone.

The *Mayflower* weighed anchor and headed for Plymouth. With a stiff breeze blowing from the northwest, Jones slipped between the long sandspits that almost enclosed the harbor. He hauled around to the north, dropping anchor just as dark fell.

The entire company came on deck, ignoring the cold, to stare at the land, their journey's end.

A long arm of sand lay between the ship and the land. In the opposite direction a mile of uneven mud flats stretched from inner water to shore, intersected by many pools. It looked barren, huge, like the earth after the Flood receded and exposed a dying world. But far off lay the solid land, a virgin land of timber, hill, and plain.

"A miracle that we got in," Captain Jones said quietly to William Brewster who stood by him. "Another hour and the wind would have changed again."

"A miracle, Captain?" Brewster said quickly, with a sly gleam in his eye. "I thought you didn't believe in such things."

Jones ducked his head, then raised a hand to scratch his nose. "Well . . ." he finally grinned, "I suppose there are always exceptions."

Then the voice of Coffin giving instructions to the seamen up in the yards came loud and clear: "Drop the mainsail—but reef it for easy flyin'. This is their graveyard, ain't it now? We'll be off in a couple of days and they can start their dyin'!"

Jones opened his mouth to rebuke the man, but Brewster put a restraining hand on his arm. "He's partly right, you know."

"What?"

"Why, the land has only two uses for man—to live on and to bury each other in. And if we do the first according to God's will, why, the other will not be difficult."

The next day was the Sabbath, and once more the saints from Leyden refused to violate it. Many of the crew had come to respect the iron-firm convictions of the settlers, even to admire the way these people lived their faith. "They ain't no Sunday men!" was the way John Parker put it. "Always the same!"

Early on Monday, a party was sent ashore to explore. They probed the wide mouth of a brook which emptied into the bay and found good soil, supporting a thick cover of pine, walnut, beech, ash, birch, hazel, and sassafras. But the ground was too heavily wooded to be cleared quickly. They called on God for direction, and decided to settle on the high ground along the brook in the southern part of the harbor, just behind the huge rock that reached up out of the sea.

That night Mary Allerton, the tailor's wife, was brought to bed and delivered of a son, but he was stillborn.

"God grant we get off this ship before we all die," William Mullins groaned. He was ill, and a dozen others lay prostrate in their bunks. That night Richard Bitteridge of London was sewed into his shroud. He had died on shore at dawn, and braving the wind and rain, they dug a shallow grave for him on the low hill just above the shore. All that day and all the next day the storm continued to beat down on the shivering men ashore, but then the weather improved and on Monday, December 25, work began in earnest.

All able-bodied men went ashore—some to fell timber, some to saw, some to rive, and some to carry. On the north side of the brook, just above the beach, they chose a site and laid the foundations of what they called their Common House. Close by, to house the workers left ashore each night, they threw up a number of temporary shelters, conical huts of branches and turf. Late in the afternoon an Indian alarm had sent all running for their muskets, but nothing came of it.

Captain Jones watched the weary men drag themselves on board. "Not much of a Christmas for them, is it?"

Brewster smiled and tugged at his gray beard. "We don't observe the day, Captain. To us it's just a human invention—a Roman corruption—just a survival from heathen days."

"No special meal, no gifts?"

"Well . . ." Brewster admitted slowly, "We *do* like to have a good meal, a little better than usual. But I suppose we'll have to forego that. We drank the last of our beer some days ago, and the larder is pretty lean."

Jones smiled and excused himself. Later as the settlers were sitting down to a sparse meal with plain water, he appeared with seaman O'Neal behind him carrying a keg, and Davis, a hulking sailor with one arm, carrying a large box.

"Why, Captain Jones!" Carver said in surprise, looking up from his plate. "You've come to join us?"

"If I may. And since I'm unexpected company, I brought a little something to add to the supper."

A hum went up as the seamen set their burdens down, and Jones asked innocently, "I am not familiar with your customs,

Governor. Are you allowed to drink beer?"

"Beer!" Carver beamed, and looking around with pleasure, he nodded rapidly and said, "There's nothing in our doctrine that forbids that!"

"Ah—and nothing against plum cake and these few dainties?"

"Indeed not!" Carver said. He looked on the neat form of Jones and said, "Bless you, Captain Jones!"

"I was afraid you might think I was trying to corrupt you into celebrating Christmas, Mr. Carver," Jones said with a sly smile touching his gray eyes.

Carver gave him a direct look, then said seriously, "No, sir. You are a good man, Captain. We all know that. I would that you were of our faith."

Jones stared at Carver, started to say something, then apparently changed his mind. "That is a rare compliment, and I shall treasure it, Mr. Carver," he said simply.

Humility had found Peter Brown seated beside her at the meal, and for the next week, he found an excuse to talk to her every day. She wrote to her best friend in Leyden, Hope Stewart:

> My dear Hope, there is no way to mail this letter, of course, but one day a ship will come and bring it to your door.
>
> The men started building our houses on December 25, and although the weather was bad the next day, on Wednesday and Thursday, all was clear and the party was back at work.
>
> It was decided to assign unmarried men to each family to save time, so there will only be nineteen houses, the size of the plot adjusted to the size of the family.
>
> Building the houses is very difficult, not at all like at home. A foundation of stone must be laid, then an open frame erected. Trees have to be cut and trimmed to square sections with a broadax, then finished with an adze. Are you impressed with my knowledge? I have been talking a great deal to a young man named Peter Brown, one of the strangers from London. He is not really a carpenter, but has done some work in that line. He is teaching me how to sharpen tools so that I can be of some help.
>
> I can hear you say, "Oh, Humility, what does he look like? Is he handsome? Is he married?" Well, perhaps you would ask that last question *first*! He looks very well, he is not married. I might add, at the risk of being vain, he is the

most eligible bachelor on the ship, and I would be blind if I had not noted the attention he pays to me. But I am not ever going to marry.

I find this hard to write, my dear Hope, but I have no one to talk to here. It is a great sin on my part, but I must confess it, even if just in this letter that may never be seen by any eyes other than mine—I have not been able to forgive Gilbert Winslow for his behavior toward me.

I have prayed and wept and tried to *feel* that I have forgiven him, for has not God said we must forgive if we would be forgiven?

The worst of it is that I hate him not because he planned to betray Mr. Brewster, which was the real evil. No, I must set it down—I hate him because he made me love him—and he did not love me!

Now, it is down, and I look at it, read the words. But Hope, he had done me more wrong than he knows, for I gave him my love—my first love—and when the discovery came that he cared not for me, something happened deep in my soul. I do not know how to say it right, but I know that never will I be able to love a man again!

Peter Brown was satisfied. There had been a drawing for the position of lots, and he had drawn one at the foot of the street, right next to William Brewster and his large household, which included Bradford and others.

He drew Humility down to see it, and she smiled at his excitement.

"It's the best lot of all, Peter," she smiled. "It's very close to the brook, isn't it?"

She listened as he drew in the air with his hands the plan of the house, and he went on to outline how he intended to have his fields and his stock just over a rise to the east. He had been talking rapidly, his eyes bright with excitement, and suddenly he gave her a look, then laughed shortly, his face reddening. He picked up a large stick and broke it in two. Throwing half of it away, he began to trace lines in the hard earth. There was a shyness in him that drew his eyes down, but finally he looked up and said quietly, "You know why I wanted you to see this, Humility?"

She stirred and shook her head, but there was a knowing light in her green eyes. "Why?"

"Because a house without a wife in it is just a pile of sticks."

He threw the stick away and pulled her to her feet, holding on to her shoulders and there was a rough insistence in his voice. "You must know that I've thought about that!"

She said slowly, "I—I've seen your interest, Peter."

He bit his lip, then said quickly, "Is there any hope for me, Humility?"

She did not move, did not stir. Far away there came from the deep woods the cry of a hunting bird, and over the cold air she heard the sound of someone chopping a tree down.

When she did not move, he suddenly pulled her into his arms and kissed her.

She did not resist; indeed, she moved forward to meet him. He was an attractive man, full-blooded and strong. He stirred her in a strange way; whatever Gilbert Winslow had done to her, he had not destroyed or warped that side of her nature.

"Humility!" Brown smiled and nodded his head. "You care for me a little, I know."

"Peter . . . I can't say. . . !" she began, then bit her lip. With a quick shake of her head, she added, "You must not ask me to marry you, Peter."

"Why not?"

"Because I don't think I'll ever marry."

With a laugh, he seized her hand and kissed it. She had shared his kiss, and he had caught a glimpse of the passion that lay beneath her smooth, even ways. "I know—I know," he laughed. "You women have to be courted. I'll ask, and you'll say no. But finally, I'll ask often enough and you'll say yes—maybe just to hush me up."

The two of them were often together, and soon they were firmly linked in the minds of most.

Gilbert heard of it, of course. Alden asked him once, "Did you know Brown is courting Miss Humility?"

The question did queer things to Gilbert. He had noted the pair, but to hear it said made him restless. "No, I didn't know that, John."

"I suppose they'll get married. Won't do for a girl not to get married in this place."

Gilbert had met her later, at the beach. It had been almost dark, and the wind was cold as they encountered each other on a short walk—he coming from the north, she from the south.

They were both looking down at the sand, and were startled when they glanced up. Each waited awkwardly, a silence that comes when two alienated people are forced to speak.

Finally she said, "Your brother got a nice lot. I suppose you'll be staying with him?"

"No, Humility, I'll be going back with Captain Jones to be hanged." Her trivial remark irritated him, and he planted his feet firmly, and looking down on her, added, "That should make you very happy."

"That's—that's not fair!" she cried, and a wave of anger colored her high cheekbones. "I wouldn't want anyone to hang!"

He felt a stab of remorse, but there was a perverse spirit in him that made him declare, "You've not been much of a Christian, have you now?"

She stared at him, and her face grew agitated. "I—I don't know what you mean."

"It sticks out like a sore thumb!" he snapped. Taking her arm in a strong grasp, he said, "You've hated me from the second you found out what I'd done!"

She grew pale in the fading light, and the streak of honesty that ran deep in her surfaced. "Yes! And I always will!" Then tears filled her eyes and she broke his grasp and ran sobbing along the beach, nearly stumbling over the driftwood.

"Nicely done, old boy!" Gilbert nodded. He kicked viciously at a half-submerged log, and the pain gave him a savage sense of delight. He stared at the figure of the sobbing girl fading into the twilight and shook his head.

Why shouldn't she hate me? She can't despise me any more than I despise myself!

He slept on the shore that night, walking the beach, and the chilling wind was a match for his spirit.

By January 3, New Plymouth was beginning to take shape, but the progress was slow. Fieldstone had to be gathered for fireplace and hearth, two-inch planks had to be sawed for walls, and the joints and cracks had to be daubed with clay.

One of the most difficult and time-consuming tasks was thatching the roofs. They were made as they had been for generations in England, but thatch was hard to come by in Plymouth. It meant miles of tramping through the meadows and along the creek banks to gather it, with the constant possibility of being cut off by a surprise Indian attack.

"Have you seen the columns of smoke over to the west, Miles?" Gilbert asked one morning.

"I'm taking a small party out this morning to have a look. Come along, will you, Gilbert?" Standish asked.

Sick of the grinding labor, Gilbert readily agreed, and an hour later Standish took four men on a scouting expedition. They stumbled onto a few abandoned Indian huts, but saw no fresh signs. Gilbert shot a fish hawk, and they stopped long enough to cook and devour it.

"Not bad," Standish said. He licked his fingers, adding, "Once in Spain we had nothing to eat but an owl for six of us. Made a pretty fair soup."

Gilbert grinned, tearing at the tough meat with his strong white teeth. "You soldiers are a rude bunch. You'd eat anything." He got up, wiped his hands on his shirt, and asked, "You think we'll be attacked sooner or later, Miles?"

"Probably."

Gilbert grinned at the stolid pessimism of the soldier; then a sober light crossed his face. "I suppose Jones will be taking the ship back to England soon."

Standish was whittling a toothpick out of a twig, and he finished it carefully, then began probing his teeth before he gave the younger man a sharp glance, saying, "You going back with him?"

"What choice do I have?"

Standish waved his hand in a wide circle and shook his head. "There's a million square miles in this land. Our royal sovereign King James may be an idiot in many ways, but even *he* has enough sense to realize a man couldn't be caught by ten regiments if he wants to hide out."

"You mean go native?"

"There are worse things, old boy—hanging is one of them."

Gilbert stood up, stared out at the rugged woods that rose up to the west, then shrugged. "Get mighty lonesome out there."

"Take a woman with you," Standish grinned.

"Oh, yes. Why didn't I think of that?" Gilbert answered cynically. "There'd be a long waiting line, wouldn't there, Miles—women just dying to go into the wilds of America with a fugitive. Have to beat them off with a stick!"

"Don't know about a line, but all you need is one." Standish studied Gilbert intently. He had a real affection for the young man, and finally he said, "You wouldn't have to go native—not altogether. We're a long way from the King's justice out here, Gilbert—a long way." The dark eyes of Standish grew thoughtful, and he mused on an idea that had been forming in his mind for some time.

"This land—America—it's not going to be like people think. Everybody seems to think that it'll be another little colony that the King can put in his pocket. But it won't."

"Why not?"

"It's too big, too far away from England; and the wrong kind of people are coming here." He threw the toothpick away, stood up and stretched hugely. "By the *wrong* kind of people, I mean the wrong kind who won't rest easy under authority. Look at this bunch, these saints. Why, they left England to get away from having their necks stepped on by royal authority. You think they'll be more humble now that they're thousands of miles from that authority? No! There's something in the air of this place, Gilbert, something that makes a man feel—oh, I don't know! Bigger, I guess."

Gilbert had been watching Standish curiously, for something of the things the little soldier was trying to say had been in his thoughts. Finally he said, "In most of that, I'd say you were right, Miles—but I can't see running away into the woods."

"That's what I'd do if I were in your shoes," Standish shrugged. "Get that Cooper girl and go build her cabin. Raise a bunch of kids."

"Not her. She's looking at Brown."

"Is she now? Well, women are pretty much alike, boy, so just pick another. That Desire Minter, now, she's after anything in pants."

Standish got to his feet, called the other men from the woods where they were looking for signs, and as they came, he said,

"Think on it, Gilbert. This won't be the last colony. You can change your name and start a new life." In a rare gesture of affection, he threw his arm around Gilbert, having to reach high to do so, and said, "I've not got so many friends, boy, that I can spare you for the gallows!"

As they made their way back to the settlement, the words of Standish kept coming back to Gilbert's mind.

He was still turning it over when they got back to the settlement. "Something's happened," Standish said.

A crowd was milling around the beach, and when they got there, Bradford met them with a tense look on his long face. "Did you see anything of Brown and Goodman?"

"No," Standish said. "Haven't they come back?"

The two men had left on a thatch-gathering trip the day before, and had not returned before dark. "Have you looked for them?" Standish demanded.

"Only in places close by," Bradford admitted. "All the thatch close by has already been pulled. They were going over toward those hills."

"That's where we've seen smoke the last few days, Miles," Gilbert said.

"Well, we'll have to search for them." He looked up at the lead-gray sky and grimaced, "Too late to do anything today. I'll take five men out at dawn."

That night the snow that had been lurking in the biting air began to sift out of the sky. By dawn it lay in strips of white on the ground and capped the treetops. Standish led the party out, and they circled through the woods all day, returning at dusk with no sight of the pair.

"We'll try more to the north tomorrow," he said. "But it'll be fool's luck if we run on to them."

"You think the Indians may have taken them?" Humility asked. She had stayed overnight to help with the work, and she fed the scouting party, filling their plates with a stew made from herring Tink and John Alden had caught that day. When she gave Gilbert his plate, she kept her face averted and did not speak.

"I hope they're just lost," Standish said. "That's not hard to do in this place."

On Saturday at midday, Brown and Goodman came stumbling into camp, almost too weak to walk. Humility saw them first, staggering out of a clump of pines to the west of the camp, and she cried out, "Peter!" and flew to meet them.

Brown was half-carrying Goodman, and when he saw Humility running toward him, he stopped, put Goodman on the snow, and waited for her.

"Peter!" she cried and grabbed at his arms. His face was raw with the cold and exposure, and his hands were blue and stiff. "I've been half crazy!" she exclaimed.

His lips, flaked with a coat of thin ice, turned upward into a faint grin, and he whispered in a cracked voice, "Have you now? Then it's all worth it."

She touched his cheek, and then Allerton and Mullins came running up, and there was no time to say anything. Alden and John Howland came, and they picked Goodman up and carried him to one of the huts. Brown waved aside all efforts to help, leaning on Humility. "I think John's feet are frozen—but I'm all right."

As he wolfed down the fish stew, Brown told them what had happened: they'd seen a deer and gone after it, getting lost in the process. Then the snow had come, wiping out all familiar landmarks and they'd wandered around the entire time, wet and miserable. "I think I'll sleep for a week!" he declared.

Humility walked with him to the hut, and at the door he paused and looked down at her. Snow was still falling—just a few flakes, but one of them fell on her cheek and he touched it with a finger. "I thought for a while we wouldn't make it."

"What did you think about then?" she asked seriously.

"Why, I thought about you, of course," he said, surprised that she had to ask. "I thought: 'The worst thing is we'll never have a life together!' That was the worst of it all!"

She was moved by his words, and when he leaned down to kiss her, she lifted her face. It was a good kiss, not demanding, and when he lifted his head he said, "Is it all right, Humility? About us, I mean?"

She did not speak for a moment, and he was afraid she was trying to think of some gentle way to refuse him. But finally, she lifted her face; when she spoke, there was a resignation in her tone, like the turning of a key in a lock.

"It's all right with us, Peter."

His face lit up, then a thought sobered him. He said slowly, "About Winslow—that's over?"

She nodded and said evenly, "Yes, that's over." Then she added, "I was in love with him, Peter. You have a right to know that."

"But no more?"

She turned her face away, looking down gathering darkness toward the beach, then came back to him. "No more, Peter. Whatever I felt for him is gone."

He studied her face, then nodded and said, "We'll have a good life, Humility."

He did not kiss her again, but touched her cheek with his hand, then ducked inside the hut. Humility wheeled, but before going back to her cabin, she looked up into the tiny flakes criss-crossing the sky, and she said intently, as if to convince herself, "It *will* be all right!"

Then she hunched her shoulders against the cold and made her way to her cold bed.

CHAPTER TWENTY-FOUR

THE GENERAL SICKNESS

★ ★ ★ ★

Log: January 14th
    Follows the order of deaths since landing: Edward Thompson, the first to die in the New World; Jasper Moore, James Chilton, Dorothy Bradford, 11th December; Richard Britteridge, 21st December; Degory Priest, 1st January; John Langemore, Christopher Martin, 8th January, Mrs. Martin the following day. Weather continues cold, with snow and ice in abundance. Crew is restless, desiring to return to England while supplies permit. My decision is to remain at least until shelter is completed for all settlers.

"Mr. Winslow . . ."

Gilbert turned to see William Bradford looking up at him from where he sat with his back against one of the huts.

"Yes, Mr. Bradford?" Gilbert went to him at once. Snow was falling in occasional flakes, and Bradford's hair was hoary in the fading light.

"Would you have a moment for me?" Bradford looked frail, and the sickness had drained his strength. "I find myself a little weak . . ."

"Why—of course," Gilbert said. "Can I take you to your hut?"

"That would be most kind of you." Bradford put out a hand and Gilbert helped him to his feet. He led him down the hill toward the hut, and Bradford clung to his arm, almost stumbling over the rough ground. Gilbert suddenly reached around Bradford with his right arm, letting the older man hold to his left, and held him tightly, "Let me be your legs this once, sir," he said gently.

Bradford didn't answer as they moved along, and Gilbert thought he had offended the man's tremendous sense of self-sufficiency, but then he felt the body of Bradford surrender and lean close, accepting help with an uncharacteristic mildness.

When they reached the cabin, Gilbert helped the sick man inside and lowered him onto his bed. He lifted his feet, and Bradford lay back with a sigh. He closed his eyes, but as Gilbert turned to go, he said, "Thank you, Mr. Winslow—or perhaps I can call you by your familiar name—since you've practically carried me like a baby."

A small gleam of humor touched Bradford's dark eyes, and he smiled suddenly, the first Gilbert had seen since they left Holland.

"It's hard for a man like me to accept help," he said.

"You're more accustomed to giving it, Mr. Bradford."

He waved his hand and said, "That's not always a virtue, Gilbert. It can be a form of pride—the sin of Lucifer." He opened his eyes fully, musing almost to himself, "If I would change one word of Holy Scripture, it would be to make the verse read, 'It is more blessed to receive than it is to give.' "

Gilbert thought that over. "Doesn't sound right."

"That's because you're a strong man—and a proud one, like me," Bradford answered at once. There was a calculating look in his eyes not unmixed with kindness as he went on, "I never liked to have things done for me, even when I was a child. I liked to dress myself, cut my own food—all the things that parents do for children, I wanted to do for myself."

"Most children are like that," Gilbert argued. He pulled a chair over and sat down beside Bradford. He'd never liked the man—had despised him, in fact, for the way he'd treated his wife. But there was something in him now that had been lacking, and he wanted to discover what it was.

"When I became a man I should have put away childish things," Bradford quoted. "But the older I got, the more I prided myself on being strong enough to handle anything that came to me—without help."

He drew his knees up suddenly and placed his bony hands on them. They were roughened by the grueling labor of the past days, but they were the hands of an artist, a scholar—long, tapering, sensitive. He raised them to his face, made a pyramid of them, and touched them with his lips. A cloud passed over his eyes, and there was an unsteadiness in his voice as he met Gilbert's gaze and said, "If I had not been so independent, my wife would be alive."

Gilbert felt the force of the simple statement like a blow. He blinked and licked his lips, unable to answer. Bradford had confessed his guilt without apology, direct as a stone.

"You can't know that, Mr. Bradford," he said finally.

"No. We can never know what *would* have been had we taken a different course." Then he looked at Gilbert and forced a smile. "You are not a priest, are you, Gilbert?"

"A priest?"

"It occurs to me that I am making my confession to you like a loyal Catholic. And I could not say this to your brother—or to anyone else in this place. But you and I are much alike, so I burden you with my guilt."

Gilbert suddenly was struck with the incongruity of the thing. He grinned widely at Bradford and said, "No one would ever believe such a thing. You're a saint—I'm the sinner!"

Bradford did not smile. Instead, he put his thin hand on Gilbert's wrist. "There was a time when I cataloged men like that—saint or sinner; heaven or hell. But I was wrong." He sighed deeply. "And what about you, Gilbert?" Bradford continued at last.

"Me?"

"I have it in my mind that you are like the man mentioned in the Scripture—the one who was not far from the kingdom of God."

Gilbert shrugged, but an angry light suddenly smoldered in his blue eyes. The weight of Bradford's gaze became uncomfortable and he said, "I've tried that way—it may be all right for you, but not for me."

Bradford closed his eyes, and then opened them, saying, "You have tried religion, Gilbert. But you have been too strong to try Jesus Christ. You have to be desperate."

Gilbert laughed bitterly. "Desperate! I've killed two men, betrayed my friends—I'm on my way back to England to hang—and you say I'm not *desperate*?"

Bradford stared at him, shook his head, and murmured, "You're too strong, my boy. Tell me the truth; you are thinking that somehow you'll get out of it. That by some means you'll escape and everything will be all right for you, isn't that so?"

Gilbert opened his mouth to deny it, then suddenly realized what Bradford said was true. "Well—I suppose that's so, but . . . !"

"You see? You haven't come to the place where you can ask for help."

Suddenly Gilbert felt stifled in the small hut. He got to his feet, stopping long enough to say, "I'd better help the others, Mr. Bradford." He left, but not before he heard Bradford say, "Run away as hard as you can, Gilbert—the day will come when you'll be caught in a trap with no place to run!"

All that week Gilbert avoided Bradford. The weather cleared and he threw himself into the work with all his strength. Tink was with him every day, and he often had to say, "You're working too hard, Tink."

"Oh, I ain't tired, not a bit!" the boy would say. But he had developed a hacking cough and his cheeks were often tinged with an unnatural red.

On Saturday the 20th of January the Common House was finished, and on the next day the entire company of the *Mayflower* came ashore, as many as possible crowding into the small structure.

The largest building in Plymouth was only about twenty feet square, of wattle and daub construction with a high steep roof. Against one side was a lean-to for tools and supplies.

Gilbert did not go inside, but from the door he had a good view of the congregation—many of them too sick to stand, lying on beds. Humility, he saw, was with the Tilleys, and at her right was Peter Brown. She met his eyes once, and there was an adamant expression on her face, marring its softness. Brown caught the glance and stared at Gilbert intently for a moment, then ignored him.

Bradford looked around, opened his little Bible and began

to read. "Lord, thou hast been our dwelling place in all generations . . ." and as he read the 90th Psalm a hush fell over the congregation. He closed the Bible and began to speak, and there was none of the harsh directness which had been part of his manner in Leyden.

"This is the psalm of Moses, and it is now our psalm. Where is our dwelling place? Is it in Plymouth?" He smiled and lifted his hand toward heaven. "No, the Lord is our dwelling place— for when this Plymouth is no more, when the earth ceases to be, we will not be wanderers, for the Lord is our home."

As Bradford went on, encouraging his flock, Gilbert saw that his hearers were struck by the new humility of his manner. They were not bound to this man as people in England were bound to their ministers, but there was a power in him that held them all. *People believe him*, Gilbert thought. *That's the secret of being a leader.*

The sermon was short, and the boat returned to the *Mayflower* at once. As soon as Captain Jones' feet touched the deck, he sensed something was wrong. Wheeling around, he saw some of the crew advancing. Instantly, he recognized their purpose; he had been expecting it for some time.

"Cap'n Jones, we needs to have a word with you."

"Yes, what is it, Coffin?"

"We've been talking, sir, and what it comes to is—we think it's time to go back home."

"Why, so it is time," he nodded easily. "And I can't say I'll be sorry to leave this shore. Of course, we must wait just a little longer. You wouldn't throw sick people off the ship without a roof, would you, men?"

"And what about food, Captain?" Coffin asked at once.

"You won't starve—I'll see to that!"

Coffin shrugged, and glanced at his followers. "How can you feed us, Captain? There's only so much food to be had, and the longer we stay here the more of it goes to these psalm-singers. Can't deny that, can you?"

Jones forced himself to smile. "Why, I think you've sailed with me long enough to know that I've never let a man starve, Coffin! Just a few more days, and we're off—and here's the best of it—" A thought came to him, and he smiled broadly, winking at the men lined up behind the pilot's lean form, "You'll all be getting a bonus for the time you spend here."

He noted the smiles of the crew, and before Coffin or O'Neal could speak, he closed the matter in his usual dogmatic fashion. "Now, to work with you—and think about what that bonus will buy in England."

Coffin did not try to argue, but Jones knew he had only postponed the matter.

Sooner or later I'll have to keelhaul that man! he thought as he went to his cabin.

The last week in January wore the work force down, some of the workers taking to their beds with what was called the general sickness.

"What *is* this thing, Sam?" Edward Winslow asked in despair.

"It's not *one* thing, I'd say, but half a dozen—scurvy, pneumonia, tuberculosis, bad diet, lack of sanitation—take your pick."

"And not the least is the fact that sick people are working in the worst weather imaginable when they ought to be in bed." Winslow shook his head and added, "But how much worse can it get? Half of us are sick now."

"And some of the crew are pretty bad as well, so Captain Jones tells me," Brewster said.

"That man is a marvel to me," Edward mused. "Many men would have thrust us off on this shore and made for home."

"God's hand was in his choosing," Brewster said simply. "He will be rewarded for his faithfulness to us."

Fuller gave him a heavy glance and shook his massive head. "I been listenin' to some of the crew—Mr. Clark, mostly. He says if Captain Jones don't haul anchor soon, the crew will mutiny."

"No, I can't think they'd do that!" Winslow stated flatly. "They'd hang."

"According to Clark, they'd rather risk hanging as a maybe, than starving as a sure thing," Fuller grunted. He rose heavily to his feet and said, "I'm going to try a new medicine on Rose Standish."

"What is it?" Brewster asked.

"Some red berries that grow in the scrub oaks. Maybe they'll do her some good."

"You mean you're going to give her some medicine, and you don't know what it is!" Brewster was horrified. "Why, Sam, you might kill her."

Fuller stared at him, and said quietly, "She's going to die anyway, William. I'm just doing it to make Captain Standish feel better."

His blunt assertion caught both men off guard. They looked uneasily at each other, then back to Fuller. Winslow asked, "Is it that certain, Sam? There's no hope?"

Fuller dropped his head, then lifted it, and there was a finality in his eyes as he said, "She's lived a week longer than I'd thought, Edward. It will be a blessing."

"Does Standish know?"

"The funny thing is, he doesn't," Fuller mused. He pulled at his bottom lip, and added, "He's such a sharp fellow in so many ways, but he's like a child where she's concerned. I tried to tell him once that it might be well to consider the possibility of losing her—and he just stared at me as if I'd said something he couldn't understand."

"Poor fellow!" Brewster said. "I'll go with you, Samuel. Maybe I can comfort them with a scripture."

Brewster and Fuller made their way to the Common House, and found Miles Standish sitting beside Rose. He asked eagerly, "Did you bring the new medicine, Dr. Fuller?"

"Aye, right here, Captain." Fuller held out a small glass bottle and said, "Can you pull her up long enough to swallow this?"

"Sit up, Rose," Standish whispered, pulling her thin form up. She was semiconscious, and when Fuller ladled some of the medicine into her mouth it ran down her chin and off onto the cover.

"Now that will do you good, Rose," Standish murmured. "You'll be up and around in no time; isn't that right, Dr. Fuller?"

"We must pray much for her, Miles," Samuel Fuller said. "Mr. Brewster came to do that—for both of you." ·

"Why, there's nothing wrong with me!" Standish protested,

but he moved back as Brewster came to kneel beside his wife and began to pray.

When the prayer was over, Brewster turned to Standish and said gently, "She's a godly woman, Captain. I know she's made her peace with God."

"No! I won't have that kind of talk!"

Standish got up and left the room at once, his face pale and there was a madness in his eyes.

Brewster shook his head. "He's not a Christian man, Samuel. It's going to go hard with him when she dies."

"Somebody must be here at all times, William. She could go at any moment."

"I'll see to it."

Brewster got several of the women to stay with the dying woman, and she seemed to improve the next day. Standish went to get some sleep about seven o'clock, for he had not left her side.

It was long after midnight when all three men—Gilbert, Edward, and Standish—awoke instantly when a woman's voice called out, "Mr. Standish!"

Miles leaped out of bed, pulled the door open and found Humility standing there with a lantern. He stared at her, unable to say a word. Finally, she said gently, "You must come now, Mr. Standish. She's going."

"No!" Standish whirled and ran across the room. Putting his forehead on the wall, he rolled his head from side to side, saying, "No! No! No!"

Edward glanced at Gilbert and then went to the soldier. "It's hard, Miles—but you must go!"

Slowly Standish straightened, and when he turned, his face was shattered with fright. He moved like a man in his sleep, and before he reached the door, he turned and said, "Gilbert—will you go with me? I can't bear it alone!"

"Of course—but maybe you'd like one of the elders . . . ?"

"No—you come!"

Edward nodded, and Gilbert took Miles' arm and followed Humility as she went forward holding up the light.

Fuller was inside standing beside Rose, but he moved at

once to come and whisper, "She's not got long, Miles—be quick!"

Standish did not release the grip he had taken on Gilbert's arm, so the younger man was practically forced to advance and kneel with Standish. Humility came forward, her face highlighted by the lantern she held high, and Fuller stepped back into the shadows.

"Rose?" Standish put his hand on the woman's brow, and for a moment Gilbert thought she was dead. But then her eyes opened, and for the first time in days, her mind was clear.

"Miles—" she whispered, and she tried to raise her hand to touch his face.

"Sweetheart mine!" he said, the tears running down his face. He began to shake so violently that Gilbert feared he might fall, but then he caught himself and leaned forward, his lips almost touching her ear. "I love you more than life!"

Rose's face was drawn by her illness, but there was a peace in her countenance. She managed to raise her hand and put it around the neck of her husband, and he fell on her breast.

"Don't leave me, Rosie!" he sobbed.

She smiled and pulled his face up so that she could see his eyes. "I'm so tired, Miles—so very tired."

The light moved and Gilbert looked up to see Humility swaying from side to side. Her eyes were filled and her free hand was held over her mouth to stifle the sobs. She began to fall, and he leaped up, took the lamp and held her upright with his free hand. He dared not move, for the tide was going out for Rose Standish.

"Do you remember the roses you gave me—the first time— we met?" she asked, and the words came harder, "And—what you—told me?"

Standish reached down and pulled her up, holding her with both arms. "Aye! I said it was a shame that the flowers were forced to look so bad—next to your face!"

"And—you said—you loved me!"

"And so I have—so I have!"

Once more she pulled back, and looking right into his face, she whispered, "I—have loved you—always—but now, I—must go—I must go to my Lord."

She tried to touch his face, but suddenly she took one deep breath, then her hand dropped, and her head fell back.

"She's—she's gone, Miles," Fuller said. He came forward and put his heavy hand on the soldier's shoulder, and added, "She's with the Lord God."

Standish remained silent, unmoving, and Gilbert was afraid of his reaction. But carefully lowering Rose to the bed, he folded her hands, leaned over and kissed her, then stood up. His eyes were filled, but there was no panic in his voice as he said, "I never loved another woman in my life!"

Humility suddenly realized that she was being held in Gilbert's embrace, and she pulled away at once, dashing the tears from her eyes. "I'll take care of Rose, Captain Standish," she said.

Gilbert walked outside with Miles and Sam Fuller, and as they stood there looking up, a star broke through the winter sky. "See that?" Standish said quietly. "That's what she was to me— like that point of light in the dark sky." He reached up as if he could touch the star, then added, "Now my sky is dark—not a speck of light in it, Gilbert."

Gilbert Winslow wanted to say something to comfort his friend, but there was nothing in him, for his own sky was dark also.

It got darker when Fuller came to him early at dawn. "The Tinkers—they're all sick."

"Even . . . ?"

Fuller knew how much Gilbert loved Tink, and his face was grave as he nodded and put a hand on Winslow's shoulder.

"He's the worst of all, Gilbert. I fear for him—he's in God's hands!"

And since Gilbert had given up on God, who was there for him to pray to? The skies overhead were blank as he stumbled across the frozen ground to the Tinkers' hut, with not a single star to break the dull arch of the heaven.

CHAPTER TWENTY-FIVE

"Love Is Not Cold!"

★ ★ ★ ★

None of the firstcomers who survived ever forgot the month of February. Whatever visions of a summery Eden remained were drowned by the rain, the sleet and snow, and the keen winds that whipped across the sea to scrape faces raw and cut the lungs with a razor's edge.

No one was ever wholly dry, and the sickness claimed new victims almost daily. There was a fever to get houses built, for the *Mayflower* could leave any day. Indians were never seen, but smoke signals were visible and more than once they came to scream at the settlers in the night.

Death became such a common visitor that the first morning thought of Fuller was, *Who will lie dead in their beds this morning?* Rose Standish's death surprised no one but her husband, and there was great grief at her funeral and afterward concern for her husband. But as soul after soul slipped off into death, it became a ritual that had lost its primeval power.

"They go different," Edward remarked to Gilbert as they were digging the graves for Edward Fuller and his wife Ann. "There was Christopher Martin, like a bull roaring and thrashing—but he had to go. And the Fullers, why they slipped away so quiet! No final words to anyone."

Gilbert paused to rest, and looking across the open field to the row of half-finished huts, he shook his head. "How many died this month?"

"Five already this month."

"That makes twenty dead in all. That means there's fewer than twenty men and boys to stand guard, build houses, trade, and hunt food."

"Standish said that we must bury the next one at night."

"Why?"

"He doesn't want the savages to know how few we are."

Gilbert smiled grimly. "They must know that already." He struck the frozen earth a blow with his mattock, "I've been surprised at how Miles has taken his loss." Standish had joined with John Bradford to become one of the most indefatigable nurses, working all day and ministering to the sick most of the night.

Edward arched his aching back, measured the depth of the grave and said, "Miles is different. He's a pretty hard fellow— never came up against something he couldn't handle with a musket until Rose died. I think he'll not be able to get away from her going."

"You mean he might become a Christian just to get to be with Rose?" Gilbert asked. "I always hated that sort of thing!"

Edward paused, looked across at Gilbert, then smiled. "I know that. But I've come to think that even a poor motive for serving God can turn out well. In Miles' case, he'll be thinking at first, *I've got to be a Christian if I'm ever to see Rose again*, but if he keeps at it, sooner or later he'll develop more than that."

"Develop what, Edward?"

"Why, a desire to see more than Rose. He'll want to see God."

Such talk made Gilbert uncomfortable, and he asked, "Isn't this deep enough?"

"Ought to do. Let's get back." Edward paused. "I'm taking Elizabeth to the ship today. It's warmer there, and there's more room in the cabin."

"Can I help?"

Edward shook his head. "No. I know you don't like to leave the boy alone too much." A thought struck him, and he added, "You might bring him on board. He might have more chance there—and his parents won't object."

Gilbert added bitterly, "No, they wouldn't care." He thought it over, and before they got to the settlement, he had made up his mind. "I think it might be good for him to be there. When are you taking Elizabeth?"

"Right away. Alden and Ellis are taking us in the shallop."

"I'll get Tink and we'll go with you."

He went straight to the Tinkers' house and knocked on the door. Thomas Tinker, a thin man with watery blue eyes and a scraggly beard, opened the door. "Wot is it, Winslow? You want to see the boy again?"

Both Tinker and his wife had recovered from the sickness, at least enough to get around. Neither of them had been strong to begin with, and the rigors of the voyage and the sickness had weakened them more.

"I'd like to take him to the ship, if you agree," Gilbert said. "It would be easier to take care of him there."

Tinker rubbed his chin with a dirty hand, and turned round to stare at the small form of Tink on the cot. He shrugged and said, "Might as well."

Gilbert at once stepped inside, and bent to pick the boy up. Tink was awake and gave him a small smile. "Well, Tink, you think you could stand a move?"

"Where to, Mr. Winslow?"

Gilbert wrapped him in an extra blanket against the cold and picked him up. "To the ship for a little while. Say goodbye to your parents."

Tink looked over at the man and the woman who were watching without much interest. "Goodbye," he said quietly.

"Mind your manners, boy, you hear me?" Mr. Tinker threatened, then lay back on his bed.

Tink had never been large, but he seemed to weigh nothing now. His eyes seemed large in his face and there was a red spot in the center of each pale cheek. As the cold wind hit his lungs, the racking cough that had plagued him began, and Gilbert pulled the blanket over his face, saying, "You just stay under there for a bit, Tink. And when we get to the ship, I'll bet we can get cook to fix you up something nice and hot!"

Edward met him, holding Elizabeth in his arms, and they

walked down to the harbor together. Alden, Ellis, and two of the other men were at the oars of the shallop, and they rowed them to the ship, helping them up the ladder with their burdens.

The first hold, which had been packed to the bulkheads, seemed empty now. "The Mullins have the cabin next to ours," Edward said. "But the small one the Hopkins had is vacant. Why don't you put the boy in there?"

Fuller came out of one of the cabins and looked up, surprised to see them. Then he nodded and said, "I'm glad you brought her here, Edward. Who's this we have?" he asked. Lifting the blanket, he peered at Tink and smiled. "Well, now, here's my fine young helper! I shouldn't wonder but what you're up and about soon, eh?"

As soon as they got the patients into bed, Gilbert pulled Fuller off to one side. "Edward and I will have to work during the day, but we'll stay with them at night."

Fuller shrugged his burly shoulders. "Some of us will be here. Mrs. White will have her baby any time now, so I'll not stray far. The Mullins are both low, so Priscilla will be here—and some of the other women. I'll see he's not forsaken."

"Has Captain Jones said when he's leaving?"

Fuller stared at him, then shook his heavy head. "No, and I thank God for that! Half his crew is down now, and the other half is on the verge of mutiny. Think what it would be if all these sick people were dumped ashore right now!"

Gilbert nodded, and left to go see Hinge. He passed through the forecastle, filled mostly with seamen, sick on their bunks and poorly cared for. One of them, a sailor named French, lifted a thin hand and whispered feebly, "Mr. Winslow—a drink of water!"

Gilbert went to him at once, and was shocked at his appearance. He had been a muscular fellow with bright black eyes, but now he was a skeleton with cloudy eyes sunk in deep cavernous sockets.

"Why, French, I'm sorry to see you like this!" He picked up a pewter pitcher, saw it was empty and said, "I'll fetch you some water right away."

He went directly to the galley and got the little gnome of a cook to warm some broth for Tink, and added, "French wants some water."

Hinge nodded at a water barrel, and said, "It's a shame the way there ain't nobody to take care o' them chaps." He stirred something into a black pot, and added, "One of 'em died last night, went out cursin' his mates, but they didn't not a one of 'em stay with the poor chap when he went out!"

Gilbert filled the pitcher with fresh water and made his way back to French. "Here we are—let me help you sit up." The man had not been cared for in any way, and the stench from his soiled clothing and filthy blanket struck Gilbert like a blow. He forced himself to smile, however, and the poor fellow gripped the glass, drinking in noisy gulps.

"Thankee! Thankee, Mr. Winslow!" he gasped as he lay down.

Gilbert looked around the room, taking in the six other seamen who were lying in the room, some in hammocks some in bunks. "You're in poor shape here, French," he said. "Who takes care of you?"

"Why, nobody. Them as can takes care of themselves. 'Course, Mr. Fuller he come by yesterday, I think it was. But he's mighty busy with his own sick folks." A sadness rose in the haunted eye of French, and he mumbled, "We already lost five men—and I reckon as how I won't be here long."

Gilbert forced himself to smile and speak heartily, "Now, that's not like you, French. Cheer up! I'll see if something can't be done for you. A little care and you'll be fine!"

"You think so, Mr. Winslow?" The little encouragement brought tears to French's eyes, and he turned his face to the bulkhead, mumbling, "Thankee!"

Gilbert went at once to the Great Cabin. Finding Captain Jones inside, he said directly, "Captain, your sick seamen are not being cared for."

Jones put down the pen he was writing with and stared at Gilbert, his eyes frosty. "Are you telling me I'm remiss in my duty, Mr. Winslow?"

"I didn't say that; you're a busy man, but the men are in bad shape."

Jones got up and went to stare out the window. He said suddenly, "I know it—but there's no way I can force the men to take care of them."

"I can do a little, with your permission."

"Certainly you have it," Jones said at once. Then he came back and sat down in his chair. He toyed with a compass, then looked up with a strange expression in his eye. "You may have an opportunity to be a nurse to them on the way back to England."

"You still intend to take me back with you?"

"I don't know!" Jones leaned back, and suddenly there was a light of humor in his gray eyes. "I don't know anything that a captain of a vessel should know. I don't know why I've stayed in this frozen land so long; don't know why I've given our food and beer to a bunch of fanatics. Don't know why I'm having trouble making up my mind about you." He grinned and summed up: "Don't know much do I?"

Gilbert met his smile, and said, "Let me know when you decide if I'm going back to hang or not. In the meanwhile, I'll see what I can do for the men."

He went back to the galley, got the broth from Hinge, and carried it to Tink. He spooned it down, and the warm food along with the clean warm blankets made the boy so sleepy he dropped off at once in a natural sleep.

Gilbert heard Fuller's voice rumbling in the Mullins' cabin and waited until he came out. "How are they?" he asked.

"Bad!" The stark answer came out sharply, and Fuller shook his head. "Don't expect them to make it. How's the boy?"

"Like for you to keep him under your eye. He's sleeping now."

"The young ones are standing it better than the older people."

Gilbert thought about that, then nodded, turned to go, then paused. "Those sailors are in poor shape, aren't they? French said you were in to see them."

"They'd be better off if the well ones would look after the sick—but they won't do it."

Gilbert gnawed his lip, considering the matter. He hated sickness, and except for Tink, had spent as little time as possible with sick people. He wanted to let it drop, but then thought of Miles Standish and the way he had done the most menial sickroom tasks since Rose's death.

"Well, I thought I'd try to do a little for them, Fuller."

The doctor stared at him; then turning his head to one side he remarked, "Never would have taken you for such a thing."

Defensively Gilbert hastened to add, "I'll be working days, but I've got the rest of today and after I get through on shore. I'll be sleeping here anyway to be near the boy. Guess it'll not kill me to give the poor chaps a hand."

"All right. I'll see to it you get some supplies and a little help."

Two hours later Gilbert was exhausted. *Why, this is worse than digging graves!* he thought as he went around the forecastle picking up the filthy clothes and blankets on the beds, emptied the chamber pots, put fresh water in the pitchers, and tried to say a word of cheer to each of them.

While he had been busy with this, Coffin and another seaman had trooped through on their way to the galley. Taking in what Gilbert was doing, Coffin said loudly, "Well, we got us one of the holy ones here today, ain't we now?"

French raised himself up on an elbow, stared with angry eyes at the pilot, and said, "You let us lie here like dogs, Coffin! Shut your foul mouth!"

Coffin cursed and moved toward French, but Gilbert moved one step, placing himself between the two. Coffin's hand dropped to the dirk in his belt, but when Gilbert merely smiled at him, he cursed and led the other sailor out of the forecastle.

As Gilbert stooped to pick up some of the soiled blankets, a sailor named Pike raised his voice. "We all thanks you, Mr. Winslow—'deed we do. You're a real Christian!"

The others were echoing Pike's sentiment when Gilbert heard the door open behind his back. Expecting Fuller, he was taken off guard when he turned to find Humility standing there.

"Mr. Fuller sent me to help," she said quietly. Their eyes met, and something stirred in him at the sight of her. The weather had roughened her skin, but the sea-green eyes were still bright and her figure erect as a soldier. He felt a loss, for a wall had sprung up between them. Suddenly he thought back to the time they had stood on the small bridge that arched the canal in Leyden, staring down at the ripples in the water, talking about love.

"Why, that's good of you," he said hastily. Then he looked down at the soiled blanket, aware that he had absorbed some of the rank smells of the sick men, and he was embarrassed. "I—I guess I'll take these blankets to be washed."

"I'll help you." She picked up the rest of the clothes and blankets, then smiled at the men. "Cook is making you something tasty, and the captain says you're all to have something special to drink for supper. I'll be back with it soon."

She turned and Gilbert followed her up on deck. "Just put those things here; I'll take them to shore tomorrow and see they're washed in fresh water."

"They're pretty filthy." He looked down at himself, and added, "So am I, for that matter."

She looked at him squarely, and there was a determined set to her jaw. Leaning back against the rail, she said, "I'm marrying Peter Brown."

"I see." He stood there waiting, for he knew she had taken this opportunity to tell him. The ship lifted and fell gently, and there was a salty tang in the wintry air. A lantern hanging on the mainmast cast flickering gleams over the deck, and her face looked like an Indian mask—planed down to simple carves and hollows.

"You love him?" he asked finally. He did not miss the quick response that swept her face—not disgust, but distrust that hardened the soft green eyes.

"I respect him; he's a good man."

"You could say that of Mr. Brewster or Mr. Bradford, I dare say. Is that enough for you—respect?"

"It's better than what I got from you!" she cried out, and despite her intention to keep her emotions under control, anger raced through her as she faced him. "I got *love* from you, didn't I? Kisses and promises that made my head swim! Oh, what a fool I was!"

He bowed his head, taking the force of her wrath as he would submit to a rightful judgment. But he could not let it all go.

"All right, I was wrong—I've admitted that. But I want to tell you two things, Miss Humility Cooper."

"What could you tell me that I would possibly want to hear?"

"When I first met you, it was all a hoax. All I wanted to do was to use you." He paused and their eyes locked, and he said intently, "But later on, after I got to know you—it wasn't all pretense."

She laughed harshly, then said mockingly, "Oh, don't tell me that you really fell in love with me! I'm not as gullible as I was then, Gilbert!"

He shrugged and said, "All right, think what you will, but I'm telling you the truth. The other thing, Humility, is that even if I am the world's greatest hypocrite and liar, that's no excuse for you to run away from love."

"You don't know what love is!"

"I know one thing—love is not cold!"

A streak of anger ran through him, and he caught her wrist as she turned to leave. "You can't bear to hear the truth, can you? But you're going to hear it this once!"

"Let me go!"

He ignored her struggles and taking her other arm, held her fast. "Rogue I am and will probably always be, Humility—liar, traitor, manslayer! But I tell you this one thing, when I kissed you on that bridge, it was not treason! It was the beginning of something I'd never known. I'd kissed other women, some as beautiful as you, but there's something in you that held me!" He forced himself to speak quietly, but there was an intensity in his blue eyes that held her fixed in his grasp.

"You are a woman of God," he continued. "But you are flesh and blood, as you found out when I kissed you. Can you deny it?"

She whispered, "You taunt me with that?"

"No! You were honest then—but you are not now."

"I am!"

He shook her like a reed and said passionately, "You are *not*! How can you be honest and marry a man you don't love? Marriage is not spirit; it's flesh and blood, Humility! And you were more honest then than now."

"It's a lie!" she whispered. "I don't want that sort of thing!"

He suddenly pulled her closer, saying, "You're afraid of love—that's why you're afraid of me right now!"

She braced herself against him, her face pale in the flickering yellow light. Desperately she cried out, "I'm not! I'm not afraid of love—nor of you either!"

He had no hopes, but he had a strong memory of her from the past, fragrant and clear as a flower. He would never have her, but he hated to see her turn into a dry-lipped, sour woman. He pulled her forward until the soft curves of her body pressed against him, and whispered, "Is this what you're afraid of, Humility?" and then he gathered her closer until they made one shadow on the deck.

She uttered one short cry before his lips silenced her, and she beat at his back with her fists, but she might as well have beaten on the huge rock in Plymouth Harbor. Furiously she struggled, kicking at his legs with all her might, but he swung her around and trapped her against the rail so that she could not move.

His lips were hard against hers, and there was no gentleness in him. His muscular arms pulled her even closer and she stopped struggling. Her hands rose involuntarily and rested on his neck, and she was aware of nothing but the pressure of his lips and the warmth of his body against hers.

Then he lifted his head, and whispered, "Never be afraid of what you're feeling right now."

She came to herself with a jerk, and her cheeks flushed as she pushed him away. With a trembling voice she said, "You're stronger than I am—that's all you've proved! You think all you have to do is touch a woman and, no matter who she is, she'll fall in love with you!" She was close to tears, but she bit her lip and made herself say coldly, "I've asked you to leave me alone, and you take advantage of me the first chance you get. Is there no honor in you, Gilbert Winslow?"

He saw that she was locked in, incapable of understanding anything he might say. He nodded once, and said, "Don't marry a man who can't make you angry—or one who can't stir your blood."

"I'm marrying Peter Brown," she said steadily. "Please don't ever make any of your foolish advances to me again!"

"I can promise you that," he said quietly. He stepped back, and she left the deck, walking unsteadily down the ladder to the first hold.

Blindly Humility went to the cabin she shared with Bess Tilley, and for a long time she sat on her bunk, fists clenched tightly together, staring at the wall.

Finally she got up, lit the lantern, and began to add to her letter to Hope Stewart.

February 28, 1621.
Dear Hope,

I cannot tell you how dark the future is for us. Over half our number lies sick, and the rest of us are half dead with fatigue.

Only one thing makes life bearable, at least for me. I have agreed to marry Peter Brown. This will be difficult for you to understand, since only a few weeks ago I expressed my intention never to marry. That was false pride on my part. I see clearly now that marriage is a duty ordained by God. I am only grateful that my earlier delusions about "romance" and "love" have been replaced by a more sensible and mature attitude.

Peter Brown is a good man, and I will make him a good wife. Neither of us expect the "romance" some people put such stock in. Thank God that it's all settled!

A knock at the door interrupted her, and she started up, thrusting the small notebook into a chest and shoving it under the bunk. Opening the door, she saw Sam Fuller, who said at once, "Can you help me, Humility? Susanna's baby is coming."

"Of course." She followed him to Whites' cabin, and for the next four hours they were both very busy.

Edward Winslow was getting ready to go to shore at dawn when Fuller approached, his face lined with fatigue. "Well, the first baby in the New World is here."

"Susanna?" Winslow asked quickly.

"Very well. She had a hard time."

"Sam, would it be all right if I saw her?"

He went quickly to the cabin and entered; Susanna looked up at him with eyes like diamonds. Out of a bundle of white, a tiny black crown stuck out, and he thought he had never seen anything more beautiful than the two of them.

"His name is Peregrin," she smiled.

"An odd name," he murmured softly. Pulling the blanket back, he asked, "What does it mean, Susanna?"

"It means 'pilgrim,' " she said.

"A little pilgrim," he mused, and the tiny fist waved in the air and grasped the tip of his finger. "Peregrin White. That's a fine name—and he's a fine boy. Now Resolved will have a little brother to play with."

"Yes—but no father."

Winslow started and cried out, "Susanna, no!"

"You didn't know?" she said. In a gesture old as the world, she held the baby to her breast and kissed his head. "He and Mr. Mullins went together yesterday."

Death had become so common that the chilling shock should have passed, but Winslow's mind was numb. "Both of them gone! I—I can't grasp it!"

Susanna rocked the child slightly, and he began to cry feebly. "He hated to go before the baby came—but he knew it was time, and he endured his going better than anyone I've ever known."

"He was a good man, Susanna—no, he was a noble man! Great courage!"

She nodded. "I think he knew he'd never stand this trip—but he wanted the little ones—and me, to have a better chance."

He rose and stood over her for one moment. "I must catch the longboat." He leaned down and touched the tiny crop of hair in a gentle caress. "Peregrin, may you be as good a man as your father and a blessing to your good mother!"

Then he nodded and left her. She stared at the door, listening to his footfalls, then looked at the child. As he began to cry, she smiled a secret smile, and fell asleep.

CHAPTER TWENTY-SIX

MIRACLES ARE TROUBLESOME

★ ★ ★ ★

February was Plymouth's worst month. Seventeen of their number perished, and work came to a complete standstill. The weather continued to be miserably cold and rainy. Gilbert had worn himself to a fine edge, working in all kinds of weather during the day and caring for the sick of the *Mayflower's* crew and for Tink through the nights.

He had finished his chores one night and gone to the galley to see if there was anything to eat. To his surprise he found Captain Jones and Samuel Fuller sitting before the small fire talking.

"Come in, Winslow," Jones said. He took a heavy pot and scooped some of its contents into a bowl. "Have a little of this warm soup."

"That would go down well," Gilbert said wearily.

Jones turned to Gilbert, considered him with a direct glance, then said, "You've been a great help, Winslow, with the sick men."

Gilbert answered, "I think French will make it now."

"How's the boy?"

Gloomily Gilbert said, "No better. Would you have a look at him before you go to bed, Fuller? I couldn't get him to eat much."

"The boy's parents died last week, didn't they?" Fuller

asked, getting to his feet. "Maybe he's grieving for them."

"Perhaps. But he's had that fever for so long!"

"I know. I'd bleed him, but he's so weak already," Fuller said. He left the galley, saying, "I'll look in on him."

The two sat there, not speaking for some time. Winslow was an enigma to the captain. He had failed completely to find an answer to his problem: what to do with him when the ship left.

Jones got up, stretched and then gave Gilbert a long look. "Been expecting you to make a run for it, Winslow. Hide out in the woods until after the ship left."

"Thought about it."

"But you haven't gone." The fact brought perplexed lines across Jones's forehead, and then he slapped his leg and said, "This is a rough crew; it wouldn't be hard for the mutineers to take over and sail the ship back to England themselves."

"What about you?"

"Maybe washed overboard in a storm. Maybe just put ashore. They'd be long vanished by the time I could file a report against 'em."

Gilbert asked suddenly, "Why haven't you left, Jones? You're not getting rich sitting here in this harbor."

"Scratch me if I can say!" Christopher Jones exploded, and there was a strange mixture of wonder and anger in his gray eyes. "I think I must be getting old!"

Gilbert smiled wryly, humor lurking in his face. "I think you're getting religion, Captain."

"No, it's worse than that, Winslow," Jones said shaking his head. "I've had religion for a long time. What I may be coming down with is a bad case of whatever fanaticism these people have."

"It can be dangerous to your health." Gilbert got to his feet, started for the door, then paused to look back. "Best be on your guard, Captain Jones. I'd hate to see you lose this ship to Coffin and the rest."

Leaving the captain to stare at the fire, Gilbert trudged wearily down to the cabin. The single candle guttered low in its own pool of wax, stretching his shadow, grotesque and malformed, from deck to ceiling. Fatigue dragged him down; he moved like an old man and his thinking was sluggish. He took a long drink from the waterjug, replaced it, and went to look down at the boy.

Tink was so thin he could see the pulse in his throat, beating irregularly. He put his hand on the boy's forehead. *Burning up! He'll die if that fever doesn't go down!*

Despair ran through him, and he sank down on his bunk, throwing his arms over his face.

Sleep eluded him, and when he dozed he had fitful dreams that flitted across his mind like stones skipping across water. Once he dreamed of a dog he'd had when he was ten—then of his mother, whom he could barely remember. Finally he drifted off into a fitful half sleep, tossing and turning on the narrow bunk.

Gilbert awoke to Tink's coughing spasm. He held the helpless boy in his arms, trying to get a swallow of water down the dry throat, but the racking coughing did not stop until it seemed even a strong heart would burst.

The words of William Bradford came floating into his mind: *"You're not desperate enough to trust God."*

Sitting there in the murky darkness with the dying boy, the hopelessness of his life settled on him like a leaden blanket. He put his head back on the bulkhead and closed his eyes, trying not to think of the future, to block everything out completely, hearing Tink's labored breathing and rasping cough.

He had almost dropped off to sleep when he was awakened by a sound from Tink. He sprang up and was beside him in a heartbeat. The boy's eyes were rolled back in his head, his chest was heaving wildly, and the cabin was filled with a rattle that came from his throat.

Then there was a *clicking* sound and the boy's body went completely limp, the arms and head flopping down nervelessly.

"Tink! Don't die, Tink!" Gilbert cried wildly. He leaped to his feet and holding the motionless boy up high in his arms, he called on God as he never had before.

"O God! Don't let Tink die!—Please!"

The tears streamed down his upturned face, and even as the echoes of his plea died out, he called again, "I love him, Lord God—don't you love him, too?"

He stood there in the murky darkness listening to the echoes of his own voice fade away until there was no sound at all save his own sobbing.

Then something happened.

Gilbert had never been a mystic, never believed in such things. When people had said, "God told me to do this," he had scoffed.

He realized suddenly that his wild fear was gone; his trembling had ceased and the racking sobs had stopped. His breathing slowed and then there was a faint ringing in his ears, like little silver bells far, far away. The cold of the cabin seemed to fade, and he felt warm. His eyes were closed, but he had the sensation of light surrounding him.

Somehow he was aware of words coming together in his mind. At first they were blurred and distorted. Then they began to come together forming a complete thought—but still not his own thought. Of that he was very sure, both then, and for the rest of his life.

Standing there holding Tink, with his mind cut off from fear and the terror of death, the words came before him:

Yes, I love him, and I will give him life. One day you will love me even more than you love this boy. You will love me more than your own life.

The cold and the darkness came back with a rush, when Tink's body twitched suddenly. The boy caught a great gulp of air, then expelled it like a swimmer surfacing after being too long under water.

"Tink!" Gilbert said huskily, and the boy's eyes opened slowly, and then he smiled.

"Hello—Gilbert . . ." he said; then he closed his eyes, and for one dreadful instant the man thought he was gone. Then he saw the boy's even breathing, and put him gently on the bed.

Two hours later, Sam Fuller came in yawning and scratching. "You better eat a good breakfast this morning, Gilbert. It's going to be cold out there. Well, let me have a look at—"

He had stepped beside Tink and bent over to look at the boy's face, placing his hand on the forehead at the same time.

"Bless my soul!" he exclaimed, then turned wildly to Gilbert, he cried, "Look at this, man! It's a miracle!"

Gilbert came to look down at Tink. "He's better, isn't he, Sam?"

"Why, his fever is completely gone—and his breathing is— why, I can't hear a thing in his chest, Gilbert!"

Tink opened his eyes then and saw the two men bending over him. "Hello," he said cheerfully though in a weak voice. Then he licked his lips and said, "I'm awful hungry! Could I have something to eat? And a lot of it, please?"

Fuller gave a burst of roaring laughter and rubbed his hands together with pleasure, "I should say so, my boy! Well, I must be a better doctor than I've been thinking lately, eh, Winslow?"

Gilbert was staring at Tink's face, and he murmured quietly, "I'll get you something right away, Tink." He touched the boy's cheek with his hand, and there was wonder in his blue eyes.

As he walked toward the galley with Fuller, the doctor could not contain himself. He clapped Gilbert on the back and cried, "I told Edward last night the boy couldn't last two days—and now look at him! Good color, clear eyes, and a ravenous appetite! Thank God! We've lost so many I was about to lose my faith, but this boy is a miracle, Winslow!"

Gilbert stopped so suddenly that Fuller stumbled. He put one hand on the rail, then with the most sober look the doctor had ever seen on his face, he said, "I never believed in miracles. But now I've seen one."

Fuller stared at him, then said, "Well, what will it do for you, son?"

Gilbert rubbed his jaw, stared out over the rail at the rolling tide, and then finally said softly, "A miracle, now, can be a pretty troublesome thing, Fuller. Once you've seen one, you can't ever go back to the old ways of thinking."

"Would you want to?" Fuller inquired gently.

Gilbert thought it over for a long moment, then said, "No, if there's something like that in this universe, I wouldn't want to miss it." Then he moved along the deck toward the galley, leaving Fuller to stare at him with open eyes.

"Well, now," the physician said in wonder, "What'll be the end of *that*, I wonder?"

March brought the end of the general sickness—and the Indians.

On March 16, Standish had called a meeting to reorganize the men into a more efficient body when they were interrupted in a most astonishing manner. Armed with bow and arrows, a tall powerful warrior emerged from the wood, crossed the clearing, and came striding down toward the Common House where the meeting was in session. He walked right up to the astonished group, raised his hand in friendly salute, and said in English, "Welcome."

There was a sudden burst of activity, and the men surrounded the Indian, everyone trying to talk at once. Finally Standish shouted, "Silence!" Then while the others listened, he questioned the Indian.

His name, he said, was Samoset. He talked for a long time, answering freely all questions put to him. He was an Algonquin and had spent much time with an English sailor named Captain Dermer, a name they all knew well. He had been sent out by the Council for New England to explore the coast but had not returned when they had sailed from England.

When they asked him about Plymouth, he explained that the place was called Patuxet in his tongue, but that a terrible plague had wiped out the tribe that had planted the corn they had found. He told them the Wampanoags ruled by Massasoit were the most powerful tribe in the area.

Finally he ate a meal of biscuit, butter, cheese and pudding washed down with beer.

There was some disagreement about what to do with him. Billington and others thought he should be held lest he be a spy come to discover their strength, but Bradford demurred, and the next morning, he left, promising to return soon with some of the leaders of the surrounding tribes.

A week passed and Gilbert met Edward as he came in from working on Standish's emplacements. There was such a pallor on his brother's face that Gilbert was alarmed. "Edward, what's wrong?"

"Elizabeth is dying."

Gilbert stood there helpless to say a word; then he put his arm around his brother's shoulder, and walked with him to their little house. Inside they found Fuller, Priscilla, and Humility watching over the dying woman.

Gilbert took a seat on a stool, his back against the wall, while Edward slumped in a chair holding his wife's hand.

Fuller came over and sat down by Gilbert, whispering, "She'll not see another day, I'm afraid."

She died an hour later without awakening. One minute she was laboring for breath, then she coughed once and the breathing stopped.

Edward stood up as Fuller went quickly. He searched for life, and then turned and said softly, "She's gone, Edward."

Edward Winslow stood there, tears in his eyes. For a long time he looked down at the dead face; then he whispered huskily, "I was not a good husband to you, Elizabeth. God forgive me!"

At once Humility, who had been standing with her back to the wall, went to him. She took his arm, turned him to face her, then said, "You were a wonderful husband, Mr. Winslow! You cared for her these last months as no other man in the world would have done! I—I never knew a man could be so loving and kind to a woman!"

She turned her head and looked directly at Gilbert as she ended, then whirled and left the room.

Later that week, Samoset returned with another Indian named Squanto. His story made that of Samoset seem pale and insignificant.

He had been to England with Captain George Weymouth, and returned to Plymouth with Captain John Smith. He spoke better English than Samoset, and informed the men that Massasoit with about sixty of his braves were on their way to Plymouth. None that were there that day ever forgot the sight of the great chief striding out of the woods, wearing about his neck his badge of office, a great chain of white bone beads. His face was dyed a deep mulberry, and he was oiled from head to foot so that his body gleamed in the sun. Behind him came sixty tall, grim-looking warriors, all painted on the face and body, some black, some red, some yellow, some white, decorated with crosses, and some with grotesque loops and squares. A few wore skins. Many were naked. All were tall, muscular men.

Captain Standish and William Brewster met him at the Town Brook with a half dozen musketeers as a guard of honor. They exchanged salutes and marched together down the little main street to an unfinished house. There they had spread a green rug and three or four cushions. The chief and his most important warriors sat on these, and then Governor Carver appeared, preceded by a drum and trumpet. Miles Standish was the stage manager for this performance. He was determined to impress the Indians with all the military pomp and bravado that his handful of soldiers could muster.

All afternoon the business went on, and Tink finally got his fill of watching. "Do we have to stay for all this?" he asked.

"Why, you're seeing history made, Tink!" Gilbert said in amusement. "What would you rather do?"

"Catch a fish!"

Gilbert nodded and said, "Me too, son. Let's let these folks make history while we try our luck at that deep pool by the big elm."

Late that afternoon when they came back with a stringer of fish, the Indians were gone.

"What happened, Miles?" Gilbert asked as he pulled off his shoes and went to bed.

Standish rolled over and gave him a roguish look. "Same thing that always happens at these meetings. We agreed to be nice to them, and they did the same."

Gilbert closed his eyes and asked, "Think it'll work?"

"Certainly—until one side gets a better offer! Not much different here than in the courts of Europe."

Gilbert lifted his head at that, then shook his head. "Think you might be wrong, Miles. These people are different. They'll do what they say."

Standish thought about that, then let his head fall back, as he muttered, "Well—*that* will be a change, won't it now?"

CHAPTER TWENTY-SEVEN

A NEW SERVICE

★   ★   ★   ★

Tink grew better every day, but now that others were getting out of their beds and making rapid recoveries, Gilbert developed a nagging cold accompanied by a dry cough and a ringing in his ears. He said nothing about it, but Edward noted it.

Since the night in Tink's cabin, he'd been quieter, spending his time alone, walking in the woods. He read a great deal from William Brewster's small library—mostly books of sermons and from the Bible. He hadn't told anyone about the experience, but it was impossible for him to forget it; rather, as time went on, the memory of it burned more deeply into his consciousness.

The closest he came to speaking of it was once when he'd been sitting late one night reading, and Edward had sat across from him writing a history of New Plymouth.

His eyes began to burn, and he coughed and put the book down. Edward looked up and said, "You ought to get some rest. You look terrible!"

"I'm all right." Then he leaned forward and stared at his brother, and asked suddenly, "Edward, do you love God?"

"Do I love God? Of course I do!"

"Tell me how it is."

Edward looked confused. He started to speak once, then cleared his throat and thought hard. Finally he said, "Why, man was made to love God. I'd be a heathen if I didn't!"

Gilbert rubbed his eyes, then shook his head. "I don't love Him." He looked across at Edward with a strange expression in his eyes, and said almost to himself, "I love people that I can see and touch and hear. But God is far away and I've got no picture of Him in my mind. It's like trying to love a dim fog."

Edward put his pen down, folded his hands and put them on the table as he considered what Gilbert had said. "You're not the first to have a problem with that. The Scripture says, 'No man hath seen God at any time.' And that's what the gospel is all about, Gilbert. Did you ever hear the word *Emmanuel*? Well, that means literally 'God with us.' And that's what Jesus is—the God who cannot be seen became flesh and dwelt among us."

"And do you love Jesus Christ?" Gilbert asked at once. "You haven't seen Him either."

"In one way I have—or rather, in two." Edward touched the Bible in Gilbert's hand, saying, "In the Gospels we have the picture of the Lord Jesus. As I read about His life—how He went about giving sight to the blind, healing the lame, it soaks into me and I get an impression of Him that way."

"I can understand that," Gilbert nodded. "He isn't like any other man, is He? I mean can you imagine any other human being saying to another, 'I forgive your sins'? And not sins done against Him, either—just sins." He paused then asked, "What's the other thing that makes you love Him?"

Edward shifted uncomfortably, and there was a trace of embarrassment in his eyes. "Well—I don't know exactly how to put it without sounding like some sort of wild-eyed prophet. It's something that some people go into error on quite often." He searched for a way of putting it, then shrugged. "I can only say that in some way I can't explain, since I gave my heart to God, there's been a—a *presence* inside me."

"A presence!" Gilbert's head came up and there was a sharp light in his eyes.

"That sounds fantastic to you, I suppose, but I can't think of any way to explain it."

Gilbert stared across the table, then asked tensely, "Do— have you ever *heard* anything?"

Edward laughed and slapped the table. "Do I hear voices, you're asking! Well, not really, but several times I've had what you might call *impressions*. Thoughts that came from somewhere outside my own mind—and that keep coming back.''

He glanced at his brother, ''Having quite a struggle with God, aren't you, lad?''

Gilbert retreated behind the Bible and nodded, ''Just thinking about things, Edward.''

He never missed the services held in the Common House, and it came to him once as he sat there listening to Bradford preach, how much more real God was in his life than ever before. Always before, God had been something academic, a vague force that had to be acknowledged. But as he listened to the sermons and the day-by-day conversation of the people around him and as he immersed himself in the Scripture, the figure of Jesus Christ loomed ever larger in his thoughts.

One day you will love me with all your heart.

A hundred times a day that flickered through his mind, but he still had not sense of what it all meant.

Two days later he was eating a quick breakfast with Miles and Edward when they heard footsteps approach; then a knock sounded on the door, loud and urgent.

''Come in!'' Edward called, and they looked up to see the door open and Captain Christopher Jones enter.

He had been there often, seeming to enjoy the company of the three men, but now his eyes were burning with anger, his lips white and compressed.

''What's wrong?'' Standish demanded, as all three of them got to their feet.

''The crew's taken the ship,'' he said tightly.

''Mutiny?'' Edward breathed, then shook his head. ''I didn't think they'd dare!''

''They dared, right enough,'' Jones said. ''And they'll get away with it, too!''

''We'll put a stop to this nonsense!'' Standish said angrily. ''Get the men up, Edward—we'll send a boarding party and take that ship!''

Jones shook his head, saying bitterly. ''Not a chance of that, Standish. Coffin is in charge, and he was a gunner in the navy. He's got your cannon in place, and he says he'll blow any craft out of the water that comes near enough.''

Standish stood there, breathless with rage. He blustered and swore, but Edward said, "We must have a meeting at once! When will they leave, Captain? A week or so?"

A bitter light gleamed in Jones's gray eyes. "They weigh anchor at dusk tonight—when the tide rises enough to get them over the shoals."

"Tonight! Why, we'll have to do something right away!" Edward said.

"Nothing to do, Winslow," Captain Jones shrugged. "There's only about fifteen of them, and only about six who are mutinous. But Coffin knows his business. He can navigate and he can do what he says with the gun. They'll be on their way at dusk."

In less than half an hour every man who could walk was crowded into the Common House. Edward asked Captain Jones to repeat his story, which he did, adding only, "It's bad luck, for me—and for you, too. I wish we'd gotten all your tools and supplies off the ship before this happened."

"Why, most of our seed corn is on the ship!" Governor Carver said in a shocked tone.

"And my cannon! How can we defend ourselves without arms?" Miles Standish cried, his face red with anger. "And most of our powder hasn't been moved to the powder house."

Everyone began talking at once, and finally Bradford held up his hand for silence. "We are helpless—but God is not. Let us pray that God will help us as He has done so often in the past. And let us be specific in our prayers. The Savior said, did He not, 'Whatsoever things ye ask believing, ye shall receive'? We are His people and the sheep of His pasture, so let us call upon the Great Shepherd to meet our dire need."

Gilbert was familiar with this method. He had seen it often used in Leyden, and it took one specific form. A need would be voiced, the people would pray, and then after a time of waiting, quite often someone would stand and give a simple message of some sort. Sometimes no one did, but often one of the congregation would give a "word of exhortation" in which the congregation would be encouraged to have faith until God answered.

Expecting something like this from one of the leaders, shock ran along Gilbert's nerves when out of the long silence he heard the voice of William Brewster say clearly, "The Lord will deliver us from this calamity—and He will do so by the hand of Gilbert Winslow!"

A wave of silence filled the room and Gilbert's face flushed as every eye turned toward him. He leaped to his feet.

"I'm not one of your number, Mr. Bradford." He took a deep breath and added so softly that those in the back had to lean forward to catch his words. "I—I am not a man of God like the rest of you."

The silence ran so deep that the sound of a woodpecker far off rang clearly through the room, and Gilbert coughed twice, then lifted his head and stared straight at William Brewster, saying, "You must be mistaken in this instance, sir. I am not a man that God would care to use."

"God longs to use all men, Gilbert!" Brewster nodded, and then he added with a fine smile, "Especially those men who are willing to confess their inadequacy. I ask you plainly, do you have anything to say concerning this trouble we are in?"

Then William Bradford said, "Perhaps this time you are desperate enough, Mr. Winslow."

Suddenly Gilbert raised his head and he said clearly. "I make no claim to being God's agent—but a way of taking the ship has been taking shape in my mind."

A hubbub of voices began, but the voice of Christopher Jones rose above it. "For God's sake, man, out with it!"

A burden lifted from Gilbert's shoulders, and from where she stood, Humility saw his wide lips break into a reckless grin, lightening the gloom that had rested on his face for so long.

"The thing is impossible," he began, "but you of all people should not be put off by that. One thing is clear, they'll watch the shallop like a hawk!"

"That they will!" Jones nodded. He had his attention fixed on Gilbert, and added, "There'll be no using that craft to get on board."

"No, but there's a way to board the ship," Gilbert said.

"How do you propose to get on board?" Bradford asked, his face perplexed.

"The only way there is—swim."

"What!" Jones yelped. "Why that's insane, Winslow! The

ship is half a mile out—and you'd have to circle behind—!"

"It'll be about a mile and a half, Captain," Gilbert said quietly. "I've done that distance and more many a time."

"That he has," Edward said. "But not when you were sick. That water is icy still with the winter's chill."

"Besides, what could you do if you *did* get there?" Standish asked. "You couldn't carry a pistol of any kind in the water."

"I could take my sword."

Something about the way he said the thing—so simply and so quietly—caught at them all. He made a flat high shape outlined against the shadows of the lanterns; there was a tough and resilient vigor all about him, a hard physical power to his body. Discipline lay along the pressed lines of his broad mouth, but a rash and reckless will was in his eyes, struggling against it.

"One sword against a crew of armed men? It makes no sense!" Samuel Fuller lowered his head, staring at Gilbert steadily, doubt in his face.

"Not the whole crew," Gilbert said. "Get to Coffin, and the rest will be easier."

Standish said, "Man, I'd go with you in a second—but I can't swim no more than a nail!"

Gilbert shrugged. "Not too many can, Miles." He looked around the room and asked, "Any of you men think you can make it to the ship?"

"I can."

Peter Brown stepped forward to stand in front of Gilbert. "I grew up on the sea, Winslow. Once I swam three miles to a reef, then back five hours later."

There was a challenge in Brown's face, and Gilbert met it directly. "There'll be a little more to it than a long swim."

"Don't worry about that, Winslow. I'll do my share of the fighting."

William Bradford stepped in to say, "I am not at all certain of this. Captain Standish, you must decide, since this is a military affair."

Miles Standish stared at Gilbert, his eyes stern, and he nodded. "It's the only way, Mr. Bradford. If Mr. Winslow has luck, it could work."

"I dislike the word *luck*," Bradford insisted, "I would much rather he had the favor of the Lord."

"Amen—Amen!" A wave of agreement swept the crowd; then Standish said, "All right, we'll do it, but with one change in your plan. We'll make a run at the ship with loaded muskets and grappling hooks in plain sight. We'll carry all the loaded muskets we can handle and keep up what fire we can. Probably won't hit anything but it'll keep those scoundrels' attention, I'll warrant!"

"What about the cannon?" Jones asked.

"If we keep the bow of the shallop straight, she'll be a mighty small target. They won't be able to get off more than two or three shots."

"But they'll be firing at us with muskets as well," Edward said.

Standish gave him a tight grin. "Yes, Mr. Winslow, that's what happens when men fight in a war. You get shot at—and sometimes you get killed."

Bradford said, "I feel that the thing must be attempted. Mr. Brewster, Governor Carver, do you agree?" Receiving their nods, he turned and went to Gilbert. Putting both his hands on the young man's head in a gesture going far back in history, he blessed him, then turned to Peter Brown and did the same.

"God will be with you," he said softly.

Gilbert looked into the older man's eyes, and there was a peace in his face as he murmured with a tone of wonder, "He already is, Mr. Bradford!"

All day the preparations for the attack kept the men busy. The skies were beginning to turn dark when Gilbert came to look at the shallop. Howland had made, in effect, a shooting platform in the prow of the craft.

Gilbert stepped in to stand on the platform with Standish, and the little captain's face beamed as he picked up one of the muskets from the rack built midway in the shallop. "Look! Just the right height to rest a musket on—and only my head's exposed to their fire!"

"Can't hurt *you* with a shot to your head," Gilbert grinned. "Just so they don't shoot you in the foot, where your brains are."

Standish gave him a wide grin, then, leaning the musket

against the rail, he grew serious.

"It's a wild thing, Gilbert—and your chances are not good. According to Jones those rascals are a pretty tough bunch, and if there's one slip they have you."

Gilbert stared out at the *Mayflower* sitting quietly in the harbor half a mile off. "Miles, one thing I'd like to be sure of—in case I don't make it."

"Name it, boy!"

"Watch out for Tink, will you?"

"Like he was my own son!" Standish said instantly. "Have no fears on that score." He hesitated and then with some difficulty asked, "Have you any fears about what happens if you die?"

Gilbert rested his hand on the upper plank of the barricade, then put his chin on it. A squadron of gulls wheeled by, dipping down to touch the long, low swells of gray water, then with cacophonous screams, rose high in the sky. "I've thought of that, Miles. Most men do before a thing like this, I suppose."

"Always before a battle," Standish agreed.

"I've never had much use for deathbed confessions—seems like a cheap way for a man to act. Live like the devil, then when death comes, go whining to God making promises to be good." He lifted his head, turned to face Standish and there was no strain in his wedge-shaped face. His eyes were steady and his broad lips were half smiling. When he spoke his husky voice was even, as if he were talking about fishing instead of his own death.

"I've not given God much thought, Miles—but these people have forced me to it. You know, I'd always thought that getting into heaven was a matter of accounting. I'd stand before some angel, and he'd put all my good deeds in one arm of the balance and all my sins in the other—then if the good weighed a pound or so more than the bad, why, I was all right."

Standish nodded. "Aye, I've thought about the same most of my life."

"It's not like that, Miles," Gilbert said soberly. "I'm not sure about many things, but I have learned this from Brewster and Bradford: getting to heaven is tied up with where you stand with Jesus Christ—and right now all I can say, I guess, is that I'm looking for Him."

"From what I get from the preaching of these men," Standish said, "I think Christ is looking for you—even more than you're looking for Him."

Gilbert nodded, then said, "God be with you when you make the attack, Miles."

"And with you, boy!" Awkwardly Standish threw his arm around the taller man, gave him a fierce hug, then wheeled and leaped out of the boat, embarrassed by his own action.

Gilbert grinned, then saw Brown standing by watching. "Ready?" he asked.

"Yes." The young man's face was pale, and he was holding a sword and a sheathed knife in his hands, looking at them strangely.

"I've been thinking about a way to carry our weapons, Peter," Gilbert said. He took the sword and measured it carefully with his eyes. "Can't carry the swords as we normally would— too much in the way for swimming. I think we can make some sort of harness out of thin strips of leather. Tie them around the neck so that the blade is out of the way on our backs."

"Yes, I think that might work," Brown said.

"I've got some leather in the hut. I'll run up and get it. We'll need to start in ten minutes."

He turned and ran up the hill, and after a short search he found several strips of leather. Picking up his sword and a dagger and a couple of sheaths, he left the hut and turned toward the sea.

"Gilbert!"

Humility had appeared from higher up the hill, and she came to stand stiffly before him. Her hands were long and slender and supple as she held a piece of cloth. A feeble slanting beam of sunlight reached through the clouds to accent the yellow luster in her hair; and that rich color deepened the ivory tints of her skin.

"I—I wanted to speak to you," she said, and color touched her cheeks as she stood before him. "There's been a wrong feeling in my spirit about you, Gilbert." The words came hard, but she kept her back straight, and her eyes fixed on his. "I've hated you for what you did—but I ask you to forgive me for that. Will you?"

"Of course!"

"Thank you." She put out her hand and he took it in his own. "I can't lie to you. I never could, could I? You know I loved you."

He nodded and started to speak, but she took her hand back and said quickly, "No, don't say anything. I don't know why you're doing this thing—risking your life, but I do know that you're not what I thought. You're honest. But we can never be more than friends."

"Humility—!"

"Peter is a reliable man. You're like the wind, Gilbert—wild and exciting, but I'd never know what to expect. That's important to me, you know."

He looked at her, then said soberly, "I know you think that." He searched her face carefully, then shook his head, saying, "You're wrong, Humility! You're more of a woman than you know—but I guess you'll never find that out."

"Why do you *say* things like that!" she cried, clenching her fists.

"Sorry." He glanced up toward the sky, then back to her. "I must go. Goodbye, then."

He turned and ran down toward the beach. If he had turned he would have seen her drop the cloth and throw her arms up in a strange manner—then put her hands over her face and retreat back up the street with her shoulders shaking as she went blindly along.

"You'd best be on the way," Standish said as he returned. "By the time you get out there, it'll be almost dark."

"All right. Here's the leather, Peter." He fashioned a simple harness for Brown's sword that allowed freedom of action and kept the blade resting on his back. "That ought to do." He made another for himself and Brown helped him settle the sword into position. "This will do for the knives." They belted the knives about their waists and then were ready.

"God be with you!" Standish cried as the two men left, running quickly up the beach.

"This will do," Gilbert said. He kicked off his shoes and Brown did the same, then they stripped out of their breeches. Wearing only undergarments and their weapons, they ran together and plunged into the sea.

The cold water hit Gilbert like a knife, taking his breath for a moment, but he forged ahead with long, slow strokes. The sea was calm inside the reef, but he could see that the water was choppy farther out. *Make it harder for them to see us*, he thought.

They passed the reef and the water became rougher, slapping at their faces and lifting them high, then dropping them down in the troughs.

After fifteen minutes he turned to float on his back, calling out, "Are you all right?"

Brown gave him a wide-eyed look and yelled back, "Yes—how about you?"

"Cold—but not too tired. Can you see the ship?"

Brown looked over his shoulder, peered into the falling gloom. "No, I can't."

Gilbert had excellent eyesight; he looked south and said, "She's right over there. We can bear south now."

They made the swim without another pause, Gilbert fearing that they'd cut it too fine. *Got to be in position when Miles attacks— if I know him, he won't stop until he rams the ship and tries to board her. Got to be on deck by then—they'd cut our men to pieces as they try to board!*

Brown got confused and finally dropped behind, but he was swimming strongly. Gilbert stayed less than two hundred yards north of the ship, then swung south and finally pulled up. Lying on his back and gasping for breath, he said, "I'm about done! How about you?"

"I—I'm pretty tired."

They lay there getting their breath back, and watching the dim shadow of the *Mayflower* outlined in the falling darkness.

"When we go up, we'll use the ladder. I'll go first, but I'll wait until you're on the ladder."

"What then?"

"The problem will be with Coffin, O'Neal, Davis, and a couple more. Some of the men aren't really in this. Don't hurt French or Pike." He suddenly threw his head back. "There's a shot—let's go!"

He threw himself forward, making for the ship as fast as he could propel himself through the sea, and by the time he pulled himself up the wooden ladder and helped Brown up beside him, the firing from the deck had started.

Gilbert pulled his knife, sliced the harness and, holding his sword in readiness, moved up the ladder, Brown right behind him. The cannon went off just as they reached the rail, and Gilbert raised his head carefully.

Four men, including French, Pike and another seaman named Morton served the gun, with Coffin standing behind it to aim the weapon.

Stationed along the rail seven seamen were ranged firing their muskets at the approaching shallop.

"Give it to 'em!" Coffin screamed, and he touched a match to the venthole. The cannon boomed, and recoiled to the end of the rope that made it fast to the rail.

"Hi! Good shot!" O'Neal yelled. "Not more'n a foot wide. You'll get a hit next time, Coffin!"

Gilbert risked standing up and saw the shallop coming full at the ship, Standish ignoring the barricade and standing up to get a better shot with his musket. He fired and splinters flew from the rail between two of the seamen.

"They're coming in," Gilbert said leaning over to speak to Brown. "I'll take Coffin and you try to put O'Neal down."

"You mean—kill him?" Brown said. There was a wild look in his eyes, and every time a gun went off he flinched.

"Put him down any way you can—or those men in that boat will be butchered! Come on!"

He had not much hope Brown would be of help, but there was no time to think. As he leaped over the rail he saw that two of the men were busy loading their muskets, and two others fired off a shot. *Three with charged muskets*, he thought, but he concentrated on Coffin who was cursing the gun crew for their slowness.

Gilbert knew that the action would last only a few seconds, and that he and Brown would not live if they failed. Coffin's narrow back was toward him, and every instinct in him urged him to drive his blade home, but he did not. Switching his sword to his left hand he lifted his right arm high and brought his forearm down on Coffin's neck with a tremendous blow that snapped his head backward and drove him to the deck, his arms and legs flapping loosely.

"What . . . !" A muscular seaman named Prine had just dropped the ball down the mouth of the cannon. He looked up to see Coffin sprawl on the deck, and his eyes caught sight of Gilbert who had put his sword in his right hand. Prine howled, "O'Neal! Over here!" He pulled a sword from his belt and glanced over his shoulder. "French—get 'em!"

French and Pike looked up at the same time, with startled eyes, and taking one look at Gilbert, they both stepped back. The other man, a seaman that Gilbert didn't know, drew his sword and joined Prine in a sudden attack on Gilbert.

Neither of them were expert, and in a single duel, Gilbert would have played with them—but they came at him in tandem, and he took a step back, parrying the blade of Prine, then with a slashing backstroke struck the other's sword with a force that drove it out of the man's hands to the deck.

Prine backed off, looked where the others were attacking by the rail, and over his head Gilbert saw that everything had gone wrong.

Brown must have been slow or had been too scrupulous, for O'Neal had avoided him. Even as Gilbert watched, the thick sailor took a step back, snatched a loaded musket from one of the men along the rail, and cried out, "Shoot them!"

Gilbert saw Prine and the other man, who had recovered his sword, closing in on him, but there across the deck he saw that Peter Brown would soon be a dead man!

Both O'Neal and one of the other men were swinging their muskets around toward the helpless Brown, and there was no doubt about their intention. They could not miss at that range. Brown turned his head suddenly, his fear-stricken eyes meeting those of Gilbert.

In that split second, with the sound of firing around him and with the blades of the two men reaching for him, Gilbert made a decision. With a catlike leap he sprang past his own adversaries. There was a low railing around the mainmast, and without breaking stride, he used it for a springboard. The muzzles of the weapons were lowering as he crouched, then drove himself in a headlong drive at O'Neal and the other man. As he flew through the air, he twisted his body, so that he went crashing with his torso on O'Neal's squat body, driving him into the rail and touching off his musket with a roar of explosion right in his face. His legs hit the other man waist high, but though he was staggered, he didn't go down.

"Peter! Cut them down!" Gilbert yelled, and a red mist seemed to fall over his eyes, the rage of battle driving him beyond logic or reason.

Gilbert saw Brown being backed to the mast by two men beating his sword down with their blades, and others were rushing to help them and Prine.

He did his best, twisting as Prine's naked blade shot forward, and by twisting his body to one side, he managed to take only a minor wound, a raking shallow cut across his back, high up.

Then he was through, for he was practically on his face after his last lunge. *Now it's over*, he thought; he was sad at what he would never have, but not afraid.

Then he heard a chorus of yelling and, rolling over quickly, saw Pike, French, and two other men come up to attack Prine.

He heaved himself to his feet, grabbed his sword and with a yell threw himself at the two men about to finish off Brown.

One of them turned with a startled look of rage and made a pass at Gilbert. He parried it with ease and drove his own blade through the man's heart, withdrew it and turned to meet an attack from the rear.

It was well he did, for he found himself face-to-face with Coffin!

The tall, thin form of the man was twisted sideways, one foot out with knee bent, left foot back and at right angles—the classic position, and the moment their blades touched, Gilbert knew he had never crossed blades with a better swordsman.

He saw in a flash that men, led by Standish, were swarming over the rail, and that the loyal portion of the crew had united with them to herd the renegades into a huddle next to the rail.

"It's over, Coffin!" he cried. "Throw down your sword."

"No, it's not over, not till you're dead meat!" Coffin snarled and moved ahead with a rapid attack such as Gilbert had never seen!

Coffin's blade darted faster than a snake's tongue, and only by falling back in a half-stumble did Gilbert survive. He was

exhausted after the swim, and the wound in his back was drain-
ing his strength. Back, back he went, staving off death by the
last fraction of a second as he pushed aside Coffin's darting blade
time and time again.

His back struck the wall of the quarterdeck, and he twisted
to one side, missing death by inches as Coffin's blade struck the
wood where he had been an instant earlier.

Gilbert turned, driven back by the brilliance of the man's
swordsmanship; never once was he able to mount an attack of
his own. Dimly he was aware that the fight below was almost
over; soon, Standish and others would come to his aid—but it
would be too late.

For he could back up no more. His legs struck the rail, and
for a few seconds the blades made a ringing clash so rapid it was
impossible to separate them. He was fighting on instinct now,
his mind not able to keep up with Coffin's tactics. Parry, parry,
parry—twist and turn. But now he was getting slower and he
saw the fiery light of victory in Coffin's eyes as he crouched for
the final lunge.

Do what he nevair expect! The words came to his mind like a
flash of light from his past—the words of his old master, Dupree.
And in a desperation born of despair, he did exactly that. He
threw the book away in one instant. With a wild yell he leaped
at Coffin, lifting his sword high over his head like a club! If Coffin
had kept his head he could have run Gilbert through the body
at that moment, but he did not.

The wild yell and the totally unexpected abandonment of
the classic style for the rough, vicious swing of the sword rattled
him. He took one step back and when the downward stroke of
his raging opponent struck, it nearly tore his own blade from his
hand!

He had only time to lift his blade to catch the next wild
sweep which Gilbert threw at him crossways like a scythe.

Screaming like a banshee, Gilbert drove Coffin across the
deck by brute force. None of the smooth exact science he had
spent years learning! He swung his blade like a wild Irishman
swings a shillelah in a brawl, and it shattered Coffin's cool confidence.

He caught himself for one last try, but as he went into the

classic stance, Gilbert kicked him in the knee and Coffin went down with a cry of agony.

Instantly Gilbert was over him, his eyes mad with battle fury, his sword poised over the fallen man's body.

Coffin looked up, and there was no fear in his eyes. He spat out, "Do it, then! I ain't afraid to die!"

Still Gilbert stood there, the sword drawn back, quivering and ready to drop.

"Well, you going to kill him or not?"

Gilbert twisted his head to see that Standish had come up the ladder and was watching the scene with clinical interest.

The roar of blood in Gilbert's ears quieted, and he looked down at Coffin, glaring at him with pale-eyed hatred.

Then he slowly pulled his sword back and there was a look of wonder in his cornflower blue eyes.

"No, I'm not—and there's your miracle right there!"

Even as he spoke, a violent tremor shook his body, and Standish at once whipped off his cloak and draped it over his shoulders. "We'd best get you to Fuller at once. That's a bad cut you took—and that freezing swim didn't do you any good!"

By the time they'd returned and Fuller had finished taking a few stitches in his back, Gilbert's head was swimming, and he seemed to be burning up.

"W-what's wrong with m-me?" he asked feebly.

Fuller threw the needle down and cried, "Curse it all, you've got a case of the sickness coming on, or I'm no doctor! Just when the thing has left, it comes back and tries to take another one of us!" Then he caught himself and said quickly, "But we'll pull you through, my boy—don't doubt it!"

But Gilbert heard only the first part of his statement. His head was swimming and he slipped into a black hole that seemed to be waiting to swallow him up like a huge beast.

CHAPTER TWENTY-EIGHT

THE *MAYFLOWER* SAILS

★   ★   ★   ★

Sometimes he was falling down into a dark hole, and he would tense his muscles for the terrible moment when he would strike the bottom. A roaring would fill his ears, like a mighty rushing wind, but when he opened his mouth to cry out, the wind rushed in, stifling him like a massive blanket.

At other times he seemed to be floating lightly in air, in a strange quietness so hollow that tiny sounds seemed to echo deep down in his brain. At those times there would be a bright light, not harsh but soft and gentle, bathing him in warmth, shielding him from the bone-cracking chill that racked him.

"It's all right, Gilbert! You're not falling!"

His eyes opened and closed abruptly as the light hit them, but he blinked and his vision cleared.

He was sitting up in bed, in a room that was dark except for a low-burning lamp on the table. The shadows flickered over the woman who was kneeling to hold him by the shoulders as he swayed and tried to throw the covers off.

"Humility!" He recognized her, and his lips were so dry her name came out in a croaking sound.

Keeping a hand on his shoulder, she picked up a mug from a table, held it to his lips, saying, "Drink this."

He found he had a raging thirst, and swallowed frantically at the water until she pulled it back, saying, "You can have more later." Putting the mug down, she asked, "How do you feel?"

He licked his lips and answered slowly, "All right. How long have I been here?"

"About ten days." She took her hand off his shoulder and said, "Can you eat something?"

"Anything!" He had a hunger to match his thirst. He ate the bowl of soup she brought him and asked for more.

"You'd better wait until Mr. Fuller gets here. Too much at first might be bad for you." She turned to leave, but came back and put her hand on his chest. Shoving him back flat on the bed, she said, "You'd better rest—you haven't had much normal sleep."

Her face was thinner, he thought, and lined with fatigue. "Have you been here all this time?"

She hesitated, then nodded. "Some of the time. Edward stayed with you as well."

He was so sleepy he couldn't keep his eyes open, but he said as he dropped off, "I don't think Peter will like it."

He woke up some time later to find clear light streaming in through the open window. A bird was singing, and the room seemed stuffy. He sat up in bed, swung his feet to the floor, then stood up. The room swung round in an alarming fashion, but he held to the wall until it stopped.

He was wearing only a pair of short underpants, and could not find his clothes, so he wrapped the blanket around him and staggered outside. He sat down at once on a rude bench against the side of the hut and looked around.

Spring had made an assault on Plymouth during his sickness, driving out the cold winds and clammy air. He took a deep breath of the warm April breeze, smelling of the sea and of green trees and warming earth, and for a long time he sat there, enjoying the warmth.

A slight figure was wending up the steep hill, and he recognized Captain Christopher Jones. There was an odd look on the seaman's face, Gilbert saw, as he came closer, but he smiled when he came up to the cabin, saying with energy, "Why, you're not dead, are you, Winslow?"

"I guess not, Captain."

"You came pretty close, I can tell you! I sat with you a few times with Edward, and it looked like you weren't going to make it." His face crinkled in a smile and he added, "If it hadn't been for that young woman caring for you like a sick baby, why, I reckon you'd not be sitting here enjoying this sunshine."

Gilbert stared at him. "She did that?" he asked.

Jones cocked his head, suddenly sober as he remarked. "I tell you, it's hard to figure these folks out, Winslow. I got the idea she had nothing but hate for you after what you did; then she goes and pulls a stunt like this!"

Gilbert bit his lip, then shook his head. "These folks believe in turning the other cheek. Humility believes in doing her Christian duty."

"That so?" Jones asked, and there was a light of humor in his gray eyes. "Well, I guess there's more to it than that—but in any case, you're looking better."

Something in Christopher Jones's face made Gilbert consider him more closely. He finally asked, "I think you've got something to tell me."

"Well, I didn't know how I'd find you . . ."

"What is it, Captain?" He glanced toward the sea, and it came to him. "You're taking the *Mayflower* back home?"

"Well, yes. Today's the fourth—we'll set sail tomorrow."

Gilbert dropped his head and considered it. He was still weak and his thinking was confused. Finally he said, "I'll be ready."

"Well, the thing is . . ." Jones cleared his throat, and seemed to be having trouble with his words. Then he slapped his thigh and cried out, "Oh, a plague on it! Why didn't you stay sick!"

"What?"

"Why, I couldn't take a dying man on board, could I? I had my plan all made to get away while you were still unconscious— then you have to wake up and spoil it all!"

Gilbert smiled at his red face, and said, "Sorry to be such a bother, Captain."

Jones stared at him, gnawing at his lip. "You saved my ship, Winslow. Chances are those roughs would have piled her up or sold her for scrap when they got home. It was you that gave her back to me. What do I do about *that*?"

"You might make me a partner," Gilbert said.

Jones grinned. "Well, that would be going a little *too* far. But you won't be going back with me to England." He grew serious then and said, "I'd never be able to look myself in the face if I took you back to face a rope—and it's not only that you saved the ship. You're not the same man that stowed aboard, are you?"

Gilbert shook his head. "No, I'm not—but I'm still a fugitive and you can get in trouble for concealing me."

"I'll be careful to keep myself clear," the captain said. "But you have to realize that the next ship that comes will probably have someone aboard with a warrant from the King." He shook his head then added, "I'll do this for you; let me take you. When we're in the Channel and I touch at Calais, you can hide yourself in France."

Gilbert shook his head at once. "I'm grateful to you, Captain—but I'll take my chances here."

Jones rose with a puzzled look on his face. "Scratch me! I knew you'd say that! I've offered to take anybody who wants to go back home, and you know how many have accepted my offer?"

"Not many, I'd venture."

"None! Not a bloody one!"

"I'm not too surprised. Even Billington and Hopkins have found something here they'll never give up."

"Found what?" Jones demanded.

"I guess it's freedom, Captain." Gilbert knew that was not altogether right, but he shrugged, and then a thought struck him. "Could you take a letter for me to England?"

"I'm taking one for everybody else, so why not?"

The next morning, despite dire warnings from Sam Fuller and Edward, Gilbert insisted on walking down to the harbor to see the departure.

In the morning light fifty-six people stood watching as Captain Jones stood on the poop deck of the *Mayflower* waving his hand. Gilbert studied them as the sails were being run up. "Why are they all staying, Edward?" he asked quietly. "Only fifty-six people, and twenty-five of those are children. Just thirty-one adults perched on the edge of a continent so big we can't even imagine how far it stretches!"

Edward nodded, and his eyes sought out Susanna White where she stood holding the baby in one arm and Resolved with the other. His cheeks were hollowed, making his large nose seem even larger, but there was a satisfaction in his clear blue eyes. "I know, Gilbert. It looks foolish to the world, but I tell you, there's a victory here! The sickness got half of us—but not a one accepted Jones's offer to go back to an easy life in Holland or England. Listen—" He broke off as Bradford raised his voice in a hymn of thanksgiving. They sang, their thin faces tear-marked, but radiating a joy that could not be denied. "The God of this universe has not let us go unnoticed!"

The women's headcloths flapped in the breeze and men's hair and beards ruffled as they sang. Old John Carver, Brewster, Bradford, and Allerton sang at the top of their lungs as the wind puffed the sails of the ship; soon only the declining speck of the *Mayflower* could be seen, then nothing broke the flat plane of the wide horizon of the sea.

The firstcomers were alone in their New World.

Gilbert regained his strength quickly, and only Edward commented on his remaining in Plymouth instead of returning with the *Mayflower*. "Jones couldn't take you back. He talked about it quite a bit while you were ill."

"I'll have to go back sometime, Edward. They won't forget about Lord Roth back in England."

But he put that in the back of his mind, working hard with the others at planting their corn under Squanto's direction. He often hunted and fished with Tink, the two becoming proficient at finding both game and a variety of ocean and freshwater fish. The boy was happy, but from time to time he got a worried look, and Gilbert knew he was worried about the next ship which might separate them. Gilbert forced the thoughts of that from his mind.

He saw Brown often. The first time they'd met, Brown had been awkward. "You saved my life on the ship. I'm—grateful to you, Winslow."

"You did a good job, Peter. I couldn't have done it without your help."

The tall young man ducked his head, his neck red with

embarrassment; then he looked up and said quietly, "I'm sorry about—about the way it turned out for you. About Humility, I mean."

"You're getting a fine woman, Peter. Any man would be proud to have a wife like her."

"Yes—but what . . . ?"

Gilbert cut off his question. "I wish you both the best, Peter."

Humility had met his gaze with her steady eyes the first time they'd met, but she avoided his company whenever possible.

On Sundays the entire town assembled in the main street, and with every man carrying his musket, they followed Governor Carver to the Common House, where they worshiped. They wore their best clothes for the occasion, Carver having on a fine red cloak. The blues, red, and greens of their coats and smocks made a splash against the plain walls, and William Brewster had a violet suit that almost hurt the eyes. The bands, flat white collars worn by the men, were white and glistening, and some of them wore high-crowned hats.

Elder Brewster served as pastor. He did not give communion since he was not ordained, but he was an excellent preacher. Bradford recorded of him in the history he was writing: "In teaching he was very stirring, and moving the affections; also very plain and distinct in what he taught; by which means he became the more profitable to the hearers. He had a singular good gift in prayer, in ripping up the heart and conscience before God."

They suffered a loss that month, in Governor Carver. The old man had insisted on working alongside the younger men in the fields, and on a very hot day he suddenly dropped his hoe and complained of a terrific pain in the head. Everyone assumed he had too much sun, but after lying down for a few hours, he lapsed into a coma and died two days later.

After the old man was buried with a guard of honor, the next order of business was the election of a new governor. William Brewster was the most obvious choice, but he was eliminated by his position as ruling elder of the church.

"We must always keep the church and the state separate,"

Brewster said, when asked to serve. "We have seen the disastrous effects of its union in England!"

Unanimously, the choice fell on William Bradford, and from his first days in office, a new vigor entered Plymouth's public affairs. Up to this time affairs had rested largely in the hands of Elder Brewster, Pastor Robinson, Deacon Cushman, and Deacon Carver—all older men. Now this group was scattered—one was dead, another in London, a third in Leyden, so the thirty-two-year-old Bradford picked up the reins firmly.

Edward Winslow worked as hard as any man, but something drove him to walk in the woods in the twilight hours. He became absent-minded with Gilbert, his attention hard to hold.

He was walking back to the town late one night, tired and dissatisfied with he knew not what. The spring peepers in the brook made a shrill chorus as he walked slowly, not looking up at the moon that was beginning to peer with a silver face through the velvet sky.

"Edward."

He lifted his head instantly, knowing the voice at once. "Susanna . . ."

He hesitated, then stepped to her side. She stood before him, watching his face in the close and personal way she had; and the warm light of her eyes grew and her face was changed in a way he could not describe. Suddenly she was a shape and a substance before him, and a fragrance and a melody all around him, so that the loneliness that had lived in him so long grew insupportable. The wall he had built against tradition and ritual went down. She was before him, and there was nothing between them. But still he hesitated.

"Edward, would you think of marrying me?" she asked quietly.

He was caught by her direct honesty, and he moved ahead and put his arms around her. Watching her lips lift, he saw that she was smiling—and so he kissed her.

When they broke into the cabin to find Gilbert sitting at the table reading, their faces shone. He rose at once, a wide smile on his face, and put his arms around Susanna, saying, "Well, I have a new sister!" and they all laughed.

Edward Winslow and Susanna White were married in May

when the wild plums put on their white blossoms. The soft, sweet warmth of New England's spring was all about them, and everyone was delighted to have something to celebrate after the long winter of sickness, disaster, and gloom.

They were low on some food, but Gilbert and Tink saw that there was enough fish to cover a wide table in the Common House, and Peter Brown brought down two fat deer.

As Gilbert watched the festivities, he remarked to Bradford, who had joined him, "I remember how I once thought all you people sat around dressed in black and hated mirth and singing . . ."

Bradford gave Gilbert a smile and said, "You have changed many of your ideas recently, haven't you?"

Gilbert said soberly, "I can't believe what a fool I was, Elder! I can't think of a thing I was *right* about!"

Bradford studied him, then asked, "What will you do with your life?"

"I don't know."

"Will you go back to England?"

"To the gallows?" Gilbert stared at the people moving along and piling their plates high with food. There was a strong streak of fatalism underneath his light manner, and he said thoughtfully, "Only a little while ago I was headed for a promising career under Lord North. Money, pleasure—and maybe even a marriage with his daughter. Now I'll probably spend the rest of my life waiting for a door to open and some officer to come through it with the warrant to drag me back to a rope."

Bradford's dark eyes fixed on the face of the younger man, and he let the silence run on before he said, "You think that would have brought you happiness, Gilbert?"

The question raked against the young man's nerves. "Why, I don't know. Why wouldn't it, Elder? Aren't those the things every man wants?"

"And were the people you met in the higher realms of society happy? Did they have peace and contentment?"

Gilbert was suddenly silent, for he knew that such was not the case. "No, they weren't. Most of them wore themselves out chasing after money or pleasure."

"If you were free to do so, would you go back and take up that life?"

Gilbert did not answer; he was glad that John Alden had stood up suddenly and called for quiet.

"Friends, we celebrate the wedding of our good friends, and we all wish them long life and happiness." A chorus of "amen's" met this, and when they subsided, John continued, "I want to invite you to another wedding—mine and Miss Priscilla Mullins!"

This came as no great shock to anyone, but there was a wave of applause and there was much hugging of Priscilla by the women and much beating on John's broad back by the men.

Then Peter Brown moved out from the side of the room where he had been standing with Humility, and with a slight pallor under his tan, he said, "Friends, since weddings and marriage is the purpose of our gathering, I congratulate Mr. and Mrs. Winslow, and I wish Mr. Alden and Miss Mullins joy." He cleared his throat before he added, "And Miss Humility Cooper and I invite you to share in our joy as well."

He moved back to take Humility's hand, and the two were surrounded at once by a wave of people crowding around to congratulate them.

Gilbert was startled to hear a voice in his ear, "It would be nice if you would join in with the well-wishers, Gilbert."

He turned to see Edward standing beside him, and Gilbert at once said, "Thank you, Edward." He moved forward slowly, and finally stood before the two. A silence fell on the room, and all eyes were fastened on the three.

"You are to be congratulated—both of you," he said quickly. Humility took Peter's arm in a quick gesture. She was not smiling as she had been, but her voice was steady and clear as she said, "Thank you, Mr. Winslow."

Brown put his hand out, and when Gilbert gripped it, he said, "I appreciate your good wishes, Gilbert."

Then it was over, and someone started a song. "That was well done," Edward said quietly as Gilbert returned to stand beside him.

"All my loose ends tied up, eh, Edward—" Then his wide mouth turned up in a sudden wry smile as he added, ". . . except the one the hangman's probably getting ready for me at the tower!"

Gilbert discovered that it was impossible to maintain his spirit of apprehension. As the weeks went by he was less and less likely to gaze at the sea and wonder if a sail would appear with the law on board.

The work kept him busy. He helped all the other families finish their houses, and since he had no house or fields of his own, he got to know all of them. The three families still intact were allotted houses, and they each took in several single men and women. Young Priscilla Mullins lived with Elder Brewster and his family, while Humility and Bess stayed with the Allertons.

Gilbert had seen Humility practically every day for months, but had said nothing more intimate than, "Would you pass the water jug?"

He had gone down to the creek to fill two water buckets and met her, awkwardly trying to fill one of the large, wooden kegs from the stream. The brook was deep only in the middle, and she was trying to shove the keg out to deeper water without getting her shoes muddy.

"Let me help you."

She whirled at his words and dropped the keg, which would have floated downstream if Gilbert had not abandoned his buckets and plunged in to retrieve it. "This is too heavy for you," he remarked as the cool water spilled into the container.

She stood there watching him, and finally she said, "I have something to say to you." She spread her hands over the front of her dress, looked out across the woods, then brought her gaze back to meet his. "You said something to me once that I feel is unfair."

"I know." He filled the keg, carried it back to the bank, then turned to face her. She took a step back as if he meant to attack her, and he smiled. "I said you were afraid of life." A loon gave his eerie cry, and then in the silence that followed, he said directly, "I still say it."

She was a tall girl, and the strong lines of her body were outlined beneath the plain dress she wore by the pressure of the

October wind. Her high cheekbones and wide-spaced eyes gave her face an Oriental cast, but the firm chin and green eyes were English. She had been hurt by this man, more than she had dreamed a woman could be hurt, and often she had found herself feeding on her bruised pride, greedily hoping that someday she would find a way to pay him back in kind.

Now she cried out, "You're wrong! So very wrong!"

"I've been wrong about almost everything—but not about this." He asked her suddenly, "When are you marrying?"

The question flustered her, and she raised one hand to tuck a blonde tress under her cap. She was restless under his gaze, and finally burst out, "Oh, I don't know! Why do you ask?"

When he didn't answer, she suddenly struck his chest with her fist, crying out, "You think you're better than Peter, don't you?"

Catching her hand, he held it, shook his head. There was a sadness in his lean face as he said slowly, "No, I don't. I don't think that at all."

She stared at him. "Then what *is* it, Gilbert? Why do you look at me like you do?" A bitterness ran through her tone, and she flushed as she said, "You didn't want me—but you don't want another man to have me, is that it?"

He was unhappy with the scene, and could not answer her question. She was not the woman he'd imagined in his own life, but he could not dislodge the pictures of her that kept coming back to his mind.

"I've made a ruin of my own life, Humility," he said finally. "I hate to see you do the same."

She stared at him, her cheeks suddenly still. He was not the same man she'd known in Holland; not even the same as when they'd landed in Plymouth. The soft lines of his face, the easy laugh, and the confident manner had faded. Now he looked older, and there was a maturity in his face that had been lacking. He smiled often, but it was not the same, for now beneath the smile there was a knowledge of the razor-sharp edge of life that can cut a man down in one instant.

She shook her head, then asked without warning, "You're still in love with that woman, Cecily."

He stared at her, then shook his head. "That's over. She's

in England. Probably married to some Count by now."

"You called her name when you were sick. You wouldn't have done that if you'd forgotten her."

He shrugged, saying quietly, "We don't forget anybody. But . . ."

Whatever he was going to say was cut off by the boom of the cannon, followed by another.

"Both guns," he said looking toward the town. "Something's happened!"

They began to run, and she was as fast as he was. When they got to the edge of the woods, they saw a crowd gathered around the rampart that Standish had built for the weapons. The captain was standing beside one of the cannons, pointing with his sword out toward the sea.

Gilbert looked that way, and saw a tiny flash of white, a sail catching the sun.

"It's a ship." He stared at it steadily, then felt her touch on his arm.

"Run away!"

"What?"

"You can go stay with Squanto and the Indians," she said, and there was an urgency in her manner. "Don't go back to England!"

He stood there, caught by her intense manner, but then he shook his head. "I can't run like a frightened rabbit every time a ship appears." He left her and started to walk down toward the beach, then turned and said with a warmth in his blue eyes, "Humility, whatever happens, I'll always have one thing."

"One thing? What will you have?" she asked.

He grinned and lifted his hand as if he held his sword in a salute.

"I'll always remember that once at least, I loved a real woman!"

As he walked away, her lips trembled, and she whispered, *You fool! You fool! You're throwing yourself away!*

She could not bear to see the straight set of his back as he went to meet whatever fate had for him. Blindly she turned and walked slowly away from the beach and the ship that came closer with every gust of wind.

CHAPTER TWENTY-NINE

OUT OF THE PAST

★ ★ ★ ★

Every man, woman, and child in Plymouth gathered at the beach to welcome the longboat from the ship. Standing slightly apart from the main body, Gilbert ran his eyes over familiar faces, and was swept with a wave of regret; there was little doubt in his mind that he was seeing the last of them.

The prow of the boat grated on the beach, then two seamen jumped out and made her fast, while the passengers disembarked.

"Elder Brewster!" a smallish man cried out, and he was greeted warmly by Brewster and many others. Gilbert heard the name *Cushman*, and looked with interest at the man about whom he had met at Southampton.

There was a swirl of people talking and moving, but Gilbert's attention was riveted on William Brewster. He stood there in the midst of the crowd like a statue, his eyes fixed on a man who got off the longboat last. Gilbert had never seen him, but he thought at once, *This is Brewster's son.* He was in his late twenties, and was in size and appearance what William Brewster must have been like as a young man. The older man's face was moved with emotion, and then he held out his arms and his son stepped into them.

There was much confusion as Cushman began introducing

the newcomers to the settlers, but one by one all were made known.

All but one. A tall, thick-bodied man with inquiring brown eyes had stood slightly apart from the group. He was well dressed in a gray suit, over which he wore a black greatcoat with a beaver collar turned up. There was an air of authority about him, and at first Gilbert thought he might be the captain of the ship, yet he did not seem to fit in that role.

Bradford raised his voice above the babble of talk. "Friends, let us go to the Common House. You must be hungry for fresh food after your long voyage." He led them up the hill, but Gilbert noted that the tall man in the brown suit stopped John Alden to ask a question. Alden paused, looked surprised, then looked around. Finding Gilbert with his eyes, he nodded his head, said something briefly, then with a long look at the man, turned and followed the others up the hill.

The man came at once to stand before Gilbert. For all his size he was light on his feet, and paused slightly before saying, "Mr. Gilbert Winslow?" His voice was deep and resonant, giving the impression that if he cared to raise it, the volume would overcome all other sounds.

"That is my name."

A light of interest stirred in the man's quick glance, eyes running over Gilbert as though taking inventory. Then he said, "My name is Wellington. Caleb Wellington of London."

Gilbert nodded but made no reply. Everything about the man signaled power and authority. His hands were strong but well cared for, and the diamond on the ring finger of his right hand would have fed the colonists for six months. His lips were broad with deep creases running along the corners, and the cleft chin was like the prow of a ship, invincible, daring anyone to get in its way. The eyes were set in deep sockets and shadowed by heavy brows, and his forehead was broad, with a mane of thick brown hair that sometimes fell over it in the brisk breeze.

"We have some business to discuss, Mr. Winslow," Wellington said finally. "Would you come aboard to my cabin?"

His manner puzzled Gilbert. There was no question of his mission, since he had asked by name for Gilbert Winslow. *He's not one of the new colonists,* Gilbert thought swiftly. *He's come for me—but why this smooth approach? Why not a brace of armed guards and a pair of manacles for me?*

"Why not here, Mr. Wellington?" Gilbert was curious to see what effect resistance would have on him. This was obviously a man accustomed to being obeyed, but he was surprised at the reaction.

"Why, if you please, but this air is chilly and our business may take a little time."

"Very well." Gilbert followed him to the longboat and they seated themselves. The six sailors manning the oars put about quickly.

"What ship is this?" Gilbert asked.

"The *Fortune*—fifty-five-ton, Robert Logan, captain. Four months out of Southampton." Wellington rattled the facts off in a practiced manner, then asked, "Has your plantation here been successful, Mr. Winslow?"

Gilbert gave him a direct stare, then shrugged. "Half our number are dead. I'm sure most would say that's a high price to pay for a dozen huts and a few acres of Indian corn."

The blunt speech jarred the big man out of his smooth manner. "Half dead! Did the savages attack?"

"Sickness."

Wellington shook his head. "I spent quite a few hours playing chess with Mr. Cushman. He talked quite a bit about his people here. Must say he's not what I expected, Mr. Winslow." His direct brown eyes searched Gilbert's face, and he asked curiously, "I've been wondering how you fit in with these people— different in so many ways from yourself."

"How am I different, Mr. Wellington?"

Gilbert's instant question broke through the man's calm. He blinked, and there was a trace of irritation in his manner as he realized he'd said more than he meant to. He was not a man to endure much pressure, so he turned to face Gilbert squarely, and a hard-edged streak surfaced, breaking the smoothness of his face. "You're not of the Brownist persuasion, Mr. Winslow— or you were not a year ago."

"Who are you, Mr. Wellington?" Gilbert asked. "Are you an agent of the Crown?"

"We're almost to the ship," Wellington said. He looked up

at the red and white cross of St. George flying from the mast. "Our business can wait until we are alone."

The firm set of Wellington's jaw told Gilbert that it would do no good to protest. He had the feeling that he was caught up in some force that was pulling him closer to a dangerous end, but there was no fear as the longboat made fast, and he followed Wellington up the ladder to stand on deck.

"This way." Gilbert followed Wellington as he walked toward the stern, and entered the oak door under the poop deck. Ordinarily there would be a single door inside leading to the captain's Great Cabin, but there were two, one of them old and one obviously new. Removing a key from his vest pocket, Wellington unlocked the one on the left, stepped back to wave Gilbert inside, then followed him.

The room was not large, not more than ten feet wide and twelve feet long. A new partition had been built, Gilbert saw, taking space from the Great Cabin. Most of the space was taken up by a bed, a large oak cabinet that almost touched the low ceiling, two upholstered chairs, a small desk and a small table by the bed. The only decoration was a colorful blanket or shawl on the newly built wall. It looked Oriental and was made of some fine material.

"You must have a very hospitable captain."

"Ah?"

"To allow you to take part of his space." Gilbert nodded at the wall to his left. "You had that put in just before you sailed, I take it."

Wellington was surprised; then he smiled. "You have sharp eyes, Mr. Winslow."

Gilbert didn't respond to that, but said, "About our business?"

"Ah, yes. Well, sit down, Mr. Winslow. Perhaps a glass of wine?"

Gilbert stared at him, then sat down with a smile and took the glass of wine that Wellington poured from a small glass decanter on the table, and tasted it.

"Very fine, sir." He took another swallow and said with a smile, "Probably the best wine I've ever shared with a man who's taking me to the gallows."

He had expected to catch Wellington off guard with the statement, but the big man merely looked at him, then sipped his own wine.

Gilbert grew angry then, and put the glass down before saying, "You like to torment the mouse a little before the kill—is that it?"

"Is it?"

Gilbert leaned forward, his cornflower blue eyes snapping, and he raised his voice. "You're a policeman—but you must be a lawyer too, judging from the way you hate plain speech!"

"Are you married, Mr. Winslow?"

It was the last question Gilbert expected. He blinked and stared blankly at Wellington, who returned the stare with bland attention. "No, I'm not married. Why do you ask—don't you arrest married men?"

"You expect to be arrested?"

"Another question!" Gilbert said. He stood up and his voice was hard as he said, "I won't play your game, Wellington. Put me in irons, but I'll not be questioned!"

Wellington leaned back in his chair, laced his strong fingers, and said coolly, "A year of hard labor hasn't done much for your temper, has it now? Hasn't it gotten you into enough trouble?"

"The death of Lord Roth was not a matter of temper!"

"Was it not? As I understand the thing, you were employed to run William Brewster to earth and then turn him over to the authorities. Why did you turn on Roth and Johnson?"

"It's—very personal," Gilbert said.

"Murder is usually a personal business, Mr. Winslow!" Wellington's voice was sharp, but he moderated it at once. "Look now, I know you have no reason to trust me . . ."

"*That* is true!"

" . . . but we are alone here, and I may be more of a friend to you than you now believe."

"A friend? How can that be? I don't know you."

"But I know you—or to put it more literally, I know *about* you," Wellington smiled. "Now, I have a proposition to make you, sir. In short, I may be able to help you to some degree. . . ." He put up his hand to ward off Gilbert's question. "Now I said *may* be able to help you, and I said to *some* degree."

"Why should you?" Gilbert knew he was no match for the wits of the man across from him, but he could not for the life of him think of any reason why Wellington or anyone else should help him.

"That question I will answer—after you have done one thing for me."

"Which is?"

"I want a complete and thorough report of your activities from the time you entered the service of Lord North until this day."

Gilbert stared at him. "You must think me quite a fool, sir, to think that I would give such a thing to a stranger."

"You would be exactly that, Mr. Winslow, if you spoke so freely to anyone else—but you would be foolish *not* to speak to me. For believe me, I am one of the very few who have the means of getting you out of this snare you have gotten yourself into. But I will not beg. This is my final offer, if you will do as I ask, and give me a complete and thorough account of the period I mentioned, I shall—if I am convinced that you are honest—let you know my reasons for being here. Now, I will not add to that. What is your decision?"

Wellington settled back, laced his fingers, and there was an adamant set to his face that told Gilbert he meant exactly what he said. The thought flashed through Gilbert's mind, *It's a trap— say nothing!* But the more he considered the man, the more inclined he was to comply with his strange request. Finally he shrugged, "You realize that what I say here, I will not repeat in a court of law?"

"Of course." Wellington got up and pulled his chair around to the small desk. He picked up a pen, trimmed it with a silver knife from his vest pocket, dipped it into the ink well. Then he pulled a sheet of paper close and with his pen poised, said, "Proceed, Mr. Winslow. I may interrupt you from time to time for fine details. It would save time if you give them on your own. I must ask you to give me—insofar as possible—not only what you *did*, but *why* you did it. In other words, lay your soul bare." He looked up with a slight smile on his heavy mouth and added, "I have seen a bit of the world, Winslow, so do not fear you'll shock me with your confession."

Gilbert turned his head to stare out of the mullioned windows cut into the high stern of the *Fortune*. The ship was anchored with the bow facing away from the shore, thus he could see the harbor and the main street of Plymouth plainly. For months he had worked on the small houses that mounted up the slope, but only now as he sat across from the man who might take him away from the small group of people he had been tied to, only then did it strike him forcibly that he might be taking his last look at Plymouth.

He thought of how he'd come to revere Brewster and Carver—and even Bradford, though he'd disliked the man at first. He thought of the young men he'd worked beside—John Alden, John Howland, Thomas Fletcher. Of the children who had stood the trip better than most of the adults. He thought of those now buried in shallow graves or in the sea. He thought of Humility.

Then he said, "I've done many foolish things in my life, Mr. Wellington. Putting my confidence in you will probably wind up at the top of that list . . ." He watched Wellington's face closely, but there was not a break in the smooth countenance of the man. Gilbert smiled grimly, then went over to stand beside the window.

"I hated my brother Edward because I thought he had robbed me of my inheritance . . ." he began, and for the next hour he went over the whole thing, beginning with his first meeting with Lord North down to the time the sails of *Fortune* had appeared over the horizon.

He began awkwardly, embarrassed to lay his memories before a stranger. But Wellington never looked up from his writing desk. He sat there motionless, making a note from time to time, but he spoke only to ask a few questions.

The questions were not the ones Gilbert had expected. He was prepared for snares concerning the death of Lord Roth, but Wellington seemed to have more appetite for other things.

"This young woman—Humility Cooper," he asked quietly. "Did you find her attractive?"

"Very much."

"So that made your task easier?"

"No, sir, it did *not*!" Gilbert shot back at once.

"You did have relations with her, of course." There was no rebuke in the smooth voice; Wellington might have been stating that it was a pleasant day.

Gilbert turned from the window, his face flushed; he took one step toward Wellington, then stopped.

The big man did not even look up from his notes. "Did you hear me, Mr. Winslow? I asked if you had intimate relations with the woman."

Gilbert forced himself to be as calm as Wellington, at least outwardly. "No, I did not."

That brought Wellington's head up, and his dark piercing eyes met Gilbert's. "Why not?" he asked.

"It's not a question I care to answer, sir. If you insist on one, the interrogation is over."

Wellington stared at the young man as if he were an interesting specimen he had discovered, then smiled slightly, turned back to his notes, and said calmly, "Proceed with the account."

Gilbert went on with his story, and Wellington stopped him at one point with a question about his relationship with Lord North.

"I admire him very much."

"And his daughter?"

"Why, she's one of the loveliest women I've ever seen."

"Is that all?"

"I—I don't understand you."

"I think you do."

Stung by the man's calm assurance, Gilbert bit his lip, then said, "Well—I will admit, sir—it *was* more than admiration."

"I see. How much more?"

Gilbert shrugged. "I was very much attracted to her—but you know how little that means, Mr. Wellington. I was a poor man, with no name and no fortune."

"There have been matches of that sort, I believe."

Gilbert struck the windowsill with his fist, and cried out, "Yes! and what is your opinion of poor young men who marry wealthy women?"

"I would have no general opinion," Wellington said, giving Gilbert a straight glance. "I know there are some scoundrels who have married women for their fortune; I know some men of impeccable honor who have married women of wealth for love. I am asking you, Mr. Winslow, what was your feeling for Cecily North?"

Gilbert sat down in the chair, poured himself a glass of wine, drank it down. Then he asked quietly, "Did you ever go through a bad time in your life, Mr. Wellington?"

"Yes."

Gilbert smiled and said, "You're no lawyer, as I thought at first. No lawyer ever spoke so certainly and so shortly. But— during that difficult time, did you ever dream of earlier days when things were better?"

"Yes, many times."

"Well, how accurate were those dreams, in all honesty? Weren't they shaped by the agony of the present trial?"

"I believe that's very accurate," Wellington nodded. "And that is, I take it, your answer as to how you felt about the young woman at that time."

"I was intoxicated by her—who wouldn't be?" Gilbert murmured. "Those brief times we shared—I've dreamed about them over and over during this past year. When death was at my right hand every day, those memories kept me sane, I think."

Wellington let the silence run on, then he said, "I have one more question. It has to do with the tragedy of Lord Roth."

Gilbert said evenly, "I thought we'd get to that!"

"Yes, now, Mr. Winslow, think carefully before you answer my question." Wellington put his paper down and leaned forward holding Gilbert's eyes with his own.

"You left Leyden with the intention of being faithful to the task you'd committed yourself to?"

"Yes."

"Then when the moment came for you to do that, you did just the opposite."

"Yes."

"My question is this: *why* did you change your mind? I have heard Johnson's story—I warn you of that—and he indicates that Lord Roth threatened to have you charged with being derelict in your duty. He was not correct, was he?" Wellington's eyes narrowed and Gilbert knew that the answer to this question was the one that could lead him to the gallows.

He looked straight at Wellington, saying, "Lord Roth was quite correct in believing that I intended to help William Brewster escape."

"But—you did not feel that way when you left Leyden, by your own statement. Why did you change your mind?"

Gilbert paused, searching for the right words, but nothing he thought of sounded like the sort of thing that would satisfy this man. Finally he looked Wellington in the eye and said simply, "I found out I couldn't be a traitor. It was a matter of honor."

"I see." Clearly that answer was a problem for the big man, but Gilbert could not find another way to put it.

"I suggest, Mr. Winslow, that it is possible that you did this for the young woman? That you had fallen in love with her and could not bear to betray her. Am I correct?"

"No, sir, you are *not!*" Gilbert spoke crisply, and got to his feet. "I would have done the same if she had been ninety years old, or if William Brewster had been the only one involved."

Wellington's large eyes narrowed. Letting the silence run on until it grew uncomfortable, finally he nodded and said, "Very well, I think that will do."

"Now perhaps you can tell me who you are."

"You have been most cooperative, Mr. Winslow." Wellington rose to his feet, walked to the door, and turned to face Gilbert with the suggestion of a smile on his lips. "If you will remain in this room for just a short while, you will receive your reward."

"But—!" Gilbert started to protest, but the big man stepped through the door and shut it firmly. The key turned, and Gilbert said under his breath angrily, "Remain in this room—where in the name of heaven could I go?"

He paced about the room, pausing at the desk to open a drawer and look through the contents thoroughly. There was nothing to indicate the profession of Wellington—only a few small books on the New World, well-thumbed, with his name on the inside cover.

He moved toward the windows to look outside, and as he passed the colorful hanging on the inner wall, his eye caught a faint movement of the fabric. He was within arm's reach, and when he stopped to face it, he heard a small sound—very much like an intake of breath.

It was a trap! he thought at once, assuming that whoever was behind the drapery had been put there so he might serve as a witness at a murder trial. Anger swept him, and he plucked up one of the heavy chairs, intending to drive it through the colorful fabric; then a thought came, and he put it down softly.

He crouched slightly in front of the hanging, his knees bent, his arms outstretched, and uncoiled his body in an explosive drive that sent him through the thin material like a cannon shot. His outstretched arms wrapped around a figure, as he had expected, but he was surprised at the small size of Wellington's man—more like a boy than an adult, and the strength of his powerful arms wrapping around his prey cut off all resistance.

The hanging ripped from its fastenings made a shroud of sorts, and when he fell on the helpless body, there was a cry of pain as the breath was driven out.

Gilbert rolled off, and cast a quick look around, noting that it was furnished in a much more elaborate fashion than the adjoining room. But it was empty save for whoever was squirming wildly beneath the folds of the covering at his feet.

He reached down and plucking up the figure, ripped the thin fabric away from the head, saying, "All right, if you're so interested in me, take a good . . . !"

Gilbert stopped abruptly as the emblazoned cloth fell away, and he found himself face-to-face with Cecily North!

He stood there in total disbelief, his mind reeling, but it was no other. He licked his lips, and said finally, "Cecily! I can't believe it!"

Cecily had a slight redness on her right cheek—accentuated, no doubt, by the pallor brought on by the shock of Gilbert's charge. But the sleek black hair still framed a face that had haunted Gilbert for months. The bold black eyes opened wide, only inches away from his own, and she said breathlessly, "Are you going to hold me like this forever, Gilbert?"

He realized that he was holding her tightly, and there was a light of laughter in her eyes as her smooth lips turned upward in a smile. "Well, since you evidently refuse to let me go—what are your intentions?"

The pressure of her body against his suddenly awakened all the old hungers, and the past and the future faded like mist—

there was only this time and this place and her full red lips.

Finally she leaned back, then whispered huskily, "It's been a long time!"

She pulled away, her hands going up to her hair—they were not steady, Gilbert noted. His thoughts were confused, and the kiss had brought back many memories.

"I remember that dress," he said, more to gain time than for any other reason. "You wore it the night we went to the Duke's ball in Bath."

She was wearing a gown with vertical stripes of silver set off by sky blue trim. Suddenly she laughed and her black eyes danced. "I love that! Here we meet for the first time in months— you're running from a hangman—and you pay compliments on my dress!"

Her laughter forced him to smile, and he shrugged, "I still think I'm having a dream."

She sobered, and pulled him to a small sofa covered with green embroidery. "Sit down—we have a lot to talk about."

Gilbert shook his head, and asked, "First, what are you doing here?"

She lay back against the thick cushion, her lips curving upward. "You can't guess?" she asked.

"Well, surely not for a holiday!" he answered with a frown and a wave toward the land. "This isn't exactly the land of Eden the travel books make it out to be."

"But it has *one* feature that interests me—Gilbert Winslow!"

He kissed her hand, and that simple gesture stirred him so that he shifted uncomfortably and shook his head. "Does any mental problem run in the North family, Cecily?"

"Why, no!"

"Then you are the first to lose your mind," he said, and a grim line etched itself between his eyes. He got up suddenly, walked to the window, and stared out blindly at the coast. "It's all very romantic, Cecily, but so hopeless!"

"Why do you say that?" Cecily asked. She got up and went to him, turning him with a hand on his arm. "It's not very complimentary to me, Gilbert, is it? Here I sail thousands of miles to see you, and all you can say is that it's hopeless."

He looked down at her and smiled. "You are the same," he said.

"Yes. Are you the same, too?"

He bit his lip, and then said quietly, "No, I'm not. A year ago I didn't have name or fortune, and I still don't. But no man can kill another as I have—and spend a year in this place—without being changed."

She nodded, her face still, then said, "You've struggled with thoughts of the future—about Roth, I mean."

"Why, of course," he said in surprise.

She looked down at the floor, and her hand toyed with a small silver chain around her neck. Then she looked up with a strange light in her dark eyes. "Suppose all that were settled, what would you do then, Gilbert?"

He smiled grimly, his jaw tense and his lips thin. "Why even think about it? It's not going to disappear."

She stood there, and then said slowly, "I've thought about you a great deal this year. For a long time I didn't do anything. I stayed at home, went to France—anything to fill the time. All the time I was trying to forget you."

"I see."

"Do you? I doubt it!" Her eyes flashed then, and she was sober. "I was sure that you'd fallen in love with that woman you were mixed up with in Leyden. I think I would have killed both of you if I'd had the chance!"

"Cecily—!"

"Wait, I want this to be very clear," she said, putting her fingers over his lips to cut off his protest. "I hated you both, and when it didn't pass away—as some said it would—I knew I had to find out the truth about us. That's why I came to this new Eden."

He stared at her blankly. "But—don't you realize it doesn't *matter* how I feel about you! No matter how much I loved you, I could never speak, for what could I offer you except an invitation to watch me hang!"

She kept her eyes fixed on his for a long moment, then walked to the door. Before she opened it, she said, "We'll have the truth about us in a few moments."

She opened the door, and said, "Come in, sir."

Caleb Wellington must have been less than a foot from the door, for he came in at once, planted his feet and said, "Now, Mr. Winslow, it is your turn to interrogate *me!*"

"Who are you?" Gilbert threw the question at him sharply, and got an instant answer.

"A lawyer in the service of Lord North." He laughed quietly, adding, "*Not* an agent for the King looking for wayward theological students, as you have supposed."

"And what is your purpose, sir?"

"To bring you back to England with me."

Shock ran along Gilbert's nerves, but he only asked mildly, "And the charges against me?"

"There are no charges, Mr. Winslow."

"It is no longer against English law to slay a peer of the realm?"

Wellington did not rise to meet Gilbert's ironic manner. He said evenly, "Certainly it is—or any other man in the English kingdom."

Gilbert stared at him, then asked directly, "What about Lord Roth?"

"Lord Simon Roth was slain approximately one year ago. His assailant remains at large, but the authorities have little hope that he will be found after all this time, and with no witnesses."

"But there *was* a witness," Gilbert said at once. "What about the man named Johnson? Surely he must have had something to say to the law."

"There *was* a certain Johnson who was alleged to be in the company of Lord Roth during the time of his death—but he cannot testify."

"Why not?"

"Because he is dead." Wellington did not blink as he said this, but he went on to explain. "I will tell you two facts about Johnson, and no more. First of all, you may know that Johnson did talk not long after Lord Roth's death to Mr. Lucas Tiddle, a gentleman in Lord North's service."

"What did he tell Tiddle?"

"Ah, that is between the two of them!" Wellington said with a frown. "And I have not found Mr. Tiddle a man who takes his calling lightly. It is highly unlikely that you will ever know what passed between the two. All I can say is that Johnson talked to Mr. Tiddle, then immediately left England on a ship—the *Defiant*, bound for Australia."

Tiddle bought him off! Gilbert knew instantly. "And he died—how?"

"The *Defiant* went down in a storm in May—broke up on the Great Barrier Reef, with all hands lost."

"I see." Gilbert stared at Wellington, trying to see past the smooth face and the hooded eyes. Finally he asked slowly, "Then—I can go back to England a free man?"

A trace of humor broke the expression of Wellington. "I doubt that any of us are completely free, Mr. Winslow—but the answer to your question is—'yes'!"

The suddenness of it caught Gilbert unprepared. He covered his confusion by saying, "I—I'm grateful to you, Mr. Wellington—"

"I am very well paid, Mr. Winslow, for carrying out Lord North's wishes. In this case, his wishes were that I accompany his daughter on a voyage and give you an item of information." He reached into his inside pocket and took out a thin envelope which he handed to Gilbert. "This is from Lord North."

Gilbert stared at the envelope, then opened it.

> Winslow, if you have finished making a fool of yourself, you may come home and pick up your duties where you left off with Tiddle. If you have *not*, I will attempt to carry on without you.

Gilbert looked at Cecily. She did not speak, but her eyes met his with reckless invitation.

Folding the paper carefully and tucking it away into his pocket, he said softly, "Not many men get a second chance, do they? Thank God I've been given one!"

Wellington gave him a careful stare. "I was afraid that you might have changed your views, Winslow. I mean, these people are rather unworldly, aren't they? Denying the flesh and all that sort of thing? The way Deacon Cushman put it, it would be difficult to be a pilgrim and at the same time keep both feet planted in this world—as any man of Lord North's will surely have to do."

This was no idle remark, Gilbert sensed instantly. *North told him to check me out*, he thought. *And Tiddle will have had something to say about my sense of "honor."*

He looked at Cecily, then back to Wellington. Finally he laughed and said, "You know, I once told Brewster that I'd never be able to trust God completely—that if I were ever to be a pilgrim, why, I'd be a pilgrim with a sword." His eyes narrowed and he took a deep breath and looked straight toward Cecily.

"There are only two swords for a man to carry in this world—his own blade to cut his way to the top against all odds— or the Sword of the Lord." He paused and there was regret in his face as he dropped his head and said, "I have had some hope of being the kind of man who would love God with all his heart— but I am not that man." Gilbert smiled grimly, then went over to stand beside the window. From deep within rose the words, *You will love me with all your heart*, and he began very rapidly to drown them out.

CHAPTER THIRTY

"WITH ALL YOUR HEART!"

★　★　★　★

The arrival of the *Fortune* stirred every member of the small settlement, and for two days there was joy and sorrow over the letters and reports that Deacon Cushman brought from Leyden. Death had come for some that had remained behind as well as for the firstcomers. Cushman was so shocked over the decimation among the ranks through the sickness that he was past comfort for a time, but when he saw that the faith of the others remained unshaken, he plunged into action with zeal.

On Wednesday, November 13, two days after the arrival of the ship, Bradford assembled the men for a meeting in the Common House, saying, "Our brother, Mr. Cushman, has news for us," and then sat down with the others.

Cushman smiled and held a parchment high for them to see; it was tan with a bright red ribbon around it. Unrolling it, and spreading it so that all present could see, he said, "This is the most important document our colony could have, brethren. As you all know, New Plymouth does not lie within the territory of our original charter. This could be very serious—we could be ordered to leave by the Crown."

"They'll not push me off my land!" Stephen Hopkins cried out, red-faced and angry.

As several others began to take up the cry, Cushman raised his hand for silence and said, "We have been in the hands of

God; this document that I hold in my hand is a patent signed by Sir Ferdinando Gorges and the other members of the Council for New England."

"What is that?" Samuel Fuller demanded.

"It is a reorganized form of the Plymouth Company."

"I hope it's better than the old one!" Billington snapped.

"You will think so, Mr. Billington, when you hear that under this patent every one of you will receive 100 acres of land at the end of seven years!"

A shout of joy went up, and every face was beaming.

"It is the hand of the Lord!" William Brewster said after Deacon Cushman went over the details, which were indeed more generous than any of them had expected.

Then John Alden asked, "May I ask if—if Mr. Brewster will be . . . ?" He seemed unable to get his question out, and his face grew red with embarrassment. All of them knew his question dealt with the legal status of Brewster; most of them had heard that Captain Jones had ignored the matter, but the *Fortune* was another thing.

"I've heard that there's a man aboard the ship sent to bring back Mr. Brewster," Isaac Allerton said. "That's not so, I hope, Mr. Brewster?"

"No, it is not. I will be staying on," Brewster said with a smile. "I think the King has more important things to do than send for a poor preacher clean across the ocean."

"What about Gilbert? Is he going to stay, too?"

All looked to Edward, who shifted uncomfortably, then shook his head, saying, "I believe my brother will return to England."

"What about the—the charges we heard were lodged against him?" Peter Brown asked.

"There have been no charges." Edward Winslow's tone shut the door on further discussion, and the meeting moved on to other matters.

After the meeting, Peter Brown left and went directly to the Common House. As he expected, he found Humility helping the other women as they cooked and prepared, decorating the place as well as they could with such little trimming as they could manage.

"How was the meeting?" she asked when he came to stand beside her. She was cutting a large cod into steaks for baking, her hair bound underneath a white cloth.

"Very good." He told her the details, ending by saying, "We'll have 100 acres, Humility, after only seven years. Of course, that's just a beginning. We can get more later on."

"Why should you want more?" she asked. Her eyes rested on him, and there was a puzzled look in them. "You can't farm even *that* much, can you?"

"I'll hire men to work it, then buy more. Before we're through, why, I'll have as much land as any man in Plymouth."

"If that's what you want, Peter." The subject seemed to hold no interest for her, and she picked up the knife and began slicing fish.

He was disappointed in her reaction, for he was an ambitious man and wanted her to share in his dreams. "Don't you want to get ahead?"

A wry smile crept across her lips, and she said, "Is a man with 200 acres ahead more than a man with only 100?"

"Why, of course!" The question troubled Brown, and he bit his lip, staring at her. She was not one for small talk, but he had run on this streak in her before, and it bothered him. "Shouldn't a man do his best, Humility?"

"Yes—but there's more to a person's best than getting and spending."

He stared at her, then a thought struck him, and he said diffidently, "Winslow—he's going back to England."

He watched her very closely, and did not miss the fact that she paused in her work, the knife suspended for an instant after he spoke.

Carefully she resumed cutting and did not look up as she asked quietly, "Is he?"

"Humility, don't do that to me!"

She was startled at the quick anger in his voice. He never showed bad temper to her, but now as she looked up there were harsh lines on his face and his lips were drawn thin.

"Why, what did I do?" she asked in confusion.

"You're an honest girl, but you aren't being honest now,"

he said. "You cared for the man once. I can't believe you've no interest in him now."

She started to shake her head, but instead lifted her eyes to his, and there was a faint color in her face. "I *was* dishonest, Peter," she said suddenly. "Maybe I'm still ashamed of—of being interested in him. . . ."

"Why don't you say it—being in love with him!"

She stiffened her back and said quietly, "All right, then, if you think it's important, Peter. I was in love with him. I suppose you can't be indifferent to someone you've been in love with, can you?"

"I hope so!" Brown answered like a shot. "I'd hate for my wife to have thoughts of another man."

She stared at him, as if seeing something in him she'd never noted. "But you have your thoughts and your memories, Peter, that I can never really share."

He was confused and angry, but could not tell why. If he had been calmer he would not have said what he did then.

"You're still in love with him!"

She put down the knife carefully and wiped her hands on the cloth tied around her waist. "If you think that, Peter, you'd be a fool to marry me. Do you want me to release you from that?"

"Oh, no! No, Humility!" Brown caught up her hand and said earnestly, "I'm sorry—I didn't mean to say that! Why, I can't lose you, Humility!"

"You could do better." She stated this as a fact, and there was a steady look in her eyes as she added, "I'm not ambitious, Peter."

He smiled in relief, kissed her hand, then said, "I'll be ambitious for the two of us."

"Very well." She picked up the knife and began to slice the pink steaks. "I knew he would go—and I've been worried about what awaits him when he gets to England."

Brown laughed then, which surprised her. He said, "So *that's* it! I'm glad to hear it—but you can worry about someone else. Winslow's going back to what most men would love to have!"

"But—he's going back to be tried for murder!"

"I've been talking to Deacon Cushman," Brown said. "He's a natural gossip, I fear, and it didn't take long to get out of him that the charges have all been dropped."

"Dropped!" Humility stared in unbelief at him. "That's impossible! How could—?"

"My dear girl," Brown smiled sourly, "with money all things are possible. Evidently Winslow was in favor with Lord North, and when that gentleman wants something, he usually gets it!"

"I can't believe it!"

"Can you believe this—" Brown watched her closely, and continued evenly, "Lord North's daughter is on board the *Fortune*—and it's Cushman's feeling that she's come for Winslow."

"Cecily!" The word slipped out before Humility thought, and she reddened. "He—called for her when he had the sickness."

"Well, he called well," Brown said with a wry smile. "She heard him, apparently, and will wed him as soon as she gets him back to England."

Humility said slowly, "She'll be coming to the reception this afternoon along with the rest." She looked around the rough-hewn logs making up the Common House. "This won't impress her much after a mansion, will it?"

"I suppose she'll do the impressing," Brown shrugged, then kissed the cheek that Humility offered and left.

Peter Brown was neither a prophet nor the son of a prophet—yet his words came to pass.

The area around the Common House served as a dining room for many, and the weather was good. Tables were set up outside for those who could not get inside the single community building, and the air was filled with laughter and singing as the new settlers—thirty-five in all, joined with the firstcomers in the festive affair.

They had just seated themselves when there was a scraping of chairs, and the men rose as a small group entered. A middle-aged man, balding but with quick, intelligent eyes entered first, and Cushman said at once, "Friends, may I introduce Captain Robert Logan—and this is Mr. Evans, his mate—and Mr. Caleb Wellington of London."

There was a slight pause, then a silence as Cushman said,

"Mr. Gilbert Winslow, you know, of course, and this is Lady Cecily North."

He was partly mistaken, for the company did not "know" the Gilbert Winslow who stepped through the door. They were not looking at the plainly dressed brother of Edward who had labored in the mud and cold. Gilbert wore a smooth dark blue velvet coat trimmed in light blue ribbon. It was long, reaching halfway to his knee, but loose with a short line of silver buttons down the right side. His neckband carried a shortfall of lace, down over a long red satin waistcoat slashed with white. The dark blue velvet breeches and the snowy white hose completed his dress, except for the Clemens Hornn sword buckled under the coat at his left hip.

Startled as they were at Gilbert's transformation, he was forgotten as they took in Lady Cecily North.

She wore a short pellise of black ermine which reached to her elbows, which she removed at once and handed to Mr. Wellington. Her gown had vertical stripes of black and scarlet, with a very low bodice edged in small white and black ruffles. A small purse, gold-dusted and set with a circle of rubies swung at her right hip, and her skirt flared in vivid scarlet; under it she wore so many petticoats that when she moved she sounded like a small rain shower.

A cluster of fiery stones hung from her neck, suspended by a golden chain; two diamonds flashed from her earlobes. She had full red lips and flawless olive skin; a small mole on her left cheek, far from being a flaw, served as a natural beauty mark.

Bradford indicated their places, and soon the meal was under way. Peter was sitting at Humility's left, and he talked easily to the man across from him—a new settler named Duncan—about the year's events in England.

After the meal there were many speeches, and Humility was relieved when finally Captain Logan thanked them for their hospitality, but said he wished to get back to his ship before dark.

"You must see my guns, Captain," Standish said, and the captain, being an ex-soldier himself, gave in. The two men left and most of the crowd followed them up the steep hill to the miniature fortress overlooking the town.

As the room cleared, Humility moved around stacking the

trenchers and mugs. Hearing a sound, she turned and found herself face-to-face with Cecily North and Gilbert.

"It's a little cool for such a long walk," Cecily said with a smile. "Do you mind if we wait inside?"

"No. Of course not."

Cecily waited for a moment, then looked at Gilbert. "I have not met this lady," she said.

Gilbert cleared his throat, then made the introduction. "This is Miss Humility Cooper—Lady Cecily North."

Instantly Cecily's eyes riveted on the girl in front of her, taking in the plain gray smock, the lack of adornment. She did not, however, miss the fine green eyes set off by blonde hair and fair skin.

A challenge filled Cecily's dark eyes suddenly, and she drew herself up, saying, "Ah, yes, Miss Cooper—I've heard of you."

Knowing what she had heard brought the color to Humility's cheeks, but she said, "We're happy to have you here, Lady North."

"Even if I'm taking part of your small company away from you?" It was a playful remark on the surface, but Cecily took Gilbert's arm with a possessive gesture, and a predatory curl marred the line of her full lips as she watched the effect of her words on the other woman.

Humility deliberately looked from the dark girl into Gilbert's face. He was watching her intently, and the vertical lines between his heavy brows indicated he was displeased. He met her gaze, and there was a short, charged silence.

"Mr. Winslow will be a great loss to the colony," Humility said, and a shock ran along her nerves as she discovered it was true. "He has served the company well, and will be greatly missed."

Gilbert blinked his eyes in surprise, then bit his lip. "That's kind of you; but then, you're always one to find something good in the worst of us."

Cecily did not care for the sudden flash of intimacy that seemed to exclude her. "Perhaps," she said with a small smile, her voice drawing Gilbert's attention, "you'll come to visit us after we're married."

Humility did not miss the startled glance that Gilbert shot

at Cecily, but ignored it. "That's very kind of you, Lady North—but very unlikely."

"Well, you *are* cut off out here, aren't you, Miss Cooper?"

"From what?"

"Why—!" Cecily was taken off guard and looked confused, "Why, from the world, I suppose I meant."

Humility stood there, and the smile on her face softened her features. The quietness that Gilbert had learned to appreciate was never so clearly in evidence as at that moment.

"We're far from England," she said, "but we're not far from God." Then she nodded and said, "I hope you enjoy your visit, Lady North."

After she left, Cecily stared at the door, and then looked directly into Gilbert's eyes. "You didn't tell me she was so attractive."

Gilbert said at once, "She is very beautiful, Cecily—and very strong."

"Yes, that's true. I wonder she's not married."

Gilbert's gaze swept Cecily's face, and he said tonelessly, "She's engaged to marry a man named Brown."

"How nice!" Cecily's dark eyes sparkled and she leaned against him, saying, "We must send them something very nice for a wedding gift."

"When did you say we sail from this dreadful place, Mr. Wellington?"

Cecily threw her book down and went to stare at the bleak coastline out of the windows of her cabin.

Caleb Wellington lifted his big head from where he sat beside an oil lamp. "We've been here three weeks. Logan says we'll leave soon—next week, I'd venture."

"How can they stand it?" Cecily threw herself down, and raked her nails across the fabric of her chair. "I'd go *insane* if I had to spend a winter here!"

"Well, you won't have to, my dear," Wellington said calmly. Then he asked curiously, "Where's Mr. Winslow been the last three days?"

"How should *I* know?" Cecily said shortly. "He said something about making some sort of trip inland for Mr. Bradford—

business with the Indians of some sort."

"Well, he'll be back soon, and we'll sail—then it'll be over."

Cecily stared at him, and there was a puzzled look on her face. She asked, "Have you found Gilbert—different lately?"

"Different? How different?"

"I don't know how to put it," she said. "He's attentive—but when I try to talk about our life when we get home, why, he just doesn't seem *interested*."

"He's been through a lot. He'll be all right when we get him away from these preachers."

She stared at him, then nodded, saying, "I think you've hit on it—he's more caught up with all this holy living than he knows. I noticed it almost from the first day we got here. And lately it's worse! He's always reading the Bible or some sermon. He reads parts of them to me and I try to be interested, but they're so *dreary*."

The big lawyer shrugged, "You'll take that out of him soon enough, I should think. Get him back home, give him a taste of good living and what service with your father can bring—he'll forget all this!"

Cecily leaned back and there was a calculating light in her eyes as she said softly, "He'll have to, Mr. Wellington—there's no room for pilgrims in my world!"

At the very moment they were speaking, Miles Standish was giving Edward Winslow a report on his brother.

"You talked to him before he left, Miles?" Edward asked. There was a worried frown on his face, and he shook his head doubtfully. "We're in for bad weather. He could get lost and freeze." They were standing on the hill looking down on the scattered houses lightly coated with fine-grained snow. "I don't understand why he went. He was all tied up with that North woman on the ship."

Miles looked at the larger man, and there was a flicker of humor in his sharp eyes. "Well, if you want my opinion, he's coming down with a bad case of God-fearing conviction."

"What?"

Standish smiled and said, "You're on your honeymoon, Edward, and you don't notice things. Gilbert hasn't been happy.

Truth to tell, he's been bone-achin' miserable!"

"But he's got what he wants, Miles!" Edward protested. "He's always wanted to rise in the world, be rich—now he'll have it."

"Well, all I know is, he came to me three days ago, and he was at the end of his tether! I thought he was sick, he looked so bad, but then after a while, I saw it was something else." Standish was a man of action, and he had trouble finding his words, but finally he shrugged and said, "He came to me because he didn't want any sermons, Edward. He knew I'd been through the fire after Rose died, and he knew I wouldn't have a sermon for him." Then the fiery little captain laughed and said, "He was wrong about that!"

"What did you tell him?"

"Well, I listened to him at first. He went over the whole thing, all his life wanting to be somebody, to be rich. And when he was finished, he looked at me with pure misery in his eyes, and he said, 'Now I've got it, Miles—so why am I so unhappy?' "

Edward stared at Standish, then shook his head. "I should have seen it! Should have helped!"

"I think the boy covered it up pretty well," Standish observed.

"Why'd he leave town?" Edward asked.

"Well, I told him how I'd forgot about God until it was a shame—and then I said, 'You'll never be happy, Gilbert, until you get Christ!' Well, it touched a nerve, I tell you! He turned pale as a ghost and seemed to melt. So I told him he ought to do what I had to do—back when I lost Rose and just about went crazy."

Edward stared at him, then said quietly, "I failed you, too, Miles. What did you do?"

"Why, I went out into the forest and stayed until I found God," Standish said simply. "Like I told your brother, I went out there, and if God hadn't done something to help me, why, I'd never have come back, Edward."

Edward stared out into the gathering darkness, and there was a sadness in his voice as he said, "Poor boy! I wish I could be there to help him!"

Miles Standish said quietly, "No, he's got to that place we

all have to come to, Edward. Nobody can help us there—not father, mother, brother, or friend. A man can get help with most things, but when he goes to find God, he goes alone!"

Miles away, the object of their concern was trudging along, head down and tired to the bone. He had taken a message to Massasoit for Bradford. It had given him an excuse to leave town, and he had carried out his mission with no problem. Massasoit had attempted to convince him that he should delay his return to Plymouth, but Gilbert ignored his warning and had reached the halfway mark when the snow began to thicken, falling in chunks from an iron-gray sky.

He had thought about Cecily and England and a new life until it made his head ache. The worst thing was that he took no joy in the prospect, and he could not understand *why*.

"It's all there, Miles, all I've ever dreamed about," he had told Standish. "All I have to do is reach out and take it—but when I think about it, I just feel—I feel *empty!*"

Night was closing in, and a streak of fear ran through him as the power of the sudden winter storm rocked him with a blast of freezing wind that seared his lungs. *Got to get some shelter!* he thought, and as the last shreds of light flickered from the west, he cut a few saplings and managed to tie them together at the top, then cut evergreen boughs to make a top.

It was a pitiful sort of thing, but there was nothing else. He managed to make a fire in the small space between a tree trunk and the door to his shelter, and all night long as the rain changed to snow, he kept feeding it with small twigs.

With a shock, he realized he had only a handful of hard-baked bread and a little dried bacon. "Should have been more careful," he murmured.

When morning came, the snow turned to freezing rain, and he had to make several attempts to get to his feet. His muscles were slow to respond to the commands from his brain, and he knew then that he was in trouble.

He was halfway between Massasoit's camp and Plymouth—at least twenty miles to either, probably more. He considered heading back to the Indian camp. *Might run across some Indians*, he thought, but then realized that no one would be out in this storm.

All afternoon he floundered through the falling snow, stopping just before dark to make another shelter. He was moving so slowly that it took him a long time, and by the time he got a small fire going, he was half unconscious with cold and fatigue.

He ate the rest of the small portion of bread as slowly as possible, saving the handful of bacon for morning.

The temperature fell quickly, and he forced himself to get up and jump in the snow until the slugging blood pumped through his body, but each time it took longer. He was using up the energy he would need to fight his way through the drifts when morning came.

Some time before dawn, he drifted off to sleep, and as the cold seeped into his body, he began to lose body heat. The small fire died to a single glowing stick, and he did not move.

He never knew why he awakened, if an animal made a cry or a snow-laden branch crashed to the ground nearby.

It was like coming out of a warm bed into an icy room—there was the intense desire to slip back into the warmth, to flee from the biting cold.

You're freezing! part of his mind said, but when he tried to move, his limbs were powerless. Desperately he tried to roll over, even to lift one arm, but it was as if he were frozen in ice.

Over and over he tried, then he stopped. He knew he was dying. Part of his mind was awake enough to tell him that. He could not feel anything—neither cold nor pain.

A great regret came to him. He thought of all the things that he would never do—simple things, like watching Tink's face when a thumping fish jerked the boy's quill under, or the first bite of food after a long hunger.

Then in the midst of these last thoughts, he was conscious of something different—something that was *not* within. He was suddenly thinking some words that came from outside, somehow. For a long time they seemed to come and go, floating around his head, and he could not understand them.

Then he heard inside his head the words he'd thought of a thousand times: *Someday you'll love me.* He saw no figure; there was no strange light, but his mind suddenly became sharp and clear as a steel blade.

He began to think of all the sermons he'd heard from the

pilgrim ministers, and the words of the Scripture beat against his consciousness. "Except you repent, ye shall all likewise perish . . . Come unto me and I will give you life . . . except a man be born again, he cannot see the kingdom of God . . . confess with thy mouth the Lord Jesus . . . he that hath the Son hath life . . ."

Then he was conscious that he was in the presence of God, and he remembered how Standish had told him the same thing had happened to him when he had gone deep into the woods after Rose's death.

He lay there thinking of his misspent youth, spotted with sins of the flesh, and he knew that even if he survived, he could not go on living as he had. He opened his eyes, blinking against the light. Gathering his strength, he pulled himself to his knees, and then he lifted his hands toward the lead-gray heavens. His voice was feeble, but the cry that came through his cracked, frozen lips sounded loud in the silence of the forest: "Oh, my God . . . I—I am lost! Lost!"

Tears scored his cheeks, and in an agony of spirit, he lifted his head and with utter despair, cried, "I can't help myself, Lord God! I am only a sinner . . . but I believe you care—that you love me. I want to love you, God!"

Raw grief shut his throat, but he ignored it, and dropped face downward in the snow, crying out, "In the name of Jesus Christ, O God, save me!"

A wolf howled far off, and then there was silence. As Gilbert Winslow lay with his face pressed into the snow, something strange was happening. The agonizing bitterness in his spirit seemed to move away, and he was filled with a sense of such complete peace and joy that he was unable to move. He lay there for a long time, and finally he was aware that his tears were flowing, but they were tears of joy! He climbed to his feet, lifted his face toward heaven, and with wonder in his voice, cried out, "O God! I love you!"

Then not in words, but with a gust of knowledge, came the thought, *You love me now as a babe—but you will grow in the faith and will be my servant.*

Gilbert finally stood upright, his face stiff, his eyes slits, weaving like a tall tree cut almost in two at the base and about to topple.

He stared out into the first light, a sickly gray feebly staining the ink-black sky, and knew he could never make it back to Plymouth.

But something inside said, "Walk!" and he left the shelter, staggering through the drifts, wallowing and falling often, but always floundering to his numb feet and beginning again. He could not make a mile, he knew, and Plymouth was almost twenty miles—but there was always the feeling that he could take one more step. *Don't quit—just one more now—that's the way— good!*

Thirty minutes later he ran blindly into what he thought was a tree. His eyes had been shut, and when he opened them, he saw that he had run into one of the pine supports for the small cabin that Miles Standish had insisted on building as an outpost the previous spring.

As Gilbert fell inside the door, he remembered with a grim streak of humor he had told Standish, "It's a waste of time, Miles! The Indians will tear them down and steal the supplies."

But they hadn't. Not this one.

He stumbled around, getting a fire going in the small stone-and-clay fireplace, melting snow to make water, and cooking the best meal of his life—boiled corn that tasted like ambrosia to him.

As he sat there eating and soaking up the heat from the fire, he reached into his pocket and pulled out a small black book— the Bible.

He stared at it until he finished his meal, then put a few branches on the fire.

Settling with his back to the fire, he opened the Bible and said softly, "God, I'll not leave this place until I find your will!"

He stayed there for two days, going outside only three times for wood. The rest of the time he was either reading from the Bible or praying.

The snow fell intermittently, but he paid no heed. Sometimes he would eat a little food, but he didn't sleep at all, or not for long.

He could never tell anyone much about what went on in that cabin, any more than he could tell them how, out of all the directions he might have gone, he'd taken the only one that had led to the outpost.

What he did say to a few people later on was simple and to the point: "When I went inside that hut, I didn't love God much. When I came out, I loved Him with all my heart!"

When he came walking into camp, he was met with a great shout by the first man he saw, John Howland, who ran and caught him with a wild embrace.

"Gilbert! You're alive!"

He gave a shout, and soon Gilbert was inside the Common House telling his story to all that could get inside. His shoulders were sore with the thumping they had taken, and looking around at his friends, he got a lump in his throat and his eyes burned.

"Here, let the lad be," William Bradford said, seeing the trouble Gilbert was having. "It's a miracle, but we don't want to kill him with kindness, do we now?" He patted Gilbert's shoulder fondly, which was unusual for him, and added in a gentle voice, "You're home now, Gilbert. We've been praying for you constantly."

Gilbert raised his head, and there were tears in his eyes and on his cheeks. He looked around the room and noted each face, dearer to him now than anything in England.

"Mr. Bradford, He heard your prayer—and He saved more than my body—Jesus Christ is now my Savior!"

A cry went up from Bradford's throat, and that stern man threw his arms about Gilbert, and someone began to sing a song of praise as they all tried to get closer—to touch the newest pilgrim.

The hull of the *Fortune* dipped below the horizon two days later; the sails followed, and finally she was gone, leaving nothing but a smooth, clean line for Gilbert to watch.

He had climbed the hill to watch her clear the harbor, and now stood beside one of Miles' guns. He had left early, and for a long time he'd stood there after the ship left, his mind going over the last few days.

"Gilbert!"

He wheeled, startled, and there she was, her face flushed with the exertion of the climb, her sea-green eyes wide and her lips parted as she stood before him.

Gilbert looked past her, but saw no one. "You came alone?"

Humility didn't answer, but came to stand so close that he could smell her hair. She faced him squarely, tall and slim in the bright November sunshine. Her face was filled with wonder. "You didn't go back!"

"No. There's nothing there for me to go back to."

She shook her head and asked with a catch of her breath. "But—I thought you and Lady North . . . ?"

He laughed and his eyes crinkled as he said, "Well, *I* thought so, too, but she told me that she'd never be satisfied with half a man!"

"She said that?"

"Yes—and she was right," Gilbert said. "I told her that something had come into my life, something wonderful, but that it would make a difference in our plans. Then when I told her that the New World was for me, she couldn't believe it." He laughed and said, "I guess living in a cabin with a minister didn't appeal to her much."

Humility stared at him. "With a minister!"

He seemed embarrassed, and the smile he gave her wasn't very strong. He dropped it, and his face was honest and open in some new way. "I'm so ignorant, Humility! Here I've wasted my life, and now I stand here saying I'm going to be a minister! Isn't that the most insane thing you ever heard of!"

"No."

He stared at her. "You—you don't think so?"

"Gilbert Winslow!" Humility said with a gust of emotion, "I expect you can do just about anything you set your mind to!"

His mouth dropped open, and he stared at her. "Why, I've never done anything *right* in my whole life, Humility! Look at what I did to you, and—!"

She put her hand on his lips, and he felt her tremble. "Hush! I want to ask you a question. Do you love God with all your heart?"

He took her hand from his lips with his own, but did not release it. "Yes!" he said firmly.

She nodded, and made no attempt to reclaim her hand. "Then you'll be His man, Gilbert Winslow!"

He stared at her, stirred as always by the clean beauty of

her face. "Humility, I wish that you and I—" he broke off suddenly, then dropped her hand.

"I have another question for you," she said, and her voice was so unsteady that he looked up quickly.

"Another question? What is it, Humility?"

She swallowed and her voice trembled as she whispered, "Would—would you marry me?"

He stared at her, thinking he had misunderstood, but she returned his look, her eyes shining like diamonds.

"But—what about you and Peter Brown?"

She shook her head, saying, "He told me he needed more than half a woman! He said . . ." She turned away from him, then, and her voice was so soft he had to lean forward to hear it— ". . . he said that any fool could see I was still in love with you—just like I've always been!"

A great joy filled his heart, and he turned her around. He looked down at her, and she tried to smile, saying with a sob, "And he was—he was *right*! I'll always love you!"

She tried to turn and run, but his strong arms made her captive, and he waited until she grew calm.

"I love you, Humility Cooper!" he whispered in her ear. Then he kissed her, and there was a union as they held each other, their lips sealing what they felt in their hearts.

Finally he pulled his head back, and there was light of pure joy in his brilliant blue eyes, and a wide smile on his lips. "What a life we're going to have!"

Humility leaned back to gaze into his face, and her lips curved into a beautiful smile, then she asked quietly, "Will you ever miss it all, dear?"

He shook his head, "Never! I'll have *you* and I'll have my sword! What man could ask for more?"

"Your sword?" she asked. "But . . . !"

He pulled the worn black Bible from his pocket and held it high, as if it were his Clemens Hornn blade.

"The Sword of the Lord, Humility!" he cried out gaily.

"The sword that gives life," she murmured, "and a man who wields it well. Who could ask for greater adventure?"